Zvi Ankori
As A Palm Tree In The Desert

Zvi Ankori

# As a Palm Tree in the Desert

PART TWO

gefen
publishing house
JERUSALEM ♦ NEW YORK

Copyright © Zvi Ankori
Jerusalem 2008 / 5769

All rights reserved. No part of this publication may be translated, reproduced, stored in a retrieval system or transmitted, in any form or by any means, electronic, mechanical, photocopying, recording or otherwise, without express written permission from the publishers.

"KaDekel Bamidbar" Part Two translated from the Hebrew by
Evelyn Abel (chap 1–3) and Jessica Setbon (chap 4–7)

All Polish songs and poems translated by Z. Ankori; Poems in other languages translated by Ankori or in collaboration with Evelyn Abel

Layout: Marzel A.S. — Jerusalem
Cover Design: Yanai Segal

ISBN: 978-965-229-436-4
Edition   1 3 5 7 9 8 6 4 2

Gefen Publishing House Ltd.
6 Hatzvi St.
Jerusalem 94386, Israel
972-2-538-0247
orders@gefenpublishing.com

Gefen Books
600 Broadway
Lynbrook, NY 11563, USA
1-516-593-1234
orders@gefenpublishing.com

www.israelbooks.com

Printed in Israel              *Send for our free catalogue*

*To the Memory of My Parents*
*Father Aazik Wróbel*
*Mother Golda (Née Weinmann)*
*And My Youngest Sister, Gunia*
*who perished in the Tarnów Holocaust*

*And to My Older Sister Mala*
*who fled the Nazis to the Soviet Union*
*and was condemned to forced labor in Siberia*
*And luckily returned and lived*
*sixty more years in the State of Israel*

# Table of Contents

| | | |
|---|---|---|
| Prologue | From Jerusalem to Tarnów in Uniform. | . . . . 1 |
| Chapter One | The Story of Jewish Company 178 A. From Asia to Africa . . . . . . . . . . . . . . | 7 |
| Chapter Two | The Story of Jewish Company 178 B. From Africa to the Threshold of Europe. . . . . . . . . . . . . . . . . . . . . | 87 |
| Chapter Three | The Story of Jewish Company 178 C. On the Banks of the Tiber . . . . . . . . | 175 |
| Chapter Four | The Story of Jewish Company 178 D. With the Brigade. . . . . . . . . . . . . . | 231 |
| Chapter Five | Each and All Took to the Road . . . . . . . | 303 |
| Chapter Six | Mala. . . . . . . . . . . . . . . . . . . . . . | 381 |
| Epilogue | Four Executions and One More Death . . . | 457 |

*PROLOGUE*
# From Jerusalem to Tarnów in Uniform

*Jerusalem, 28/2/1941*

*Dear Mother,*

*This letter I will not be mailing, I'll hold onto it until I can hand it to you personally. A savage foe has cut us off from one another and it is a year and a half since I've had any news from home. I assume that you haven't heard from me either. The twenty-five words you were permitted to send on January 16, 1941 via the International Red Cross were approved by the censor only four weeks later (as evident from the date stamps on the page) and reached me after another two weeks. Nevertheless, their arrival lit up my room, momentarily mitigating our forced severance. I say "momentarily", because that's how long it takes to read twenty-five words — the puzzling amount set by the Red Cross. I read the letter again and again, and many more times still, finding, to my amazement, that the more I scan the text, the longer it takes to read, for I taste every word and delight in the taste and turn each word over, hoping to discover some hint that I may have missed before. I imagine you over there, Mother, choosing one version from the drafts you composed; the version which managed to squeeze the main points into the draconian pillory of twenty-five words. Your handwriting is strong and I hope that reflects your mood, as also Father's and Gunia's, as much as is possible under the circumstances.*

*Our home address (as the letter indicates) hasn't changed, and that's no doubt a good sign. The fact that you jotted down Mala's address in Siberia tells me that the Molotov-Ribbentrop Pact between the two powers permits contact between the USSR and the territory under German control. The one and only letter I received from Mala at the start of the war was from Lwów — proof that she had managed to cross the border to the other side. She asked for a new passport, since, in her flight, she had either forgotten to take hers or lost it en route. I sent her an alternative passport issued by the Polish Consulate in Jerusalem, but who knows whether it ever reached her or whether it is still valid in these times. In any case, I'm glad to have her address. You may be sure that I will move mountains to get Mala out of there. Even without knowing her whereabouts, I applied to the Mandate government several times. It, however, displayed utter obtuseness, as if the world were not at war.*

*As for myself, from the heights of Hanita (the kibbutz at the Lebanese border I have lived on this past year), I saw, dozens of kilometers away, a series of fires caused by Italian aircraft in their bombardment of Haifa and Haifa Bay. I understood that the foe is* ante portas, *a situation in which a Zionist like myself must stand up and be counted. I have therefore waived the exemption from army service granted advanced university students and, like many other young people of Eretz-Israel, I have volunteered for the British army. I purposefully enlisted in the transport corps, which operates abroad and moves with the army, so that when the time comes I will get to Europe. I have completed basic training and the drivers course, and tomorrow I leave for Egypt where the main body of the British army is encamped. Yes, Mother, I am coming in uniform to you; I am coming to you, Father; I am coming to you both, Gunia and Mala. Even though I have memorized Mala's address, and will remember it wherever I go, I decided in any case that as long as I am making my way to you, underneath my British uniform I will carry your twenty-five-word Red Cross letter with Mala's Siberian address. This is the*

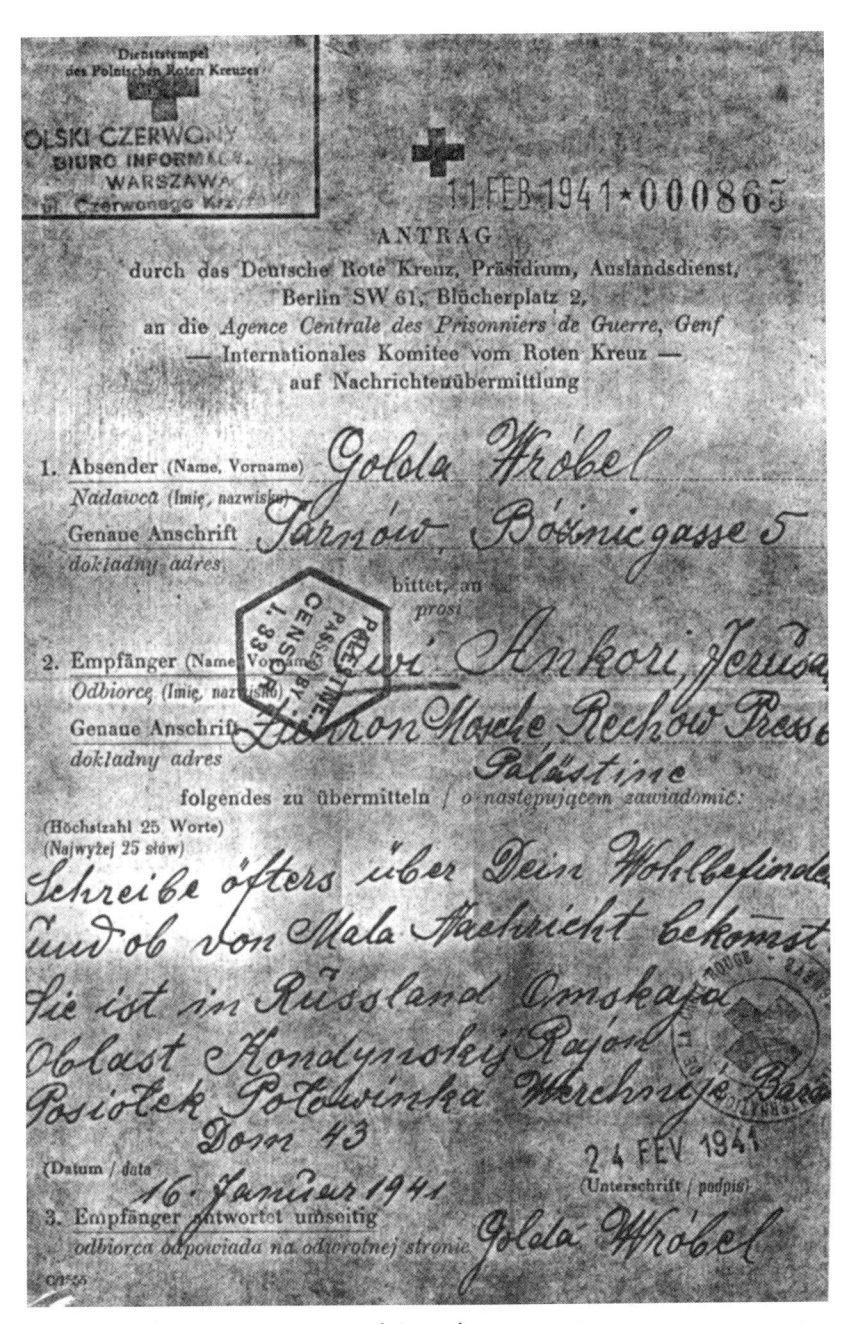

Red Cross letter

*address that will stay with me until I have done what I am setting out to do, and somewhere we shall meet up:*

— Omskaja Oblast, Kondynskij Rayon,
Posiolek Polowinka,
Wierchneje Baraki, Dom 43

*No doubt you remember, Mother, that our voyage, mine and Mala's, from Tarnów to Jerusalem in 1937 took only ten days. Who knows how long this voyage of mine will take me from Jerusalem to Tarnów as a soldier, in the midst of war. Months? Years perhaps? No matter how long it takes, you may be sure I'll come!*

*It is for this reason that I have donned a soldier's uniform and tomorrow I start towards you, Mother, Father, Mala and Gunia — it seems strange, but I will be coming from Africa. The road is hard and dangerous. But I am not afraid. The word "afraid" was never in my lexicon. The main thing is that you hold on there! And in due time I will arrive to bring you all to Jerusalem.*

*Yours as always*

# As a Palm Tree in the Desert

## PART TWO

The Wróbel children in Tarnów, 1937
Mala (18.5), Hesiek (17), both on the eve of departure for Palestine,
and Gunia (12) who remained in Tarnów

*CHAPTER ONE*

# The Story of Jewish Company 178
## A. From Asia to Africa

### I

The small train depot in the Rehovot colony did not pretend to be the kind of large railway station the soldier knew from Poland, either on his childhood trips with Mother to Kraków or on his "grand tour" of Polish cities in 1934, when train travel was declared free for youth under fourteen. Nor did the depot resemble its Jerusalem counterpart, a beautiful stone building from Turkish times. The Rehovot station was the exit point of cargo trains heading for the ports of Haifa and Jaffa and laden with citrus export from Jewish and Arab orchards. The fruit was first packed in crates of plywood slats, held together with iron wire ("of the sort I used to make my bookcase in Jerusalem" — the student-soldier chuckled). Prior to loading, they were stored near the depot in large shacks, roofed with tin that glinted from afar in the generous sunlight. Only with the outbreak of the Second World War did the Rehovot train depot, due to its unique location on the country's only railway track to Egypt, enter history as the dispatch point of means and men for combat. Egypt was the gateway to the North African front. The largest force of British troops in the Near East was stationed there, waiting for a bold commander to lead it to victory over the Italian-German Axis.

The train waited at the platform. Next to it stood an erect, clean-shaven British sergeant, his Brasso-polished belt buckles gleaming "smartly". He made sure every soldier had the necessary Movement Orders that allowed groups and individuals to travel to fill out the ranks of companies serving in Egypt. The Jerusalem tyro was assigned to the new Jewish Transport Company 178, which succeeded and had internalized the myth of the 5MT, the oldest Jewish transport unit in the British army. After 5MT's promising penetration of Cyrenaica under Field Marshal Wavell and lengthy service in the Western Desert; after its heroic epos of besieged Tobruq and hasty retreat from there with the defeated British troops; and, on the other hand, after its campaign over the right to hoist the Zionist flag and use Hebrew as the language of command within the Eretz-Israel contingent — 5MT had transferred the mantle of glory to 178, whose reputation was to shine both because of its predecessor and in its own right.

"What then? Off to the front?"

"Yes, sir".

The sergeant recognized the tyro with no trouble; he had been his instructor for a month of basic training at Sarafend. But, unlike Sarafend, where he had been properly stern and kept his distance from his underlings as befits the military hierarchy, he now went out of his way to endear himself to the "Palestinian" (as the volunteers of Palestine's Jewish Yishuv were officially called in WWII), especially as he was familiar with the tyro's academic background after perusing his personal file.

"Forget the 'sir'. Call me Jack" — the sergeant unpeeled his stern exterior. Embarrassed, opposite a legendary product of the British school for professional sergeants (the touted "backbone of the British army"), the soldier refrained from addressing his (albeit ex-) commander by his first name. This particular "backbone" — as gossipmongers jealous of his senior-instructor position would have had it — had been overly fond of drinking and misbehaved under the influence, which cost him promotion during his seventeen years of service in India. Nonetheless, some of his India background had been retained: unable to curse his subordinates in Eretz-Israel as "bloody Jews" — and curse one must, for "how do you make soldiers out of citizens without cursing?" — he made do with calling them "bloody Indians".

"I envy you, old chap. What I would give to return to active duty on the front! But things happened in the past, and they won't let me." And as if he felt he had said too much, his face hardened once more; the rare human moment passed, the mask was back. "Take care" — he uttered the standard farewell, erasing his brief openness and turning to the next person on line.

Confused by the abrupt goodbye, the soldier boarded the train. With his left arm, he tugged at the heavy kitbag, packed with khaki uniforms, a change of underwear and socks. Just beneath the bag rope, he had placed a small Bible which he always carried with him ever since he had begun his Saturday tours of Jerusalem with his youth movement charges. The fingers of his right hand meanwhile struggled with the pocket button of the battledress as he tried to reinsert his "Soldier's Service and Pay Book" and the Movement Order that had just been checked. On board, he was pleased to find an empty window seat on the right side of the car, knowing that later on, it would afford a view of the sea.

Squeezing into the corner between the window frame and the backrest, he tried to isolate himself from the tumult and crush filling the car, as he sought to unravel the secret that the sergeant had unwittingly given away in their chat. The soldier had never really believed the Sarafend rumor that the sergeant's lack of promotion was due to his drinking. If drinking were an impediment to military advancement, it would have put half of the British command out of commission. What's more, during basic training the tyros had never seen the sergeant drunk, not even on Sundays. He was always sober, conducting himself with the spit and polish of army decorum. If so, what unforgivable crime hung over his head? Had a stray bullet of his killed a fellow soldier? Had he been guilty of a severe breach of discipline? On the other hand, if he had already served his sentence and for years now had earned high praise as a top sergeant — why wasn't he made officer?

The socialist in the soldier could not quash another cause that came to mind. Though no one had ever mentioned it, it struck him as more transparent and reasonable, even if the sergeant himself seemed to have accepted it as a law of nature. Now at least 40, the sergeant must have enlisted a generation ago, when imperial Britain (whose revival Churchill still dreamt of), and particularly the upper classes, conceived of the officer ranks as reserved for the nobility and the privileged. Recruits from the lower classes, even excellent ones, could rise as far as NCOs (Non-commissioned Officers) and no further. The current war and its needs and general conscription might well change that conception and sprout a new generation of officers from "the ranks of the people", whose talents, rather than lineage, would decide appointments — the socialist soldier summed up his views and hopes. Nevertheless, even if change would come, this sergeant would probably not benefit from it. After decades in the army, he was close to retirement. Ankori was sorry that he had not found out his surname (he knew him only as Jack, and there were a great many "Jacks" in the army) or his British address; he might have been able to pay him a visit on his planned journey to London after the war.

The soldier looked around as if noticing his fellow-travelers for the first time. His absorption with the injustice done the sergeant — which he regarded as a metaphor for society's built-in tyranny even as that very society called for war against external tyranny — had diverted his attention from the body of soldiers, a random, motley crowd, physically united by the closed car of the train.

Several soldiers were dozing in various positions, heeding the supreme military rule attributed to Napoleon himself and always valid for all armies: "Wherever you don't have to stand — sit; if you don't have to sit — lie down; whatever the case, whenever possible — doze!" Others were watching the scenery through the window either out of interest or boredom. A solitary Scots Highlander took up his bagpipes and played a homesick tune for his faraway country. His neighbors however silenced him; perhaps they refused to acknowledge their own similar sentiments. The bulk of the soldiers had grouped themselves on the floor of the car and were playing cards.

They included Englishmen, brawny Scots Highlanders (whom the Eretz-Israel transportation unit would meet again and again on their North Africa missions), short Indians and tall, turbaned, bearded Sikhs (their hair rolled up on their napes), as well as New Zealanders and Australians. The soldier smiled at those hailing from the southern hemisphere who "walked with their legs in the air" as Eretz-Israel children were fond of saying.

"This is what the International Brigade in Spain could have looked like and, given its motivation, the republic might have stood a chance" — the soldier lamented, reflecting on the 1936–39 Spanish Civil War from the perspective of 1941. "Had the Brigade operated under a single command and coordinated its firepower like the international British army, had discipline been enforced and had the different components stuck to fighting the real enemy instead of resorting to ideological in-fighting, the republic could have survived and the current world war could have been averted." The idealistic sixteen-year-old he had been then, had longed to enlist in the Brigade and to counter the self-important "experts" alienated from the idea of an ideological, worldwide voluntarism that he had championed.

The entry of two MPs cut short his thoughts about Spain and the Brigade of the not so distant past. The subject was dear to his heart and he was determined to return to it, regardless of the current new circumstances. The appearance of the MPs was a sure sign that he had dozed off at some point for he had not seen them board at the Palestine border at Rafah. He had been looking forward to the sensation of border crossing — he, the son and brother who had vowed never to return to Poland — as he made his way from Jerusalem to his dear ones in Tarnów. Yet he had missed it. The train was already entering the joint Egyptian-British zone, known as Sinai, though the peninsula's flat coastal region hardly matched the picture of Sinai lodged in his heart since childhood and based on the Pentateuch. But what was this musing about Sinai and the Pentateuch when he again had to fight the pocket button of his battledress for his "Soldier's Service and Pay Book" and the Movement Order to be checked anew by the MPs?

The train meanwhile passed the delightful palm grove of el-Arish, a long stretch that materialized without any prior indication only to vanish again like a mirage along the shining clean, sandy coastline lapped by Mediterranean waves. How had scores of palms collected on this amazing sandy tract of el-Arish? His curiosity whetted, he attempted to examine a question that travel books on Egypt and el-Arish did not even bother to ask. Suddenly, a wild thought occurred to him, based on a remembered detail from a guidebook on Crete he had come across at the high school library years earlier. The southwest corner of the island, opposite the Libyan shore, apparently also boasted a startling palm grove. Scholars surmised that pirates infiltrating the island from Libya at the corner closest to Africa, had fed on dates they brought with them and spat out the pits on the sand. Years later, the pits sprouted palms, remaining a testimony to the exploits of the pirates of the past. Might el-Arish also owe its palms to pirates? One wild thought led to another. Perhaps not pirates but Israelites, crossing the Red Sea that lay southwest of here and not content with eating manna on their wanderings, had picked dates from palms they had found, and their pits, decades (or centuries) later, had sprouted the majestic palm grove on the way from Egypt to the land of Canaan?

An inner voice mocked him: "This is how theories are born. And, as a future researcher, you had better make sure that you don't believe in theories hanging on a hair. Be careful when you sit down to write your dissertation. Now that your examination of the question is over, you may return to your memories." He in fact recalled that the entry of the MPs had intruded on his disparagement of "experts". The latter had learned nothing from history, fighting yesterday's wars in the here and now. They had thus belittled the imminent danger posed to the world by the Spanish conflagration, dismissing it as a minor skirmish "over Europe's tail". He had to admit that he and his mother, too — in their fanciful "Radanite" journey from southern France eastward with the help of the *Romer Atlas* — had ignored Spain's bottom western corner and related jocularly to the Iberian peninsula at the edge of the map: "Spain looks like a tail dangled by Europe between Africa and the waves of the Atlantic Ocean", they tittered.

But in 1936, at the outbreak of the Spanish Civil War, the titters were silenced. In the mock trial that Kresch, the teacher, conducted at school, the sixteen-year-old socialist spoke out against Leon Blum himself: "Now that the French Prime Minister has opted for neutrality and banned the export of arms to the republic across its southern border, while Nazi Germany, fascist Italy and communist Soviet Union are supplying both weapons and soldiers, each for its own reasons — we, the young, as witnesses to this disgraceful and dangerous scenario, regret the admiration we previously harbored for Blum." And to the mockers of the "tail analogy", he said: "You may dismiss the importance of the tail as much as you like, but anyone with a pet at home knows this to be a law of nature: step on the tail of a cat or a dog — like the three despots of Central and Eastern Europe are stomping on Spain and exploiting the tragedy as a laboratory to test new weapons and warfare against each other — and that tail will transmit its pain to the mind and the mind will vent its fury. The result will be a tragic historical nemesis that will shock neutral, self-righteous Western Europe." To the astonishment of both Kresch, who chaired the mock trial, and the pupils, the passionate prosecutor publicly announced his resolve to volunteer for the International Brigade and, before the school could inform his parents of his decision, he ran off to the (camouflaged) recruitment office. He was however turned down for being under age.

Frustrated by the rejection, he decided to use the pen as a weapon for the good of the cause. He wrote a street-show about the Brigade, which his youth movement friends volunteered to perform despite the risks. The danger turned out to be more concrete than anticipated but it did not come from the police, as feared. On the small square near the Skolimowski Café, where national holidays saw a stage erected in salute of the military parades, the high-schooler created an amateur backdrop with the three-arrow symbol of the International. The police apparently took it to be a youthful, foolish prank and ignored it. Not so the unfriendly crowd that gathered at the stage, their mood hardly boding well. The International symbol did not stop Leftist hooligans from wrecking the backdrop and, with cries of "*Żydy do Palestyny* (Jew-boys to Palestine)!", they put an end to the performance while, on the opposite side, Fascists hollered "*Żydo-Komuna*!" There was a huge gulf between the two factions, yet they were united in their hatred of Jews and Judaism, and in their blaming of Jews for all the world's ills. The Jewish performers, supporters of the Brigade, fled by the skin of their teeth.

"How we ran" — the rebel playwright still blushed in shame four years later as he recalled the debacle. All he had wanted to do was show solidarity with the struggle of the Spanish republic. Had the Left's conduct heralded the poisoned ideological differences in its own camp that came "to the aid of Spain" and accelerated its defeat? Who could have predicted then that most of Stalin's "vassals" returning to the USSR from Spain would be eliminated at his command?

"Either way (the rejected volunteer summed up the Spanish episode): Europe's situation today proves that my assessment was right. Spain was the starting volley of the war of the powers, i.e., of the present world war. And though I may have been rejected for the overture, may my volunteering for the main campaign do good."

His eyes suddenly flew open, alarmed, as if waking from a nightmare. He glanced at the soldiers in the car, none of whom he knew personally. He did know however of the comradeship formed in the British army. "This time it will be different. This time, together, we'll win!"

On the left side of the train a primeval desert landscape penetrated the window, with a caravan of camels on the horizon. There was no sadness in the scene. Nevertheless, the soldiers yearned for other landscapes, the familiar vistas of England, Scotland, India or the southwest tip of the Pacific. Only one soldier in this entire sundry group dreamt of Eretz-Israel, of the Jezreel Valley, the palms of the Galilee and of the Jordan Valley and, yes, of peerless Jerusalem. The card-players seemed to have had their fill of cards and of sitting on the floor, and returned to their seats. The Highlander picked up his bagpipes once more and launched into the well-known, well-loved Irish tune of "Oh Danny Boy". Bit by bit, the other soldiers joined in, humming along if they didn't know the words until the whole car finally burst into song.

The Palestinian Jewish soldier did the same, albeit pensively: instead of bare desert he again saw the delightful palms of el-Arish and those of the Upper Galilee embracing the sources of a youthful Jordan. He took out his new notebook and, retaining the tune but discarding the English lyrics, he composed his first poem on Egyptian soil.

In foreign land, my anguished heart sings out to you,
El-Arish palm, betrothed to sand and sea —
Your canopy nods warmest greetings to me too,
From your sister palm high up in Galilee.

And I know well why gloom gnaws at me night and day,
Pushing at me these foreign nameless hills —
For my homeland palm, alas, is far, so far away
Like chime of camel bells from distant desert sills.

And I know, too, the sun is rising every morn,
Waking the palms to play and bask in light —
When evening moon returns, a shining star is born,
Both lull the palms to dream through silvery night.

Yet gloomy sadness gnaws at heart all night and day,
Rolls on my chest these foreign nameless hills —
For my homeland palm, alas, is far, so far away
Like chime of camel bells from distant desert sills.

## II

Al-Qantara, a small town bridging the Asian and (opposite) African bank of the Suez Canal, was the southernmost stop of the Palestine-Egypt railway line. For the travelers of the singing car it was the end of the road, after hours filled with cigarette smoke and boredom. "We're here" — with a sigh of relief and a trace of (unacknowledged) fear, perhaps about what lay ahead — the soldiers, Englishmen, Scotsmen (including the bagpiper), Hindus, Sikhs, Australians and New Zealanders began to alight into the shock of the Egyptian sun. They had already served in the region, and, returning from leave in Palestine, they knew the way to their base. Not so the solitary Jewish soldier. This was the first time that he set foot on Egyptian soil and his destination was still far away.

"This then is the canal of Verdi's 'Aida'?!" — the Eretz-Israeli was disappointed at the sight of the narrow ribbon of water. What's more, he had read that this was the *widest* part of the hundred-and-twenty-seven-kilometer canal, which started in the city of Suez on the left bank of the Red Sea — an elongated bay, matched on the right side, by an elongated sister-bay of the same sea, with the city of Aqaba. The two arms, left and right together, embraced a heart-shaped overland triangle, the Sinai Peninsula. The guidebook had been accurate; at el-Qantara the canal broadened to enable two ships to pass alongside one another. From here, the canal, a ruler-straight princess, would swallow another forty-four kilometers of desert until in Port Said, she would kiss the prince of her dreams, the Mediterranean.

The soldier hoisted up his kitbag and went down to the ferry. Disappointed as he was at the canal's narrowness, the primitiveness of the crossing was worse still, in complete contrast to the strategic importance of that body of water. After landing on the opposite bank, he followed the signs to the office of the Town Major. There he was issued vouchers for a cold drink, a beer and a sandwich at the NAAFI canteen, as well as a new Movement Order to continue to Cairo that same night by Egyptian train. Cairo's Town Major was to provide a Movement Order for the last lap of the trip.

At the end of a tiring night on a train groping its way through the biblical "darkness of Egypt", the soldier was snatched from his hasty morning nap by an unknown hand. It may have been the tumult of the ancient-modern metropolis itself that jerked him awake: on one side, still inside the station, there were close sounds of a trail of perspiring women vendors, coaxing disembarking passengers with their hot pitta-bread and fruit; the sing-song of a peddler with a gleaming brass canister strapped across his shoulder, pouring, with amazing aim, a date drink into an outstretched cup; or perhaps the shrill cries of newspaper boys running from one end of the platform to the other. On the other side, beyond the walls of the train station, there was the commotion of the street and the square. And over all was the dominant call of the muezzin from the nearby minaret.

Or — the young man chuckled, pleased by his book knowledge of Egyptian mythology — perhaps he had been roused by Ra, the ancient Egyptian sun god, navigating his boat through the firmament by day, and now completing his nighttime voyage through the netherworld, who had sent his rays through the window of the train car while painting the desert gold? Was the god intrigued, or rather irate, at the sight of a descendant of the Israelites? *They*, after all, had demanded permission to *leave* Egypt. Indeed, Pharaoh Merneptah — in the first and only Egyptian mention of "Israel" — had ceremonially proclaimed on his victory stele that he had laid Israel waste en route to Retenu-Canaan. And now, a member of the latest generation of those "laid waste" was *returning* to Egypt, and his companions moved freely on Egyptian soil in "motorized horses", as if mocking those earlier Egyptians and their chariots lost in the deep as they pursued the Israelites. "No (the young man added from his book knowledge), it has been generations since the gods have interfered in the life of man; and even the Pharaohs — the gods' sons for whom the multitudes had built pyramids — could not, though mummified, remain concealed from the eyes of the Lord of Time. Will I see them in the museum? Will I meet them face to face?" He was excited at the very thought.

The office of the Town Major was in the train station itself and the soldier could soon arrange his Movement Order to continue on to Qenah in Upper Egypt where his unit, 178 Coy, was stationed. Once more, he was given vouchers for the NAAFI canteen but, to his regret, he was billeted at the Abbasiyeh barracks in the northwest part of town, far from the sites that interested him. At least he was allowed to leave his kitbag in the office till the evening, so as not to waste time.

"The train to Qenah leaves tomorrow morning and by the end of the day I will be with my Company" — the soldier eagerly awaited the coming experience, though glad, too, that the night trip had left him a free day for sightseeing in Cairo. It could be no more than an initial taste, opening the way for later visits. Little did he know then that fateful events on the war front would totally distance him from Cairo, or that dramatic post-war changes in Egypt itself and in the map of the region, upon the establishment of the State of Israel, would block his return to Cairo for decades. Only after a peace treaty was signed with Egypt, would he be invited to lecture in Cairo and acquaint himself with all the sections of the city.

The Egyptian sun blinded him as he stepped out of the train station onto the Midan Raamses Square, named for Raamses II. Coming out of that same station years later, on his second visit, he would find a huge statue of Raamses on the square in front of the station. Was it to be placed there by Gamal Abdel Nasser who perhaps regarded himself as Raamses' successor, just as the Shah of Iran linked his name to Cyrus, the ancient King of Persia? Some scholars believe that the Israelites had been enslaved in Egypt from the start of the period known as the New Kingdom, and that only at the end of the thirteenth century BCE had the Israelite passage from bondage to freedom taken place, indelibly imprinting the national memory. Had Raamses II in the sixty-seven years of his reign been the last of the enslaving pharaohs "who knew not Joseph" as the Bible relates? And was it his son, Merneptah, that had been the pharaoh of the Exodus and was it his army that had drowned in the Red Sea?

"Where to, now?" — the soldier wondered, wishing to make wise use of the time that had dropped into his hands like manna from heaven. "I have only one day. So what first?" Clearly, he would have to leave the tour of the Misr al-Qahra Muslim section of the city to another time, even though he had written a seminar paper that had earned him recognition as a promising scholar of the Fatimid and Mameluk periods. So where should he go now — to the pyramids or the Egyptian Museum? He opted for the second choice, assuming that after the museum closed in the late afternoon he could take a taxi to Giza to commune with the pyramids and the Sphinx in moonlight. In any case, the museum was first: there he would meet the pharaohs themselves — not pharaohs in official finery but embalmed as mummies, a process that had protected them from the teeth of time for three thousand years, while cunning, heavy pyramids with false doors and other deceptive devices had not managed to protect them from grave robbers.

The gem of Cairo was set in the north of the Midan Ismailiya. The name — as he would find years later when he returned as a guest — was to be changed to Midan a-Tahrir (Liberation Square).

The Egyptian Museum almost touched the "*Ye'or*" — yes, the *Ye'or*, as the soldier had learned to call the Nile in his childhood reading of the Pentateuch. And he, like every child that learned the Pentaeuch in *heder* or in the lower grades of Hebrew elementary school, had imagined the *Ye'or* as a static body of water in the great land of Egypt: a lake behind the Israelite homes there, near Pharaoh's palace. What could be better than the papyri growing on the banks to hide a babe in a basket? What offered a better vantage point than the path descending to the water's edge to ensure that Pharaoh's daughter on her way to bathe would discover the basket? It was not until the Fourth Grade that he had learned in geography class about the 6,671 kilometers of water slashing the desert from the heart of Africa to the Mediterranean. Only then did the *Ye'or* become the "Nile", the longest river in the world.

Ah, if only Mother could see the river (the young man enthused)! If only she had been able to walk on its banks, just as she had liked to walk on the banks of the Wisła in Kraków! And the Wisła, after all, erupting from the green Carpathians rather than from a desert and bisecting Poland over a mere 1,068 kilometers to the Baltic Sea, was a midget compared to the Nile — some six and one quarter times longer. Moreover — if Mother were here, she would see not one but two real deserts framing Egypt to the east and to the west of the Nile; up to the Suez Canal and the Red Sea on one side, and towards Libya and the Sahara, on the other.

As if obeying the command of Mother's blue eyes, the son delayed his entry into the museum though time was short. For her sake he strolled along the bank (and a good thing too, for on his later visit he was to find a bank clasped and obscured by modern hotels). Unasked questions from the past suddenly flew through his mind: why had Mother never suggested Egypt as a destination of their imaginary voyages? Why, if she had her sights set on China, the final destination, had she chosen the fourth route of the Radanites, the overland route to China, and ignored the initial part of the route they had taken through North Africa and Egypt? Why had she not followed in Egypt in the footsteps of Benjamin of Tudela whose trips she had cherished? The son had no answers. Cheerless and pensive, he entered the museum.

## III

"How odd" — the soldier muttered. Here he was sitting in a train puffing white steam en route to Qenah, his first exciting destination in active field service in the British army, whereas, only yesterday, from the moment he had trod on Egyptian soil, he had been lucky enough to enjoy a different sort of excitement, the sort that any student could wish for: a whole, packed day of taking in the archeology and art of ancient Egypt, a subject to which he had devoted many hours of reading and study. And yet his present excitement surpassed all these: gazing at the Egyptian countryside through the window of the moving train, he caught his first sunlight glimpse (as opposed to the previous lap in the dead of night) of a glorious scene! Beyond the ribbon of the Nile's green water, and beyond the bulrushes and papyrus reeds rising naturally at its edges, broad brown-green strips of settlements and tilled soil clung to the riverbanks. They owed the miracle of their life and breath not only to the Nile's seasonal flooding but to manifold small irrigation canals dug out and filled with water over thousands of years of human effort. The Nile water spilled out from revolving wheels hung with pails that drew-and-dumped, drew-and-dumped the liquid over and over again; ostensibly primitive devices yet remarkably efficient, creating an unequalled geographic wonder — a new stretch of green land between two primeval yellow deserts: Egypt! From his train window, the traveler watched the villagers toiling to bring forth bread from the earth much as generations before them had done. And he knew that they comprised no more than a fraction of the total inhabitants of the Nile River Valley, densely pressed together, for, apart from this valley, there was nothing but desert, and desert did not support life.

His Fourth Grade geography textbook had introduced him to

Herodotus' assertion, by now a hackneyed truism, that "Egypt is the gift of the Nile". But if so — he wondered — why did the "gift" not work along the thousands of kilometers traversed by the river before reaching Egypt? It had to be due to the other partner in the gift's realization in Egypt. Properly speaking, the saying demanded a complement: the Nile, as wonderful as it might be in Egypt, was mere infrastructure, that man had since ancient times learned to develop with his hands and his wisdom. Thus Egypt had risen and endured. The young traveler took the country to his heart, scarcely understanding the source of his love.

Shutting his eyes briefly, he allowed his mind to return to the previous evening's thrilling experience: the pyramids in moonlight, a fantastic picture! In the darkness, however, they were two-dimensional, lacking depth and masking the age differences between the three pyramids. The three suspended, giant black triangles appeared as if hung by a master craftsman between heaven and earth. Pure romance! He recalled that the ancients had regarded the pyramids as one of the seven wonders of the world. But his critical faculties soon quashed the romanticism. "The wonder is very impressive" — he noted soundlessly — "but entirely sterile and, like all sterility, disturbing and saddening." Furthermore: "it has no continuity, no expectation of realization". As a student of history, albeit temporarily in uniform, viewing history as both his future profession and his hobby, he looked to history as the ultimate interpreter of human endeavor and motivation, and the concomitant physical changes they wrought. "A pyramid was simply the caprice of an omnipotent, megalomaniac Egyptian despot who believed that he was god's incarnation on earth. He thus considered himself entitled to indulge his whim and recruit untold numbers of working hands, while draining the state coffers, to build himself a tomb. One day, another megalomaniac rose, who also decided that he needed a pyramid, maybe even bigger than the previous ones. He would have it constructed separately, with no connection to its predecessors, no historical continuum, as if proclaiming: 'History ends with me'. As such, the pyramids — which in Herodotus' day were already considered the most ancient historical monuments — are anti-historical and anti-human, and despite their beauty, their fame, and the technological accomplishment of their construction, it would have been better had they not come into the world."

He opened his eyes. The splendor of the living, green Nile Valley, basking in the golden libation of the Egyptian sun, vied with the memory of the dark triangles suspended between heaven and earth the night before. The Nile flowed against the direction of the train, as if promising the southward travelers a safe return from the desert. The wheels of the pails in the canals squeaked and turned, drawing-and-dumping Nile water, drawing-and-pouring it without cease. "*That's* the real wonder, the wonder of life, not the pyramids that subordinated human life and toil to death. The stillness of the pyramids is the stillness of the grave, but so long as the Nile flows and the wheels of the pails squeak in the canals, there is life in Egypt!"

At the start of the previous day's museum visit, even before he had seen the pyramids and mentally castigated the megalomania of their builders, the soldier had found the museum's display of more other pharaonic megalomania stiflingly oppressive; the huge statues of pharaohs of different dynasties reflected a preference for size over beauty, for quantity over artistic quality. The marble giants obviously meant to daunt and dwarf man, and enslave the human spirit. Trapped between equally-repulsive look-alike giants that overshadowed the impressive exhibits beneath glass panels, the soldier-student felt as if he had strayed in here by mistake and almost turned to leave. He reconsidered however: he had so longed to visit this treasure of ancient Egypt, the richest and most beautiful in the world, and had been so happy at the windfall of a whole free day at the museum from opening to closing. Mustering self-discipline, he banished the *colossi* from his thoughts as if they had never existed and began examining the display cases with enthusiasm and rapt eyes.

## IV

Only on reaching the hall devoted to the "Amarna Revolution", could he enjoy a liberating respite from the stern, petrified atmosphere that had been dictated for generations by the dynasties of the realm and by the priests of the gods in the shrines. The revolution — a daring deed of the poet-king, Pharaoh Akhenaten, in the second half of the fourteenth century BCE — had annulled polytheism and sanctified a monotheism that worshiped the Great Disc of the sun. It had established a new capital at Amarna in Central Egypt and downsized the figures of artworks, putting an end to the shock of bombast. Instead, it lent the figures a "human" visage, and a tender gaze emanated from every exhibit in the hall.

There seemed to have been a spare ironic message that the curators of the permanent exhibition of Amarna art intended to drive home, by importing from the Karnak shrine, colossi of Amenhotep IV (Akhenaten's pre-revolutionary name). "A clever ruse" — the soldier enjoyed the deed — "this juxtaposition of expressionless colossi of Thebe, devoid of all spirituality, and detached from humans that sought shelter in their shadow, as against Amarna's delicate human art under the inspiration of Akhenaten, the poet immersed in beauty and the most human of kings. He acted in cooperation with his sister-wife, Nefertiti, the most human of queens and the loveliest of women.

"What can be more human than these sights?" — a group of Amarna reliefs attracted the student's attention. "Look at the pair of pharaohs, Akhenaten and Nefertiti, being immortalized before a domestic altar while worshiping the Sun Disc. And what could be more surprising than the (human) representation of the disc, emitting rays of light and warmth to the world with human hands at their tips? What did the prophet of the new religion mean by this anthropomorphosis: that the hands, the hands of the sun, lovingly embrace all humanity and protect man, fending off any danger that might befall him?

"And what can be more human and idyllic than the sight of His Majesty the Pharaoh, playing with his children as any ordinary man would? He, Nefertiti and their daughters appear in the relief all clad in plain, non-ceremonial, comfortable house clothes — a relaxed family scene at the royal palace at Tel-Amarna. Can one even imagine such a scene in the stuffy, sanctimonious Theban art? Prior to the rise of Amarna art, was a pharaoh ever depicted holding his youngest daughter on his lap and kissing her, as was Akhenaten, a loving father just like any other?"

The soldier moved back and forth between the display cases, each time discovering a new detail. Here was a toy! A painted chariot harnessed to monkeys. "Which of Pharaoh's daughters played with it, stroking the monkeys? The one Akhenaten had kissed a moment earlier, or the other princesses whose clay heads looked out at the viewer?" And here was a surviving fragment of a fresco from the Tel-Amarna palace: colorful birds and butterflies, animals romping in the reeds, and plant specimens drawn by a practiced hand. "Did Nefertiti, the mother, have the girls' rooms decorated with them? Or, had Pharaoh and his spouse, nature lovers, have the fresco installed in their own room? And what about the painted floor, a piece of which was brought to the museum from the ruined Amarna palace — in whose room was that?"

And here was the exhibit that the soldier's eye had searched for from the moment he had entered the museum: Nefertiti's bust, molded in clay. Mesmerized, the young man gazed at the embodiment of beauty. The face of the queen, radiating both divine serenity and determination, painted in colors that seemed to bring her back to life.

This was not his introduction to Nefertiti. Their initial, incidental and unexpected encounter had taken place ten years earlier, when he had been a twelve-year-old high school pupil. It had been love at first sight, and like every case of first love, it had lodged in his heart ever since. Browsing through the elegant German edition of *Ancient Egyptian Art* drawn from "Mother's bookshelf", he had come across a reproduction captioned "The Bust of Nefertiti". To his astonishment at the time, unlike most of the photographs in the book portraying the objects and sites of Egypt, the bust was said to be displayed at the Berlin Museum. Berlin? Great! Close by! Egypt — in the eyes of the Galicians — was as faraway as the Hills of Darkness and hadn't even featured in the imaginary atlas voyages of Mother and son. But Berlin? It was around the corner, a mere train trip. What's more: Galicians were familiar with the German language. Thus, when Golda saw that her son could not put down the book, she promised that they would visit Berlin the following year (1933), as a *bar-mitzvah* gift to him, and see Nefertiti. However, Hitler's rise to power in January 1933 had preceded the boy's *bar-mitzvah* in August of that year, just as it had preempted the parents' *aliya* in 1939.

Before many years had passed, the high-schooler became a university student and the war made the student a soldier, and the soldier finally laid eyes on Nefertiti's bust. True, it was a different clay model, but it was in its most natural setting — in Egypt. Yet the Berlin representation that he had seen only on paper, stayed with him. "No matter" — he promised his fellow soldiers, who resigned themselves to his obsession and stopped teasing him — "when we enter defeated Berlin on our victory march, I'll take you to the museum to say 'hello' to Nefertiti. And you'll see for yourselves that my praise was justified. There never was, and there never will be, a more beautiful woman!"

At the time that these words were said, none of the Eretz-Israel soldiers in Egypt knew what had happened to the Jews of Europe. Nor could they imagine that it would not be the West's Allied forces that entered Berlin on a victory march when the war was over. No, it would be the Red Army that took hold of the destroyed city, and the Iron Curtain would bisect the continent and the whole world into "West" and "East", with the Berlin museums lodging in the "East" and remaining closed to "Western" soldiers. Only at the end of the twentieth century and the fall of the Berlin Wall, would the student, who had meanwhile become a professor, and the British soldier who had become an Israeli officer — manage, accompanied by his wife, to call on Nefertiti in Berlin.

The tour of the Amarna hall took longer than expected, and it was soon two hours to closing time. The final part of the tour, visually and emotionally the most difficult, required some preparation on the part of the visitor and it had intentionally been left for the end. This meant that important halls would have to be skipped, including the treasures from Tutenkhamun's tomb, found twenty years earlier in the Valley of Kings in the desert west of the Nile. Nevertheless, he felt that he had not yet exhausted the main substance of the Amarna hall and, no matter how late it was, he had to at least stop at one more display case, unique and famous. He could not leave without locating the Tel-Amarna Tablets, both because of their importance and because they reminded him of a high school experience. "It's ironic (he chuckled) that this site, breathing of pure antiquity — the antiquity of generations and peoples and rulers and historic events, and the antiquity of exhibits, such as these, that fill the building's two stories and ten rooms — harbors a youthful memory for me; and all, all are tied together by a hidden, unbreakable thread."

He approached the display case he sought. Unlike the others, containing fine or popular Egyptian art objects, wood or stone carvings, statues and figurines, jewelry etc., this particular one sheltered burnt or dried clay tablets with no pretense to art. They were the "writing paper" so to speak of ancient Assyrian and Babylonian civilization inscribed in cuneiform. The "letters" had been discovered in 1887, apparently a remnant of the Amarna royal archive. They include pleas to the King of Egypt from his vassals (among them, Abd-Hibah, King of Jerusalem) who, by the grace of the Egyptian patron, ruled the tiny city-states of the land of Canaan. The soldier recalled how excited he and his classmates had been at the Tarnów Hebrew high school eight years earlier when parts of the letters had been quoted in a history lesson: the various peoples of Canaan were apprehensive and entreated the pharaoh to intervene, for the tribes of "Habiru" — possibly "Ivrim [*Hebrews*]"

— were invading and settling Canaan. Was the identification as "Hebrews" accurate? If so, it was the first extra-biblical mention of Hebrews, although some scholars rejected the identification for various reasons. The schoolboys were nonetheless overjoyed to be Habirus — as if they had discovered their roots.

## V

Entering the hall of the mummies on the second floor, his final destination at the museum, the soldier was gripped by both anxiety — the natural human anxiety in the face of death — and pangs of conscience. Was it right or ethical to disturb a mummy's rest and change its position etc., especially when it was not even for the sake of science but to satisfy an ostensibly legitimate interest in history? Wasn't it voyeurism of a macabre and hair-raising sort? "No" — the small, shameless demon that had helped him plan the museum visit whispered to him — "there's nothing wrong with a bit of voyeurism! Don't you want to glimpse at Raamses' face from up close — the despot who enslaved the Israelites in his land; on the other hand, don't you want to see the megalomaniac with pretences to omnipotence laid out in the misery of shrouds, his embalmed body a mere shell, emptied in the process of guts, heart and everything that once gave him life?"

The young soldier-visitor quashed the inner voice and bared his unsure conscience to the person in charge of the gallery. The erudite Egyptian calmed him with a smile (smiling in the room of the dead?!): he told him that professionals had stolen a march on him by more than three thousand years, in the period of the twentieth dynasty; grave robbers who had not only disturbed the peace of the dead and fallen on the riches of the grand pharaonic tombs of the New Kingdom (the eighteenth and nineteenth dynasties) in the Valley of the Kings across the Nile, but had also disfigured the mummies. Over time, priests managed to collect the damaged mummies and rebury them at two concealed sites.

These buried treasures had only come to light about a century ago and "here they are before you", the Egyptian summed up. Pleased that an intelligent visitor had crossed his path, he led the soldier from one mummy to another, addressing each one by name. When they arrived at the mummy No. 12, he said in a monotone, "this is Raamses II", and continued straight on to the additional eight male and six female mummies. He did not notice that he had left the young man behind. The soldier's shoes were glued to the floor as his lips uttered: "This is Raamses II": a head on a wooden board, impressive despite its ninety-year life and unlike the huge statues of him. Balding. Hairs on the crown and nape. An aquiline nose. Large ears. Eyes shut. Clamped lips. Protruding cheekbones. A sharp chin. All power and dignity — even after thousands of years.

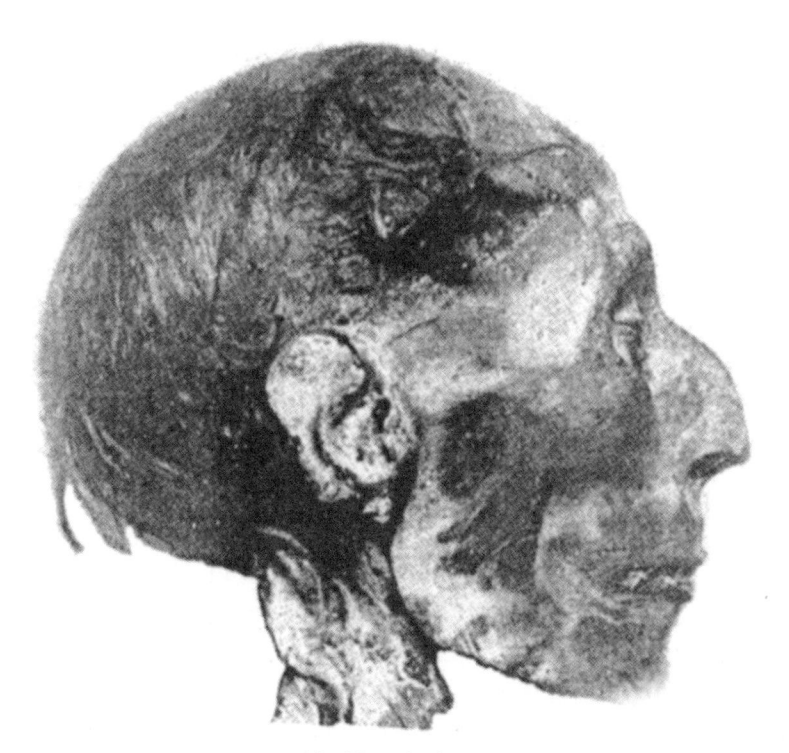

Mummified head of Raamses II

He could not take his eyes off the mummy. "Strange" — he debated with himself. Here he was gazing at the figure of the dead Raamses and he had the feeling that he had seen the face before. Where? In his imagination? While reading the Pentateuch? Moreover, he had no doubt that, had Raamses opened his eyes, he would certainly have been appalled to see him here. "Yes, it's me. I am more of an intruder on your rest than all the grave robbers down all the generations" — the young man said soundlessly — "for I am the new Hebrew. I am your nemesis. The son of Hebrews enslaved by you and your predecessors, and the son of Hebrews freed from slavery, and now I am a Hebrew soldier defending *your* country from the enemy. In addition, since half the world adopted the Hebrew Bible and the story of the Israelites under your oppressive rule, history remembers you because of the Hebrews, not because of all the steles and colossi you had erected in the years of your reign. And not only yours: of the hundreds of pharaonic steles decipherable to a handful of present-day scholars, one stele alone is mentioned in books: your son's, Merneptah's. And he and his stele only entered history because of a single word carved in stone, 'Israel'."

The soldier was worked up. The longer he stared at the king's face, the blurrier its facial features. In its place, another ancient face arose, expressing equal resolve, leadership and power. This one however sprouted a hoary beard and it, too, was known to the soldier: from imaginary scenes while reading the Pentateuch? Or from Mother's art books? *Moses!*

The train plied its way south. It passed Luxor, but the soldier was still under the lingering influence of the museum mummies, particularly of Moses' revelation against the background of the Raamses mummy. A real revelation or fanciful? The stages of his acquaintance with Moses flashed before his eyes, from the Pentateuch of his childhood to the heated debates with students years later on the question of monotheism: though it was reasonable to assume that Moses derived his monotheism from Akhenaten, as many argued, he, in contrast, stressed that Moses had gone beyond annulling polytheism; he had also repudiated the picture of the one god as the Sun Disc: *"Thou shalt not make unto thee a graven image, nor any manner of likeness, of any thing that is in heaven above"* — Moses demanded. Yet another argument had been sparked by the publication of Freud's last book (1939) which attributed Egyptian origins to Moses. Ankori, then in his third year at university, had summoned the lessons of history as witnesses: revolutionaries do not spring from the common folk but from classes above the people they are fighting for, and from a more advanced culture absorbed from the outside. Such was the Hebrew Moses.

There he was. The Hebrew infant snatched from the bulrushes of the Nile by Pharaoh's daughter and taken into the palace of her father, Pharaoh Seti I, where he was raised as an Egyptian along with his peer and playmate, Raamses, the king's son and designated successor. His head shaven according to Egyptian custom and dressed like a young Egyptian notable, he bore an undeniably Egyptian name: "Meses" or "Mosis", as in Tuthmosis, Ahmosis and Raamses (but Hebraized to *Moshe* [Moses] and without the prefix of the god). There he grew up and became a man, living comfortably like all assimilants in every period, until he was jolted back to reality by what may be termed an anti-Semitic event, which restored him to his people. Similarly, the Dreyfus trial was Herzl's rude awakening from assimilation, and other incidents acted on lesser people, such as Regina Seiden in Tarnów. Moses and Herzl, ex-assimilants, understood that the solution was exodus from the Diaspora and independence. This understanding returned Moses to the palace of Raamses, his former friend and now the Pharaoh, who respected his cultured, Hebrew childhood mate and allowed him to come and go as he pleased in the palace. But Moses looked straight into the Pharaoh's open eyes (shut in the mummy, of course), and boldly demanded of the friend, the ruler, the oppressive despot: *"Let my people go!"* Tirelessly, he repeated the demand for years until he wrested what he sought from the Pharaoh — perhaps no longer from Raamses but from his son, Merneptah, whose mummy is also on display at the museum — his resignation to the Israelite departure from Egypt.

"Incredible! Overwhelming! However important and reasonable the assumptions about Moses may be (including my own) — they don't even come close to what I experienced that one moment as I stood with Moses before Raamses' mummy. Both of us, Moses and myself, beheld that same face, Raamses', the face of sovereign arrogance and power — albeit three thousand years apart. Moses understood my language and I understand his, and our hearts beat as one. This, yes, *this* is the essence — and the secret — of history."

The train groaned from the long journey even though it must have been aware that most of the travelers had alighted in Luxor, easing its load. The soldier was finally able to stretch out in his seat and smile at the Nile Valley, persistently invading the car and painting the windows green. His visit to the museum yesterday had also ended with a smile, he recalled, despite the presence of the mummies. The gallery director, who had returned to Raamses when he realized that the guest had no interest in the other mummies, not even Merneptah's which was next to his father's, stood silently to the side, presumably alert to the young man's inner turmoil. At last, he tapped him gently on the shoulder, like a tour guide who felt he had to ease the visitor's distress, and whispered: "Only fifteen minutes to closing. Enough time to end with a refreshing sight". He led him to a collection of thousands of scarabs of every sort and material — granite, stone, clay and metal — and every size and from every period: they had filled a religious role (to the sun god), made reference to the pharaohs and their reign, served as seals with inscriptions engraved on their flat bases, and their oval form had been found suitable for necklaces and signet rings. The "tour guide" explained that in the New Kingdom, the period of the mummies they had seen, it had been the custom to place a large stone scarab inside a mummy's shrouds, etched with a chapter from *The Book of the Dead*. Popular with the public inside Egypt and, in time, also outside of Egypt, they were all artistic renderings of real scarabs. A pair of huge green granite scarabs, in particular, caught the soldier's eye. Little did he know that he would come across them again.

Musing about the marvelous scarabs, he was hardly aware that the train had stopped. "Qenah!" the conductor thundered. The soldier took his kitbag and got off. He had finally reached his destination.

## VI

As soon as he arrived at 178 Coy, the soldier sensed the dejected mood at the base. He reported to the Company Sergeant Major, CSM Bankover — who had received his initial stripes in the first Royal (Eretz-Israeli) Auxiliary Military Pioneer Corps (AMPC) units in Greece, avoided German captivity and had been promoted upon his transfer to the (Palestine) Jewish Transport Unit some time before the arrival of the Jerusalem volunteer in Qenah. "Private Zvi Ankori, No. 30653, reporting for service, sir" — recited the newcomer as taught at Sarafend and handed over his Movement Order. "At ease", the Ramat HaKovesh kibbutznik smiled at the recent graduate of British Sarafend — "here, orders are in Hebrew, as you are familiar with them from the Haganah. Discipline is the same as in every army, but relations are friendly and you'll feel at home. We've heard about you and know something of your background. We expect you'll fit in well and be an asset to the Company beyond your daily duties. Come back after you get organized and we'll chat." The tyro '178er' in fact soon found his feet in B Platoon, where he was to remain for five years until the end of his service (or "for the duration", according to official British phrasing).

"So the dejection is not due to personal antagonisms" — the new soldier dismissed his first natural assumption. That was encouraging but also doubly dismaying, for he had no idea what to attribute the gloom to. He, in any case, was determined to do something to keep up his own spirits, even if he could not improve the camp atmosphere. The first thing was to talk to Bankover, as the latter had suggested. On Saturday, when they were both free, the CSM and the Private met for what was possibly an unprecedented army chat in terms of length, informality and instant rapport despite differences in rank and age. Subsequently, he got to know the rank and file — tyros, veterans, sergeants, and even a number of officers. Though none of the tyros knew him personally, the kibbutzniks among them may have opened their hearts to him because of his Hanita background; other freshmen tyros, who may have been beginner-students, sought his friendship possibly because they knew him as a graduate student. Either way, after mulling over what they told him, he felt that he had gotten to the bottom of the problem:

It's hard to contend with a *myth*, especially one that had holes punched in it. It's hard to contend with *frustration*, when it was basically justified. And the bitter blend of the two was that much harder still.

The *myth* was the eulogy of 5MT, the first Jewish transport unit to enter Libya's Cyrenaica region upon the British attack and was stationed at Tobruq. The period — as Churchill had said in a different context — was "their finest hour". But the Wehrmacht had trounced the British and torn eastward, and on its way it had laid siege to pockets of resistance such as Tobruq. The *victorious* myth of Tobruq thus made way for a more glorious myth: *besieged* Tobruq. On July 23, 1941 the besieged fled and the myth of Tobruq dissolved. The veterans of 5MT, wearied of their role after the trauma of retreat, began to quit the army on various pretexts. Not a few however continued to serve in the successor Company, the new 178, passing on to the latter's soldiers the distress of the disintegrated myth that gnawed at their minds and hearts.

The *frustration* stemmed from the location of the base after the retreat, in Egypt's backyard so to speak, far from both the Libyan front and Palestine. The Company's mission too appeared petty: providing transport for the paving of a road from Qenah via the eastern desert to Safaga on the Red Sea. "What? No longer supplying ammunition, fuel and food to troops entrenched only a hundred kilometers from Alexandria, but provisions for a rear escape route and the complete retreat from Egypt?" — 178's experts protested. Archive documents on the war actually corroborate their assumption. "Optimistic pessimists" whispered that it was "better to be in Safaga": in a hidden hangar somewhere on the coast, a ship was being built and when the critical order came — "Help yourselves!" — we'll sail home. The Jerusalemites were quiet: in those days, there were no swimming pools in the city and Jerusalemites didn't know how to swim. Tel Avivians wondered whether it was worth sailing to Aqaba or, if the Suez Canal was still operational, directly to Tel Aviv. Tel Aviv? Yes, to the port that had opened with great fanfare during the "Disturbances" and was immortalized in a photograph of two sacks of cement en route to the museum, amid an enthusiastic rendition of "We are building a port here". No one of course saw a ship or builders, no one had come across any hangar on the coast. The idea, despite its Zionist destination — Eretz-Israel — was from the start defeatist. And yet the talk was not entirely unfounded: if not by sea, then maybe overland, through the Eastern Desert along the canal? Ultimately, the plans were all dropped.

Ankori and other soldiers who, like him, believed that it was possible, indeed necessary, to change matters, tried out new approaches to limit the number of absentees from Sabbath parties and "cultural" programs ("sh-h-h! A dirty word"). In their new format, the get-togethers featured Capt. Sakharov in a review of "The week in politics" and "The week in war"; Hazan did what Shalom Aleikhem had never even dreamed of doing: he had soldier Menahem Mendl dispatch military news on a weekly basis to his spouse, Shaineh-Sheindl; Flaschman contributed a feuilleton; Dubi Levine sang Yiddish songs from home; and Shklar and Ankori vied every week over an intra-company song. Ankori also formed a choir and the evening rehearsals, in spite of a hard day's driving on desert roads, attracted participants. Moreover, at every opportunity, there were of course sing-alongs which always included the learning of a new song.

The choir reaped its first reward on July 24, 1942, with the performance of a skit for the night of Tish'a BeAv (the Ninth of Av, the anniversary of the Temple's destruction). The full title appeared in the Company's newsletter *HaHayal HaIvri* (The Hebrew Soldier): "*'MiHurban LeVinyan'* (From Destruction to Upbuilding), arranged and adapted by soldier Zvi Ankori and delivered by the Unit choir." The paper also printed the full version of the skit. It was performed in the formation yard before the whole Company, with vehicles parked in a "three-sided box" as a natural backdrop, and torches furnishing lighting. For a while, the skit's production seemed to signal a turning point in the unit's self-image. It was the talk of the Company for a day or two, but it made a slight dent only in the apathy and emotional fatigue of the rank and file.

Three weeks after the much-lauded performance, quite a few people continued to absent themselves from the Sabbath gatherings. Ankori was not content with "a dent"; he sought to tear the mantle of apathy to shreds. He published a "Letter to a Friend" (under the signature of Z.A.) in the *HaHayal HaIvri* of August 14, 1942. The opening lines and a few closing lines cited here reflect the mood of the soldiers, especially the veterans:

> "You left me a note and it spoke for you thus, self-abashed:
>
> "I've grown weary, my friend, I beg you, don't censure me. In Eretz-Israel, my place was also with the activists, the visionaries, the doers. I, too, have tasted of the trials of Tobruq. But, now, I have done my duty: I am a soldier. May my soldiering continue softly, without constant striving for —"

❖ ❖ ❖

"You left me a note and it spoke for you, self-abashed:

I do not know you — —
 I do not know you by name but I see you, in every corner of our base I see you. I saw you arising anew on one of our Sabbath evenings, entirely decided to break out of your alien shell. And then I saw you sinking back into inaction and mindlessness...
 Arise, friend, and say your piece. If you are embittered — say so. If your light has been extinguished — read in the dark.
 Let's link arms and march together, together —"

The lads that persisted in the activities, despite their disappointment at the poor turnout for Sabbath get-togethers, had the loving and loyal support of Moshe Mosenzon of Kibbutz Naan, editor of the Company's *HaHayal HaIvri*. He regularly reported on the Sabbath gatherings, sometimes citing the songs, just as he printed hundreds of copies of the full version of the Tish'a BeAv skit as a supplement to the newspaper and distributed them to the soldiers of 178 and of other Eretz-Israeli units. He did it out of a sense of mission (as he wrote in the paper): "the matter is of interest to us as a memento of the evening and to other units as a blueprint for their holiday celebrations."

It soon became clear that the standard Sabbath gatherings had little impact on the general dejection and the active core tried to introduce informative pastimes such as lectures on ancient Egypt and tours of the area, to Luxor and to Aswan. In one of the lectures Ankori surprised the soldiers by telling them that 178 was not the first Jewish unit in the history of the area. In the time of Ezra and Nehemia, the fifth century BCE, with Egypt under Persian rule, a Jewish military colony in Yev, opposite Aswan, had guarded the southern Persian border. The story of the historical continuity stirred interest, but it did not dislodge the gloom. The truth was that the dispiritedness of the Jewish unit, made up of highly-motivated volunteers, reflected the greater and more general gloom of the British army in the Middle East. The General Staff was alert to the low morale on the North African front; it stemmed from a string of defeats and the lack of a suitable response to the new German war methods. The panicked retreat over hundreds of kilometers inside Egypt, the frequent replacement of failing commanders, and the absence of any sign of a more successful course of action did not escape the soldiers; they experienced it all first hand. From officers in stripes down to the very last private, everyone hoped for a quick change in the personnel conducting the war.

## VII

The change came on August 7, 1942. General Montgomery was appointed commander of the Eighth Army and of the Allied forces on the North African front.

A new spirit now fired the large army base facing Rommel and the German-Italian armies. It was felt that under "Monty" — who had scored previous successes, including the rescue at Dunkirk during the miserable stage of war in Europe — the string of defeats would end, opening the door to major historical developments in North Africa. The soldiers of the Eighth Army and 178 among them were glad to be part of the campaign that was to prove decisive.

On August 14, the Unit was ordered to leave Upper Egypt and redeploy at Geneifa in the Suez Canal area to await new orders. In light of the expected action, backs straightened, frustration dissolved, apathy and listlessness were banished. A new era dawned.

Apart from transport missions to sites along the Suez Canal — Kibrit, Kasasin, Fa'id, Port Sa'id, Port Fuad, Suez, Port Tawfiq and, above all, lovely Ismailiya — and beyond the anticipation of the great day itself, the move to Geneifa provided two novelties. One was almost immediately evident and hung in the air until the transfer to the front — the Unit's encounter with ATS 509, a Company of Eretz-Israel female soldiers. It was almost a family reunion ("178 are like older brothers", as one of the nurses put it), not to mention the fact that after long months in the Qenah-Safaga desert, the male soldiers saw every young woman as a princess of dreams. Meetings usually took place on Sundays, when most of the young servicemen and women were free, on the lawn above the Canal at Ismailiya. The seat of the Canal administration, Ismailiya was a specially planted, wide-ranging, surprisingly green, wondrous island in a sea of ochre desert. Joint cultural activities were quickly set up. The female choir joined the male choir and in September 1942, under Ankori's baton, both performed his skit for the Jewish New Year, "*Likrat HaBaot* (Towards Things to Come)", solo parts alternating between men and women. This text, too, was published in full in *HaHayal HaIvri*.

In advent of the performance, choir rehearsals were intensive, taking place every evening after the drivers returned from duty. Choirmaster Ankori was given permission to hold separate rehearsals in the women's camp, provoking the chaps to jest that he was in mortal danger from the jealous non-Jewish guards at the gate ("and maybe from my green-eyed peers as well?" — he chuckled in pleasure). On the evening of the celebration, the camp of 178 donned a festive air. Unlike the first performance held in the formation yard at Qenah, the veteran, orderly Geneifa base had permanent buildings and a large auditorium, and the skit could be staged indoors along with a holiday meal for hundreds of guests. Decked out in white tablecloths, the tables boasted fine dishes, including the traditional apple and honey, and even vases with roses in honor of the female soldiers (though everyone wondered how the flowers had been brought in). The united choir earned lengthy, resounding applause.

The second novelty, awaiting Unit 178 at the Canal, related to the vehicles. The old vehicles that had served the Unit in Qenah and Safaga were put out to pasture — a "motley crowd" of every type of conveyance with "historical" production dates, collected or impounded by the army before it had been ready for war, to hastily equip the first transport units. These were now replaced by standard U.S.-made Bedford trucks (or, in British English, "lorries"). The workshop soon painted a blue Star of David against a white background on the doors of the lorries, and spry drivers procured paint so they could festoon the front fenders with the names — and namesakes — of their Shoshannas, Rinas, Sarahs, Dahlias and their sisters, who, without jealousy or rivalry, trusted their private drivers to neither bend the fenders nor — dear oh dear — injure them in an accident. The vehicle mechanics of the 178 workshop — a virtually autonomous section under Second Lieutenant Silberstein and the Regimental Sergeant Major (RSM), who was universally known as "Tayyish" (Goat) even though he had no hint of a beard — relished their initiation into the secrets of the Bedfords and, at every stop, no matter how temporary, eagerly stood at the ready to administer repairs to real or imaginary problems.

As a matter of fact, there was no lack of problems, either of the regular sort of malfunctioning components, or due to incautious driving and accidents, or because of built-in faults; in the urgency of war, the Bedfords had been hastily constructed and handed over to the British for immediate use before they were properly tested.

Now, it happened that some men gained glory for their care of the Bedfords, though the lorries were crushed or facing "cardiac arrest", while to others, the Bedfords, healthy and in good working order, brought shame and setback. The two instances cited here were neither concurrent nor connected; their common denominator was that they occurred in the desert and took their place in the mythology of Company 178.

The first instance concerned the workshop and reflected the work ethic of 178. It was totally contrary to the conception of the striped English servicemen who limited their duties to command and supervision. Sixty years later, "Tayyish", looking back on his days as RSM of the 178 workshop, recounted: "The English were bowled over to find a Regimental Sergeant Major lying under a vehicle and doing repairs with his own hands along with the workshop NCOs and mechanic privates busy at the very same job." The elderly Abraham Silberstein, who had been workshop commander sixty years earlier, fills in the story: "After that many convoys on desert roads, the vehicles required repairs for further use. The many trucks were scattered over a large area, every driver standing next to his truck and waiting for a mechanic. By chance or not by chance, the Brigadier appeared; he was in charge of all the transport units of the Eighth Army. At the sight of the number of vehicles waiting to be fixed, he asked me how I meant to tackle all the work. Since I knew my men's dedication, I said unhesitatingly: 'Tomorrow morning, all the Bedfords will be ready, sir.' The veteran officer, used to the British pace of work, found it hard to believe. The next day, entirely not by chance, he returned. The lot was empty. 'Well done, Captain Silberstein'. 'I am a Second Lieutenant, sir', I tried to correct him. 'As of this moment you are a captain', he declared. On the following day a motorcyclist arrived at 178 headquarters, with formal approval of the promotion."

The workshop RSM continues the story: "Captain Silberstein — yes, Captain! — still excited and hardly believing that it was true, assembled all the workshop men who knew nothing of what had transpired (I hadn't said a word, for I wanted the appointee himself to tell them), and reported on the turn of events, thanking and praising them all, and saying that it was only due to their devoted work that he had been promoted."

The second instance concerned the present author and his new Bedford. Ankori understood the importance of exchanging the old wrecks for cars capable of working around the clock, as would be expected of the Unit in the coming days and weeks. Yet he mourned his Albion, which had seen better days in the First World War and had not been produced in years. Its high front seat afforded an open view into the distance.

The Albion's high seat remained a fond memory for years, as the former 178er, from time to time conjured up the fierce desert sandstorm between Qenah and Safaga that had covered the windshield in thick dust. The sandstorm caused limited visibility and blinded the driver of a standard vehicle that was moving forward

— straight into the side of the Albion. Ankori was saved from sure injury only because of the high seat.

The Albion furnished another fond memory as well. The man attached to Ankori as second-driver was Shlomo Lavie of Kibbutz Ein-Harod. Lavie was one of the older soldiers who had volunteered for army service in answer to the call of conscience. Whatever their real contribution, there is no doubt about their sincerity — with the exception of one or two functionaries who regarded their service as a personal springboard.

From the height of the Albion, Ankori and Lavie gazed out on the desert landscape and chatted about home and homeland — the sixty-year-old Second Aliya pioneer and the twenty-two-year-old Fifth Aliya pioneer both belonged to Eretz-Israel's Labor movement, the one a pioneer at Ein-Harod, the other at Hanita. The scornful may have ridiculed Lavie as he roamed about with an open tin to collect old screws and nails — "the kibbutz will find this useful" — but Ankori considered every trip with him a privilege and etched their conversations on his memory. Like the Albion that disappeared with the arrival of the Bedfords, though unconnected to it, Lavie too disappeared from the Unit one day. There was not a word of explanation, nor did he take leave of his young friend.

Was he discharged due to age before the impending battle? The mystery was solved in a letter by Lavie to *HaHayal HaIvri*: after being shuttled about, he reported, he was absorbed by Unit 468 on the home front. His young driving partner did not meet up with him again.

Banishing his grief for the Albion, the cocky Ankori did not bother to have a dry run on his new Bedford as did some of the men. The next morning, he took his place behind the wheel near the head of a long convoy, when suddenly, there was a screech and a knock-knock — the kiss of death. Death? Puzzling in a horse so young. His attempts to revive the engine were greeted by dying grunts. Pressing on the starter, he managed to move the truck to the side of the road and place a warning triangle several paces behind it — all according to rule. Other trucks in the convoy passed him.

Drivers waved as if to say "never mind" and he responded in kind, cheerful and well-disposed. Mentally, he reviewed the lessons in the theory of mechanics, pleased to remember that he had been deemed an excellent student. On one occasion, the instructor had asked, "which screw in the car is the most important?" The men tried their luck, mentioning every screw they could think of. The Englishman shook his head: "No!" Ankori didn't know either, but he decided to try a jest: "The missing one!" he said. To his astonishment, the sergeant cried: "That's it! — You're smart". This was the first time that the soldier heard the word "smart" used in the sense of "clever". In His Majesty's army, it usually meant trim and tidy — and was a supreme value and necessary condition: "If you get into trouble, do so smartly!" In other words: Shave! The Tobruqites, he recalled, had recounted that after the heavy, two-day battle ending in the siege of Tobruq, an English major had assembled his company for roll call and inspected the ranks, as customary. Finding an exhausted soldier unshaven, he lifted the poor culprit's chin with his stick and declared out loud so that justice could be heard as well as seen: "Because of you, Tobruq fell!"

Ankori took out his messtin, poured in some water from the canteen, dipped in his brush and spread shaving cream on his cheeks and chin. He submitted to the ministrations of the Gillette, which, at first stroke, posed as sharp. Finishing the cosmetic treatment, he rinsed his face. He had thus paid his dues to "smartness". Now — to work! Screw. Pliers. Monkey wrench. He dismantled this and that, blew into this or that pipe to the best of his ability, screwed, tightened, and put the whole lot back together again. The engine grunted briefly and died a clinical death.

"There's no choice" — the penny-mechanic diagnosed — "but to wait for the rearguard." He put the tools back into the box along with his pride and self-confidence. The rearguard vehicle arrived and deposited Sergeant Miller. The soldier sighed: "Miller is from A Platoon. He doesn't know me."

"What's the problem?"

"The car won't budge. The engine's dead."

"Just like that? It went and died?" The irony was lost on Ankori. "So what have you tried?"

Ankori went into detail about his efforts and the tools he used. In vain.

"Good. Very good. You're a busy lad, are you?" Ankori still didn't get the irony.

"Would you be so kind as to permit me into the cabin?" Only then did the grounded driver realize that the A Platoon sergeant, who must have heard about the driver as a "culture-vulture", was mocking him just as he mocked all touted culture lovers. Miller climbed into the cabin, glanced at the dashboard and got out.

"Go to my car, get a jerrycan of petrol from my driver, and bring it here. Understood?"

"Now unscrew the cap of the petrol tank (not there, in Bedfords the tank is on the other side) and pour in the petrol. Done? Now get into the cabin and start the engine."

"Well done! Drive!" The sergeant left, but soon returned, ostensibly because he had forgotten the empty jerry can.

"Hey, Ankori, what sign are you?"

"Cancer."

"Cancer. The crab. You know why crabs walk on their sides?"

"Why?"

"Because they have no brains!"

In the afternoon of October 20, 1942 the base was dismantled and 178 moved out. They were to drive and stop, drive and stop — the lorry serving the soldiers as both road vehicles and homes, their bedding being the ammunition crates making their way to the front, i.e. el-Alamein, inside Egypt itself — oh, oh! — only a hundred kilometers west of Alexandria, the location of the earlier trouncing. Now, the frontline soldiers were flexing their muscles in anticipation of the longed-for order from Monty: Charge!

The moon of October 23, 1942 crept quietly up the hidden heavenly ladder, unsuspecting that anyone was plotting to disrupt its tranquil passage across the sky. In utter neutrality, it gazed from above at two armies stationed along the non-sandy, desert coastal belt girding North Africa. Passable on foot, by horse and vehicle (unlike the southern desert of heavy sand), the coastal belt had been settled since ancient times: whether by the Phoenicians who came by sea from Lebanon and established their colonies there, or the Greeks, Romans, Byzantines, Vandals, Arabs, Turks and French, or twentieth-century Italians who came to realize Mussolini's imperial dreams, driving the native Sanusi (i.e. Libyans) and Berbers from their land and their desert way of life. Now the Italians were allied to the Germans in a political, belligerent Axis, poised against the British and the Commonwealth, including the volunteers of the Jewish Yishuv in Palestine. The coastal strip, down the generations, had taken them all in.

Not straying from its millennial routine, the moon dispatched jets of light at the historic desert, painting it silver; at the same time, it poured ewers of silver-sheen onto the Mediterranean blue — the sea we admired in our youth from the Tel Aviv walkway; now we saw it spreading out further and further up to the Atlantic Ocean — its African border hugging the coast. And thus the two remain embraced, the Mediterranean Sea and the Western Desert, in peace and in war, for eternity.

Had the moon that evening turned its glance on the army behind the line of the earlier defeat at el-Alamein, and peeked into the commander's tent, it would have learned that the commander considered it, the moon, a friend and ally, enlisting its light in the plan that would bring the British victory in Africa. Suddenly, as the moon strewed silver light onto sea and desert, there was a clap of thunder unprecedented to African ears: 900 cannons under Monty, across the entire el-Alamein line, opened their jaws in flashing bombardment and paved the way for the moonlit charge of the infantry and armored corps. In contrast to previous commanders, who had not managed to come up with a response to German warfare, Monty wisely borrowed the German method itself and used it to wear down the German forces. Thus, on November 4, 1942, the Battle of el-Alamein ended with the complete routing of the enemy. The fleeing forces were pursued for half a year until their full surrender. Rommel was left with thirty-six tanks!

# VIII

His eyes blinked in the dark and the wind crooned through the soldier's dusty forelock. Somewhere in the distance, the stubborn engines of German Stuka planes still chugged, in a last-ditch attempt to make up for the drubbing of their infantry and armored corps comrades on the new front line, relentlessly pushed back by Monty's troops. The Stukas tended to tail convoys, including 178's, and spray them with machine gun fire. The danger aside, the convoys moved back and forth, back and forth, bringing ammunition to the front, bombs for vanguard aircraft, spare parts, petrol and food, administering constant transfusions to the front's vital, life-giving transportation artery.

As protection against the machine gun, three suggestions — suggestions, not solutions — were offered. Huge signs posted along the route warned drivers: "Keep your distance". Within range of the front, the signs — now red — were a tad more inelegant: "Don't be a bloody fool — Keep your distance". Keeping one's distance of course didn't dispel the danger; it simply lowered the number of potential casualties. One morning, two heavy Macs passed the 178 convoy at dizzying speed. Ten minutes later, by the time the 178 convoy reached the site, the English soldiers were already burying the two Mac drivers, their deaths credited to a Stuka pilot. One convoy vehicle stopped to help. From pieces of broken wood scattered on the sand, drivers of 178 improvised two crosses and the English wrote the names of the dead men on them; the Mac drivers had apparently been from their unit.

The second suggestion applied to face-to-face encounters with a Stuka: "Stop the car, jump into a trench at the side of the road or into any ditch for cover. Crouch as best you can, cover your head with your hands and…. pray."

The third suggestion was not advice at all but a strict order: It called for utter blackout during nighttime driving, including around bends, no matter how perilous.

Squinting and straining from the effort, the last car groped its way between blocks of darkness on every side. A last parking-order was snuffed out in the night breeze. This, then, was the new camp. Not much of a camp. One tent, the HQ's. Where was it? Couldn't say for sure. Dazed, you drove all evening along not much of a road, your hands clutching the steering wheel, your eyes painfully trying to make out a black rectangle moving ahead of you, blacker than the black night, while keeping a steady distance from it. There was some comfort in the thought that you had a friend in that rectangle: like you, he was hunched over the steering wheel. And in front of that rectangle, there was another, with another friend, and another, just like all the rectangles behind you, and like you they all couldn't wait to finally reach the camp on this endless black night. During the six days that the convoy had been on the road, driving into the unknown, the HQ platoon had been ordered to move forward and set up temporary camp a hundred and eighty kilometers west of el-Alamein. El-Daba and Bir-Foqa had been passed, and we were now in the Egyptian capital of the desert, Mersa Matruh. Yes, until a week ago, all this had been conquered territory. From here, the convoy was to continue westward to Sollum, high up on the Libyan border overlooking Cyrenaica.

Still squinting, your eyes soon isolated blocks in the darkness. This was the camp-no-camp. No tents apart from the HQ's. As in the convoys, so here, too, at this more or less orderly stop, drivers would bed down in Bedfords camouflaged with tarpaulin. Over there, the large block behind the HQ tent was presumably the workshop; the three blocks of vehicles, in semi-circle in front of the HQ tent, were the three platoons:

B Platoon, yours, was in the center, A Platoon was to its right, C Platoon to its left. The next morning, you reconnoitered the area in daylight. There was the Mersa Matruh Plain spread out before you. To the right, i.e., *to your right* as you faced the convoy's next destination, lay the white shore and blue sea. From here on, the sun would always rise *behind you*, and in the afternoon, slowly gliding from the slopes on the horizon, the sun would always set *before you*. And a good thing too: for it was towards the sunset that you were heading, westward, and you would get there in the end, with Monty.

And tomorrow you would set out again with the convoy. And the road would be littered with fallen aircraft, broken tanks, vehicles bereft of wheels and orphaned stores, as well as crosses upon crosses upon crosses along the roadside. And the crosses would reach out, one arm eastward and the other, westward. Arrogant Prussian crosses, straining upward, the largest for the high and mighty, the lower ones for lifelong underlings, the lowliness of their lives still bearing down in death like an irremovable hump. And two miserable sticks would stand near a charred tank or an upside-down vehicle or a heap of twisted steel. And a smashed aircraft lying on the ground would stretch its wings like a black cross, in expired splendor as it were. And a lonely mound that friends or a passing soldier had piled up in haste (for fear of renewed bombing) would sport a rusty steel helmet or a random bottle — in memory to the *human being* that had been. And at an intersection, a smooth piece of wood would show two signs in the form of a cross and, on them, an inscription in modest Italian and in round and proud Gothic German — in memory to the *power* that had been. Only after the war were the crosses to be salvaged and replaced by burial in cemeteries large and small, their symmetric flowerbeds carefully measured and installed with geometric accuracy. Crosses on the way of the convoy, one arm reaching eastward, the other, westward. Eastward was the destination of those who hadn't made it. Westward was where we were advancing — —

A week later you returned to Mersa Matruh. This time, you noticed that the sea at Mersa Matruh was not blue, as you had thought before; this time it was purple with a shade of blue.

And it gave you pause: the Indian soldier in the next unit looked out at the same sea and saw the shore of Bombay, his hometown;

and the English soldier with his hair singed saw in the sea Dover, his hometown, just as you, looking at the Egyptian sea, imagined the Carmel Coast and Bay, and the Sea of Galilee. All at once, each and every man remembered that the sea *there*, in the landscape of his heart, was just as purple as here, with a shade of blue.

And you thought further: only ten days ago, an Italian soldier had stood here. In his love letter to his sweetheart, he wrote that the Mersa Matruh sea was just like that of Naples, purple with a shade of blue. And the German next to him thought of Hamburg, seeing in his mind's eye the sea of his hometown, and it was purple with a shade of blue, like here, in Mersa Matruh. And yet, we were enemies. A chilling thought...

Tomorrow we would be setting out again with the convoy. And as the Eighth Army advanced in pursuit of the enemy, now in retreat but fighting for every inch, the supply lines from Mersa Matruh to the front line would grow longer. El-Alamein! Unforgettable! As was the bitter battle of Englishmen, Australians, New Zealanders, Indians, South Africans as well as soldiers from outside the Commonwealth, Poles and Frenchmen. They suffered heavy losses but fought bravely on to victory under Monty, while Rommel lost 500 tanks and 1,200 cannons, and forty thousand of his soldiers were captured. Unforgettable el-Alamein! In the distant future each and every soldier would proudly tell his grandchildren: "I was there!"

Daytime driving was pleasant regardless of the Stuka threat. Your eyes would sometimes discover something new, and the distances were no longer unknown as they had been at first. Daytime driving, unlike the demands of blackout, did not force you to fix your eyes on the moving rectangle of the lorry in front of you. It was enough to keep your distance, as the signs warned. By day, in coordination with your hand on the steering wheel, your eyes were free to absorb the war landscape, while your heart could do what every soldier's heart did best: complain. Not a complaint of frustration — far be it — as in Qenah (Qenah? Where was that? When were we there? Years ago?). For now, you were here, where you had volunteered to be — in the thick of a crucial campaign to decide the outcome of the war. And, as if in keeping with the Law of Connected Vessels, you carried out your mission, without which the forward infantry and tanks could not do theirs. All were inter-dependent. So what was there to complain about?

Actually, there were two causes for complaint. One was a practical issue: since by the dint of hard work, the supply stores had been advanced from Egypt to the Cyrenaica region on Libya's doorstep, to be close to the front — why didn't our base move there as well? Obviously, even without the complaints, the move was imminent — but, if at all possible, why not complain; within limits of course? The other cause was more of an ineffable wish, merely whispered in intimate groups. Why should 178 see to supplying tanks and tank forces? Couldn't 178ers themselves have been those very tank forces? Formally, we were drivers, there being no Eretz-Israel tank units at that time. But if soldiers could be upgraded to officers after proving their dedication, why couldn't Unit 178 be upgraded too? It had proved its capability in every respect.

## IX

The convoy of B Platoon returned to base Friday afternoon. By fluke (or by order unknown to us) the convoys of the other two platoons also arrived and parked their empty lorries at the designated site. For the first time since leaving the Suez Canal area, the entire Company was together in one place. According to rumor, it was the Company's last Sabbath at Mersa Matruh. Tomorrow, the HQ tent and the workshop were to be dismantled. On Sunday, after the new base was erected on the pattern of the previous one, every platoon would set out in a separate convoy for reasons of safety, and eventually meet up in Cyrenaica.

In the dark valley behind the gleaming sandy shore, the Company assembled for its first party after Geneifa. Such powerful singing as broke out that Sabbath eve at Mersa Matruh had not been heard between the desert and the sea (albeit the Mediterranean rather than the Red Sea) since the telling of Exodus — "*Then sang Moses and the children of Israel this song... for He is highly exalted; the horse and his rider hath He thrown into the sea*". After the sing-along, Ankori surprised his fellow soldiers with "The Ballad of Mersa Matruh" to the tune of a music box. It was both a farewell to the site and to Egypt, and an echo of what was on the mind of every 178 soldier.

>  Whooshing and rustling, embracing the sand,
>  The wind sings last ballad in Egypt's dark land.
>  The wind's passing by, the wind's in a squall —
>  The convoy rides roads that are no roads at all.
>      A convoy crawls slowly on a night dark and black \x2
>      To Mersa Matruh on a desert trek. \
>
>  The horizon is black for dark is the night —
>  "Darkness of Egypt" (the Bible was right),
>  "Darkness of Egypt", crosses line the way,
>  Charred tanks with swastikas in silent array.
>      A road that's no road, all hopes nearly dashed, \x2
>      A German tank — oops! How sudden the crash. \
>
>  Bum-galli-galla, the storm not yet gone,
>  Here's how the ballad starts moving on.
>  Black are the heavens, the wind gusts in bouts,
>  From inside the tank, two eyes seek me out.
>      Good God, give me strength before I go under! \x2
>      Inside the tank I make out my commander. \
>
>  Sitting so sadly with his lips pressed tight,
>  No scepter or frills, or trappings of might.
>  Then, disillusioned, he smiled with dismay
>  And secretly this he decided to say:
>      The tank is a peerless contraption, see? \x2
>      I dreamed of it often in old 5MT. \

Bum-galli-galla, their head and their mind,
Lead on the ballad forthwith to unwind.
Darkness outside, but inside the sun
Brings Private and Major dream on as one.
    Dream on as one of the desert, of course \x2
    Of tanks and of battles and a proud Hebrew force. \

To drive not lorries but battle-ready tanks
Is the hope that excites for weeks all ranks —
How great is the hope, enchanting and neat:
Star-of-David tanks will the enemy meet!
    Then sudden boom-boom, I quickly came to, \x2
    Enter the Sergeant. His next step I knew: \

"What's this?" he shouts, "On duty you sleep?
Your lorry and a Mac were nigh in a heap.
So what if it's dark, so what if it's night?
Here in the desert you do your work right!
    No resting here, or having a stop — \x2
    Night or no night, get on with the job." \

"What idle talk's this? Oh, demon so cunning!
What night do you fancy? The sun is asunning.
Your lecture on jobs deserves no thanks!
We leave in the morning driving our tanks!
    And be it mere fancy, be distant the day, \x2
    Let me hold on to my dream all the way!" \

Bum-galli-galla, no stopping or rest,
The thread of the ballad moves further with zest:
Darkness… but inside shine rays of the sun,
Private and Sergeant dream on as one —
    Dreaming as one of the desert, of course, \x2
    Of tanks and of battles and a Hebrew force. \

Rumor takes wing down the vale and uphill,
All three platoon convoys come to standstill.

Hearts of the dreamers, whatever their rank,
Make truck they are driving Valentina tank.
    Each driver now puts his Bedford aside \×2
    Stands proud in the turret commanding the ride. \

Bum-galli-galla, valid non-valid,
The story reached top, and so does the ballad:
Darkness… but inside shine rays of the sun,
The Company in full is dreaming as one.
    Rumor flies high straight to its fate: \×2
    Hebrew Tank Company One-Seven-Eight. \

Bum-galli-galla, the ballad is done,
Dawn spawns a new day awaiting the sun.
The ballad is done, the sun is agleam.
But a Jewish tank remains still a dream.
    A dream we dreamt driving through night dark and black
    To Mersa Matruh on the desert track.
    A dream we dreamt driving through night dark and black
    To Mersa Matruh on the desert track.

There was no need to teach the catchy "music box" tune. After one or two verses, the men began to hum along excitedly with the songwriter. There were no song sheets, useless in any case in conditions of total blackout. Ankori was asked to go over the song again and again, and the soldiers followed his lead, learning the words. Even when the get-together broke up, each man going to his vehicle, the tune and the words stayed with him, searing his lips as if coming from the heart. In the next issue of *HaHayal Halvri*, Moshe Mosenzon wrote about the ballad "written by Ankori, who sang it full of feeling, and the audience, following him, repeated the daydream of a driver and a major of a Hebrew tank. And pride filled the heart with the ballad's unwinding."

    Ankori was too excited to shut his eyes beneath the Bedford tarpaulin. When the dale emptied of people, he stretched out on the good earth drenched with dew, aware, without seeing it, that the Tel Aviv sea watched over his head. A soothing, velvety stillness hovered over the valley. No hum of a plane, no roar of cannon, no war in the world, no crosses, no bloodshed. There was only the night scent of the earth, the same scent that had filled the lungs of the young man in Hanita as he lay on the ground of Lower Hanita at night, and Shaikeh, his instructor, initiated him in the secrets of the stars, suspended high above there much like here, at Mersa Matruh... And blessed be the unforgettable valley of Mersa Matruh and blessed the nighttime stillness, for momentarily *Eretz-Israel* descended unto them.

When he opened his eyes, the sun ushered in 178's last Saturday at Mersa Matruh; no day of rest but brisk and busy with the dismantling of the base.

## X

The B Platoon convoy was the last to leave this time. The road to Sollum veered from the coast and passed Sidi Barani. Those who remembered the war's start in Africa could not repress a chuckle. Two and a half years earlier, in July 1940, under Marshal Graziani, an Italian division from Libya, the great Italian colony, had invaded Sidi Barani with much fanfare. The target was to reach Mersa Matruh, some hundred and forty kilometers to the east and Mussolini's first short-lived victory on Egyptian soil. The 178 traveled in the opposite direction. In order to penetrate westward into the Cyrenaica region, the Sollum Pass had to be taken. The road was steep and winding, and behind it — the abyss. Driver, you had better grip the steering wheel and wisely manage the overheating-prone engine. For the ascent was long and treacherous. There below — no, don't turn your head — is *Sollum*, in a hidden shaft on the slope. Correction: That's where Sollum *used to be*. Furthermore, beyond that point was the border. The portal to new endeavors, new trials, new experiences. And you had better realize that it was a mountainous border, a formidable tower, its slopes sheer and slippery, that had to be scaled, each bit anew; as if its capture by the vanguard had not been enough, as if every soldier had to fight it to recapture its peak.

What a good thing that such was the gateway to a new country: hard and high. Behind it — a chasm. From above you looked down on Cyrenaica, green, fresh, lovely, a wonder of nature between the Egyptian and Libyan deserts. And now, for the descent. At a snail's pace. The ancient terraces seemed to lead to a hidden shrine of old, more legendary than real. And here was the gem of the sea, set in the hillside shade — *Tobruq*! It was late afternoon already. A light rain added a sheen to Tobruq's walls. Walls? What *had been* its walls — now they were ruins; the ruins of a city that had twice changed hands. The seven-hued rainbow came out to welcome the mountain scalers, while their vehicles groaned under the effort. As kitschy or contrived as it might sound — it was the truth. That's how it was. The rainbow dipped one foot into the Bay of Tobruq, wading briefly in the wadi; its other foot climbing up the mother of all mountains. A rare moment of grace, not to be missed. And here you are, Tobruq — another minute and we would be within your gates. Wait for us. And in case your gates were destroyed by the enemy, we will remember your former glory. *Shalom to you, Tobruq. 178 greets you.*

To the regret of 5MT veterans, 178 entered the city for a short while only. A courtesy call. In the coming weeks the old-timers would be able to visit it and linger there to their heart's desire. But now haste was in order. The new base was far off and had to be reached before dark. The veterans ran to and fro among the ruins, afire to save the handful of nostalgic moments they remembered. Each of them then grabbed the sleeve of a young soldier to guide him through the ruins. This was Main Street. They had named it "Tel Aviv Street"; the Hebrew street sign still fluttering over the ruins. The next street, amazingly, was called Me'ah She'arim — probably not after the Jerusalem Ultra-Orthodox neighborhood, but rather the small lane near Allenby Street and the Tel Aviv beach. Maybe, one of the soldiers had lived nearby. A Hebrew inscription on a former building reads: "Café Ziona" — only the inscription remained. And here are the ghetto ruins: the remains of a synagogue, and next to it what was left of its yeshivah. The small Jewish community no longer existed.

And so the Company came full circle. The shadow of the myth that had divided the mother-unit from the daughter-unit was put to rest. Rest? 5MTers huddled together. A roll call? Speeches? No — the majority decided, and not only because it was so late but also because 5MT no longer existed. An informal get-together — please. But Tobruq now belonged to us all. Mosenzon whispered something to Ankori. The latter moved off to the side, his notepad open. Slight embarrassment. About fifteen minutes later, a page was plucked from the notepad.

> *To the tune of "Volga Volga"*
>
> Tobruq Tobruq, fort of fame
> 'tween the desert and the sea.
> We shall always hail your name
> And the name of 5MT.
>
> Besieged yet sheltered in the wadi.
> Neither in nor out you go —
> On the harmonica played Gil'adi,
> Guns responded with noise their own.
>
> Tobruq A, 5MT City.
> Enemy guns produce a show.
> Enemy planes bomb with no pity.
> Soldiers crouch in a ditch below.
>
> For you, Tobruq, they suffered pain
> And sorry flight to ships in bay —
> But you must know 'twas not in vain,
> Victory's nearer every day.

Tobruq, Tobruq, Tobruq B
We're knocking on your ruined gate:
In the wake of 5MT
Comes to you 178.

I don't know what greater treat:
The Tobruq then or that of now?
Back on Tobruq's Tel Aviv Street
To old-timers let's take a bow.

Let Tobruq A-B be one to all,
To vets and youngsters in friendly bond!
Let the harmonica send out the call.
The guys harmoniously will respond.

# XI

Station after station on desert roads. And so large and deep and endless the desert, and not always yellow. Sometimes, in winter, it surprises even itself; after a few hours of flooding, it makes up its face like a young miss, putting beauty marks on the earth's fresh cheeks — petal buds of bold tiny blossoms that cling to the ground as if not trusting their curved stems and drawing security from the damp soil instead. But the miracle of green is fleeting. Like all miracles — it is singular, appearing suddenly and then retreating fast. All too soon, the yellow regains its mastery, the desert reverts to the heat of day and the chill of night.

Daily routine marked convoy life afresh: some convoys covered short distances, others stretched over days. The one change was in the number of trucks heading for the same destination; sometimes only four or five trucks set out together. The change was perhaps dictated by safety precautions, to avoid aerial attacks on long convoys. The attacks were stepped up, coming not only from aircraft on the front, which had already been pushed back to Tunisia, but from planes taking off at Axis airports in Greece or

Italy and crossing the short Mediterranean air route to target also Allied naval vessels.

The soldiers preferred the small intimate groups. After five hours on the road, a driver would stop some distance from his mate for safety reasons and, closing his cabin door, stream out a puddle that had long waited for release, like a dog raising its leg to proclaim its presence and mark its territory. On one occasion, after the lorries parked, Ankori felt a need to donate to the desert a weight heavier than a puddle. Golden sands gleamed in the noon sun and a dune crafted shapes as if helping the Supreme Architect in the wonders of Creation. Ankori considered a conundrum: was it at all permissible in this sort of situation to invoke the Creator (albeit metaphorically) and confound the dune's pristine purity? He soon came to his senses: didn't an explicit biblical verse consider the very matter, and in desert conditions at that? How amazed he had been as a *heder* boy at the ways of Torah: the Torah did not merely speak in human language, it gave detailed instructions even about human emissions:

> *Thou shalt have a place also without the camp, whither thou shalt go forth abroad. And thou shalt have a paddle among thy weapons; and it shall be, when thou sittest down abroad, thou shalt dig therewith, and shalt turn back and cover that which cometh from thee. For the Lord thy God walketh in the midst of thy camp … therefore shall thy camp be holy*
> (Deuteronomy 23:13–15)

A paddle he did not have, his weapon had been left in the cabin. The only part of the verse he could thus carry out was "when thou sittest down abroad" — which he did instinctively in any case, regardless of the decree from on high. And yet behold the marvel! No sooner did he rise when two giant beetles appeared out of nowhere — as similar as two peas in a pod to the pharaonic granite scarabs that had so impressed him at the Egyptian Museum in Cairo. And just as fast, in a split second, the astounding guests vanished along with the bodily waste, the sand dune again gleaming in pristine purity like before, as if nothing had occurred: the *"camp be holy"*. The little perverse demon, a seasoned instigator in the recesses of Ankori's heart, teased him with the notion that the two heroines were none other than the original pharaonic scarabs from the museum, who had donned the form of living insects and followed him through the desert — their natural habitat — begging him to deliver them from their stifling glass case.

"What's up?" — his mates called out in concern — "You look like you saw a ghost."

"On the contrary, I saw a living spirit."

His mates looked at him with compassion. A clear case of sunstroke.

"So where were you?"

"Never mind. But I must tell you. The verse is explicit: *'the Lord thy God walketh in the midst of our camp'.*"

Now they were sure that a screw had come loose in the head of their (apostate) friend.

"Are you up to driving?"

"Don't be ridiculous! What's wrong with you — have you gone mad?" Yet further corroboration of his state of mind. If *we're* nuts, *he* must be *arop fun dakh* (off his rocker). Sergeant Listenberg, who was on rearguard detail in the convoy, asked if he might join him and ride in his cabin. Ankori was pleased; he suspected no ulterior motive. When they returned from the mission, Listenberg reported to the chaps that he had really enjoyed the conversation with Ankori. "He's fine, forget it" — was his diagnosis.

From that day forward (unconnected to the dune episode), Sergeant Listenberg was a permanent resident of Ankori's cabin, riding with him during the day and resting next to him at night on the crates of ammunition beneath the Bedford's friendly tarp. The arrangement moved Ankori's lorry to the back of the line so that Sergeant Listenberg could continue to be on rearguard detail. The two soldiers got along fabulously. Only one petty problem irritated the "landlord" even as he knew that his irritation was unfounded. At night, in the desert loneliness and ominous silence, as enemy planes repeatedly circled overhead, supposedly targeting from above the four or five defenseless trucks, Ankori would lie awake, not truly frightened, though following the planes' circles and trying to guess the number of scheming aircraft from the hum of the engines. Listenberg — much to Ankori's annoyance — slept on throughout, oblivious of the action in the sky. The host-driver finally put himself to sleep by counting airplane circles as if they were sheep, the way he would be advised as a boy on sleepless nights: "count sheep". After one such instance, the morning revealed that the wicked angels had poured their wrath onto British Lancasters parked about half a kilometer away. The 178 convoy was not harmed. The morning also erased the night's foolish, innocent irritation, turning the whole business into a good-spirited jest.

The five drivers continued to enjoy the smaller-scale convoys. On cold desert nights, they would gather together in one truck, connect an inspection lamp to the truck battery and succeed, under cover of the tarp, to pass the evening in normal activity and full light. Flaschman, of Kibbutz Gesher, would write to his wife, Ora, every night; Listenberg and two others (whose names unfortunately escape the author's memory) read Eretz-Israel newspapers borrowed from the editorial board of *HaHayal HaIvri*, which received them, as a gift to soldiers, directly from the editors, after a two-week gap; while Ankori wrote a letter to Ila, his girlfriend, composed a song for the coming Sabbath eve, or struggled on bravely with *Gone with the Wind*, sent to him by his neighbor, Leah Kofman, who had earlier helped him compose letters to the Mandate authorities about his sister's matter. It was the first thick English book he read and mastered. When sleep beckoned, everyone returned to his own truck, leaving Listenberg and Ankori in theirs.

## XII

Gradually, step by step, as the convoys made their way to and from Libya's borders, and single cars were sent back on special missions to Egypt or Palestine, Unit 178 managed to build a real base on the outskirts of Benghazi. The new character of the Jewish unit was largely determined by the entry into the large liberated city and the encounter with local inhabitants and passers-by, especially with women and children, after long months of male loneliness in geographic and human wastelands. Crowning the encounter was the meeting with Benghazi's old Jewish community whose suffering had come to an end with the defeat of Libya's Italian rule. Reaching as far as Tripoli and the Tunisian border, the convoys continued their duties in a yellow desert now grown monotonous, whereas previously its purity had been a curiosity. For fear of falling asleep at the wheel, drivers, in the loneliness of their cabins, would burst into sky-rending solos of songs from here and there or pin up a piece of green cloth on the windshield to refresh their eyes from time to time.

"Hey, Ankori, forget Zionism for a minute and make up a love song!" — one of the drivers called out on Maintenance Day, as every soldier serviced his truck, changing oil, tightening wheel screws, changing a worn tire or hosing off desert dust. The whole Company was assembled that day, albeit not as a group but as individuals, all doing their own thing together.

"Or write something about the convoys and Benghazi!" — one soldier cried.

"Better still, about all three combined — convoys, Benghazi, love!" — another added.

"And set the words to a popular tune so we don't have to learn it."

Ankori looked around and chuckled. "This is precisely what great artists wish for — to have lyrics or tunes commissioned from them. And here, it has fallen into my lap without my having asked for it." He had no interest in writing about Benghazi. But he would create a symbolic Benghazi girl open to fantasy, with each driver entering the name of his girlfriend. The tunes of two well-known Hebrew songs suited the unit's lifestyle on the roads: "*HaDerekh Nir'et Li Kol Kakh Aruka*" (The Road Seems So Long) and "*HaTender Nose'a*" (The Tender is Driving), which could easily become "*HaConvoy Nose'a*".

(To the tune of *HaDerekh*)

Driving in convoy 'tween desert and sea
Four heavy wheels and their tread —
Mersa Matruh is way back behind me
El-Ageila is just up ahead.
Mersa Matruh is way back behind me
El-Ageila is just up ahead.

A week has just passed in the convoy parade
We'll get back to base before long —
In the town of Benghazi awaits a young maid
I've dreamt of and sung her a song…
In the town of Benghazi awaits a young maid
I've dreamt of and sung her a song…

With ebony eyes and ebony hair
Like a Yemenite from Rehov Shabbazi —
The sergeant lost only a kitbag back there
While I lost my heart in Benghazi.
The sergeant lost only a kitbag back there
While I lost my heart in Benghazi.

The flame in her eyes was lit by the moon
One look and my mind, oh, was heady —
And then comes the order: "We're leaving town soon,
At dawn the convoy be ready."
And then comes the order: "We're leaving town soon,
At dawn the convoy be ready."

The convoy is driving — Tripoli walls
Rise from afar — rightward veer!
Without your sweet smile my doll-of-dolls
The cabin is lonely, I fear —
Without your sweet smile, my pretty doll-of-dolls
The cabin is lonely, I fear.

Out of pity for the readers, "The Convoy is Driving" will remain in the notepad unquoted. What's more, it was never really completed. Since it was so catchy, verses were occasionally added by popular request to reflect the life of the Unit; thus the song constantly lengthened along the thousand kilometers from Benghazi to Tripoli. The Culture Committee decided to devote one Sabbath party to parodies of the Sabbath gatherings themselves. Benny Zuker delivered an antithetical version of Shalom Aleikhem, having the writer ape Eliahu Hazan's pretence of reading Menahem-Mendel's letters to his wife; Levitza wrote a parody of Flaschman's feuilleton; Ankori sang a parody of his very own "The Convoy is Driving". And since Sergeant Major Bankover had just returned from consultations in Palestine during which time the Unit had "fled" to Tripoli, Ankori was asked to address the matter. There was no censorship apart from the bounds of good taste and, within these, Ankori liked to poke fun at the command from time to time: "Opposite one poor Private, bone-weary and blue/ Corporals by the dozen, a sergeant and officer too." Bankover also laughed good-naturedly at Ankori's parody of his opus, *"Pages from the Diary"*.

Winter on the Libyan coast, the location of the convoy roads, of the bases and the cities, could not be compared to the dry winter of the Egyptian desert. In Libya, the short winter is filled with heavy rain and storms. Driving in convoys grew progressively harder and, even on nice days — particularly nice after the rain washed away the haze and swept clean the desert dust — there was no feeling safe from the highly changeable weather. In fact, there was no feeling safe at all, not on the base nor at road stops nor in the bivouac, your personal small tent. The idea of building "homes" was of unknown parentage — perhaps, it was the natural nesting instinct embedded in every living being. In any case, the lads found themselves competing over the most attractive and comfortable "dwelling". They began collecting empty petrol containers and asked the workshop to cut them in half so they could be filled with sand. These were the "bricks", making up three walls and topped by a bivouac as roof. The problem was the fourth side, for it had to both serve as an entrance and ensure light, air and privacy.

While scouting the area, the soldiers reached the Italian colony in Libya. Its pretty houses were set in gardens and gleamed white, except for the black fascist inscriptions printed on the walls ("*Molti nemici — molto onore*" — Many foes, much honor), and the black salute to *Duce*. *Duce* covered every vacant meter, while the center displayed the bust of Mussolini with a steel helmet and the look of a ruler who knew his worth and his purpose. The colonies bore Italian names. The largest was called Madelena; likely the regional capital. Everything seemed to run on orders from above and yet there was no sense of affluence, but of toil rewarded. The area was now empty, though the homes had not been damaged or looted. Whether or not the population had been evacuated by the Italian government before or on the eve of the war in Africa — was unknown. It had probably been assumed that the colonists would be interested in temporarily leaving for reasons of safety. Mussolini, after all, was sure that the Axis would be victorious and the colony would flourish again, and perhaps even have the conquered part of Egypt annexed to it. In any case, whether the authorities had evacuated the colonists in an orderly fashion or the colonists had fled at a later stage of fighting, after British gains became clear, they must have been confident that they would return. This impression was cemented at a well-to-do, though not ostentatious, home where the soldiers stopped.

"Ankori, you read Italian, don't you? There's a note on the door here. See what it says." The polished door shone both naturally and with the pride of its owners.

"*Soldiers* (the note whispered), *please do not damage the house.*

*We are not rich. This house is our sole property. We earned it by hard work. Watch over it for us. We are not enemies."*

The note had obviously been jotted down in haste, maybe at the last minute before leaving. It had mistakes and looked like it had been penned by an uneducated woman. There may have been another reason for the haste: the woman may have wanted to hide the deed from her fascist husband who wouldn't be eager to proclaim, "We are not enemies."

"Either way, this is the first voice we've heard from simple folk on the other side, erupting through the boastful inscriptions, the settlers had either been forced to or had chosen to write. Sad."

"The note may be sad but it's misguided" — Ankori reflected out loud, the others nodding in agreement. "Mussolini duped his subjects into believing that they would return, as is obvious from the note. They'll never return. They've lost Africa. After the war, the Libyans will probably demand independence, and rightly so."

"Let's take the door" — Listenberg concluded, knowing the hesitations of his friend, the 'conscientious agonizer'. "Our conscience is clear. If we don't take it, the Sanusis will use it for firewood. We can use it for the fourth side of the small "home" we built against the cold and rain."

The "agonizer" hesitated only momentarily. With gusto, he then lifted the door off the hinges, the note still stuck to it, and he and Listenberg hoisted it onto the empty truck and brought it back to the "housing base". There, they fixed it in place at the entrance to the tin-and-sand structure they had designed. That same night, a typical Libyan storm hit. The door held, protecting its new owners from the chill and wind. The note, however, as was discovered the next day, had been blown away — where to? Northward, to Italy? Or southward, to the Saharan Sanusis and Berbers?

One thing was sure: wherever the note was, the door-pilferers were never to forget it.

Libya's stormy wintry rain (350–500 mm. precipitation) — or "this cloudburst, this Shevat-pluvial", as Mosenzon wrote with his magic pen, waxing lyrical and elevating *HaHayal HaIvri* to the sacred. Combined with the monotony of driving to replace the euphoria of el-Alamein and Tobruq, Mosenzon surprisingly romanticized: "the heart yearns for the heat of Qenah in Upper Egypt". To raise morale, the Sabbath party was deferred from Friday night to Saturday, January 30, 1943, to enable the participation of the platoon that had just returned to camp after days on the road.

In the same breath, *HeHayal HaIvri* mentioned another aspect of the party as well. This was its report: "Ankori, who that same day capsized in his truck, its wheels in the air, and was miraculously saved, nevertheless taught a new song to the surprise of those concerned about him." Indeed, Ankori emerged without a scratch from the accident, which was caused by a blowout in the front tire. The person to suffer was Sergeant Listenberg, occupying his regular spot next to the driver. The Bedford's designer had apparently not foreseen the possible consequences of placing the battery under the passenger seat in the event that the vehicle turned over. Listenberg, too, emerged from the tumble without a scratch. But when the two men fell down from their seats, the battery acid spilt and trickled onto the sergeant's forehead and face. The resulting burns and scars disfigured him and it was weeks before the scabs fell off.

And yet, even the cloud of the accident had a silver lining. A week later, again in order to raise morale, B Platoon decided to mark the "ten-thousand miles" traversed by its drivers since leaving el-Alamein. No one knew who had dreamt up the idea, just as no one knew who had calculated the mileage; but no questions were asked, nor doubts voiced, and the total mileage did not seem at all unreasonable: after all, only one Benghazi-Tripoli return trip measured 1300 miles, and there had been many such trips. Everyone felt that "something had to be done" to ward off the feeling that "their duty was done"; nothing is more dangerous in an army. The songwriter used the upset of his truck as an excuse for a cheerful quasi-reckoning after being given back his life. Thus was born the "Ten-Thousand Miles Song", which, as usual, carried a mile-long string of stanzas. Its refrain made it a platoon hit both because it was short and catchy and because it again spelled out the war aims.

> Sing out Hey! Hey! Song of drivers' life,
> Ten thousand miles or more have just weighed in:
> From Alamein to Tobruq and Benghazi,
> From Tripoli to Rome, from Rome straight to Berlin.

## XIII

"Daddy, Daddy, Jewish soldiers have arrived! One of them has 'Eretz-Israel' written on his shoulder band with letters from the prayerbook!" — the small son of the community rabbi cried at the sight of 178's Hebrew soldiers. The Unit reached Benghazi's Jewish street on the first Sabbath after the city's liberation, December 19, 1942, six weeks after the Battle of el-Alamein. The child had not been mistaken. The girlfriend of one of the 178ers had embroidered "Eretz-Israel" in Hebrew letters on the shoulder of his battledress when he had been on home leave, next to the English "Palestine", the official insignia of the uniforms of the Hebrew units in the British army.

"Father, why don't you go out to greet them? Everyone at all the balconies and windows is happy to see them and say 'Shabbat Shalom'. Some of the neighbors have gone downstairs and are talking to them." The child could not understand his father's reluctance to go out to the soldiers. But while the child was too young to remember, the father had cause for caution. He must have seen the events of recent years flash before his eyes: the festive thanksgiving prayer he had conducted at the synagogue upon Benghazi's liberation by the Allies, the reception for Jewish soldiers in the various Allied divisions and, above all, the community assembly in honor of the soldiers of the 5MT Hebrew unit from Eretz-Israel. The joy was short-lived. The Allies retreated. Oh, the revenge on the Jews unleashed by the Italian authorities for showing sympathy to Allied forces! "And now, until Tripoli is liberated, who can assure me that *this* victory is final, that the outrages will stop?" In 1941, the British retreating from Libya managed eventually to stabilize the line at el-Alamein. In the fighting, Benghazi changed hands five times, and was nearly razed to the ground. The authorities were viciously vindictive.

The rabbi opened the door to go onto the street. At that very moment, a group of 178ers came up the stairs, accompanied by local youngsters who led them from one ruined house to another with explanations of who had lived where and what had happened to them. They reached the rabbi. Gnawed by fear, he welcomed them with reticence. But when he caught sight of the soldier with the Hebrew "Eretz-Israel" insignia, he stooped and kissed each letter. The horror stories of what had befallen the community were endless. 5MT veterans asked about families they had befriended during the first British conquest. The answer was uniform — they were gone: some were killed in cold blood, some were hung at the town square for all to see, some were sent for forced labor in battle areas and had not been heard of since, some were led off to the concentration camp at Jado in the desert, about 200 kilometers south of Tripoli. Of the thousands of Jews in Benghazi and the thousands of residents from small communities deported to Benghazi, two hundred Jewish households remained, along with the hope that the Jado prisoners would return upon liberation. In fact, the two hundred surviving households had also been earmarked for the last transport to the camp. They had only been saved by the panicked retreat of the Axis army before the British Eighth Army offensive. Tripoli still had thirty thousand Jews and, according to rumor, the Germans had meant to imprison them in extermination camps to be erected in Tunisia. But Tripoli had also fallen in Montgomery's assault and the whole of Libya was liberated. The prisoners of Jado were starting to return.

178 Coy arrived in Tripoli with the first convoy in mid-February 1943. At the sight of vehicles with the Star of David on the streets, the local Jews burst into tears. They approached the truck doors

and put their lips to the emblem in awe. The young asked the soldiers to direct them to the enlistment office so that they could take part in the rest of the war effort. The conquest of Libya released the initial, timid restraint shown by public leaders in Benghazi. Hearts opened up. Benghazi's, thanks to the stationing of 178 in the neighborhood, was the first Libyan Jewish community to practice Jewish brotherhood: the Hebrew army unit and the community cooperated in rehabilitating Jewish life in the city, mainly seeing to the needs of children and youth. At a meeting of the representatives of the Jewish units, Officer Reifenberg of the Hebrew University suggested that 178 launch a Hebrew school for Benghazi's children.

*HaHayal HaIvri* reported that community volunteers applied themselves enthusiastically to adapting the old Talmud-Torah building to its new role, and the names of children were collated from every household. The Unit's active members could not conceal their excitement at the public's total response to a project that they, the soldiers, had initiated and were to implement. Not a single family held back, every child was enrolled. All Jewish pupils had been expelled from government schools before the war, when Italy adopted the Racial Laws and, in 1940, all Jewish teaching institutions had been shut down. Of the seventy youngsters remaining in Benghazi, the younger ones had never sat on a school bench, while the older ones failed to grasp the change — addressing the Jewish revivers of education with the fascist salute, as they had done in the past.

On March 1, 1943, the school was festively opened. All the age groups were assembled in a single classroom and the community chairman, in his opening words in Italian (translated into fluent Hebrew by Yitzhak Gueta, community secretary), thanked God for saving the city, and the Hebrew soldiers for their unforgettable spiritual and moral service, as well as their practical assistance, to their brethren in the Diaspora. He asked the children to show diligence in their studies after four years of enforced idleness from Torah learning.

Ankori, an experienced teacher and counselor of youth in

Jerusalem, who was charged with running the school, spoke on behalf of 178's soldiers. He decided to talk directly to the children, delivering suitably simple messages. The school (he said) aimed to transmit three messages: love of Eretz-Israel as the homeland of the Jewish people; study and love of the Hebrew language as the renewed ancient language of the Jewish people; and the resolution to make *aliya* to Eretz-Israel and take part in its upbuilding. The designated teacher wondered if he should use the language they understood — Italian — so as to dispel any anxiety they might have about lack of communication and let them see the open channel between them. On reflection, however, he chose to speak in Hebrew (translated into Italian by Gueta), to distinguish between Hebrew — the language of Eretz-Israel and of the Hebrew soldiers — and Italian, which was identified with the fascist salute and the Italian soldiers.

*HaHayal HaIvri* reported his words:

> "Until now, you've been used to seeing soldiers as your enemies and enemies of your people. We also wear uniforms, but we are brothers in uniform. We come from the Land of Israel. And, as the name says, from the land of the people of Israel. For many generations we have been scattered over all ends of the world. Only a few decades ago, young men and women arose with the name 'Israel' in their hearts and decided to rebuild the land. And the land was like the wilderness around this city. With sweat and toil the desert turned into a blossoming garden, like Cyrenaica. But in our generation, there arose a wicked tyrant who wanted to destroy us. Young Israelite men left the land of their own free will and went down to Egypt. Together with the British army, they crossed the borders into Libya, freeing the Jewish communities. God came to our help and victory was ours. And the day is not far off that the wicked tyrant will be destroyed, and we, the Hebrew soldiers, will return to Eretz-Israel. There, we will

wait for you, children of the Libyan Diaspora, to come and build our homeland together with us."

The pupils required a few days before the gaiety of childhood and the joy of youth lit up their faces once more. The nearby yard was taken over by ball games after the new Benghazi municipality cleared away the rubble strewn there since the last fatal bombing. The sadness in the eyes of children with black bands on their lapels naturally persisted, though, gradually, they too learned to smile and play like their peers. As opposed to the children, it took longer for the parents to recover. The dread did not dissolve all at once, the fear lingered even if subconsciously.

As it happened, one mother, who like all parents came to collect her son at the end of the school day, did, for some reason, arrive early and stood at the classroom window waiting for the lesson to end. Suddenly she grew alarmed. Through the open window, she could hear the strains of "*HaTikvah* (The Hope)", the Jewish national anthem. In trepidation, she looked up and down the street to make sure that there were no passers-by to identify the tune; under the Italians the song had been banned. It was several moments before she realized that it was no longer dangerous to sing "*HaTikvah*" and when she did — she burst into tears of release. Upon regaining her composure, she remembered that the district political officer of the British army had formally approved both the school opening and the curriculum. He had even accepted the invitation of the Community Council to lend his patronage to the upcoming Purim party, to be arranged by the Jewish school and no doubt to include "*HaTikvah*". The Purim celebration, in fact, took place three-and-a-half weeks after the school opening. It was the first public Zionist performance in the history of the Jews of Cyrenaica, and it marked a true turning point in the social life of Benghazi's Jewish community.

Typically, *HaHayal HaIvri* in Mosenzon's ardent high-sounding style reported: "We were privileged to taste handfuls of emotional and refreshing experiences with the Jewish children." It was leap year on the Jewish calendar and the Purim holiday, caressed by an evening breeze in the Benghazi spring of Adar II, waited till March 23, 1943 before it appeared in all its splendor. The party was held in the hall of the former fascist bank, confiscated by the British military government and lent to the Jewish community for the evening. This circumstance afforded the community both pleasure and occasion for crowing. Freedom has seventy faces; one of them is to hold a celebration in an erstwhile fascist institution once barred to Jews. The hall was jam-packed. Apart from community members, their faces grooved with pain and grief, guests included soldiers from Jewish units stationed in the area. The nearest unit was 178, but there were also a group of Jewish soldiers from England; seamen from the Royal Navy anchored at Benghazi, and invited guests from the military government HQ, headed by the district governor. The Eretz-Israel soldiers burst into spontaneous Hebrew songs, their voices amplified by the pupils of the Hebrew school. The sounds resonated wonderfully in the space of the hall that had never heard a note of Hebrew.

The interval between the school opening on the first of the month and March 23 had allowed the children to learn holiday songs and recitations in the Hebrew of Eretz-Israel. Parents were moved to tears. But there was laughter, too, in the pantomime on Ahasuerus King of Persia, Mordekhai the Jew and Esther the Queen, clad in royal costumes produced by volunteer mothers. Other volunteers had baked the three-cornered *hamantaschen* pastries served at the end of the evening. The great surprise of the evening, however, was the unexpected presence of a Benghazi woman who always turned down invitations. A respected community member and known for her fine voice, she had lost her husband in one of the early bombings and had worn black ever since, retiring from all social activity. One day, on passing the school she heard the children singing. She introduced herself as a musician and asked to borrow the notes of the songs. Ankori knew neither her name nor her story, but complied with alacrity. Tearing out a page from an exercise book, he drew the five-line staves and entered the notes of three Purim songs. On the back of the page, he jotted down the lyrics in Latin letters, accenting the syllables that were to be stressed. Then he read each song aloud to her and translated its substance. She thanked him and departed, her curiosity apparently satisfied.

Ankori wondered why a musician would take interest in children's songs, but since she did not return, he put the matter from his mind. To his surprise, on the evening of the Purim party he saw the lady in the audience, and they nodded to one another. He noticed that instead of the black she had worn on her school visit, she was in an elegant floral dress. "Why not?" — he chided himself, without knowing anything about her bereavement. He was even bemused that he remembered her attire at all.

When it was time for the performance, he went up on stage to conduct the mixed choir of boys and girls. The remainder of the program, he directed from the sidelines. At the end of the second part and the lingering applause it earned, he mingled with the audience. The musician was waiting for him.

"I have a request" — she whispered — "I'd like to go up on stage and sing."

"Excellent" — he said, glad that he managed to conceal his surprise.

"I will sing the songs that you gave me. But, please, no preliminaries, no introduction."

Ankori signaled to the choir's piano accompanist to return to the stage. The pianist took his seat and the audience believed the stage appearance of the singer and the pianist to be part of the continuing, planned program. The residents of Benghazi, however, were astounded at the sight of the musician. She briefly conferred with the pianist who at her request, improvised an overture, and then struck an erect, imposing stance, as if straight out of an Italian opera. She delivered the first Purim song and immediately launched into the other two without pause. Professional and polished, her acting conveyed a pampered little girl. The audience was in raptures, the applause rocked the foundations of the building. "*Bis!*" "*Bis!*"

Next, she asked the children crowding together in the corners of the stage to come up and they and she together sang the songs again as the audience joined in. But the program surprises were not yet over. The audience was treated to arias by Verdi and Puccini, followed by the climax of the evening, an aria from "Carmen". The singer was patently enjoying herself as much as the audience. She left the stage to the sound of roaring applause and as she passed Ankori, her lips hovered briefly over his cheek, like the wings of a butterfly. She made her exit from the hall.

After the Sabbath, she dropped in at the school towards the end of the day. Ankori welcomed her happily, expressing his warm thanks for her splendid performance.

"No" — she said — "I'm the one that has to thank you for allowing me to perform. It's been three years that I haven't sung, I've led a reclusive life since my husband was killed in the bombing. Now, with the soldiers of Eretz-Israel around me, I've started living again."

She took out a small box from her purse and extended it to Ankori.

"Open it, please." The box contained a pair of gold cuff-links.

"They were my late husband's. Please accept them as a token of my gratitude for what you did for me."

"I did? "Me?" — Ankori tried to decline the gift. "I did nothing."

"You've restored my *joie de vivre*."

## XIV

The spontaneous kinship between Unit 178 and the Jews of Benghazi grew increasingly closer.

The Unit's Sabbath parties often hosted active community members. The first guest to be invited, on April 2, was Yitzhak

Gueta, whose fluent Hebrew had been commended when he acted as translator at the school's opening. Ankori's reports on the school became a permanent feature of the parties. Beyond furnishing details on the children's progress and their rehabilitation from the traumas of war, he was also asked to report on the social contacts with the town's Jews. One anecdote he related concerned an invitation he had received to a Sabbath meal with a family living near the synagogue. Because of the distance from the base, he had been forced to drive, but out of respect for Benghazi's observant community, he parked around the corner. The synagogue beadle, an elderly religious Jew, noticed and said: "Never mind. Leave your car here. You are a saint." Ankori recounted the episode both for its piquancy and because it reflected the love and recognition of Benghazi Jews for Hebrew soldiers.

The focus of the soldiering work done for Benghazi Jewry was the Hebrew school, a community asset that grew firmer with time. The return of Jado prisoners swelled the pupil population to 400 and the school had to move to larger premises. The project's very success, however, and source of pride for all involved, remained an equally justifiable cause for concern. Armies, by their very nature, move on as called for by circumstance and it was only a matter of time before 178 was to advance with the Eighth Army. The soldiers in fact eagerly awaited the development. But luck was on Benghazi's side: other Hebrew units (water suppliers, engineering corps, etc.) were to be stationed nearby, making it possible to recruit from their ranks a dedicated teaching force to continue 178's work. Long after 178 pushed out to a remote Libyan location, on the puzzling orders of the supreme HQ, visitors from Benghazi brought the Unit heart-warming reports about the school's development and the fond memories reserved for the first wave of 178 Coy soldiers.

For example, military rabbi Ephraim Urbach (later a professor at Hebrew University), participated in a 178 Sabbath party two months after the Unit's departure and gave the following account (as reported in *HaHayal HaIvri*) of his visit to the Benghazi school where soldiers continued to serve as teachers:

"Here I must mention that your Unit left a lasting monument with the project in which several of you invested much energy and in which you all took an interest and may be proud of. Ankori's name is mentioned fondly and gratefully by both pupils and adults."

Further, the rabbi stated: "When I was in Tunis, a large city with sixty thousand Jews, I was sorry that Jewish units have not yet got there. The Jews there welcomed all the Allied Jewish soldiers with unparalleled enthusiasm, but of course they are primarily awaiting soldiers from Eretz-Israel."

On April 23–24, 1944, almost a year after 178 left Benghazi, teacher-soldier Ben-Ami of Water Supply Unit 405 reported in *Hahayal HaIvri* that "the project in which Ankori was involved continues to develop".

Similar comments about the Benghazi school and the people who had set it on a solid footing were relayed to *Hahayal HaIvri* from various visitors, and Mosenzon was only too pleased to print them for the benefit of his readers. The newspaper in fact continued to serve as a quasi-Poste Restante (mobile letterbox) for correspondence from Benghazi's children.

### Letters from the Children and Adults of Benghazi

"I received your regards from Mr. Gueta and thank you, dear teacher, I remember you always and will never forget — I send you greetings, my teacher."

Miriam Zakhut

"My dear teacher, this is little Norma, I remember you, my dear teacher. Write me, and remember me always — thank you very much and bye".

from Norma Zaruk

"My dear teacher, Zvi, Mr. Gueta told me that you send

your regards. Thank you very much for remembering me, dear teacher. I hope to see you in Eretz-Israel and goodbye".

Miriam Zaruk

"I wrote you about a month ago and have not yet received an answer — you are always on our minds and we constantly talk about you — now the school is closed, hopefully it will open in October. — Ben-Ami and Yehuda have also left already: so none of the old-time teachers are here. — Don't forget us — I want you to know that there is not a single person in Benghazi who doesn't remember you and all of you".

In great friendship,<br>Yitzhak Gueta, Community Secretary

"Dear Zvi, first of all I bring you good news: a month ago I got engaged to Y.G. [Yitzhak Gueta], as he himself wrote you. I'm happy to be progressing in Hebrew but I'm sorry that you're not here with us to help me progress further. I hope you'll come here soon, I send you warm regards.

Lilliana

Benghazi, 23.7.43
Benzion Tito

To my dear teacher, Zvi,

It's a long time since you parted from us, and you may even have forgotten us. But we, especially I, can't forget you so fast. — — At this time, I want to infirm (inform) you that I passed into the next grade (2). I'm the only one that got ahead like this in our class. Meanwhile there have been changes in our lives, a lot of children came back from Jado.

# As a Palm Tree in the Desert

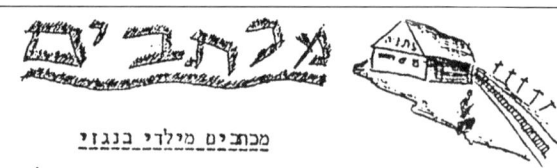

**מכתבים מילדי בנגזי**

"קבלתי את דרישת שלומך עם אדון גוויטה וחודה לך מורי היקר, אני זוכרת אותך תמיד ולא אשכחך - - - שלום לך מורי."
מרים זכות

"מורי היקר, אני גורמה הקטנה, אני זוכרת אותך מורי היקר. מפתחובלב, וחדור אותי תמיד - - - תודה רבה ושלום."
גנורמה זרוק

"מורי צבי היקר, אדון גוויטה אמר לי שמחה דורש בשלומי. תודה רבה לך מורי היקר שזכרת אותי. אני מקוה שאתראה בארץ-ישראל ושלום לך."
מרים זרוק

"כתבתי לך לפני חודש ולא קבלתי ממך עוד שום תשובה - - - אנחנו זוכרים תמיד אותך ותמיד מדברים עליך - - - עכשיו בית הספר סגור ומקוים לפתוח אותו באוקטובר. - - בן-עפר ויהודה כבר נסעו גם הם; כך כל הסדרים הותיקים אינם אצלנו. - אל תשכחנו - וחדע לך כי בבנגזי אין אף אחד שלא זוכר אותך ואותכם. בכל הידידות - יצחק גנניטה שאכיד חקהילה

"לכבוד צבי, ראשית כל אני נותנת לך בשורה טובה: זה חודש אחד אני ארוסה של י. ג. כמו שכתב לך חגוא. אגי שמחה שאני מתקדמת בעברית אבל אני מצטערת שאינך פה אצלנו ושאינך עוזר לי להתקדם יותר. אני מקוה שתחיה אצלנו בקרוב ושולחת לך דרישת שלום לבביח."
לילאנה

---

ב.ה.
בנגזי 23.7.43

לאורי יקר ב.ג., שפת רב!

[handwritten Hebrew letter]

Letters from Benghazi

The old school was too small, so the authorities gave us a big school (the one on the sea shore). It's really more comfortable there and a lot of children go there. My teacher now is Israel, he is a good teacher and we like him and the teacher of First Grade is Mordekhai. — I hope to see you soon but I don't know when. But maybe in Eretz-Israel. If you happen to pass Benghazi, come to us. We'll welcome you nicely and be happy to see you. I'm ending my letter with the hope that you are well. Your loving pupil,

Benzion Tito

— My father and mother send regards —

## XV

As happy as the reports were from visitors to Benghazi, impressed by the solidity of the Hebrew school despite changing teachers, and as moving as the children's letters were along with the fact that they missed their first teacher, the Unit knew that Libya was only the first lap on their road. Their war role was only fully beginning in Europe and it was mainly there that the task of the Jewish soldiers was to be fulfilled. The Benghazi school had been a laboratory and the experiment succeeded; a model devised on the basis of prior teaching knowledge and experience, combined with the improvised dictates of time and circumstance. It was to serve Unit 178 in its future activities as well, which would certainly be far harder than the Benghazi case.

The future however tarried. The return to routine caused open restlessness — not the dejection of Qenah but a mixture of boredom and impatience. There was no "moving" in sight, no advance towards the real target: Europe. Nor, on the other hand, was there any ray of light on the horizon, or any temporary alternative: home leave after a lengthy stretch of intensive service. At Sabbath parties or in the loneliness of the cabin, the chaps would break into the hallowed army song — "Booms, we're moving/Moving and done" — written before 178's exit for el-Alamein, to the tune of an erstwhile German youth movement song. Like all army songs, it too had innumerable verses, every move after el-Alamein adding many more or modifying the original as the situation demanded.

The song was sung over and over again like a mantra, as if the incantation of "moving" flung into the air and backed up by "booms" would make the "big bang" happen. But nothing happened. Africa, after Monty's stunning victory, was the backyard of the war; instead of a battle zone, it became a cauldron of political intrigue centered in Cairo. The machinations could not fail to reach the soldiers, especially as some of the goings-on concerned the future of Palestine. All eyes were glued on the fateful campaigns taking place in Sicily and southern Italy, and despite the praise showered on the experienced Hebrew units, there seemed, regrettably, to be no visible intention of incorporating them in the Eighth Army's forward march.

The days stretched like the indifferent, yellow desert road, marking the soldiers' faces with restlessness. A general fatigue descended on the drivers and the vehicles. In addition, upon the opening of the Benghazi Port, convoy distances had shortened and convoy routine had been significantly downsized. Inadvertently, this turned out to be a good thing in view of the dilapidated state of the vehicles. The Bedfords, adopted in anticipation of el-Alamein, had been a hasty product, thrown together on a conveyor belt and handed over by the U.S. to Britain as part of the Lend-and-Lease agreement. They had been planned for a total distance of some six thousand miles. 178 squeezed them to the maximum; with their dying breath, the Bedfords swallowed up thousands of miles more than the "ten thousand" immortalized in the B Platoon song. Regular "patients" at the workshop, the vehicles were diagnosed by the engine doctor, Master Sergeant "Tayyish", as being beyond artificial respiration: in other words, they were old heaps.

The culture medics again tried to inject some spirit and brake the drop in morale. The prescription was not unlike that tried at

Qenah during the period of dejection in Upper Egypt. Now, however, it was far more successful, perhaps because of the glory of the Benghazi Jewish school in which the entire Unit felt it had a share. Sabbath parties were held regularly and sing-alongs were boosted by an important ally: the editor of *HaHayal HaIvri* collected the songs sung by 178 at Sabbath parties from Qenah to Libya and stenciled them off. Mosenzon brought the songbook to Ankori, having written on the front: "To you, Zvi. The first copy". At that moment the two, giver and receiver, were gratified by their public work.

A pleasant diversion was provided by tours of the most important Roman site in Libya, Leptis Magna. Ankori surprised his listeners with two stories of Jewish fighters preceding 178 in Libya, just as he had done in Qenah with the story of the Jewish fighters at Yev opposite Aswan. Jewish soldiers from Eretz-Israel, defeated by the Roman Legions, had settled in Cyrene, the regional capital (and origin of the region's name), which resembled the landscape of Eretz-Israel. The similarity had excited also 178's soldiers when, on their journey from the Egyptian desert, they had entered green Cyrenaica and exited it into the Libyan desert. The region's unique link to Eretz-Israel, however, went beyond landscape and was underscored by the lingering identification of its settlers with the Jewish population in the Land of Judea, their never-to-be-fogotten homeland.

Forty-five years after the destruction of the Second Temple, the Jews of Cyrenaica picked up the sword and rose up against Trajan, the Roman Emperor. The rebellion spread to many Jewish communities in the Roman Diaspora. Yet it failed, because the people of conquered Judea did not join it, and Cyrenaica's Jewish uprising was quashed. Conversely, when some years later Bar Kokhba led his revolt in Eretz-Israel, the Diaspora did not join him.

The second instance of Jewish fighting in Libya was during the period of Arab conquest in Africa, in the 680s. The Berbers, natives of the desert, resisted the Muslim invaders. Two clashes in particular went down in history, in the decade between 687 and

697. The Berber struggle was led by Dahiyah, a Jewish woman usually referred to as Al-Cahinah (the Priestess) and sometimes as the Queen of the Berbers. She is depicted as a sort of Jewish-Berber Jeanne d'Arc who fell in battle. The mere fact of Jewish fighting alongside Berbers is a permanent motif in the writings of classic Arab historians. To this day, the Berbers have preserved their separateness but they are scattered over various North-African countries and have remained without independence.

The restlessness of 178 continued. In Tripoli the British army opened a supervised brothel for soldiers. Every day, some 300 men, including some 178ers, waited on line for their turn. The Talmud advises those overcome by sexual urges to don black and scuttle off to some place where they are not known. Where was a soldier to get hold of black clothes and where could he have gone so as not to be recognized? No one said anything. But many hearts were filled with sadness.

A hint of "moving" finally came. There was a change of vehicles — The Bedfords were swapped for Dodges that were in the hands of a colonial unit. Sixty years later, in a phone conversation with the author, the Master-Sergeant in charge of the workshop recalled: "The mileage gauge in every car showed less than 2,000 kilometers, in other words, the vehicles were practically new. Yet not one car was whole. They were all badly damaged — from reckless driving? From sabotage? — all banged up. What a sight! Unbelievable!" 178's workshop began to work around the clock. "Moving" was in the air. The damage had to be fixed and the cars made road-worthy. Without a doubt, 178 was "moving". But where to? As a rule, the army withheld information on the destination until moving was well under way. The name "MALTA" suddenly cropped up — though how, and by whom, remained unknown. More rumors: the Unit had been chosen for a "selected job".

Doubt was rife. But a "selected job" was not to be sneered at. Sworn optimists and doom-seeing pessimists continued to argue until the very last minute. Why Malta of all places? Why not straight to Italy? Maybe there was a secret plan, that had nothing to do with Malta? There was no lack of fear either: Malta was a prime target of enemy bombing. What about the sea crossing? Wasn't it sure prey for German and Italian pilots? And back to square one: was it Malta after all? It didn't matter as long as a "selected job" was assured. The main thing was the "selected job". Such as? — the elitists wanted to know. Dreamers spun great scenarios. Ankori listened to it all and jotted down a light-hearted ditty:

| | |
|---|---|
| Oho! Oho! | We'll stay there but a week |
| Is it Malta? Yes or no? | To replenish the physique |
| What's the job? We don't know. | And also get a stealthy peek |
| A "selected job" — that's so. | At the invasion date — — |
| | |
| Oho! Oho! | With David Star on lorry |
| Off to Malta sure we go, | And a splendid job of glory |
| *"Fohren yunge un alte"* | And a kid school for Ankori — |
| Maybe to Malta | No, no we won't be sorry, |
| For a "selected job"! | It surely will be great! |

   Oho! Oho! You're at anchor "City of Florence" —
      We won't renege,
      Let's fly the flag
    Straight to the "selected job!"
  Oho! Oho! We'll sail with you "City of Florence"-
     Sail northward, "Florence".
     Hoist proudly the flag —
   A "selected job" is not a gag.

❖ ❖ ❖

Two days before sailing, on April 28, 1943, the cranes began hoisting the trucks with the Star of David on their doors onto the "City of Florence" cargo ship, anchored in Tripoli Harbor. Unit drivers suddenly — suddenly, despite the fervent anticipation of "moving" — found themselves grief-stricken. Without their trucks, they had no taste for life and wandered about aimlessly.

One sat on a rock and wrote a last letter from Libya, to be mailed from an unknown destination.

Another stared out at the open sea.

A third wondered what could have caused the break with Africa.

The final sunset painted the sea rose. Ankori remembered that upon coming to Libya he had written that the sunset would always be before him: he was marching towards the sunset, westward, and he would get there at the end of the road.

Yes, he had arrived. This was the end of the westbound road.

Now it was time to pursue a different direction: northward, to Europe. He opened his notepad and in the light of the last sunset, wrote:

"LIBYA — FAREWELL".

The desert is a book,
Its parchment dried-out yellow —
Each letter painted bleeding-red.
On unnamed two-stick crosses,
Unseen, a sobbing halo
Relates the price it took
To leave the area dead.
Remain but undreamt dreams,
Defeated, won't relent;
Remains an unprayed prayer
Raising a silent hand —

> The storm will fell the crosses before long
> And heave instead high mounds of sand,
> While an anguished, painful song-of-songs
> Roams war-torn Libyan land.

The desert is a road
With no beginning or end,
With neither yesterday nor tomorrow.
Heavy convoys approach, behold!
Others follow faster still.
The convoy driver never tires,
No time for crying over a fallen friend,
No time for stopping in joy or sorrow —
Even though the sandstorm covers
Every trace of other tires,
Drive he must and drive he will.

> Our African job is done. No more
> Benghazi, Mersa Matruh, Alamein —
> But the memory of Libya and the African War
> Our hearts will forever retain.

*CHAPTER TWO*

# The Story of Jewish Company 178
## B. From Africa to the Threshold of Europe

### I

Mysterious are the ways weaving an individual's life, beliefs and loves into the web of general events beyond one's control and into a tapestry of landscapes beyond one's ken — Ankori reflected as he strained to make out the Libyan shoreline in the dark. The shoreline seemed to be physically receding in the distance while the ship deck on which he sat was frozen, unmoving on the Mediterranean waves, obeying the command of the enchanted evening of May 1, 1943 to maintain utter calm. As usual, after midnight the waves would rebel and thrash the sides of the ship that had invaded their territory and bisected it on the northward sea crossing. But for now the moment was precious, made for introspection, for an intimate debate with his own self.

The men had chosen to gather on the ship's prow when the Major had officially announced that Malta was the current destination, after all. A new spirit of awakening opened hearts and lips and the soldiers' mighty song was their way of showing relief from the uncertainty of recent weeks — the worst sort of situation in a soldier's life — uncertainty about the journey's final destination. True, Malta's name had come up in the pros and cons of the arguments and he, Ankori, had even made up a light ditty about it and taught it to a laughing audience at the farewell party from Libya. Now, he chuckled almost secretively: for two years he had been teaching songs in his Unit, including of his own composition. Yet, at this moment, he was not with the guys in song, having opted for solitude as he gazed, to the extent that the dark night permitted, at the coastline that he would most likely never see again. The farewell words he had jotted down in his notepad while the cranes loaded vehicles onto the ship, resurfaced in his mind:

> Our African job is done. No more
> Benghazi, Mersa Matruh, Alamein,
> But the memory of Libya and the African War
> Our hearts will forever retain.

He had not shown the words to anyone and maybe never would. For it was his confession, the confession of his love for Libya which had seared his heart in all its blaze. And confessions are not made for strange ears. They are between a man and himself, between a man and his beloved.

Libya, yes, one of a kind. When driving his vehicle in Libya westward — he remembered having remarked on this — he knew that to the right of North Africa's narrow continental belt, where the road stretched for thousands of kilometers from Egypt to Tunisia, he would have the sea as his constant companion. This twinning of sea and land inspired a sense of security, faith in the world order. Land and water and union with the entire universe. This would not be the case in Malta. He said this even though he had never been to Malta, merely on the basis of his knowledge of the island's history and topography.

Ringed by water, the small island was far away from any continental landmass — between Africa to the south, from which they had just sailed, and Europe to the north, which they would reach one day in the invasion of Italy; and between Sicily to the west, where Monty might co-opt Unit 178 to his corps (which, possibly, was the rumored "selected job"); and Eretz-Israel to the east, to which the soldier would return at war's end. In Malta he would be cut off from the rest of the world. That was the nature of an island as small as Malta, a mere twenty-seven kilometers in circumference with the sea closing in on all sides. He chuckled once more as he thought of the episode that had made the Turkish fleet the laughing stock of Europe for three hundred years. Circling the Mediterranean back and forth on a mission against Malta, the fleet consulted Turkish and European maps, used a pointer to check distances, yet ultimately it failed to locate the island. Giving up, it humbly notified the Sultan: "Your Majesty, Malta *yok*" — there is no Malta.

On an island — whatever its strategic importance — man was alone, locked in as if in prison, no matter that the whole Eighth Army was with him. On the island, he would have to draw on his own inner resources. No, there was no reason to fear coming to Malta, nor, however, was there cause to rejoice in being conducted there. No, he would not join his merry friends in song at the prow. Instead, he would scan the Libyan coastline once more — except that the coastline was gone, vanishing in the distance. "*Yok*". Offsetting the black emptiness of the sea, boats took shape in the dark, gliding behind one another like giants descended from heaven — a long flotilla escorted by so many warships and so many destroyers, their cannons sticking up as Spitfires circled overhead like a flock of eagles. Onward, to Malta then! Malta ahoy!

Malta's population welcomed the flotilla into its Grand Harbor with endless enthusiasm. The day was pronounced a holiday and cause for celebration. After months of brutal aerial pounding by day and night, the consequences were starkly evident from the deck. This tiny dot in the Mediterranean, in March and April 1942, is said to have suffered twice the number of bombs poured down on London in the Blitz. Now, after protracted siege and dearth bordering on malnutrition, the flotilla had broken through to the beleaguered island bringing longed-for supplies and tidings of the blockade's lifting. One of the Spitfire pilots, who had repeatedly circled above the "City of Florence" during the night, as if grown emotionally attached to the ship's passengers, waved to them as he watched them disembark, well but shaky, along the bridge from ship to land. Did he already know what had befallen the other flotilla at sea? The soldiers were greeted on the pier by the Unit Major, the first to debark, according to form. He had six words to say to them, instantly turning their joy into grief: "462 is gone. It was sunk."

As more details were revealed, the picture of the disaster and its prelude gradually became clearer. While 178 was preparing to sail from the port of Tripoli to its destination, the sister unit in Tripoli, 462, was returning to Egypt. For some reason, there had been rumors that it had received a week's leave in Eretz-Israel, much to the open and understandable envy of 178's soldiers. But this was not the case. The unit had been ordered to leave its vehicles in Alexandria and join up there with a flotilla of 80 vessels headed for Malta. Ahead of 178 by four days, the 334 soldiers of 462 had boarded an Indian ship (under English command), the "Erinpura", carrying also some 750 infantry from Basutoland in South Africa, as well as other English and Indian military personnel. The Company's vehicles were dispatched separately on a cargo ship with a team of twenty guards and maintenance men. The RSM (Regimental Sergeant Major), nicknamed "Tayyish [Goat]", remembers that, when the morning mist cleared, he caught sight of the vehicles and their familiar Hebrew symbol arrayed on the deck of the flotilla's other cargo ship. At the time, the "Erinpura" and its passengers were cruising along the Libyan coast. Near Benghazi, the ship was both bombed from the air and torpedoed by submarine. It sank within four minutes. The Hebrew unit lost 140 men. Some 700 foot soldiers from Basutoland and others perished. The first Sabbath party of Unit 178 in Malta (14 May) opened with a memorial to 462's fallen soldiers. Ankori, the MC, read out from the Bible David's lament for Saul and his son, Jonathan.

Two months after 178's arrival in Malta, the editor of *HaHayal HaIvri* wrote — "Only now have we been given free rein to express the depth of our grief: the list [of 462's casualties] has reached me."

"Man looks out for his own interests" — the Sages noted in the *Yevamot* tractate of the Talmud, and reiterated the saying in the tractate of *Sanhedrin*. "Our Sages were able to read the soul" — Ankori acknowledged — "they were sober psychologists, having no need to hide behind diplomas." And woe, they had been right. For all the grief — true, sincere grief — a blush of shame suffused his face as he remembered the words he had said in all honesty to his comrades: "Did you stop to think it could have been us? Praise and thanks wherever it is owed: we were spared." Yet the blush continued to burn his cheek, for the "*we* were spared" meant, in fact, "*I* was spared". "All I can say in my defense is that this admission does not detract from my grief for my comrades of 462."

One blow followed another. Newspapers reached us from Eretz-Israel. It appeared that while we sat relaxed amid warm hosts at a Passover *seder* in Tripoli, there had been an uprising in the Warsaw Ghetto. "Mother, I wrote you that I am coming. Am I too late?" — Ankori, in turmoil, waited for a sign from his mother. None came. He rose to moderate the evening, opening with a portrait of HeHalutz members Zivia Lubetkin and Tossya Altman, who had fallen in the ghetto battle. But his heart betrayed him and he broke down. He hoped that no one plumbed his inner agitation, for when he said "Zivia", his heart cried out "Mother", and in mentioning Tossya, his heart wept for "Gunia", his seventeen-year-old sister, and when, in pain and pride, he uttered "Mordekhai Anilewicz", his heart choked on "Father" —

Ankori did not know then and was not to know until the end of the war that, in June 1942, while he was organizing the choir at Qenah, the villains murdered Father, Mother and Gunia.

The platoon was housed in a monastic edifice, one of the buildings that had been erected by the Sovereign Military Hospitaler Order of Malta. Christian mercy had named it the Luca Poorhouse. As it transpired, this was a euphemism for a lepers hospital. The charity institution had once played an important role in earlier sanitary conditions, though it had apparently exhausted its original function. Apart from a small lepers wing, it had been abandoned, disinfected, and prepared as military quarters.

The lepers, confined to "one small wing" in the Malta "poorhouse", piqued Ankori's curiosity. Lepers had fascinated him since his youth, perhaps because in studying Leviticus, Father had always skipped over the weekly Torah portions of "Tazria" (on a woman's impure period following childbirth) and "Metzora" (on lepers), saying that they "were not for children". Of course, the boy had covertly read the chapters for this very reason. Though he found little interest in the priestly ritual "treatment" prescribed in Chapter 14 in the weekly portion of "Metzora", the description of the symptoms of the plague in Chapter 13 had left a lasting impression. As a result, on one of his walks in Malta, a strange impulse brought him to the back of the "poorhouse". From afar he saw people sitting on the entrance stairs and beckoning him to come in. Only as he drew nearer did he take in the noseless faces, crooked jaws and warped bodies — and he fled in alarm. His mind went back to a similar irrational fear that had gripped him, at the age of four, in the Carpathian resort of Rabka. He had wandered off quite far, with a new net in hand in pursuit of butterflies. Suddenly he heard noises, the sounds of a motley crowd: "A Gypsy camp?" — he had frozen in fright. "Yes, Gypsies! Didn't everyone know that Gypsies were kidnappers?!" He had run for his life, back to where his mother was calmly sitting and reading a book.

Unit 178 formed close ties with the British club of Jewish soldiers, the military chaplain helping the 150 young men create their own unique experience. Natural friendships sprang up, both public and individual, with 178 as a whole and its soldiers singly who emitted the aura of Eretz-Israel and the volunteering spirit (as opposed to compulsory conscription in Britain). A decision was taken to join forces for Sabbath and holiday gatherings where English and Yiddish mixed with the Hebrew of Eretz-Israel, so different from the prayer-book Hebrew that the English lads remembered from their *bar-mitzvah* days.

As strange as it may sound, though the region was at war, daily work proceeded on still waters: the island functioned as a "peacetime base", as it had done in the Victorian era with all the "bullshit" and the ease that that entailed. The "bullshit" — in soldierly jargon, meant perfectly buffed army boots; Brasso-polished buckles gleaming like gold; never to be caught without a close shave or a bare head — in short, a "smart" look. To be sure, the island command repeatedly rebuked 178 for the slipshod appearance manifested by the graduates of the desert school. As for the "ease" — the daily driving quota was dictated by the island's scant dimensions and the procedures of a peacetime base. There weren't — and couldn't be — any long exhausting trips as in Libya. Work usually broke off in the early afternoon and Sundays were of course free.

Most of 178's work consisted of transporting goods from the Grand Harbor to the bases under construction, the supply stores and the ammunition depots, scattered over the island's length (twenty kilometers) and breadth (fourteen kilometers); "in advent of the great invasion" — 178 strategists pronounced, the assessment colored by wishful thinking and their interpretation of the future "selected job" awaiting them one fine day. The lads quickly got used to driving on the left (as in England) and, as far as one remembers, not a single accident could be laid at the door of this change. What's more, rural roads running between stone fences were so narrow that one could hardly speak of left and right sides. The protruding stones of the fences lining the roads scratched both sides of a vehicle equally.

But it was not comfortable housing and easy work conditions that had caused the men of 178 to happily respond to Malta's call; it was the promised "selected job". Either it had been a lie, plain and simple, or a joke by someone at army HQ poking fun at these unusual, spirited soldiers, who, sought action rather than enjoy the quiet life and hope, as any sane person might, to emerge from the damn war unscathed. Fallacy or joke — both were cruel, frustrating the Unit as a whole and each soldier separately. For the region was a battle arena at the time and history was being decided. Five weeks after 178 arrived in Malta, Monty invaded the small island of Pantellaria as his starting line and, a month later, east Sicily, while American soldiers landed on the identical target in the west. Meanwhile, 178, brought here for a special assignment, looked on at what was happening a hundred kilometers away from their base, and suffered with longing. "Selected job" — where are you?

The strategists of 178 had not been wrong. The stores, depots and other supply centers that the Unit drivers helped erect in the first four months of their Malta service came to life. A vast invasion fleet assembled in the Grand Harbor's fortified inlets, and the drivers of 178, who till then had distributed military resources over every inch of the island's free space, now reversed their direction and began to cart soldiers from the bases, collect supplies and war tools from the stores and the depots to the boats and warships within the orb of the Grand Harbor's ports. On September 3, 1943, two weeks after the war action ended in Sicily with that island's conquest — and exactly four months after Unit 178 reached Malta (on May 3 of that year) — the Eighth Army invaded Italy. "And what about us?" — 178 soldiers were galled — "After faithfully laying the groundwork, we are to be forgotten? We *have* been forgotten!"

Some drowned their disappointment in the arms of Maltese local damsels ("tyfflas" in very respectable Maltese). The friendships and flirtations of the soldiers and tyfflas took the normal course of young romance and were the butt of good-natured banter from soldiers who did abstain from this type of diversion. Particularly amusing was the insistence of the girls — good Catholics each and every one of them with a dangling cross around her neck — on dubbing their Jewish friends with the diabolic nomenclature of "Jewish Catholics". To them, it was inconceivable that anyone could not be Catholic.

As opposed to these innocent relations, Valetta — the capital with its magnificent buildings bequeathed by previous generations and the traditional jewel of the knightly order betokened by the Maltese Cross — was far from pure. A meeting point for tens of thousands of men of every corps and race, changing over in turn, and a huge anchorage for a fleet and cargo ships with thousands of sailors, Valetta concentrated its dens of sin in separate sections of the town so as not to disturb its respectable citizens. Here, day and night, dozens of shady bars, taverns and night clubs, drunkenness and prostitution lurked for soldiers and sailors craving their offerings. The most notorious venue the soldiers came upon was called, strangely enough, Straight Street, but the sages of anatomy slang more judiciously labeled it "The Gut". It was not long before bored groups of 178 soldiers discovered the street and its one "club", where the not-young prostitute-hostess, a seasoned psychologist, immediately saw that she was dealing with greenhorns, "babes", who were interested not in her professional offerings but in her company, her sharp, crude tongue making them blush up to their ears and squeezing titillating, embarrassed snickers out of them.

The "babes" would drop in for an hour in the early evening, and she, available since the place had not yet filled up with real clients, liked to sit with them so long as they kept ordering drinks for her, colored water that cost the price of alcoholic beverages. From time to time, one or another member of the group decided to order a drink for himself at which point she, by now on close terms with them, would issue a word of caution, "not this one", "don't drink that", or she would go to fetch the drink herself.

Not unlike drinkers, it was typical of this breed of patrons to become missionaries of transgression, as if it were their duty to convince others to try the club, if only once, for the sake of untold adventure. They particularly targeted the disinterested who disdained the entertainment form. Ankori thus presented a special challenge: a "culture-vulture" who had not befriended any of the tyfflas and — for all anyone knew — might still have been a "virgin". Introducing him to the paradise or purgatory could have been a real feather in their cap.

"Be a sport (they begged). We feel at home at the club and you will too." One of them, himself a semi-"culture-vulture" though careful to present himself as one of the guys, tried an intellectual tack: "You're a man of arts and letters. Don't you remember Zola's *Nana*? Didn't you see Toulouse-Lautrec wallow at the feet of brothel women? And why did Van Gogh cut off his ear? Come, you won't compromise a grain of your culture. What do you say — shall we go?"

"Of course we'll go" — Ankori astounded the guys who had expected protracted persuasion and a final "no". "Happily, but as an anthropological exercise, as a student of human nature. Though I think we should also take someone else along, someone older maybe, an establishment figure. What do you think? He'll no doubt refuse at first: '*S'past nisht*' (It's unseemly). But I'll convince him."

The lads couldn't understand how matters had gotten so out of hand. With his instant agreement, Ankori had reshuffled the deck, robbing the club patrons of the joy of achievement. Either they didn't really know him, or he was having them on. "Let's see if he brings that older guy."

The sun was already setting and the dark trying to paint The Gut black, though it had to admit defeat and retreat. Strong electric light spilled out of the taverns and bars on both sides of the street while a red light flickered above every doorway. Radios blasted the area with war hits. The "freshman" and his elderly guest walked behind the four patrons, looking with curiosity left and right until they came to a lit-up glass door. "It's here" — one of them whispered, pushing the door open.

Ankori, on his free Sundays, usually went to Valetta's main street to stroll up and down the Cathedral Square and watch the Maltese decked out in their finery and celebrating their Catholicism rather than the Sovereign's Anglicism; displaying, by their civilian garb, their segregation from the medley of uniforms flooding the island; and greeting and chatting with one another volubly in Maltese, though they spoke English very well indeed.

On the day after the visit to the Gut Club, the indefatigable walker again mingled with the Maltese masses marking the Christian Sabbath, and he even entered the Cathedral of St. John (who lent his name to the knightly order). There were so many worshipers that it was impossible to see the floor, which was entirely paved, like a quasi-mosaic, with tombstones installed down the generations over the graves of knights.

When he returned to the square, he froze in his tracks. It was moments before he was sure that his eyes were not deceiving him, that the sight before him was real. A woman in an elegant powder pink suit and a proper church hat — her Sunday best — was going up the cathedral stairs with a red-edged prayer book under her right arm.

Her left hand held that of a five-year-old child in a hatless sailor's outfit and not a hair out of place. The woman looked straight at Ankori, confidently, somewhat ironically and even challengingly — he was certain that the previous evening's madonna, the queen of the club and its handmaid, recognized him. She vanished from sight to be swallowed up by the cathedral gates.

His mind went back to the interesting conversation that had developed at the last Sabbath party: the soldiers had expressed disappointment and frustration at being tricked by both the bait of a "selected job" and the location which they were eager to leave. The MC had tried to tone down the criticism. He claimed that we did not really know the place or its inhabitants. Now, two days after that talk and one day after his visit to The Gut, Ankori sat down opposite the cathedral, reached into his pocket for his notepad, his bosom friend, and sketched a portrait of Malta, a smile painting over his disappointment:

**Malta: a Portrait** *(to the tune of "Rina…")*

Malta, you wondrous isle awash by sea,
Malta, we loved you dearly through the year —
Malta, we'll love you twice as much when free,
Free of you, Malta, and moving far away from here.

Here you've Valletta and Hamroon
And Luca Poorhouse and MPs —
And you did welcome us as soon
As you did realize that we ain't "Ingliz";

Here's boot paste more than we may need
And Brasso for the metal parts —
And since the siege the legs of girls ache and bleed
And undernourished, break our hearts.

Refrain: Malta etc…

Here's every pub named for a saint,
And divides 'tween girls and women blurry,
And whether it's serious or it ain't
The flirting's blessed by Virgin Mary.

In brief, dear Malta, on every ground
You're a mix of things, some nice some less:
King George in color on each pound,
But all the rest is filth and bloody mess.

And so — —

Malta, you crazy isle awash by sea,
Malta, we suffered you almost a year —
And now please, Malta, do finally set us free,
And be sure, we won't shed for you a single tear!

## II

As usual, they were sitting in the truck cabin for their lunch break after strenuously unloading the ammunition stores, kept, at the time, in a field hangar near Hamroon, and transferring them to the port in preparation for the imminent invasion: the Basuto of the Pioneer Company (acting, this time, as porter) did the heavy work and then took his place in the cabin next to Ankori, the driver, who made the twenty-minute trip with the laden truck to one of the side bays of the Grand Harbor. Here the Basuto foot soldier would unload the cargo and set it on the pier, where other men of the Pioneer Corps would take it to the waiting cargo ship. The Basuto porter would then return to the cabin and his partner would drive the empty truck back to Hamroon. He would reverse the truck up to the hangar opening and the whole operation would start all over again: loading, port, unloading, return.

All the stages of the operation, which from beginning to end took about an hour and-a-half, were repeated three times (depending on the components and their weight) before lunchtime. Other soldiers of Unit 178 were similarly employed with different stores, some nearer, some farther away, each driver and his own foot soldier. Now and then Mauritians replaced the Basutos, for a day or two or a week, though the four phases of the work — loading, port, unloading, return — never varied. At times, his conscience pricking him, the Gordonite socialist from Hanita tried to assist the foot soldier, only to be chastised by the British sergeant. The division of labor in the army (or was it racial segregation?) remained sacred as ever.

Now they were sitting in the cabin, opening the tins of bully-beef they had each brought from their own base. After the meal, there would be one more four-stage operation and at about three o'clock another truck would arrive, making the rounds of all the operational sites that day to collect the weary infantrymen and take them back to their bases. The drivers of 178, each in his own truck, would return to the "Poorhouse".

The Jewish socialist loved the lunch break, not so much because of the rest it offered — the porter needed it more than he did — but because of the utterly egalitarian comradeship of "sitting together". It sometimes seemed to him that the African beside him came from another planet. And he, the intellectually curious student, regretted that he knew so little about black Africa, which was so very different from the North African Mediterranean belt. Recalling reproductions on Mother's bookshelf, he knew that, were it not for the influence of *African art*, Picasso would never have painted the "Demoiselles d'Avignon" as he did. That painting had launched cubism in 1907 — but he, Ankori, did not know the *man of Africa* and, presumably, neither had Picasso.

"Ha! Again that soft English bread that you don't need to get your teeth into since it almost melts in the mouth. English bread is not good" — the Jewish driver determined one day as his fork foraged in the tin of bully-beef meant to complement the bread. The Basuto turned his upper body toward the white driver. He was a large man, broad-shouldered, his chest muscles bulging out of his army shirt. But it was his hands that commanded the most attention; they were huge, with the fine, tapered fingers of a Thai dancer.

"You don't revile bread" — he said, in the tone of a preacher. "You may say: the English don't know how to bake bread to your taste — OK. It's not to my taste either. But it's not the bread — the basis of life and man's earliest invention — that's not good; it's the baker, who either doesn't know how to bake it properly or doesn't care." The lesson was delivered. A blush tinted the cheeks of the picky white man. And as if wishing to add from his observations of the world, the Basuto continued: "Africa has masses of animals. They all eat one thing or another because you have to eat to sustain life. Some prey on the flesh of other animals, some eat grass. But none make their own bread. Only man does that, for he is man." The Basuto was silent, returning to his meal as if nothing had been said.

Ankori, stunned, sat at the steering wheel speechless at the unexpected rebuke his African friend had dealt him. The only other person ever to rebuke him, albeit on a different topic, had been his father, and that had been more than fifteen years ago when he had been only six or seven. On the other hand, himself a teacher and educator, he received the words of the "Basuto philosopher" (as he respectfully referred to him inwardly) as confirmation of things that he too had voiced at various forums where he was rebuffed by what he termed the "academic guild": namely, that "formal education (he declared) undoubtedly enriched the resources one needed to cope with immediate problems, but it was no guarantee of original thinking. On the contrary; often, it even inhibited or stifled it." This young man, in South African conditions, had very likely been unable to complete four years of missionary schooling (where he had learned his English); yet his original thinking, fluency, logic of presentation and courage to express his ideas made him fit to take his place alongside the best of students.

Finishing the job at one depot, the drivers and porters moved on to farther hangars that had been prepared in advance of the mission. Whether at random, or because their superiors regarded Ankori and the Basuto a fine, efficient team, the two men continued to work together. But as the distance from the harbor lengthened, a single operation, loading-port-unloading-return, now took more than two hours, limiting the rounds to two before lunchtime and one in the afternoon. The men were thus able to return to camp while it was still daylight, a working arrangement quite normal for a "peacetime base".

One day, when they reached a more remote hangar in an obviously rural area, their nostrils were assailed by a pungent, unpleasant odor reminiscent of outhouses. Their supposition proved correct: in the state of siege, fertilizer could not be imported and the meager livestock (apart from sheep and goats) were unable to solve the problem of manure to raise vegetables etc. As a result, human feces had been used instead. Unlike the Eretz-Israeli who found the odor obnoxious, the Basuto accepted the situation without complaint. His friend sensed that the same system was used in his own country though he did not volunteer any information.

In contrast, the sight of sheep at pasture on one of island's rare hills excited him: "How I would like to do that!" He flexed his long fingers as if seeking to run them through the wool. "Oh, for a taste of home through the sheep's warm fleece!" Ankori envied the African and his bond to land and livestock. Presumably, he also baked his own bread.

Despite the monotony and disappointment of the work assigned 178, the Maltese daily routine did not lack for personal experiences that were to arouse pleasant memories and nostalgic smiles even years later. This was especially true of the liaisons formed by no few of the Unit's men with Maltese tyfflas, which, for all the predictable problems of such relationships, had produced joy, tangles and tears. It was also true of the comradeship Ankori developed with the Basuto of the Pioneer Corps and his Mauritian counterpart, and of his tours after work and on weekends of the island's historic sites and colorful fishing villages.

It was true too of the ties the soldiers formed with Malta's tiny, economically and socially solid, Jewish community. The Unit songwriter was right to have guessed prior to the departure from Libya that a place without Jews was unthinkable. But unlike the rest of his predictions, that there would be "a kids school for Ankori" here too — Malta's Jews required no help. They simply displayed a sense of brotherhood with the Jewish soldiers from England and the volunteers from Eretz-Israel.

Quite naturally, the well-attended Sabbath parties were the chief ray of light in an otherwise gray existence and in personal crises affecting some of the men after ever-longer stints of service. Not for nothing had the former "Indian sergeant" warned fresh recruits at Sarafend: "The army will make you or break you, bloody Indians!" The army had in fact strengthened most of the Eretz-Israel inductees into the British army, maturing and preparing them for days to come. What's more, they were highly motivated Jewish volunteers, nursing aims that others neither felt nor knew of. However, there were a handful of sorry cases too: soldiers that fell apart while their comrades looked on helplessly, unable to do a thing. Especially painful was the case of an older, educated soldier, probably an erstwhile *halutz*, who had published an occasional article in *HaHayal HaIvri*. In Malta, he became addicted to drink. He was aware of his condition and anxious about losing the regard of his two daughters, yet he failed to escape the abyss. The army, rather than send him for the available treatment, moved up his discharge, shirking its duty towards him. The Austrian army (Ankori recalled) had fifty years earlier done the same thing with his grandfather, Shloimeh, who had been crippled by decades of service. Instead of seeing to his rehabilitation, it released him and rid itself of a problem. And what, oh what, of the man who had given body and soul to the army for years? *What of the man?*

The Malta social gatherings continued the tradition of including British Jewish soldiers and other guests, and the latter occasionally contributed to the evening fare. On July 2, 1943, for example, the British Jewish pilot, Leonard Cohen, regaled the audience with a description of his flight over islands near Sicily, which had furnished a comic intermezzo at the height of the British and American invasion of Sicily — in itself the opening volley of the Allied invasion of Italy. Cohen, circling overhead on the lookout for pilots who might have parachuted into the sea or for soldiers who had survived a blow to their ship, ran out of petrol and was forced to land on the first island to come his way: Lampedusa, which was still in Italian hands. He realized that his fate was sealed. He required a moment or two to recover from the emergency landing, but when he stood up (so he told the Sabbath gathering) he found that no one had come to take him captive. He was able to take an initial glance around him. To his astonishment, he saw a large crowd of residents with white flags in their hands. From the front row, Italian officers broke rank to salute him and proffer their surrender. Cohen's aircraft was refueled so that he could alert Allied HQ of the surrender and for it to stop the bombing.

Later gatherings were nevertheless marred by sadness. The news from Palestine was bad, telling of arms searches and arrests carried out by the British Police at kibbutzim. The mood of Unit members could aptly be summed up as fury and depression: fury at the mischief wrought by the British realm against us, its loyal allies and soldiers of its army; and depression that, as part of the British military, we were unable to raise a hue and cry. Ironically, the first victim of the new British policy in Palestine was Ramat-HaKovesh, the kibbutz of 178's Sergeant Major Bankover.

> "On 16.11.1943 [Bankover wrote, via his commander, according to regulations, to the Supreme Command, describing his feelings and the event] Ramat-HaKovesh

turned into a battleground. Hundreds of British policemen and Indian soldiers swooped down to conduct an 'arms search'. From the very first moment, the search resembled an unbridled attack. The village was placed under siege, the yard was surrounded by a barbed wire fence, [the soldiers] burst into members' rooms and worksites and dragged off every male to the fenced-off area. Even the sick were forcibly removed from their beds, male and female members were beaten. Twenty-four were wounded, some of them badly and they are in hospital. One died of his wounds. 35 locals were arrested."

*(The letter appeared in full in* Sefer HaHitnadvut [The Volunteer Book], *from which this first paragraph was taken)*

Other kibbutzim came next after Ramat-HaKovesh. And we? Far from home and trapped on the island, we felt exploited, like blacks, by our white British masters.

Ankori wrote a new song about the situation, prefacing it at a Sabbath gathering with a brief explanation that was repeated in *HaHayal HaIvri*: "I recalled a Yiddish play I saw as a boy in Poland, titled 'Mississipi', about a lynch carried out on a black man who loved and was loved by a white girl. I more or less remembered the tune sung by the white girl; as for the lyrics, only the first line of the refrain rang in my ears: '*Veil ikh bin veiss un er is shvartz*' (For I am white and he is black).

"The rest is taken from the life of wartime Malta, the friendships formed by Maltese tyfflas, much like today, with black Mauritian soldiers and the ensuing tragedies due to the racist opposition of white parents to such liaisons. Thus, by way of metaphor, I tried to give voice to our own feelings of being humiliated like 'blacks' by our 'white'(British) rulers in Palestine." This indeed is how the listeners understood it. The love story per se was just a guise. Reports *HaHayal HaIvri*:

## "THE SHIPS SAILED IN AND DOCKED AT MALTA"
A Maltese tyffla sings about her crossed love for a black Mauritian soldier
*Written by Zvi Ankori in Malta — October 1943*

The ships sailed in and docked at Malta,
The faces strange, worlds far away,
The navy gleams as I behold her,
My heart feels that's my lucky day.

> For he stood there, a black Apollo,
> And waved from far a friendly hand —
> To me 'twas obvious I would follow
> My heart's desire to the end.

>> Refrain:
>> And if I am white and he is black,
>> Why must my love be held in check?
>> And 'cause he is black and I am white,
>> They trampled on my loving's right.

For he was black like night of autumn,
That sheds its stars and stands alone —
His eyes sent kisses, and when I got them
Mine sent back message of my own.

> Yes, Europe's air I breathe with zest
> And a cross hangs always on my neck —
> But tropic thunder pierced my breast
> With love no different though it's black.

>> Refrain: And if I am white etc…

He came, and to the strains of tango
My heart set sail for southern sights:
Banana trees and scent of mango
And austral sun high in the skies.

> We glided through the magic site,
> Enchanted by the jungle thrall,
> When Mother entered… and outright
> She ordered me to leave the hall.

>> Refrain: And if I am white etc…

My mother's threatening position,
Failed nip my loving in the bud,
For I belong to my Mauritian
So long as red is our blood.

> The blood is red no matter where,
> Whatever skin, whatever race,
> And, black or white, we equally share
> Our dreamy nights and bitter days.
>
> Refrain: And if I am white etc…

To every mother came the call:
'The cause is just. Send sons to war!'
But black or white, world's mothers all
Bewail the sons that are no more.

> True justice can't be cut in parts —
> Equality for each race and nation!
> Forget the skin on body and heart —
> The main thing's the MAN — the God's creation!
>
> Refrain: And if I am white etc…

And so I sit here sad and lonely,
The cross still dangling from my neck —
My beloved fights for survival only,
Not sham-justice for the black.

> My beloved fights, but no one knows
> Or cares if he's alive or not —
> Forgetful world! They praise but those
> Who filled the ranks of the ruling lot!
>
> > So 'cause I am white and he is black
> > They made of our love a wreck,
> > And for he's black and I am white
> > They trampled on our loving's right.

Three things made the song the crowning achievement of songwriting in all its periods and a popular tune at every gathering: firstly, until then the songs had been an internal affair dealing humorously with the army life of the Jewish transportation Companies; this song tackled a painful, topical national problem, rallying even people who did not usually attend the Sabbath parties. Secondly, it metaphorically dressed up a clear Zionist national problem in well-known Maltese garb. And, thirdly, it had a universal ideological theme, the call for justice in human relations beyond race and nationality, a call that any reasonable person could identify with.

Aware of this, the editor of *HaHayal HaIvri* reported on that Sabbath party thus: "A printed sheet was distributed again, this time with a new song of Ankori's. The story revolves around our sentiments as news reached us from Eretz-Israel." This was followed by a report on the audience's lively participation as they joined in, in the refrain.

Still, the song was written for soldiers alone. Its composer never dreamt that it would go public. But when he returned to Eretz-Israel, he learned that it had become a smash hit. Someone (apparently from 178) after the war gave a faulty version of it to some songstress, and registered it as his own, omitting the ideological verses and presenting it as an exotic love song. Fifty years later, Palmah doyenne and chronicler of Hebrew song Netiva Ben-Yehuda noted: "We all sang the hit even if we didn't understand it all. Thus, instead of 'Mauritian' we sang 'Moroccan', and so on." On more than one occasion, the song was aired on the radio call-in program, which took requests. Listeners wanted to know who had composed it and when. But nobody knew. Moderator Meni Pe'er had learned the truth from actress Gilat Ankori and he conducted a telephone interview with her father on his radio show. Moderators however are not in the habit of learning from their colleagues' programs. In the end, Ankori did hear the song played on the radio though it was a faulty version, which upset him. When the moderator, Haim Keynan, asked the public to help identify the writer for his next program, Ankori traveled to Tel Aviv and personally brought him the original version and documentation of *HaHayal HaIvri* from 1943. But Keynan did not bother with them nor was he interested in talking to the author. His appeal had apparently been no more than a popular radio gimmick.

To improve the mood of the Unit, downcast by the news from Eretz-Israel, or maybe out of a sense that the Maltese space could be utilized for the sort of Haganah drills, which, for obvious reasons, were impossible to be conducted in Palestine, Sergeant Levitza suggested a military exercise for the whole Company. The goal: to capture a hill (one of the few in the topography of the mostly-flat island). The operation: A Platoon was to charge from the front; B Platoon was to come in from the side through fences and trenches, and take the rear by surprise; C Platoon was to be ready as reserve. Three sergeants — whose ranks in the Haganah were much higher — Eliahu Cohen (later Ben-Hur), Hiel Teiber, and Levitza from Jerusalem — each commanded a platoon. The drill was capped a great success (even though… sh-sh-sh, Levitza's outflanking platoon, including the writer of these lines, arrived late, when they were no longer needed). The Brigadier General, who was invited to watch, was filled with marvel. "But" — he asked — "why do drivers need to learn to capture a hill?"

The mood however deteriorated as British actions in Palestine grew more severe. At a Sabbath party in early December 1943 (according to *HaHayal HaIvri*) "Ankori sang a song 'of the present' that he wrote, expressing the stormy emotions of Eretz-Israel soldiers in view of the present situation." ("The present" was a code word for news from Eretz-Israel). Did British intelligence cast its net also over the newspaper of the Hebrew soldiers at the front, warranting caution? Since the song's original lyrics have been lost, the text below is quoted from the *HaHayal HaIvri* report (though graphically different), the editor having decided to publish the most exciting stanzas. Thus, at least part of the song was saved. It was adapted to a tune from the time of the Disturbances, "*Shkhav Bni, Skhav Bimnuha*" (Lie down, my son, lie at rest), though its lyrics are quite the reverse of the original.

Arise, my son, no time now for rest,
Ominous threats fill the night —
For your sake Father went to defend our nest,
And Mother also joined the fight.

> *Refrain*: Father's a soldier and so is your mother,
> They mustn't speak out, complain or condemn —
> So what if you're a child, there is here no other,
> If they must keep silent, you speak out for them.

*And further*:

Don't believe, don't give in anyone trust,
The world is filled with foes —
There exists no truth, the law is unjust,
Pain has no tears, God knows —

*Refrain*: And Father's a soldier etc…

Nighttime, night of blackness so deep,
Not even a single star —
Son, tonight don't fall asleep,
For alone, alone you are —

*Refrain*: For Father's a soldier etc…

Nighttime, nighttime, nighttime of doom,
It's still so far to dawn —
Keep your vigil in this time of gloom
For now you're on your own —

> For Father's a soldier and so is your mother,
> They can't speak out, complain or condemn —
> So what if you're a child, there is here no other,
> If they must be silent,
> THEN YOU SPEAK FOR THEM!

(*HaHayal HaIvri* concluded: "The silence that greeted the end of the song faithfully reflected the drift of the heart…")

Along with the sense of frustration and betrayal felt by Jewish soldiers in British uniform, there was also a saving grace, a different, more positive feeling: that we would soon be moving out. The alluring, promising familiar scent of "moving" was in the air, peeking out of every corner, pausing on every threshold. Wishful thinking? Or sober observation? The possibility became more and more real. The only question was: moving to where? Would they want to include the veteran, seasoned, available Jewish unit in the Eighth Army's advance into Italy and from there, onward? Or, would they leave its soldiers to rot in Malta, perhaps even send them home? Even the dog-tired hoped that we would set out for Italy and on, towards Europe's heart. That, after all, was the reason that the Yishuv's young had volunteered for active service. The survivors of the European catastrophe (the word "Holocaust" was not yet common currency) needed them, and the hearts of the soldiers certainly went out to the Jewish remnants. Finally, amid preparations to celebrate the third day of Hanukkah candle-lighting, the order came to push up the party to the first day. The Hanukkah celebration thus turned into a farewell party from Malta, after eight months of being posted there. Two landing crafts were already anchored at the Grand Harbor, waiting for *us!* The day after the party, we sail!

# III

On December 23, 1943, two days before Christmas, the most important holiday of Catholic Malta, Unit 178 left the island. Malta's residents, men, women and children, gathered in their doorways, on their balconies and on the streets to wave a friendly "Saha" farewell to the convoy of trucks with the Star of David on their doors making its way to the Grand Harbor. Just so, eight months ago, they had cheered the same convoy of trucks when it had left the port and, led by MPs, had turned up the hill to the Luca Poorhouse and soldiers' quarters. They had similarly cheered on other ships and passengers, their joy embracing all arrivals. But it had been an interested joy: tied up with the breaking of the siege and the import of longed-for supplies to the island. Not so this time. Now, Malta was taking leave of friends. Their amber vehicles, boasting the emblem that the Maltese had come to recognize as Eretz-Israeli, had through spring, summer, fall and early winter been a fixed gemstone in the Maltese landscape: driving from shore to shore, they had sometimes picked up a tired citizen. Civilians had no access to petrol and the down-to-earth Eretz-Israel soldiers had no airs: they did not stand on ceremony as did other puffed-up British soldiers. The exit procedures were equally simple and publicly accessible. A farewell — no formal roll call. It was not like the fleet of dozens of ships that had entered on May 3 under the protection of an armada of warships and an aerial umbrella. The two landing crafts took 178 and its vehicles aboard, accompanied by a single destroyer. "May St. John protect you", devout women crossed themselves, once, twice, three times.

Arrangements were different because the circumstances of war, certainly Malta's, had changed. All of North Africa, Sicily and southern Italy itself were in Allied hands. Officially, Italy had surrendered back in September 1943. But the Germans had regained control, even managing to free the imprisoned Mussolini, who, under German patronage, succeeded in establishing a fascist microstate in the north. Yes, the war on Italian soil would take another year and four months. The Jewish Brigade — a new, entirely Jewish formation, totally under Jewish command and sprouting the Star of David on its shoulders — would join the Eighth Army at the Italian front in 1944, with 178 incorporated in it as its transportation unit. The army would break through along the Adriatic coast up to the Italian-Austrian border and 178 would then be left in charge of this borderland and, while there, fulfill a major Jewish mission.

Whereas only one destroyer accompanied the landing crafts, it is said that 178's departure from the Maltese harbor for the open sea was escorted by a bevy of local boats with weeping tyfflas, waving hands and handkerchiefs that served the additional purpose of mopping up tears. Ankori gripped the rail of the landing craft and gazed at the winter sea — gazed but saw nothing: neither boats nor tyfflas nor even the internal sea locked within the ring of the Grand Harbor. In his mind, he had already left Malta, before boarding the landing craft and, unlike his journey to the island, when he had gazed backward in parting from the receding Libyan coast, this time his imagination was with the still-distant, invisible Italian shoreline, the province of childhood visions. In fact — he was a bit ashamed to admit — he wasn't sure whether he was eager to reach Italy as a Jewish soldier, it being the dream of all Jewish soldiers to gain the European threshold and start their real mission, or whether he yearned for his own private Italy, primarily the land of Dante. That land had enchanted him and, in time, he came to know it well from books and pictures, from studying its language and literature, its art and historic sites. Now, finally seeing it face-to-face, he would be able to weigh the sights against what he had heard, read, explored, learned and dreamt.

Not surprisingly, sweet memories seemed to caress his eyelids until he forgot that he was on a military landing craft, escorted by a destroyer, whose cannons, at a safe distance from the 178 craft, stood erect and ready to open their jaws should any foreign body penetrate their zone from above or from below. He drifted back in time, savoring his childhood romance with Italy. It had started at age zero, or (to appease the pedantic) from the moment that the infant's eyes learned to discern objects in the room. At that time, when he opened his eyes in the morning, he felt stern eyes watching him from the top of the cupboard opposite his bed and he grew frightened and cried. His mother soothed him, explaining that it was Dante Alighieri who gazed at him and she promised to devote her next bedtime stories to Dante and his country. Thereafter, every morning, a one-way smile passed between the child and the bust atop the cupboard, Dante retaining his stern mien. Afterwards, as the child grew into a boy, the poet's writings became a source of boundless curiosity and extended his love of Dante to love of Italy,

Dante's homeland, which the youngster's curiosity also embraced boundlessly.

Mother kept her promise (Ankori remembered gratefully). She beaded into his evening bedtime stories a chain of details about Dante, the man, and Beatrice, his love, about his exile from Florence and his settling in Verona and finally in Ravenna, where he died. And, in passing, she described the delights of these cities, relying on the large Polish book by Edward Porębowicz, filled with pictures of Italy. So transported was the child by the sights that it led him to commit an inexcusable act: he cut out the pictures and added them to his childhood collection of photographs and postcards. That book has been the object of his search for years now. He was prepared to pay any price asked, but the book was unattainable. The entire stock is said to have been lost in Warsaw's wartime destruction. Only copies that had been purchased by libraries remained. When the boy was in the fourth grade, Mother decided that she had exhausted Dante's personal story and moved on to the three worlds beyond, where Dante roamed under Virgil's guidance and which he immortalized in the three parts of the *Divine Comedy*: "Inferno", "Purgatory" and "Paradise". She illustrated her lectures with reproductions of pictures of the inferno and of paradise as conceived in the fertile imagination of Italy's great artists.

Until one day, on entering high school, the son decided to read the words for himself: "For now, in translation, until I can read the original Italian" — he added. Golda smiled to herself. She had no doubt that he would do so. Her son would succeed where she had failed: to read Dante in the original. That same day at Seiden's store she bought a copy of *Boska Komedia*, Porębowicz's Polish translation of Dante. Reading Dante became an obsession. The boy learned whole passages by heart, as was customary in those days. He was especially fond of, though chilled by, the inscription on the gate of the Inferno:

> Przeze mnie droga w miasto utrapienia,
> Przeze mnie droga w wiekuiste męki,
> Przeze mnie droga w naród zatracenia.
>
> Ty który wchodzisz, żegnaj się z nadzieją!

> Through me is the gate to the city of sorrow:
> Through me you'll sink into pain eternal,
> Through me came the Lost with no today or tomorrow.
>
> Leave behind all hope, you, fated to enter.

The obsession did not stop with the Polish translation. It was important to the youth to also find a Hebrew translation. In the pages of *HaTekufah* he came across an article by Friedman on Dante and, in it, to his joy, the cited inscription; he also found there a complete translation of the "Inferno" by Jabotinsky.

Absorbed in rumination about Italy and the knowledge of Italian, Ankori remained oblivious to Malta. "Malta *yok*", as it were. Now, after reciting the two Hebrew translations of Dante's "Inferno" that he remembered from childhood to a hidden audience of the heart, a third translation surfaced and insisted on being heard, even though it belonged not to childhood but to the start of his immigrant-student period in Jerusalem. It happened some six years back — he smiled at the memory of his meeting with the last translator and his translation. It was after a day's touring, a pastime he had undertaken in his first year in Jerusalem so that he could get to know the city. This time it was not to the old neighborhoods which he embraced, but to drink in the air of the Rehavia Quarter with its modern streets and lovely houses. He even sneaked a look at the nameplates next to the doorbells and, childlike, was overawed by the names of the VIPs living in the neighborhood. Finally, he entered Café Hermon at the head of Rehavia, the start of Keren Kayemeth Street.

The Hermon offered fine and expensive coffee (which, for the student meant to forego lunch), and the *Haaretz* newspaper, affixed to a bamboo stand "like in Europe", as well as a German-language newspaper aimed at the "*new aliya*" (as it was called then) from Germany. This is where Ankori first met Dante's translator — a writer, linguist, *uomo universale*. To the seventeen-year-old youth, he appeared ancient, though his bass voice shook the cups and treated the saucers to a taste of coffee. He must have been a regular customer, for as soon as he came in he went straight to the telephone and boomed into the receiver — "Olswanger here — what's the time?" The switchboard operator apparently needed a moment to recover from the shock of the voice. The gentleman waited for a response with typical Olswangerian patience, tapping his fingers over every square centimeter around the instrument. The response came, the inquirer calmed down. He looked around, searching as usual for an unfamiliar face. In the end he found what he wanted. He sat down at the student's table. Now the tapping fingers waited for a waiter.

— "You're a student." It was not a question but an observation requiring no confirmation.

— "Literature, history, philosophy. In that order." The monologue continued.

— "Languages: German, French, English. Also Latin and Greek."

At this point the student felt a need to intervene. Olswanger obviously took him for a member of the German *aliya* and it never occurred to him that the student had a Slavic, East European, Yiddish background and Hebrew education. A remark from this new friend put an end to the monologue that Olswanger apparently enjoyed and which usually met with no protest. But now a real conversation developed, meandering to Dante and his translations, and the importance of knowing the Italian language and culture. The young man told him about his decision to learn Italian. As for visiting Italy — he hardly dared nursing such a dream.

— "You'll get there. Of course you will." Neither imagined that the Italy-thirsty student would first reach Italy as a soldier on a landing craft, at the height of the World War and the Holocaust.

— "Will you be here tomorrow?" The student squirmed. Olswanger understood. He too had been hard of pocket as a student in his youth. "On me" — he added with a laugh.

The next day at the noontime meeting, Olswanger gave the youth a booklet of Yiddish folklore, "*Roite Pomeranzen*" (Red Oranges), which Schocken-Berlin had published in Latin letters in 1932.

— "You said you especially liked Dante's inscription above the gate of the Inferno. Have you read Hebrew translations as well?" The student quoted from memory the translations of Friedman and Jabotinsky.

— "Here, I've brought you a third translation. "*HaTofet* [The Inferno] will, I hope, be completed in a couple of years. Meanwhile, you can copy the lines that interest you. You're the first to see them."

From his pocket, the recipient of the text withdrew a notebook that seemed to be limb of his limbs, and transcribed the translation of the four lines.

In 1938, the Italian government endowed a Chair of Italian Language and Literature at the Hebrew University of Jerusalem. The opportunity that the youth had longed for since childhood thus presented itself. He was among the first to register for the new program, and he developed excellent relations with his teacher, Dr. Haim Vardi. The latter was impressed by the student's enthusiasm and regularly invited him to his lovely home on HaNevi'im Street where he was able to browse through art books and receive informal instruction volunteered by the lecturer to acquaint him with the ideas of Benedetto Croce, whose student Vardi himself must have been. These two years of intensive study made the student the only soldier able to converse with Benghazi's trusting children and parents simply and faithfully, in the only language they knew. On the other hand, with the help of a dictionary, he was able to dive into the original text of *Divina Commedia* — and add, to the translations of the inscription above the gate of the "Inferno", the original Italian as written by Dante:

> *Per me si va nella città dolente,*
> *Per me si va nell'eterno dolore,*
> *Per me si va tra la perduta gente*
>
> ---
>
> *Lasciate ogni speranza o voi ch'entrate!*

The ships sailed in and docked at Malta, and the landing crafts would not leave before the vehicles were chained down to rings on the floor to stop them from moving and being damaged in stormy waters. Leaning on the railing, the soldier returned to Dante whose bust he had once glued back together with chestnut adhesive. Most of all his heart was with Beatrice, Dante's love and fellow in the *Divine Comedy*. In "*Vita Nuova* [New Life]", Dante dedicated a poem to her — the first that his devotee had dared translate from Italian to Hebrew and English. As he set out for both his soldierly and private Italy, the first verse rang in his ears, in both the original and the translation:

> *Tanto gentile e tanto onesta pare*
> *La donna mia quand'ella altrui saluta,*
> *Ch'ogni lingua divien tremando muta*
> *E gli occhi non ardiscon di guardare.*

> > So honest and gentle is my Lady Fair
> > When she waves greetings to each and all around,
> > So that every tongue stops mute, not emitting a sound
> > And all eyes in wonder do not dare look at her.

The love song ends with "*Sospira!*" — "Sigh!" In those days, a sigh was the epitome of lovers talk. The soldier too emitted a dutiful sigh, as witness to the sigh of his beloved poet.

A cacophony of voices suddenly wrenched him back from his

reflections. He was unaware that the landing craft had disengaged from the pier and were slowly, carefully, moving over the smooth waters of the harbor basin to the exit into the open sea. Now he also noticed the boats that had gathered alongside the landing craft with the tyfflas displaying various degrees of agitation. The juxtaposition of the sails with the love sigh of Dante to Beatrice, and the hysterical cries of the herd of girls on the boats, obliterated any trace of empathy for the demonstrative parting scene. After all (he judged mercilessly), only a few months ago the same girls had parted in similar agitation from another company that had landed in Malta, and in a month's time, they would be dating men of a new company. The superficial connections on the part of the soldiers inspired even less sympathy. But he soon bit back his harshness. Even if there was some justice for his cynicism, there were also cases of true — woefully hopeless! — relationships between two young people, and these deserved acknowledgment, not disparagement.

The landing craft meanwhile left the boisterous bevy of boats behind and entered the open water. The December sea being Maltese, hence sympathetic to the tyfflas, decided to indiscriminately wreak havoc both on the soldiers from the faraway land who had turned the heads of Malta's gullible maids and on those who had kept their battledress impeccable. Subordinate to the weather, the landing craft bowed to the evil designer, a misanthrope in league with the stormy sea, who had dictated their behavior from the very beginning. Lacking depth, the vessel's flat bottom enabled the raging waves below to lift the front half of prow, while the charging waves from above, plunged it, in turn, into the deep. This went on for the whole twenty-two-hour trip, up and down, up and down. And what about the passengers? As the prow rose, one's belly dropped to the feet, and as the craft sank, one's belly rose to the throat. All at once, all your friends were leaning over the rail as if, with all their might, they were searching for something lost in the sea, to the accompaniment of groans smacking of a swearing-in ceremony for spirits and demons. No sooner did they straighten up, believing they had been released, when they suddenly turned and ran back, to lean over the rail again, as though their previous sea search had missed something. Back were the groans and stronger still, as if the afflicted were trying to exorcise a *dybbuk* inhabiting their guts, a *dybbuk* that fled and returned, fled and returned on end.

Ankori may be writing about his fellow soldiers, but he is actually describing himself. Ultimately, he thought he had found a way to restore his spirits: he returned to the rail and instead of fleeing the wave of cold, salty water spraying his face, he allowed it to wash over his neck. But the relief was short-lived: the water cooled the body only. "This Inferno" — he mumbled, helpless — "is not the kind that consumes you from the outside, but the kind that burns up your insides, making you spew out your soul." Exhausted, he wended his way to an empty hammock (the navy's "hot bed system") and sank into merciful sleep. He dreamt that he confronted the stern-faced Dante who had stepped out of the bust to appear before him in living form. He had not seen him since coming on *aliya* to Palestine. Now, however, unlike in his childhood, the young man withheld a friendly face: "Oh, Dante, Dante, you were right to cast your foes, the Florentines, into the inferno. But what have I, your faithful admirer, done to deserve it?"

He did not manage to hear Dante's reply. The guard, finishing his shift, roused him up to take over. "Damn watch. The worst shift, from two to four A.M." He took his rifle and went up to the prow. "It's about to start all over again" — he thought apprehensively, planning where he would put his gun when it did. "Oh, for one Stuka — only one! Not to harm the guys, just to take my own head off!" But the nausea stayed away. He must have been numb, the shift passed very quickly. Had he dozed off on duty? Warm sun rays calmed the sea. He returned to his hammock and fell into sleep. When he opened his eyes again, he saw no mast as one did in films, from which a sailor would cry "Land ahoy". The workshop crew were undoing the chains that fastened down the vehicles. The landing craft opened their jaws — the forward side — and their tongue, an iron bridge, was lapping the shore of the Ionian Sea. Every driver took his seat in his truck, started the engine and under the sergeants' watchful eyes began to move to and across the bridge. Directed by an MP, the drivers parked the vehicles in an ancient olive grove next to the coast, stepped out of their cabins and for the first time set foot on Italian soil. Hmm... look at those olive trees! Hmm... fully inhale the air into your lungs! Hmm... how soft and sweet the air is! Hmm... raise your head to the sun! Do you feel it? Do you recognize it? *Eretz-Israel*!

## IV

Eretz-Israel indeed! Ankori adopted an olive tree and instead of dropping his head on the kitbag (his companion of the crossing and landing craft), he stretched out on the bare ground, pressing his limbs to the soil to relax in its silent, intoxicating breath, and to let the earth feel his love. He was no sailor nor would he ever be; he couldn't even swim. In Eretz-Israel too he felt comfortable only in the Jerusalem Hills or on the Hanita ridge of western Galilee's hills. As for sea views (visible from the top of Hanita) — he was prepared to marvel at them as one would at a lovely painting — from afar — without getting his feet wet. He was reminded of a wonderful Greek text that he had learned in his Greek class at school: "Anabasis", from the fourth century BCE, by the Greek Xenophon. At the end of the war, after an exhausting, thousand-mile overland retreat from Persia homeward, he finally spied the blue sea in the distance and cried out the famous words: "*thalasa, thalasa!*" meaning literally "sea, sea!" But what he had meant, personally and emotionally, was "homeland, homeland mine!" Not so the Jerusalem soldier, averse to the sea. After the twenty-two hour crossing and the agony that had made the distance from Malta to Italy seem as long as the thousand-mile Greek retreat, he, spying the bay in the distance, had inwardly cried "Land Ahoy!" praising the "dry land, dry land!"

His alleviation was instant as he adopted the "Eretz-Israel olive coast" as a "temporary homeland".

He semi-closed his eyes, careful not to fall asleep, though his whole, sore body needed sleep badly. Totally shaken, he simply wanted to recover as fast as he could from the sea experience and reconnect with the new landscape. It was no accident that his mind went back to his Greek lessons. He knew that though the region geographically belonged to continental Italy, for centuries it had been Greek in language and the identity of its inhabitants; thus, it had been known as *Magna Graecia*. Turning his vision inward, he conjured up ancient settlers at the end of the eighth century BCE, laying anchor on this shore which was then called Taras: they were not the regular Greek emigrants of the Mediterranean space then — from Attica and other areas of the Greek mainland and islands ruled by Athens — but Spartans, and this was their only colony outside of the Peloponnesus.

The independence and Greek nature of the colony commanding a strategically important bay such as Taras was intolerable in the eyes of the rising power of Rome, and it eventually overran the entire region, naming the city "Tarentum" in Latin. According to Hebrew tradition, recorded by the medieval "*Yossipon*", Titus exiled three thousand Judean families from Jerusalem to the Tarentum area in 70 CE, right after the destruction of the Second Temple. This was the overture to Jewish settlement in the area; its denouement was Unit 178.

The Unit reached Taranto on Christmas Eve, 1943. In the afternoon, families with children walked out to the beach, the Vittorio Emanuele Lungomare, which for the most part was dirt and dust. Tiny, isolated gray patches here and there attested to the promenade's former asphalt cover. The promenade had been crushed by tanks in the battles of September, and the pretty sea-front homes on its northern edge were destroyed in RAF bombings. Conquering the area in the fall of 1943, the British were indifferent to the fascist devastation and the huge fascist inscriptions. By the time 178 arrived, the promenade was still in ruin, the absurd-heroic slogans and grotesque portrait of the *Duce* screaming from every wall.

The mysterious ways of the calendar that year paired Christmas with the Jewish Hanukkah. The first candle of the eight-day Jewish holiday had been lit at the merry gathering in Malta as 178 hearts swelled with joy over the next day's "moving" to Europe's threshold. The majors of the two sister units, 178 and 179, reflected, in their words, what was in everyone's heart. Major Aaron gave voice to 178's exhilaration at setting out for Italy; Major Saharov expressed the hope that the two units were not really parting and that 179 would soon follow. The first Hanukkah candle was the last light in which 178 took leave of Malta. The second candle was lost at sea as its potential lighters hung over the rail of the landing craft. Even as they vomited, they found solace in the fact that the Maccabees themselves, celebrated by the Hanukkah feast, would not have behaved more bravely had there been a sea between their hometown of Modi'in and Jerusalem, and had they been tried by breakers in a landing craft. The third candle, slated to be lit as evenfall descended on Taranto and its bay, after 178 got organized amid the trees, was lit, surprisingly, in the presence of guests. Their attendance defied even the wildest dreamers and excited even the greatest skeptics. All of 178 knew that there were Jewish survivors biding their time in Italy. But no one had expected to meet them within hours of reaching the European sill.

There are various (albeit not contradictory) versions about the circumstances behind the encounter. Some said that an officer and soldier or two of 178 had taken a Company vehicle to scout the city on initial reconnaissance. Stopping on a random street, they were approached by several passers-by who were astounded to see a Star of David on the car door. They stroked the emblem in awe while confessing that they were part of a group of Jews that had managed to cross the Adriatic Sea to Italy in flight from the anti-Jewish horrors in Yugoslavia, their country. The soldiers picked them up and drove them back to their living quarters. The excited crowd that gathered around the three soldiers from Eretz-Israel were informed that, within a couple of hours, trucks would arrive to transport everyone, old and young alike, to the olive grove for the lighting of the third Hanukkah candle together with the Jewish soldiers from Eretz-Israel. The second version was similar, except that it contended that the car had expressly driven into town "in search of Jews". Informed by passers-by where the refugees lived, the soldiers drove to their camp — and the rest is known. A third version places the initiative with the refugees. A group of youngsters — whether strolling innocently along the promenade like other residents or heading purposely for the olive grove after hearing that Jewish soldiers had landed and were stationed near the shore — arrived at 178's base. They introduced themselves to a joyous welcome. Within hours, vehicles were dispatched for the rest of the refugees and a joint Hanukkah party. Meanwhile, tables and benches were set up for the guests and a double quantity of Hanukkah doughnuts prepared.

The lighting of the third holiday candle was a festive, impressive ceremony, though there was little assurance that the guests knew what it was about. Certainly, the children had no idea. The sighting of the Star of David on the vehicles and the mere presence of Eretz-Israel soldiers may have excited them. Nevertheless, in terms of Jewish consciousness, they appeared to be utterly assimilated. After the ceremony, many admitted in private conversation that they were waiting for the moment that they could return to a non-anti-Semitic Yugoslavia. Their experience had not taught them any Jewish national lessons. "We will meet many more like them" — the soldiers told themselves — "and no matter what, we must be kind, embrace them warmly, help them recover, and extend practical help. It's unfair to compare them with Libyan Jewry. One cannot 'choose' one or another type of Jew. They all deserve our love and help."

The very encounter and presence of the guests frankly and unreservedly excited the soldiers, including the sworn cynics who usually mocked the "culture vultures" and had ignored 178's educational efforts in Benghazi. Soon enough, they unexpectedly found a way to the children's hearts, singing with them and teaching them Hanukkah songs, playing circle games and lifting them onto their shoulders, so much so that one couldn't tell who was having more fun, whether the impromptu "nannies" or their "charges". Moved to the bone, the editor of *HaHayal HaIvri* devoted three densely typewritten pages to the meeting, describing every circle and listing every song. The joy was infectious. It swept up the crowd, those in uniform as well as those out of uniform. It was however to be a one-time affair as the Company very well knew, for in a couple of days, it would be pulling out, moving north to Foggia, the current boundary of the British-American advance. This fact only made that first encounter all the more precious, a quasi-pointer for future meetings with survivors wherever they might be found. Nor, at parting, was material assistance forgotten: bundles were quickly wrapped up with undergarments, socks, blankets and canned goods, and loaded onto the trucks that took the guests back to their camp amid waving farewells. Yet Mosenzon could not refrain from ending his article with a question mark: "And in leave-taking, one thought gives no rest: after this wonderful, brotherly meeting — what next? How will *they* reach calm waters?"

In the evening, the Company received good news: it being Christmas, all units were issued turkeys and the necessary ingredients for the traditional stuffing, along with gallons of beer. The cooks rose to the challenge enthusiastically, promising a feast. But it was disconcerting even to 178's non-religious Jews to feast if merely "on the occasion" or "in honor" of the birth of "that man" — as rabbinic literature refers to the Nazarene Jew whose followers served us ill through history — and then, three hours later, to light Hanukkah candles. However, just as all armies abided by the Napoleonic principle that "one was not to stand if one could sit", so the imperial axiom held sway, namely that "soldiers march on their stomachs". Jewish conscience was thus stilled as everyone looked forward to the meal scheduled for noon of Christmas Day — not, heaven forefend, in honor of the Christian holiday, but in honor of the Corsican, his name be praised, and in compliance with his order.

One bit of news came quickly on the heels of another: the Company, for the next two days, was to be at rest, doing only minimal necessary chores such as guard duty and cleaning. This second piece of news was a happy lead-in to the third: on the morning after the break, i.e., Unit 178's fourth day in Italy, the Unit would be "moving" — to its appointed destination and to work!

"So?" — Moshe Mosenzon confronted Ankori as they sat on a tree trunk relaxing from the tumult and excitement. "Here you have it, in a nutshell as they say, a brief history of the Jewish people. A villain rises up and the Jews manage to save themselves from his evils — in this case our Yugoslavs who fled to a region that never before saw a Jewish face. I've read a bit about Italian Jews — I know about the Jews that settled in Rome even before the destruction of the Second Temple; I know that the term 'ghetto' comes from Venice and was absorbed into our lexicon and the lexicon of the whole world (I may have left out a detail or two). That's it. And now, persecution has brought survivors to the sole of the Italian boot where there have never been any Jews. So tell me, Zvi, in all honesty, what's the point of your university studies, when here, before our eyes, we have the very process, the extinction of a thousand-year-old diaspora and the formation of a new diaspora at a site where there has never been one?"

"Moshe, you've looked at two issues that are only incidentally associated. You were right in your definition of the formation of diasporas through history — and I'm just as upset as you are that the Yugoslavs have learned no lesson but want to return to their diaspora in the hope that it will become more tolerant. But, let me relate to your statement that there were never any Jews in this area, where we are stationed. My university studies, it transpires, have not been in vain after all. Actually, I knew about the Jews of this region even before I entered the university where I only learned more. My first teacher was the famous traveler, Benjamin of Tudela, who paid a visit here in the 1160s and reported on his travels. Then, as today, the area was called Puglia. It's a part of Italy's Magna Graecia and was settled by Greeks for two thousand years, which explains the name. This is what Benjamin of Tudela had to say about Puglia (and I quote from memory, omitting irrelevant details):

> And from there [from Rome, Naples, Salerno, Benevento — along the extension of the Via Appia] two days to Melfi in the land of Puglia…" — Benjamin reports — "and, there are about two hundred Jews there… And from there two days to Trani which is on the seacoast, and all those errant in their religious beliefs [the Crusaders] gather there, to pass on to Jerusalem, for there is the right port. And there exists a Jewish community of about two hundred… and it is a fine large town… And from there a day's journey to Colo di Bari, the largest city destroyed by King Gulielmo of Sicily, and there are no Jews there today, nor Gentiles, for it was totally destroyed. And from there one day's travel to Taranto… and its inhabitants are Greek and it is a large town with three hundred Jews, including several Sages. And from there a day's course to Brindisi on the coast… From Brindisi two days to Otranto on the shore of Greece [i.e. of Magna Graecia] and there are about five hundred Jews there.

"I have not yet toured the region but I guess it must have changed since then. The size and importance of the towns surely have changed: Bari, which Benjamin found in ruins, in time became a sea power and the capital of Puglia. I've always thought of the city in connection with Bar in the Ukraine, my grandfather's birthplace, which was established by an Italian princess who wed the king of Poland in the sixteenth century and named it after the sound of Bari. Taranto became an important port of the Italian fleet for which it paid a heavy price in 1940 and especially in the fall of 1943 as we can see with our own eyes. The ports of the Crusaders ('those who err in their religious beliefs' in Benjamin's words) on Puglia's Adriatic coast were a hive of activity in the twelfth century. They degenerated into fishing villages, except for Brindisi. A ferry line makes the crossing from Brindisi to (the real) Greece. By the way, some of the descendants of Trani's Jews are known nowadays as *Mitrani*, even though they are unaware of the name's origin or that the *Mi* is the Hebrew prefix, meaning 'from' (Trani).

"All these places — those that Benjamin visited, where he was hosted by community leaders (mentioned by name in his book) and learned from them about the size of the Jewish communities — I would now like to see for myself", Ankori confessed. "It would be the consummation of the imaginary journey I used to make with my mother in childhood, following in Benjamin's footsteps. On the second day of our current break — obviously not tomorrow, for one can't forgo turkey and beer out of the king's pocket — I will ask for a vehicle to tour Puglia according to Benjamin's map, outlined in his account. If you like, Moshe, you're welcome to join me. Will you come?"

It was late. The two friends parted with the hope that they would be able to carry out the plan for the tour. Indifferent and somnolent, a thin moon plied its way in the heavens. It was their first night in Italy.

Exhausted from the experiences at sea and on land, Ankori couldn't fall asleep. The two books that had been the cornerstones of his childhood seemed to be watching him from across the space of years: the booklet that he knew by heart from having read it so much, i.e., *The Travels of Benjamin of Tudela*; and the large tome whose every page was photographed in his mind, the *Romer Atlas*. Mother and son perused the books together, riding, in their imagination, like the Radanites on the Silk Route or sailing with Benjamin in a galley on the Ionian Sea. In 1943, the young man was not to know that his dream of traveling to China as the Radanites had done a thousand years earlier would come true one day. But Puglia did not have to be a far-off dream. Puglia was the present! It was where his Unit was stationed. This then was an opportunity to follow the route Benjamin had taken 780 years earlier and to evoke the region's spiritual riches in the past. Not for nothing had the rabbis of distant France praised the Jewry of the region: *"For from Bari will go forth the Torah, and the word of God from Ortanto"*.

Dawn burst forth in the east. The idea of the trip pleased Benjamin's admirer and a veil of calm enveloped his shoulders. Now he felt that he could sleep in peace. In peace? The racket from the kitchen, the clatter of pots and the voluble voices of the cooks, who had risen early to keep their promise, banished all hope of sleep. It would come at another time and another place, though who knew when and where? In any case, there was nothing he could do to bring on blessed sleep.

The next morning found Ankori and Mosenzon sitting on the stairs of the Aragon Citadel, built in the eastern corner of ancient Taranto and rightly so, for it was the east — the Turks — that in the sixteenth century had boded ill for the city and southern Italy, and the fort was built as a defense position. Geography was Taranto's greatest advantage as well as its worst foe — from Roman times to Hannibal's expedition, and Rome again, then the Byzantines, the Arabs, and the Byzantines again, followed by the Normans, the region's annexation to the kingdom of Naples, and, finally, its conquest by Ferdinand II of Aragon in 1502. It was the stairs of Ferdinand's fortress that Ankori and Mosenzon reached four hundred and thirty years later, puffing but pleased with their morning walk. Their ears rang with Benjamin's prosaic words. He, in the twelfth century, had mentioned Jewish life in Puglia as a natural circumstance, free of any of the excitement accompanying the two soldiers from Eretz-Israel in the twentieth century, during World War II and the Holocaust.

They were particularly interested in what Benjamin had found at Taranto in the twelfth century and what he could not possibly have found due to later developments. Very likely, the small lanes and houses had remained as they were in his day, possibly even dating back earlier, to the Arab period at the end of the ninth century. What had certainly changed from the start of the sixteenth century when Taranto came under Aragon rule was the topography. The king, at the time, had ordered the excavation of a water channel to fortify the rocky hill supporting the city, by separating it from the shore of the open sea (*Mar Grande*). He thus had made it an island. Hence, on their way to the Old City, the two men crossed a bridge (one of two; the other had been bombed out). Benjamin of course did not mention either bridges or a citadel, since they had been built 350 years after his visit.

The lagoon resulting from the excavation of the channel (*Mar Piccolo*) created a second shore, lined today by Strada Garibaldi Street and populated by fishermen. Ankori chatted with the netcasters, his knowledge of Italian and Byzantine Greek allowing him to recognize some of the early Byzantine words that laced their Taranto Italian, though it was centuries since the decline of Byzantine culture in the region.

Time and again, the two friends were amused by the ironies of history: Spanish rule had expelled the Jews from Puglia and other areas in the realm of Naples, as it did from Spain itself. And even though Spanish rule had been ousted from Italy long ago, the region had remained almost empty of Jews until the start of the twentieth century. Now, two Jewish soldiers sat on the steps of the Spanish citadel, part of the army defeating the current rulers. History keeps records: crime and punishment, villainy and redress for villainy!

Mosenzon was not content with the brief milestones listed by the traveler of Tudela. He asked his private guide for details of the structure of the Jewish communities, their occupations, their spiritual life and contacts with Eretz-Israel. Suddenly, an idea occurred to him: "Listen. Don't tell it all just to me. How about treating all the boys to a lecture? Say — today, after the king's feast?"

"The king's feast" — an elegant euphemism for "Christmas" — was decidedly a royal fête. Interspersed between the olive trees, the tables and chairs set up for yesterday's Yugoslavian refugees and now meant solely for the boys in uniform, had never seen such a lavish, cheerful repast as the cooks of 178 had promised and delivered for December 25, 1943. The soldiers, each with his own messtin, cup, knife and fork in hand, waited for the signal in the shade of the old trees, which, with motherly compassion, had taken 178's young to heart, as if they were dear sons, and protected them from the Italian noon sun that must have confused the calendar to radiate Easter warmth on Christmas Day.

When the signal came, the soldiers took their places at the tables. Those who chose not to crowd onto a bench, sat more comfortably at the foot of an old olive tree, enjoying both the company and the solitude. Mosenzon and his friend managed to get back in time and "with luck" found two seats on a back bench. The student-friend did not appear overly excited by this piece of "good fortune" that had come their way. In his mind, he was still roaming through the lanes of old Taranto, reminiscent of old Jerusalem, or imagining himself greeting in Greek and Italian the fishermen casting their nets from the Garibaldi wharf to Mar Piccolo. Mosenzon, in contrast, who never forgot that he was the editor of *HaHayal HaIvri* and would have to report a summary of the lecture, beamed with delight. "An excellent place for the lecture" — he mumbled. "Easy for the lecturer to maintain eye contact with the whole audience and visible, unhampered, to the whole audience." The lecture's logistic aspects were probably not foremost in the mind of Benjamin of Tudela's escort.

From somewhere among the trees, or one of the tables perhaps, a soldier, apparently impatient or because his flaring nostrils could no longer endure the aroma of the stuffed roast turkey, launched into the well-known song: "*Od lo akhalnu...* [We have not yet eaten...]". His mates joined in at high pitch to the accompaniment of clanging cutlery and messtins. The cooks understood that it was time. They summoned the sergeants who had volunteered to act as waiters, and the ensuing procedure was simple: cooks and their assistants brought in clean, dry pots (in lieu of trays). Turkey had been pre-carved into generous portions and two sergeants in every group of pans, armed with long kitchen forks, lifted portion after portion out of the pot and placed it, with a smile, in one messtin after another.

The first "round" was followed by "seconds" and then "thirds", the sergeants tirelessly dipping their long forks into the pans and dishing out portion after portion of roast. Abundance and tastiness brought a flush to every cheek and a spark to every eye. But let's not forget the beer. Throughout, two average-size beer barrels stood on the table, on tap, as the light beer raised a white foam in the pouring. This part of the operation, the pouring, was controlled by the feasters themselves. But as soon as a barrel was empty, the Beer Master, also a volunteer sergeant, assiduously refilled it with the foaming gold beverage to the sound of applause from around the table.

Gradually, the glutting and drinking began to leave their mark. Someone took a stab at starting up public singing, but the attempt died at the hurdle of the song's second line. The double and triple portions of roast took their toll on heavy eyelids while the beer raged through the brain in waves and plunged to the feet. The last to present their bill were the queasiness and spinning heads of the day's heaving aboard the landing craft, and the subsequent insomnia.

By the approximate time of the planned lecture, most of the audience was already napping. They dispensed with etiquette. There was no point in asking to be excused, since their neighbors too showed glazed eyes fighting a desperate battle against sleep. Some of the men simply rose from the table and stretched out in the merciful protection of an olive tree from the inconsiderate midday sun. Mosenzon had been right to praise the back bench. Facing his audience, the lecturer could take in the whole camp at a glance. This he now did: his eyes combed the tables, assessing the percentage of his potential listeners. He realized that it was close to zero.

Like a drowning man crying for help, he turned in despair to Mosenzon. But his neighbor at the table had long since dropped his head next to his plate, and didn't even hear the question. The lecturer, too, felt that the spaces between his words and the gaps between the syllables began stretching beyond the acceptable in human speech and the desired decorum of lecturers. They gradually degenerated into gibberish; ultimately, they sank into oblivion.

Jewish Puglia's exciting story thereby dissolved in stupor, the stupor of both the audience and the designated teller. Not so had the latter imagined the onset of the blessed sleep he craved. The olive trees cradled their boughs in the light breeze as if aiming to refresh drooping eyes. But the rustle of the leaves had the opposite effect, intoning a wordless lullaby. The story of Jewish Puglia remained stored in the mind of the only person who knew it. And he, unfortunately, never did, and never would, tell it to 178's soldiers.

# V

— "Ankori, get ready, you've got half an hour!" — Sergeant Major Bankover discharged a seemingly offhand call into the tent, soft and friendly as was his way with the kibbutznik from the day that he had admitted him into the Company. Nevertheless, it was an order, loud and clear.

— "Get ready for what?"

— "To travel" — he replied shortly as if stating the obvious — "the car's waiting".

— "Travel to where?"

— "To Ferramonti."

It was the first time that the soldier heard the name and he was not convinced that he should apologize for his ignorance. Yet, it was a name that was to become identified with him in the history of the Jewish units in the Second World War, almost like an alter ego.

— "Where is this Ferramonti of yours?"

— "Don't mock. In three hours' time it'll be yours."

— "Where is it?"

— "In Calabria."
— "Meaning in the toes of the foot parading in Italy's boot?"
— "You could put it that way."
— "And what's there?"
— "The first liberated large Italian concentration camp is there."

The soldier was stunned. His lighthearted tone abruptly dissolved. He remembered that in southern Libya, at Jado, on the edge of the desert, the Italians had set up a forced labor camp for Jews, and Benghazi's schoolchildren had been waiting for their fathers to return. Real concentration camps, in the full sense of the word, he associated with Nazis.

— "And why do you want me to go there?"
— "You're to be our first envoy and the first envoy of the Jewish units in Italy."
— "And what does an envoy do at a concentration camp? I have no experience in this."
— "Nobody has any experience in it, so don't expect advice from anyone. You'll create the job as you see fit, just as you did the model Jewish school in Benghazi. Except that this time, on a far larger scale — ten times over — and not only for children but for the entire population, adults and youth, school and kindergarten."

The soldier was still, as if calculating, without pen and paper, what "ten times over" meant.

— "Enough questions already. The car is waiting. More important: *they are waiting for you there*. Move!"
— "What's the rush? I haven't got a change of socks and underwear — I did laundry only yesterday — and I have no education or information material, no book, no songbook, no map."
— "Doesn't matter. Anyway it's all in your head. Socks and underwear we'll send on in a week's time. The main thing is — go!"

The road veering westward from Taranto — quite passable despite the war damage all around — wound its way for about a hundred kilometers along the brown coastal strip hugging the bay. The passenger's eyes were glued on the Ionian Sea lying to his left, its waters calm now and sparkling in the splendor of the winter sun. But he found it hard to get over his resentment at the sea for the torment he had suffered on the crossing by landing craft on December 23. To his right, the car was escorted by Puglia's lowlands, tilled for the most part and waiting for a good harvest despite the ongoing fighting to the north. The low hills appeared to be rolling towards the shore, only to change their minds at the last moment, but they had no beauty or uniqueness to catch the eye. Thus, unable to forgive the sea for its treatment in the past, and in the absence of stimulating land sights in the present, the soldier-suddenly-turned-envoy chose to give his mind over to thoughts that alternately upset and excited him, after being called on to leave with no equipment for an unknown job.

He set out for the unexpected mission without hesitation or fear, armed with his typical exuberance and not a passing thought for the hasty, astounding and inexplicable manner that he had been sent to fill — no, to create — a job that had no definition since no one could define it. He trusted to his resources and experience. Inwardly, he had sniggered at the remark that he could get along without books since it was "all in his head", and without hiding behind false modesty he had decided not to dispute the statement.

For the first two hours of the trip, with nothing in the dull landscape to attract his attention, he looked inward, reviewing his professional qualifications: his experience and innovation in teaching workers' children; his ability as counselor and director of public summer camps in Jerusalem to condense and implement in one month a complete, varied and topical program; his lecturing before adults at the Histadrut Workers Seminar — all this without being chained to books, merely by drawing (Bankover was right) on his "head", that is, from the many layers of education and reading accumulated in his mind in years of study and activity, from diverse seminar papers that had caught the attention of teachers and colleagues, and from his command of languages, notably

German and Italian. The latter, without a doubt, were the cement that transformed a motley refugee public hailing from different countries into an organized, survivor society in adverse camp conditions.

"We're leaving the coastal road now" — the driver broke the silence, apparently noticing that his passenger had come out of his meditation — "and taking a secondary road for a stretch to the right, meaning to the north; then we drive west again, along a winding road through the mountains, the Mountains of Calabria."

— "How do you know all this? You're not using a map. Along the bay you obviously didn't need one — there *is* only one road, to the west, so you can't go wrong. Were you given directions for the route through the mountainous region?"

— "No need. I know the way."

— "But how? Have you been here before?"

— "Just yesterday. I drove back and forth. We received travel counsel, took a map and the major read aloud from the English guidebook."

This is how Ankori learned, from the Staff driver, that he — and the major's car — had been requisitioned to deliver him to his destination without mishap. So much for his fantasizing: he was not, after all, the first "Radanite" to penetrate the "unknown country" of the "Iron Mountains" (*Ferra monti*) of Calabria. The major himself had preceded him, no less. Of course, the major wouldn't be assuming the day-to-day work. But his erect stature and patently "English" appearance, along with the crown insignia of rank on his shoulders, must have made an impression. Very likely, after hearing the report of the refugee leaders, he had promised to immediately dispatch "one of my men" for an extended mission. This would explain the morning's haste. Having given his word, his honor as commander was at stake. He could, of course, have made things easier on the envoy by sharing with him the information he had been given at the camp. But information given to a major is meant for the major; majors give only orders.

The driver was openly enjoying his advantage of knowing the

lay of the land, taking credit for explanations that the major had read out loud from the guidebook the day before.

— "We're leaving the shoreline now, since it starts being steep and rocky here. We're entering an area with three mountain ranges. The highest is at an elevation of two thousand meters. Notice: the one on the right, Sila, is high, steep and wooded, though here and there, you see plateaus of pasture land. It's cut by streams, full at this time of year. In summer, they're dry, just like our wadis. The incline causes a strong current but in the last stretch, the water forms marshlands, a hotbed for malaria mosquitoes. The government has started draining the swamps. The malaria, however, has not been completely wiped out. Everything ground to a halt with the war.

"Were it not for the mist in the west" — the driver continued, pleased with himself — "we would be able to see the highest, steepest Calabrian mountain in the distance, at the sharp, mountainous tip of the Italian boot. It's called Monte Alto — "High Mount" — and is true to its name. It looks like it has its back to the Ionian Sea and nods to the Tyrrhenian Sea, west of Italy. There's no problem seeing the third range, the one to our left. It's low and bare, having greedily been plundered by earlier generations for lumber, maybe for shipbuilding. Look to the left now, past my shoulder: there, at the bottom, you'll see a partially drained plain, still plagued by malaria. You see the dozens of shacks scattered over the area? *That's Ferramonti!*"

# VI

Upon completing the mission after a month and a half's absence from his Unit, the maximum furlough permitted a soldier — furlough being the official explanation for his leaving the Unit — a car was sent to return Ankori to Foggia, the unit's destination after gaining its initial foothold in Italian soil. It had spent three pleasant days at Taranto Bay — "compensation" (the soldiers jested) for the discomforts of the landing craft. The "moving" northward had occurred the same day that Ankori had been sent west to Ferramonti.

Foggia, on the northern border of the Puglia district, was at the time the boundary of the British advance towards the center of the Italian boot. It had been overrun by the Germans following the Allied landing in Southern Italy and Italy's surrender in September 1943.

Before the month was out, Foggia had fallen to Montgomery's Eighth Army, with whom Unit 178 had broken through from el-Alamein to Tripoli. Now the Unit was to advance with Monty along Italy's eastern (Adriatic) coast, nursing great hopes that it would soon cross into Austria and Germany. In parallel, General Clark and the U.S. Fifth Army were tackling the Germans on Italy's western (Tyrrhenian) coast.

Until its conquest, Foggia had serviced Italian and German forces as a highly important military and air base, due, chiefly, to its forward airports. From these, Italian and German aircraft would raid the boats of the British fleet in the Mediterranean Sea, which was not very far away. Roaming the streets, the soldier felt queasy: he recalled that this had been the take-off point of the damn bomber responsible for the drowning of one hundred and forty men of Unit 462, the Company that was to meet up with 178 en route to Malta. Little wonder then, that when 178 reached Foggia and found it in semi-ruins, they felt no pangs of conscience at the systematic pounding to which RAF planes had subjected the town and the airports on its outskirts. Foggia's homes, whether abandoned or confiscated, were nevertheless still standing and, now, they were to house the Jewish company and other British units.

The availability of real houses and the break with army routine of erecting an outdoor tent camp was a welcome bonus that winter, given the cold and snow in the border region of the central Apennine Mountains. True, some of the roofs were said to have caved in from the weight of the snow, while several walls were undermined by bombing — and this, after the British soldiers were already billeted there; no one bothered to conduct the required engineering check. Nonetheless, the living quarters in Foggia were better than anything 178 had known to date.

Ankori soon sorted out a niche for himself and at once started browsing through the pages of *HaHayal HaIvri* lying on the table, eager to update himself on the news of his Unit during his absence. "*Visit to the Ferramonti Concentration Camp*" — a headline captured his attention. Written by Moshe Mosenzon, it was meant as a report of a first trip by a 178 delegation to Ferramonti. The site, much like Calabria itself at Italy's southwestern tip, had been shrouded in mystery and very likely not included in the itinerary of tourists.

Unfortunately, the issue that was to introduce Ferramonti to the soldier population was published after a six-week delay because the Gestetner had been badly damaged by the rampaging landing craft. Its eventual publication more or less coincided with the envoy's return, after the name "Ferramonti" had ceased to inspire awe, had become the object of visits, and was on every tongue. Ankori had written and signed an initial memo about the site and his work, and this had been sent on to the National Institutions in Eretz-Israel along with the signatures of Unit commanders Major Aaron and Sergeant Major (CSM) Joseph Bankover. So in Eretz-Israel, too, the name Ferramonti was no longer unknown.

As regarded the envoy himself — the very start of the article divulged in broad daylight both the surprise and resolution of questions that had perturbed him:

> Two days after we landed [wrote the editor of *HaHayal HaIvri*], we drove off to pay a visit to the Ferramonti Concentration Camp, about a hundred miles away; we — being the Commander, Officer Ben-Hanokh, and Moshe Mosenzon. We set out at daybreak in the Staff car. We arrived at the site after a three-hour trip. The area is surrounded by bare hills on all sides. A large camp of shacks with no tree, and no sign of normal life of a settlement.

The shacks are dismal, with mud and rainwater puddles in-between.

Quite possibly, what the editor had taken for puddles were part of the drained section, work on which had been cut short by the war. Mosenzon quoted the hosts who noted, "we suffer a good deal from malaria here because of the nature of the environment. So far, we've had thirty mortalities."

Finally, Ankori searched for and found in the newspaper a reference to the question that had briefly crossed his mind when he had left for the mission, but which his strict self-discipline had quashed so that it would not interfere with his work. Now, after returning to 178, his attention was caught by an item reprinted in *HaHayal HaIvri* from the "Bulletin of the Soldiers Association in Eretz-Israel". There, after greetings and praise on the completion of his stint of duty, he found some retrospective sympathy for what had preceded his departure:

> Zvi set out with a heavy heart. Hasty was the decision and hasty his departure. But we knew that the lacunae caused by the haste of the decision, which prevented Zvi from equipping himself with auxiliary materials, were filled with the love that Zvi carried with him for those to whom he went.

Zvi, nevertheless, believed that his personal success at the job did not make up for the impromptu manner and haste with which they had sent him off to cope alone with the problems of a large population, haunted by nightmares and horrors after four years behind barbed wire — to cope with something the envoy had no experience of, nor any way of knowing, when he left for Ferramonti, whether he would succeed or — perish the thought — fail:

> It was foreign ground [the Bulletin emphasized], much like exploring unknown worlds. Doubt gnawed at the

heart: those terror-filled years they had lived through, to what extent had they grown in the furrows of a hurting heart? There was anxiety and the decision only multiplied the hesitations, for one of us was to leave to plow our first furrow in those fields of youth."

The Bulletin article had been written after Ankori already returned from the mission. Based on the results of his work, the initial anxiety had been stilled, the doubts erased and the hesitations dissolved. The second envoy to take up the duty already found an optimistic atmosphere when he arrived:

> The youth group at Ferramonti was no longer a foreign field. Furrows had already been drawn there that deepened in the heart. Zvi's faithful hand had gone over the field with our plow — and sown within the furrows the seed found its natural place. And the field will yield its harvest. And for this, Brother Zvi, we are grateful!

The article was signed "M." There was no doubt that Moshe Mosenzon had written it himself. It was his unmistakable rhetorical style, his unquestionably sincere doubts. "One way or another (the envoy reflected), I'm not upset at the hasty departure that morning nor would I be upset had they sent me off in the dead of night. On the contrary, I would have eagerly volunteered and, in my usual way, met the challenges face to face, with double resolve."

Ferramonti was a motley crowd of internees, including small Christian "nationalist" groups and some converts, although Jews made up the largest, most dominant element. They (about 2,000 people) consisted of mixed blocks of European nationals, categorized by country of origin. The differing origins, outlooks and hopes for the future of the various blocks and individuals did not cause alienation or self-isolation — not in the four years of internment behind barbed wire nor when the gates were opened and the fence dismantled by Allied armies.

As a matter of fact, some individuals did walk out of the gates. The new gust of freedom propelled the young to try their luck in the liberated towns of Southern Italy. Most of the former *internati*, however, remained in the camp, whether because of its relative comfort, security and economic benefits, or because the organized blocks lent status and meaning to the institutionalized waiting period for *aliya* to Eretz-Israel or immigration to another country.

The organization and migration arrangements of the Yugoslavian block were an example of the advantages of remaining together in the open camp. The respected leader of the Yugoslavs, David Levy (Dalo in Serbo-Croatian), who at that time served as the elected chairman of the entire Ferramonti population, duly passed on accurate statistics to the first Eretz-Israel group on the numbers registered for *aliya*, for immigration to England and its colonies or to America.

Nonchalantly, he added: "The rest have chosen the option of returning to Europe". He was of course referring to the 250 Yugoslavs (apart from a handful of Zionists from Yugoslavia registered for *aliya*) who were to join him, within days, on the road back to their country.

Prior to his departure for Ferramonti, the envoy had no information about the makeup of the camp population or its subdivision into "national" blocks. He had however attended, after his arrival, the last assembly of the Yugoslavs, and even days later was still shocked by the memory of the chairman's speech. Never before had he heard anyone express himself so *galuth*-like ("exilically"), and he hoped that he would never hear that again. True, there had been Jewish refugees from Yugoslavia in Taranto and, after the reception organized in their honor by Unit 178, they had admitted that they hoped to return to their native land, a land that had repaid their love with hate. But these had been personal confessions, uttered quietly, perhaps even painfully. Not so Dalo's speech. He brandished a patriotic pathos and fervor — and this only five days after welcoming the Eretz-Israel major and four days after the Eretz-Israel soldier-envoy was dispatched to the camp. "I am a major in the Yugoslav army" — Dalo declared — "I pledged allegiance to my king and I will not break my oath". What's more, in a covert argument with the equal-ranking Eretz-Israel commander, he had pointed to the Yugoslav royal insignia on his lapel.

— "What about the Ustashi slaughtering Jews under the patronage of the realm?" — a member of the audience challenged this absurd ultra-patriotism. "What about Jasenovac?"

Ankori, in January 1944, never imagined that in May 1945 he would actually visit the horrid concentration camp after it was abandoned by the Ustashi jackboots for fear of the partisans. On the Sava River he would still see dozens of corpses, their faces in the water and their hands tied behind their backs. And on land — fingers, hair and feet of Jewish forced laborers, worked to death, would be protruding from the hill of bricks manufactured at the camp factory. The Eretz-Israel soldier would arrive in Jasenovac, undaunted by the warning that the Ustashi were still roaming the forests, hungry for prey.

— "And what will Tito, already ruling most of the territory, say to you? Will he be touched by your pledge to your king?" — a jeer was flung into the air of the hall. "If the major continues to sport the insignia on his lapel — it will take only one partisan and one bullet to put a stop to the show!" There was silence in the hall. No one hushed the protesting disdain of Chairman Dalo and, indirectly through him, of the king. On the other hand, no one removed their mesmerized eyes from the major and his lapel tag; everyone knew what it had represented in the past, and they clung to its authority now too.

The Jewish question was never mentioned by the different sides to the dispute over returning to Yugoslavia. Only the cry of "Jasenovac" had alluded to Jews. Apart from a few Zionists, the public was mostly with Dalo. The ensuing silence did not reflect the dilemma of choosing between Eretz-Israel and Yugoslavia, but concern about the outcome of Yugoslavia's internal, historical contest between Tito and the *ancien régime*.

Dalo ignored the interjections. In the charged silence, he announced: "The Yugoslav military delegation has organized a special train for us, which is to stop here on January 18, 1944 at 10:00 A.M. to take us to Brindisi. From there, we will sail for Egypt. The rest will be arranged later. We will therefore meet again in another ten days at 9:00, and march together to the nearby railway track. In those ten days, we will be able to prepare ourselves and our belongings for the journey, as well as part from our friends after four years of a shared fate.

"The Serbo-Croation school, which gave our children a taste of the homeland, will shut down today. We would like to thank the principal and teachers for their devoted work under difficult conditions (applause). I have been told that, at the German and Italian school, pupils are preparing farewell compositions to be presented to their departing friends. Thank you for this moving gesture of friendship! I hereby declare the assembly closed. It is our last assembly in the camp. We will thus meet again on the appointed day to bid Ferramonti farewell. *Long live Yugoslavia!*" The entire audience repeated after him: "Long live Yugoslavia! Long live Yugoslavia! Long live Yugoslavia!"

At first, despite his shock at the patriotic Yugoslavian speech, the "green" envoy took part in the sad partings of adults and children alike. The teachers suggested that every pupil present a copy of their composition to the Eretz-Israel envoy too. The latter had managed to endear himself to the children in his very first week. At the end of each day, (with the teachers' consent) he visited the classrooms to give a short talk about Eretz-Israel or teach a Hebrew song. The children were happy to address him affectionately as "Zvi", a new Hebrew name they had not encountered before.

The compositions the children gave him impressed him; the authors showed an ability for self-expression. But he was bowled over by the naïve belief the German- and Italian-speaking youngsters expressed in the compositions, namely, that the Yugoslavs were the first of the Ferramontesi to be making *aliya*, and that the remainder were to follow in their footsteps. The Yugoslav children believed the same thing.

Was it a calculated diversion on the part of the Yugoslav parents? They certainly knew that their children were friends with the children of the Zionist block, and that they participated in the activities of the youth club. The club had slowly become more Zionist. They attended the separate Serbo-Croatian school, but the club's songs and dances exposed the children to Zionist propaganda, stirring in them, perhaps, as in their friends, dreams about *aliya* to Eretz-Israel. Did the parents fear that divulging the true destination would cause the youngsters a crisis?

> Das Wiedersehen in Erez-Jisrael.
> von Judith Breuer geb. den 18 Februar 1930 in Wr.-Neustadt    Deutsche Unterklasse Ferramonti-
> 13. Februar 1943. (5.704)
>
> Mit den Jugoslaven fing das Wegfahren an. Es wird aber damit nicht aufhören. Bald wird auch an uns die Reihe kommen....
> Wenn der Tag unseres Abschiedes von Ferramonti kommen wird, wird es uns einesteils leid tun, uns von Ferramonti zu trennen. Hingegen werden wir uns freuen, daß wir uns schon endlich einmal unserem Ziele Erez-Jisrael nähern. Zu dem wir uns schon jahrelang sehnen.

One writer, Yehudit Breuer, age thirteen, understood the situation very well. She knew that the paths of the two blocks diverged. She took comfort in the hope that the Yugoslav trip to their destination heralded the imminent departure of the Zionists to their destination, to Eretz-Israel:

"13 Feb. 1943 (*correct date: 1944*). The Yugoslav people have begun moving out of here. But this is not the end of it. Soon it will be our turn... When the day comes to part with Ferramonti we will be sad, on the one hand, to cut ties with Ferramonti. On the other hand, we will be glad that at last we are getting nearer our destination — Eretz-Israel — after having longed for it for years."

Pupils of a lower grade, ten-year-olds, not illogically took a different view of things. The announcement about the journey to Egypt had apparently reached the children's ears. It did not require much from here to jump to a reasonable conclusion. And they did: Egypt's proximity to Eretz-Israel made it a natural stopover on the route to the hoped for destination, so dearly hoped for...

> Jetzt fahren alle Jugoslawen weg.
> Sie fahren über das Meer, und ich
> wünsche ihnen, dass sie bald ihr Ziel
> erreichen, nach Erez zu kommen. Ich
> hoffe dass wir uns bald in Erez
> sehen werden.
> Sie fahren wahrscheinlich nach Cairo.
> Wir werden sie vielleicht einholen.
> Lea Domnitz
> [דומניץ]

Thus, in the spirit of these conclusions, wrote Leah Dominitz: "All the Yugoslavs are now leaving here. They are sailing by sea and I wish them that they will soon realize their goal of reaching Eretz-Israel... I hope that soon we will meet in Eretz-Israel. They are apparently going to Cairo. Maybe we'll even catch up with them."

> Endlich können die Jugoslaven nach vier Jahren weg von hier nach Kairo, von wo aus sie leicht nach Erec Jisroel kommen.
> Sie sind die ersten die das Heilige Land erreichen können; sie sind die Spitze und nach Ihnen, werden wir das Ziel erreichen
> פנחס קוטנר
> [יצחק שטרנזיס]

Pinhas Kutner (signature in Hebrew) supposed the same: "Finally, after four years, the Yugoslavs are leaving here for Cairo, from where they will easily be able to reach Eretz-Israel. They are the first who will be able to enter the Holy Land; they are the spearhead, and after them, we too will reach our goal."

As did Yitzhak Sternzis (signing his name in Hebrew): "All of us, the ones remaining behind, hope to meet up with them again in Eretz-Israel."

Unlike the largely monolithic Yugoslav block that identified with the country of origin, the Zionist block encompassed Jews from various European countries, including a handful of Yugoslavs, though the largest element by far came from Slovakia. All, in principle, refused to be nationally identified with the country from which they hailed or to cooperate with the military committees of

# FROM AFRICA TO THE THRESHOLD OF EUROPE     147

*... Wir alle Übriggebliebenen hoffen, uns wieder in Erec Jisrael mit ihnen zu sehen.*

[Hebrew handwriting]

those countries, which arrived at the camp to recruit their nationals. As Zionists, they professed loyalty to their historic crucible, the young even asking to join the Jewish units in the British army.

From the moment they became refugees on Italian soil, after the fascist government dumped them, as *internati*, behind barbed wire at Ferramonti's Campo di Concentramento, the Zionists had worked clandestinely to promote their cause. They emerged from hiding to openly proclaim their hope when the Allies liberated Southern Italy (including Ferramonti) in a bid to liberate the whole of Italy, which at its surrender had been overrun by the German army. Zionist hopes swelled when rumor spread of an imminent Allied landing in France, and when news came of the Red Army's advance on the eastern front. In this atmosphere, the problem of the future became in the eyes of the refugees urgent and highly concrete. Tragically for all, the invasion of France took place only five months later and, even after that, the war continued for another whole year.

In Southern Italy, the first territory (after Sicily) to be taken by the Allies, the front remained static through the winter of

1943–44. This may have been due to the difficulty of moving large forces through the Apennines in that season, or because Germany mounted a tougher defense, knowing that the continued pushback of the Wehrmacht northward would bring it to the Austrian border, i.e. to the *Heimat*'s very doorstep. For this reason, the Germans waged a dogged battle at Monte Casino, on the way to Rome.

Still, it must be said — and anyone robbed of their personal freedom and incarcerated in an Italian Campo di Concentramento can corroborate this — that despite the similar terminology, there can be no real, inherent comparison between Italian *Concentramentos* and German *Konzentrazionslagers* — the latter, an unprecedented product of Nazi madness in the twentieth century, a factory of death and extinction.

## VII

"We got here right on time", the driver announced and tired from the journey, pulled up at the camp gate. "Look, you're expected. There's even a bigger reception party waiting for you than there was for our delegation yesterday, despite the rank of the Company Commander."

The envoy tried to play down the numerical difference: "It's because the Major arrived without prior notice, whereas today, everyone knew that an envoy would be coming." In his heart, though, he was secretly pleased that the driver had remarked on the difference: "Somehow (he thought) it will reach the right ears."

At the Ferramonti gate, beneath a large, round, arc-like sign broadcasting in Italian the site's name and character, a reception began, with three welcome speeches — in Hebrew, in German and in Italian. The speakers (whose name and public function the guest was to learn later) acquitted themselves with solemn formality and undisguised tension: after all, the arrival of an Eretz-Israel soldier at the camp, not by chance but of his own free will and for an extended stay, was an unprecedented event.

The envoy, for his part, also responded to the greetings in Hebrew, German and Italian, the intentionally lighthearted tone of his words banishing the tension. The youngsters lining the gateway on either side burst into song, "*Heiveinu Shalom Aleikhem*" (We Bring You Shalom), and the guest responded with a parallel song of Shalom: "*Osseh Shalom BiMromav*" (He Who Makes Peace on High). And without wasting any time, he straight away began teaching the crowd a line of the catchy refrain, "*Yaasseh shalom, yaasseh shalom*" (He will make peace, He will make peace). The chemistry between the envoy and the assembled Ferramontesi of all ages was instant.

The driver had meanwhile unloaded the goods sent to the camp by 178 and these were quickly absorbed by the kitchen and the clothing warehouse. He also unloaded the envoy's kitbag and waved good-bye. In minutes, his car could be seen climbing up the mountain until it was swallowed up by the woods.

Only then did the regimented lines break up and the youngsters huddled around the envoy. Handshakes. Admiring glances at the "Palestine" tag and the metal "8" on the "Africa Star" ribbon (the mark of a soldier who had served with the Eighth Army and Monty in the desert). Singing and handclapping, they escorted the envoy to his shack. "Shalom!" he parted from them, and went inside.

"And (to paraphrase the biblical verse in Genesis) it was morning and it was noon": the initial half of Ankori's first day at Ferramonti was done.

In the afternoon, as if of their own volition, his legs took him to the large courtyard between the blocks of shacks, one block on the left, one on the right. "This must be the square" (he guessed). Here, under the Italians there had been a morning and evening roll call, primarily for purposes of a daily count of the *internati*." Now, the square was deserted, the former *internati* resting in their shacks. But in the evening it would be filled by people taking the air, families with children, couples and singles, despite the bitter memories.

All at once, Ankori saw someone approaching. Yes, it was the

Hebrew speaker of the morning's reception: thin, tall (his height accentuated by his leanness); his face scored by a tormented gravity; his voice somewhat hoarse though ardent. At the end of every sentence or paragraph (it struck the listener), he seemed to wrest a weary smile from his somber face.

"Asher Dominitz" — he humbly introduced himself. Ankori embraced him warmly. Dominitz drew out the hug by several seconds as if hungry for friendship. The friendship he returned was unqualified.

— "Your words this morning moved me. It's a kind of Hebrew that is no longer heard these days."

— "You'll never understand what a Jewish soldier means for us (Dominitz replied in his own fine Hebrew that was a pleasure to hear). Time was that we too dreamt of taking up arms. The fact that a soldier has joined us in the camp and left his Company and friends for us makes it all the more precious."

— "In recompense, I have made a new friend." The new friend's smile no longer looked spent and weary. He suddenly opened up, relaxed his ostensibly-fixed facial features and broke into a free, warm laugh. Dominitz could not remember the last time he had laughed so. Four years ago? Before the blasted war had erupted and dammed up his face, so to speak, freezing it? In the coming days, the envoy was to learn that Dominitz handled everything; he opened every assembly and prepared its agenda. Hereafter, he would invite Zvi (as the envoy was known to children and adults alike) to address the assemblies either on day-to-day matters or more general topics. It was a pity that Dominitz had to waste his time smoothing ruffled feathers and making peace, mostly in affairs of ego between different chairmen jealously guarding both their irrelevant titles and their fancied self-importance. Only Dominitz shunned honor and titles.

— "Can I help you with anything?" Dominitz whispered, anxious not to offend the listener.

— "Yes, I would be most grateful. For the long term — please let me know honestly and unhesitatingly if I make any mistakes or errors due to my ignorance about the people here, their background, mentality and past, and how they came to be at the camp. As for now: it's only two o'clock, there's lots of time before nightfall. Would you kindly take me on a full tour of the camp? I would like to see its organization and institutions, and then end up at the youth club."

They set out arm-in-arm as if they had known each other for years. Dominitz spoke thoughtfully and quietly, taking no credit for what he showed nor bemoaning the shortcomings. He was apparently mulling over the envoy's request. "You asked me to advise you about how to conduct yourself here. Here's one modest suggestion for you, only one — and if I'm right in my opinion of you, based on our brief acquaintance, I'm sure you'll get my meaning and require no further counsel, not from anyone. Far be it from me to judge your officers, but the thing we found most humiliating was the patronizing attitude. Maybe, there was none. Maybe we imagined it due to an inferiority complex. Nevertheless, it grates. Yes, we need and appreciate your help from the bottom of our hearts. But even the best of intentions can steer you wrong in believing that there is nothing positive here, that it is a wasteland and only your actions turn the 'nothing' into 'something'. I sense that you are capable of giving much to the camp. You showed that this morning already. But bear in mind: build on what you find here, on the 'something' that we have created with devotion and at great risk. My advice to you therefore is: live our lives from morning to night. Identify with us in deed and dream. In short, *be one of us*. And then, even if you sport your movement's blue shirt — we'll accept you with love.

— "How do you know I wore a blue shirt? Have you been told about me and my views?"

— "No, but your face speaks of Labor Eretz-Israel. You have the mark of a *kibbutznik*."

— "But my presence here is non-ideological. I'm here for everyone. Out of love of the Jewish people, love of Eretz-Israel."

— "And because of that, out of a conviction in your integrity, even Jabotinsky's Revisionist Zionists will be happy to consider you one of them."

In fact, dozens of years after this prediction, the "commander" (as was his title) of the Betar youth group at the camp, Yehoshua Citron, listed the envoys of the Jewish units in his memoirs: "The first was Zvi Ankori (Citron wrote), of 178. *He became one of us* and we found it hard to part with him."

Mentioning the Revisionists in the camp, Dominitz took the opportunity to lay before his friend the epos of the "Pentcho", an old, ramshackle riverboat that in 1940 plied a course on the Danube to the open sea, with a dual cargo aboard: longing and hope — the longing of hundreds of Slovakian Betarniks under Citron's leadership, to steal their way to Palestine; and the hope of safely gaining the destined shore despite the war and the British White Paper that had shut the gates of Eretz-Israel at the very moment that the Jewish people most needed a safe haven. The Betarniks were joined by dozens of families and individuals who did not personally identify with the Revisionist-Zionist movement but regarded the steam emitted by the boat as a chance for what many European Jews found inconceivable: to turn their backs on the continent, before it turned its back on the Jews and stood by, while the enemy did its worst.

Dominitz described the stops made by the boat in sailing close to shore and the moment of foundering as it left for the open sea. The passengers were saved by the skin of their teeth, grasping at rocks of an isolated, uninhabited island. Thanks to the levelheadedness and wisdom shown by Citron, the commander of the transport (and not the captain who lost control of the ship and went to pieces), no one was injured. They were rescued by an Italian ship and conveyed to Rhodes. In the end, the group was deported to the Ferramonti concentration camp, where it had been for the past four years. Dominitz told the tale of the boat quietly and unemotionally, like a neutral commentator on some minor incident. Only after some time did Zvi learn that his friend had been among the passengers.

Primed and disciplined, "Pentcho"-Betar became the core of the camp's Zionist block. Their children were organized in the Trumpeldor Cadre, their boys and girls in the Ze'ev Cadre, serving as counselors (whom they called "commanders") and accepting, even in camp conditions, the authority of Citron, their supreme commander. History will judge if the "Pentcho" of 1940 was the last of the pioneering "illegal immigrant" ships to make its way to Palestine by the end of the third decade of the twentieth century — ships whose passengers did manage to reach the shore near the Sharon coast, were carried onto land on the shoulders of Haganah members and delivered to nearby kibbutzim; or whether it was the harbinger of a future wave of "illegal immigrants", composed of Holocaust survivors who were to do battle against the siege of the British war fleet and ultimately break it.

The "something" Dominitz spoke of to the envoy — a "something" that the Ferramontesi had built for themselves — was highly impressive. The *internati* had devised and diligently managed a daily routine as if the world were not at war and they, themselves, not stripped of their freedom and incarcerated because of it. But (in Zvi's private view), the format of their actions, the only format they had known before their detention, now, in 1944, appeared worn, shallow, rather outdated. The efforts spread over four fields: religious services — two synagogues, a rabbinate, ritual slaughter, a burial service; social assistance — for even though all shared a single fate, some were more needy and some were more able to offer help; education — a religious Talmud-Torah and four secular schools, their language of instruction corresponding to the languages spoken at home ("this we will change. I'll suggest to the assembly that in addition to the compulsory Hebrew, there be one language of instruction, say German" — the envoy made a mental note, then caught himself: "Am I also being patronizing?"). Dominitz seemed to read his friend's mind. He noted that the departure of the Yugoslavs was imminent and that one of the schools, the Serbo-Croatian, would in any case be shut down. The fourth field of endeavor related to political and ideological frameworks and their endless polemical sparring over problems that had become irrelevant: the Zionist Organization, the New Zionist Organization (founded by Jabotinsky five years before the internees had been detained), and the Zionist parties as they had been before the war. Only in the realm of Zionist youth movements had there been a refreshing innovation: while Betar was at one pole, HaNoar HaTzioni (Zionist Youth) embraced, at the other pole, all other members, from the religious Mizrahi down to the leftist HaShomer HaTza'ir.

There was an *aliya* office, Pal-Amt, which, at liberation, justified its raison d'être. It had begun to operate even before the Eretz-Israel office in Bari where envoy Enzo Sereni worked actively while he awaited a special assignment; and there was a Jewish National Fund office, which dreamt of planting a forest in Eretz-Israel to commemorate Ferramonti and its captives. An overseas emigration office also opened, anticipating post-war needs. Nor had sports been neglected. Still under the Italians, the assembly yard had doubled as an occasional soccer field, and there was much joy when the young Jews managed to defeat the *carabinieri*, the camp guards. There was even a café located in the space between two shacks, offering, apart from a dubious sort of coffee, a place to socialize and play chess or cards.

The half day's "orientation tour" and the reliable information supplied by Dominitz, the expert on "Ferramonti-ism", were enough for the envoy to realize that even if his dispatchers had been unable to define his assignment, their built-in conception and his own (prior to arrival) had naturally been based on an automatic comparison with the situation in Libya. The assumption was that refugees, wherever they might be, needed the same type of assistance that 178 soldiers had extended to Benghazi's Jews: food and clothing on the one hand, and education for their children, on the other. The stricken remnant of the Benghazi Jewish community — which had known trauma and vengeance as it passed back and forth from hand to hand, and which had lost numerous Jews to bombings and thousands to exile in the desert's forced labor camp — had been stripped of the cement that for generations had held the glorious community together. Depleted numerically, economically and socially, they had been left with nothing but the synagogue. Rehabilitation in Benghazi by the 178 Company had thus started from "nothing", and created "something": cultivating a leadership core, establishing and providing Hebrew schooling for children who had never attended school, drawing their parents into the school orbit, and instilling a Hebrew-Zionist atmosphere in home and community. The school, under its principal, Ankori, had thus become the cornerstone of the community's revitalization. Even after 178 was transferred to another front, the institution continued to thrive, thanks to both the strong foundation laid by 178 and the later cohorts of soldier-volunteers from other units.

Dominitz had been right to issue a word of caution. Any comparison of our future work at Ferramonti with our Benghazi experience, as natural as it might have seemed — Ankori was persuaded — was inherently false and certainly unacceptable to the proud Ferramonti public. Still keen after the extensive tour and an evening at the Youth Club where he taught movement youngsters Eretz-Israel songs and dances, he returned to his room and set down the following in his notepad:

"Ferramonti!
    Not the sort of camp one imagines.
    Not refugees that didn't know one another, randomly rounded up at the site.
    A major Jewish town,
    Its Jews sharing a sense of mutual responsibility.

"Ferramonti!
    The groups brought here for detention
    Carry a tremendous store of values on their backs.
    But the treasure is outdated — as if time has stood still,
    For four years have passed since the site was cut off from the world.

"That's Ferramonti!

Amazing at its inception, but standing still, unchanging ever since.

Given this situation — what is my role? He asks and answers: "My role is to reinvigorate the 'something'. To renew it. Update it and enrich it.

To propel it forward. To make it Hebrew. To turn it into little Eretz-Israel."

"This, then is the mission" — again and again, Zvi mentally reviewed all that he had seen and heard and learned, his mind abuzz with ideas, all resting on the "something" and yet new.

"That's my mission" — he continued to imprint the conclusion on his heart. "From here on, whatever I do will be aimed at a single objective — Eretz-Israel. Talks with the young — Eretz-Israel. Speeches at adult assemblies — Eretz-Israel. "Homeland" discussions in school classrooms — Eretz-Israel. Daily activities with movement youth and counselors — Eretz-Israel. Songs and dances — Eretz-Israel. Intensive Hebrew instruction — Eretz-Israel. Every walk of camp life (he planned) will be in a state of anticipation, so to speak, for *aliya* to Eretz-Israel, and every activity, whether educational or otherwise, will aim at preparing the population for life in Eretz-Israel. And if one day, the camp's post-liberation history is written, I would be gratified if it said that the feeling of many people, especially of the children of all ages, was that the soldier-envoy transformed the Ferramonti valley into a patch of Eretz-Israel."

"Will we create an additional 'something' out of 'nothing'?

Perhaps this too. Something's brewing in the heart and mind.

There is an idea. Exciting, visionary, dream-like. But the time is not ripe yet…"

# VIII

Yes, Ferramonti was a Jewish town in every respect. When its gates opened after the British army captured the region and the fences came down, autonomist trends swelled and the "major Jewish town" instituted self-government. The Yugoslavs left and despite the sorrow of parting, the exit of the incurable assimilants was to facilitate a Zionist Eretz-Israel atmosphere in the camp.

Of course, the old, irrelevant party polemics never stopped. Just as the arguments between the two youth movements continued with great fervor. But it was merely a special edition of the recycled fervor of old. Life together behind the fence had imbued a spirit of partnership and brotherhood that was only amplified thanks to the encounter with the Eretz-Israel units. The soldiers were the epitome of single-mindedness. Their outlook may have differed on various matters, but the blue and white flag united them all, without question.

Ferramonti youth and counselors, 1944
Circle center, Zvi Ankori; to his right, Ossi (Betar), to his left Bozho (HaNoar HaTzioni)

The envoy's day was crammed full of unflagging activity, framed by a most prosaic routine: by his morning wash and shave at the outdoor hose tap in the nearby section of the courtyard and his visits to the same tap at midnight, to wash off the sweat he had worked up in Eretz-Israel dances at the youth club. Unlike his companions who grumbled at waiting on line for the tap, Zvi regarded the line as an opportunity to chat with his neighbors and learn of their problems first-hand. A madcap thought occurred to him: there were a number of taps scattered near the shacks and maybe he should pick a different one each day so as to meet different segments of the population each time? Gradually, though, through his daily ablutions, he formed an intimate relation with the tap as if it were the navel of this severed world, the vital artery. The tap represented free will, it was not policed and hadn't been even under the Italians; if you want to drink — drink to your heart's content; if you want to wash your hands and face — be my guest; you want to wash your upper body? Take off your shirt and go for it. In his heart of hearts he promised "his" tap a daily visit: to start his day there when he rose and to end his day in its cool water at bedtime.

Basing himself on the spirit of unity that became a major component of the Ferramonti "something", Zvi established and conducted a *joint* permanent seminar for the counselors of the two youth movements. He did not do away with existing frameworks. But (on Dominitz's advice!), in friendship and with respect, he helped the movement counselors deepen their work, channeling the unity from the interpersonal to the inter-movement plane. For the first time in the history of the two, ideologically-opposed youth movements — nay, in the history of Zionism — they joined forces and, with the participation of their counselors, held common activities. Soon enough, they learned that their similarities outweighed their differences, and that the differences, even in unity, were able to leave room for what was unique to each.

In the morning, one or another teacher would invite Zvi to the classroom to tell the pupils about the Jewish soldiers and their work with the Jewish children of liberated Libya, or about the life of children on kibbutz. Nobody questioned his authority in the arena of school education or the innovations he proposed in the curriculum, just as there was no protest from the movements. Both school teachers and movement counselors deferred to his leadership, respecting the knowledge and experience he brought with him and the refreshing Eretz-Israeli atmosphere he inspired in word and deed.

The regular evening meetings with movement youth and seminar counselors centered on serious discussion of the problems faced by the Jewish people, Eretz-Israel and Zionism, while the social togetherness, including the singing and dancing Eretz-Israel dances, was reserved for the later hours that stretched to midnight. In the work with the intermediate and youngest echelons, however, the tone of the "homeland-talks", was of a different nature. Shot through with familiar songs and the teaching of new ones, these were held in the late afternoon, when the club was still empty of older members, or as part of a nature walk to a nearby wood. Frozen in their whiteness, the poplars denied all connection to the camp but, curiously enough, Zvi's singing roused and reminded them of another poplar forest and another chestnut tree in a faraway land to the north. And even more curiously: a young man's ardent tenor was suddenly replaced in his memory by the deep alto of a distant woman — the one and only, the unforgettable. She, in the land of poplars and chestnuts, was singing the old songs of Eretz-Israel to her small son, songs that she herself had learned as a child, and exposing him to the breeze that combed the treetops of Mt. Carmel's woods or carried him on the hump of a camel to a burning, yellow desert. In a moment of uncontrollable homesickness, Zvi confessed that the afternoon hours with the children were especially precious to him. But when asked why, he was embarrassed, as if fearing to give himself away. Instead of an answer, he offered only a sad smile.

Little wonder then that when he returned to his unit after an absence of a month and a half, and opened the collection of loving farewell letters presented to him by the school pupils as a memento, he was astounded to find that the thirteen-year-old Eva sensitively divined the inclinations of his adult heart:

> So war Zwi unter uns, welche uns nicht mehr als Kinder fühlten, wie ein Kind, und führte uns in das Kindesalter zurück. Er hielt uns einige „Moledetsichot." Er unterrichtete uns nicht, sondern reihte unsere Seelen ein und führte sie spazieren, durch Berge, Städte und Ebenen. Durch duftende Pardessim und durch steile Felsen. Mit den Gedanken klettern wir leicht in den Felsen herum, auf der Suche nach der wunderschönen Blume „Chavatselet" Und dann kehren wir zurück, die Seele ausgefüllt mit dem Geruch der „chavatselet" und der Orangenblüten.

"And this is how Zvi felt among us — we, who no longer felt like children — as if he himself were a child, restoring us to childhood. He did not really teach us but lined up our souls and led them on a walk through town, hill and vale, amid scented orchards and steep rocks. In our minds we easily clambered over rocks in search of the Sharon lily and, on our return, the soul was bathed in the fragrance of the lily and the blossoms of the citrus."

Within two weeks, the envoy was pleased to find that his daily focus on varied educational work — at school, in the inter-movement arena, and with the younger children — already bore fruit. From day to day, a growing joy of life and joy of youth flushed the youngsters' faces; it had not been there when he first arrived. From day to day, the splendor of a new dawn anointed boyish forelocks, and colorful ribbons seemed to come out of hiding to coquettishly adorn girlish braids. If one didn't know that the youngsters belonged to a prison camp, one might have taken them for children of Eretz-Israel. Teachers and counselors too radiated confidence and faith in the fruition of the Eretz-Israel policy sketched by the soldier-envoy for the camp, so much so that they forgot that it had not existed, had not even been imagined, two weeks earlier.

True (Zvi frankly acknowledged), he couched his stories, talks and songs in romanticism, as romantic — he recalled — as the Eretz-Israel narrative in his Tarnów childhood. Despite his close knowledge of daily life in Eretz-Israel since his *aliya*, he was swept up in the excitement and enjoyment of the romantic visions his own mouth drew for the young: the romance of the HaShomer guards, of Joseph Trumpeldor at Tel-Hai, of Deganya, the first kibbutz and of Beit Alfa, Ein Harod and Hanita that followed; the romance of young, sand-white Tel Aviv with its Herzliya Gymnasium High School and the dome of Bialik House and HaBima Theater and the symphony orchestra; the romance of the Sharon Plain and the scent of its lilies and the carpets of intoxicating, blossoming orchards; the romance of the coastal dunes and the sky-blue Sea of Galilee; and last but not least, the romance of Mt. Scopus gazing out on Jerusalem on one side, and down to the desert and the Dead Sea that seemed to lie in the palm of a hand. Romance, so what? What harm was there in the romanticism of youngsters of that age or, for that matter, of his own twenty-three years?

The picture he painted was not false, even if it was romantic. The romance, itself, was no lie; it was reality as seen through the prism of the observer's sentiments. This was what Eretz-Israel had been like when *he* made *aliya*, or this was how *he* had sensed it when he came, and this was how he wished to endear it to his charges: a country that's small but open, thinly populated but in love with its people and itself, alert to its ancient roots and preserving its biblical, primordial, landscape. Let the young make *aliya* and see for themselves: some might take a more sober view — so what? Others, like he, would cling to the visionary Eretz-Israel — what harm was there in that?

Apart from the three active arenas of daily work with youth, a fourth too required attention and action: Ferramonti's adult population. For the most part Zionists, they awaited *aliya* permits, but unlike the young, their four years of detention, dearth and worry had left scars that did not heal easily. "I must find a way to reach this population" — Zvi set himself a task — "not simply for their own sake but for the sake of a unified goal between parents and children, and between Zionist Youth counselors and Betar commanders." Only unity could bring about an idea he had nurtured since he had first sized up the mettle of Ferramonti's youth — an idea it was now time to expose.

How to win over the population to the idea? In contrast to the young, who spent most of their time together and whom he met on a daily basis in uninterrupted hours of education and experience that encouraged cohesion, the adult public was heterogeneous and naturally critical. Under Dominitz's leadership, it assembled once a week to hear a review of the current situation and the future of the camp, to discuss a specific matter that had come up or to enjoy an address by the envoy. Unlike the English love for understatement, Europeans admired a speaker who fired the heart, applauding his talents even if they disagreed with his views. By these lights, anti-Trotskyites had no problem singing the praises of the brilliant orator even though they spurned his ideology. And Zvi remembered from childhood, whenever Jabotinsky paid a visit to Tarnów, Golda, his mother, never missed a speech of his though she belonged to the main Zionist camp, opposed to the Revisionists. At the end of the evening, she would come home to share with her son her delight in the charms of her hero's art of rhetoric.

Without — perish the thought — comparing himself to the masters of oratory, Zvi knew that if he were to conquer Ferramonti's adults, it could only be with eloquence. His stint of duty after the first two weeks left him four weekly assemblies — four speeches. This meant that the message at every appearance had to be razor sharp, focused to the last word, impassioned and arousing. Already on his first evening, the entire Ferramonti public had been assembled to meet him and, as many confessed, the envoy's address, in polished German, had captivated them. Passers-by subsequently greeted him pleasantly, stopping to tell him of the impression he had made at the last assembly. Nor did people miss assemblies; they looked forward to the speeches.

In a sweeping article published in the Viennese press thirty years later, Rita Koch, then an accomplished journalist, recalled Zvi's speeches, though she had been only twelve at the time; youth too had been attracted to the adult assemblies and the speakers. Listing for posterity 178's varied forms of assistance — food, clothing etc. which Unit commanders regularly sent off to the camp with Company drivers — she summed up:

> "But the best thing they left with us was a young man from Poland, who had enlisted into the army from his kibbutz: slightly over twenty, good-looking, educated, passionate, he was able, with his fiery speeches and the songs and dances of the Holy Land, to sweep up and enthrall even the most confirmed naysayers. His name was Zvi Ankori."

> Das Beste jedoch, was sie bei uns ließen, war ein junger Mann aus Polen, der vom Kibbuz in die Armee eingetreten war, knapp über 20 Jahre alt, gut aussehend, gebildet, temperamentvoll der auch die negativst eingestellten Menschen hinreißen und begeistern konnte, mit seinen feurigen Reden, mit Gesang und Tanz aus dem Heiligen Land. Er hieß Zvi Ankori.

In the early weeks, everyone noticed that after each meeting with youth Zvi walked about lost in thoughts. He did not divulge the nature of his reflections, keeping them to himself. He honestly admitted that he had various ideas how to improve the work, but that "the time is not yet ripe". Only latterly — as week was added to week and the envoy's measures left a mark in all walks of camp life, he asked questions and probed, chewed things over and offered solutions, taking all the youngsters under his wing to the extent one could hardly imagine Ferramonti society without the involvement of the envoy. It was then that Zvi arrived at the judgment that: *"the time is ripe"*. In other words, it was time to break out of the circle of the "something" he had adhered to (albeit broadening and enriching it in countless ways), and move on, full swing, to creating "something out of nothing".

The idea that Zvi finally revealed to the public was astonishing in its daring. He suggested that movement youth and counselors be removed from the orbit of camp dependency and relocated to another region in liberated Southern Italy. There, an agricultural training (*hakhshara*) camp would be erected for them, preparing them for *aliya* to Eretz-Israel. The *hakhshara*, would resemble the immigrant Youth Aliya communities founded at the initiative of Henrietta Szold at kibbutzim throughout Eretz-Israel. Half their day would be devoted to study (with a strong emphasis on Hebrew and knowledge of Eretz-Israel), the other half would train the youngsters for a life of labor, maybe even on kibbutz. The youngsters were ready: life at the camp had matured them beyond their years and fostered a yen for independence, away from parental supervision.

Zvi was right that the young were ripe and ready for a project to express their independence. "The idea of establishing a *hakhshara* was his" — *"Der Gedanke an eine Hachschara war sein"* (Zvi's) — wrote Rita after three decades that had not succeeded in obliterating her wonder — "and was our dream that we all longed for" — *"und unser aller Wunschtraum"*. It may have been their dream and, nevertheless, the envoy's unexpected announcement stunned not only the parents and other adults and elderly attending the assembly, but the young themselves.

They, the natural candidates for the youth society depicted by the father of the idea, were the first to recover from the bolt. They were highly conscious and undoubtedly also proud of the privilege that had come their way: here, on this piece of Italian soil freed from enemy clutches, at the height of the conflagration of war and the height of the Shoah, the first European *hakhshara* camp was to rise for *aliya* to Eretz-Israel of young Jewish survivors. And they — yes they, the Ferramontesi — were to be its first builders and architects! The *first*!!

Scattered over the hall, the members of the youth movements required no signal or guiding hand to burst into a formidable song, spontaneous and surprising, with its opening words:

> We, it's we, shall be the first,
> One the other we must define,
> We will build and forge with thirst,
> Stretch the cord, hold the plumb line,
> > We will build and forge with thirst,
> > Stretch the cord, hold the plumb line!

According to Ferramonti mythology, on the evening preceding the fondly remembered assembly, as on every evening, the youngsters learned a new song from the envoy. Was it the one above? The mythology is divided between two versions. One claims that the song was expressly taught that evening with a nod to its content and without the singers guessing at the envoy's hidden motive. The other contends that the youngsters already knew the song from their many hours of public singing on previous occasions, and it was only the whim of fate that summoned it to the stage of history when they heard the glad tidings of *hakhshara*.

Either way, hereafter all disagreement was silenced. As if a heavenly voice had proclaimed the future *hakhshara* on high: *Rishonim* — in Hebrew, "the first" — so it was to be universally known, as if this were the geographical name of a site soon to feature on official Italian maps.

It was agreed, before the envoy left Ferramonti, that the next month would be set aside for "preparations": Hebrew teachers would review all that had been taught to date; youth movement counselors would prepare the young practically and emotionally for departure (after all, these were children who had never been away from home or the camp); and the parents — they knew what was expected of them. One issue, however, which the envoy insisted on as a matter of principle, was still overshadowed by doubt: he demanded that Betar's commanders — the movement opposed to the Eretz-Israel Labor alignment with its kibbutzim and training (*hakhshara*) farms — also join the HaNoar HaTzioni counselors, just as they had worked together at the Ferramonti camp, and be part of the Rishonim. After much soul-searching, Citron, the Betar supreme commander, gave his consent and instructed his commander-counselors accordingly. As a result, an inter-movement partnership was formed on an ideological question of principle — a partnership unprecedented in the relations between the official Zionist Organization and Jabotinsky's Revisionist Zionism. Citron visited the Rishonim when the *hakhshara* was already running and, in his book, published after the war, he wrote the following — and there can be no better first-hand witness:

"The first and loveliest of all was the Rishonim *hakhshara*, a paradise for our children. The children studied and worked under the supervision of their counselors, forgetting the life of the Diaspora and the wandering. The atmosphere of Eretz-Israel and of Hebrew reigned there…"

When the 178 vehicle arrived to convey Ankori (as he was to be called again in his Company) to the Foggia base after his month-and-a-half long mission at Ferramonti, the soldier knew that he had completed only the first stage of the work. Two more stages awaited him: his Unit's reception of the idea and the degree of its volunteerism in preparing the physical infrastructure fit for thirty youngsters and ten counselors; and the third stage — the running and management of the *hakhshara*.

In his book, the Regimental Sergeant Major, nicknamed "Tayyish" (Goat)", had the following to say about the second stage:

> "Zvi Ankori, one of our Company old hands, had an idea… the coming days were to prove how much the idea touched the hearts of the Unit's soldiers."

## IX

The "month of preparation" regrettably stretched into five weeks and some — through no fault of the Ferramontesi, who faithfully kept on implementing the program Zvi had outlined for them before leaving. They were presumably biting their nails in anticipation as they waited for the promised vehicle to arrive, to take them to the (as yet unknown) site where a commune and new life was to be built for each of the thirty members personally and the youth community as a whole. Nor was there a lack of volunteer spirit among the soldiers of 178; it was not they who caused the delay in work on the ground. The reason for the irritating hold-up was that the two officers responsible for scouting out a farm or rural building to house the community had not yet succeeded in their assignment. Everyone was agreed on the desirability of a location near the city of Bari, both because the Hebrew units were stationed close by and because of access to institutions, such as the Hebrew Soldiers Club and the Palestine Office of the Jewish Agency, both headquartered in Bari and able to extend assistance if need be. On the other hand, the site itself obviously had to be in a rural area so that the young could train in agriculture and because fruit trees would lend the air of a kibbutz on the Sharon Plain or in the Jezreel Valley. Eventually, an abandoned farm was found in the village of Grumo near Bari. Surrounded by a farmyard and fruit gardens, the shell of a building stood there, its exterior pleasing, its interior in ruins — an excellent opportunity for 178's volunteers to show what they were made of.

In 1993, in his book, RSM Tayyish wrote with a wonder that had not grown stale after fifty years:

> "Inside this house, a rural quasi-dormitory for youth began to go up. Zvi Ankori, with the help of Moshe Yehudai (who volunteered to serve as agricultural instructor) and other young men, with their own hands built a house and home

for boys and girls. It was, in the end, a house with all the fixtures and facilities necessary for a youth dormitory. It was an amazing story, typical of the resourcefulness, enthusiasm, and vision of these young men. 'Beit-Rishonim' — the House of the First — rose..."

On March 21, 1944, two Eighth Army trucks with the Star of David on their doors arrived at the Ferramonti gate to deliver the thirty youngsters, ten counselors and a housemother to Grumo. Where is Grumo? Nobody knew. Excitement. Joy. An end to waiting. Ferramonti bid its sons and daughters farewell. The young parted from Ferramonti hopefully forever.

This, their first time away from Ferramonti and their first four-hour trip along an unfamiliar road to an unfamiliar part of Italy, was accompanied by a sense of freedom and was in itself an experience. But an even greater experience awaited the youngsters — the sight of Beit-Rishonim, basking in almond blossoms. It surpassed their dreams. Eretz-Israel! A spontaneous rendition of the Hebrew "We... shall be the first" burst from their mouths and from that moment became the farm hymn. The hymn was sung every morning at the farmyard's quasi-roll call before the start of studies. Zvi (as he was called once more) turned to the nearby Jewish cartography unit, housed in an abandoned (or confiscated) school, with a request. At the approval of unit commander Officer Berest, their mute Italian school "lent" the Rishonim "school" fifteen double classroom benches, a blackboard with packages of chalk and a sponge, wall maps of Italy and of Europe (the Jewish Agency in Jerusalem sent a wall map of Eretz-Israel) and display boxes for butterflies and insects to be used in nature studies. Officer Berest took the farm school under his wing, frequently adding to its equipment: exercise books, pencils, writing paper, crayons, paints, compasses, rulers etc. The "classroom" fittings thus complemented the modest furnishings of the two dormitory halls, one for boys, the other for girls, of the dining room and of the clubhouse.

> "It was impossible not to marvel (RSM Tayyish wrote) at the enormous, instant change in the youngsters boarding at the house. The first yardstick of their cohesiveness, perhaps, was the language. A lot of Italian and German were heard there, the languages of the Ferramonti youth, but Hebrew began to take over quickly and surprisingly."

Another new experience was furnished by the afternoon field work. Shouldering a hoe, spade or rake, the youth marched to the words of the hymn's second verse, which matched their activities during those hours:

> We are going, we are coming,
> Work aplenty, end unseen —
> Amid the rocks, now trees aplanting,
> On the hills, in the ravine.
> > Amid the rocks, now trees aplanting,
> > On the hills, in the ravine.

Actually, Puglia was a plain with neither hill nor vale. The background for the song was the landscape of Eretz-Israel; it was, after all, *hakhshara* for Eretz-Israel. Under Moshe Yehudai's instruction, the Rishonim thus imagined themselves planting trees in the stony ground of Eretz-Israel (when, in fact they were planting potatoes, ha-ha).

Beit-Rishonim's reputation reached all the Jewish units stationed in Southern Italy. Soldiers stopping in Bari on duty or on leave made it a habit to drop by, meeting up again with the almost-Eretz-Israeli group whom they saw as their adopted charges. Some remained for the evening to take part in the folk singing and dancing.

There were also visits of a more serious nature. These included regular visits by U.S. officer-doctors, most of whom were Jews (but also non-Jews), serving at the military hospital not far from Bari. The pact with the American medical corps was sealed after natural disaster struck the Grumo region in the very first week that the Ferramontesi settled there. Heavy downpour flooded the farm area, totally cutting it off from the rest of the world. In general, the problem of communication was the farm's Achilles heel: due to the supervision of regional headquarters, 178 was unable to allot the farm a permanent military vehicle. Nor was there a telephone. Contact with the outside thus relied on visitors from the outside and the initiative of Officer Berest's nearby cartography unit or the Jewish Soldiers Club in Bari. All this was formalized only later. Truthfully, the isolation did not leave its mark on the group — for there was no lack of food and the weather-induced closure even promoted togetherness. The problems began when the children developed painful, pussy boils. Medical attention became urgent. Zvi delegated the reins to Moshe Yehudai and waded through the water to make his way on foot to Officer Berest's unit to ask for help. Berest immediately drove him to the American hospital, thereby alerting the American doctors to the presence of a group of refugee children in the area. They packed up the necessary supplies and drove Zvi back to the farm in their jeep. Thereafter, they volunteered to look after the children's health, attending to the sick as necessary and keeping the first aid box filled with medications and bandages.

Another natural disaster brought the doctors back to the farm at their own initiative. The eruption of Vesuvius sent a cloud of volcanic dust eastward over a distance of some two hundred kilometers. The black cloud crossed Southern Italy, including Puglia and the Rishonim farm, reaching all the way to the Adriatic Sea. The hospital lab tested the water for pollution, but the results showed that it was fine.

After about a month and a half, a high-level guest arrived at the farm, Moshe Shertok (later Sharett), the head of the Jewish Agency Political Department or, in other words, the Zionist Movement's "Foreign Minister". At this time, he was continuing to recruit young men and women of Eretz-Israel's Jewish Yishuv for the British army (thirty thousand volunteered) and negotiating

Rishonim Hakhshara (1944)
In circle on left — Moshe Yehudai; in circle on right — Zvi Ankori

with the British government on upgrading the existing Jewish units and forming a Jewish (fighting) Brigade, under its own command, insignia and flag. At the same time, he was battling to increase the *aliya* certificates issued by the British — with special emphasis now on refugees and Holocaust survivors who dreamt of making both *aliya* and a new life for themselves in Eretz-Israel.

Shertok was enthusiastic about the Rishonim project and he joined the group on the roof where a mast had been prepared to raise the Zionist flag. It was the first time that the flag was raised in Italy, in all its glory and to the proud rendition of "HaTikva", the Zionist anthem.

Shertok was the bearer of two bits of news: one good, one sad. The first was that all of Ferramonti's six hundred families (about two thousand people) were to be permitted to make *aliya* to Eretz-Israel despite the White Paper restrictions. The other was that the quota was to be split in two — three hundred families were to sail within days, the remainder in a year's time. The joy was thus mixed with the sorrow of disappointment and parting. The dream of the Rishonim — of immigrating together to Eretz-Israel and together establishing a kibbutz of their own to be known as Kibbutz Rishonim — shattered. Only eight of the thirty Rishonim numbered in the first allotment, and a heavy pall descended on Ferramonti when the young group returned to the camp to reunite with their parents.

The parting was hard and heartfelt. Moshe Mosenzon treated it to many pages in *HaHayal HaIvri* and the article was reprinted (ten pages) in *Sefer HaHitnadvut* (The Volunteer Book). This is what he wrote about the Ferramontesi on the day of leave-taking:

> From the moment the Ferramontesi arrived, you saw someone walking among them surrounded by a glowing aura. Loving, caressing eyes followed him, adult looks and children's arms rested on him: Ankori, the soldier-counselor. More than once I sensed how oppressive this love must be, how hard for him to contain such an abundance of love…
>
> And when Greenschlag [the chairman of the Zionist Organization in Ferramonti] hushed the singers and said: 'We would like to bid our Hebrew soldiers farewell', a tremor passed through our hearts, and you felt a shock pass through the hall. All heads turned. All. Ankori spoke. He was pale. The hundreds of loving eyes all around apparently were his undoing. He delivered his words emotionally, evidently mining them from inner depths. They fell heavily and tremulously on attentive ears. All around, there was a deadly silence. Not a rustle, not a whisper…

On one of Italy's end-of-May brilliant days, the passengers boarded the deck of the Polish ship, "Stefan Batory", which had been co-opted to the British fleet in the war, and sailed off to the east. Most probably, the passengers did not know that the ship bore the name of one of the great kings of Poland who had encouraged Jews to settle in his realm and spread his protection over them. At that hour, as they waved goodbye from the deck to their friends in the harbor, the rest of the Ferramontesi, remaining in Italy, climbed onto a 178 truck and drove westward, back to Ferramonti. It was time to mend what had been broken, to relight the flame that had been snuffed out in bitter disappointment, and to reorganize the Ferramonti public for their slated *aliya* within a year. And who remained with the Ferramontesi to infuse them once more with hope and faith? Who — if not Dominitz?

❖ ❖ ❖

When Ankori finished his mission at Ferramonti and at Rishonim, and happily took his place behind the steering wheel once more, he had time, while driving, to sum up his experience of the preceding five months. He knew that the mission at the liberated camp and the farm had been *THE* job of the entire twenty-three years of his life and, that this job, objectively, had been harder than any other ever imposed on a soldier in those early days of the encounter with Europe's survivors. Nonetheless, he was grateful to whomever had found him worthy of the mission — which had not only benefited Ferramonti's people, but had also matured him and molded his personality as a Jew, as an Eretz-Israeli, as a man.

*CHAPTER THREE*

# The Story of Jewish Company 178
## C. On the Banks of the Tiber

### I

ALL ROADS LEAD to Rome except that which prevented the Eighth Army's northward advance from the southern-Italian front, a line that remained frozen throughout the winter of 1943–44. The delay kept the Allied armies out of Rome for another nine months after Italy's surrender, since the Nazis were swift to retaliate for the betrayal of their former ally: they lost no time in seizing Rome along with central and northern Italy, and they dug in at the main highway in Monte Cassino — a name that causes shudders in every soldier who served in Italy at the time.

The top of Monte Cassino, southeast of the capital, boasts an abbey complex built by St. Benedict in the 520s. This medieval monastery was not only the heart and mind of the Benedictine Order as well as its spiritual center, but a holy site of Catholicism through the ages and a treasury of medieval manuscripts. In the course of its long history it had been attacked several times — the price it paid for its strategic location — and was destroyed by conquerors; yet it had always been restored, surrounding itself with new fortifications. The blow it took in World War II, it is universally agreed, was its hardest ever, delivered after the Allies bounced back and decided to crush the major obstacle that placed in German hands the key to blocking the road to Rome.

After a series of heavy air-raids that pulverized and punctured the site so that it resembled the landscape of the moon, it was stormed by infantry on May 17, 1944, the mission of Cassino's penetration being spearheaded by the Polish army. The latter, consisting of Polish refugees in Siberia, had been formed by the Polish government-in-exile and made its way to Italy where it was co-opted to the British Eighth Army. It was a gory battle, etched indelibly on the history of Poland and the epos of the Second World War. Indeed, on May 18, the road to Rome was opened by the blood of thousands of soldiers falling for their distant homeland, the country that in September 1939 was the first victim of the German blitz. Rome, the capital, was liberated on June 4, 1944. A new chapter began in the campaign for Italy, and it was the first time that Eretz-Israel soldiers came to the aid of Rome's Jews, a community still reeling from nine ruthless months of Nazi rule.

Unit 178 had not yet been transferred to Rome itself or its outskirts; it was to start moving there only in early December 1944 when, after four years of service, it would be incorporated into the Jewish Brigade that had only now dropped anchor in Taranto and was stationed at Fiuggi near Rome. Exerting heavy pressure on the Wehrmacht, the Eighth Army pushed back the front to central Italy and the historic cities along the Adriatic coast. In mid-May, 178 too moved from Foggia and advanced with the Eighth Army until, in November, it reached Firenze.

Three weeks after the move, when Rome was liberated, Ankori was surprisingly called to the capital on a mission and would not join up with his unit again until it was halfway to Florence. The rabbi of the Eighth Army, Capt. Urbach (later a professor at Hebrew University), had opened a Jewish Soldiers Club in Rome on Via del Tritone, not far from the Trevi Fountain, and asked 178 to dispatch Ankori to Rome to launch Zionist educational work. The rabbi was mindful of the praises earned by the soldier-teacher, which continued to be sung in Benghazi months after the end of

Ankori's mission, and had followed the story of his leadership in Ferramonti and his founding of the Rishonim farm.

Just as Benghazi, the town, had been a different sort of calling from Ferramonti, the camp — and Rishonim, the farm, had resembled neither of the two previous undertakings — so Rome made it necessary to adapt the new mission to different realities. The four stints of service, however, did share a common denominator; most of the energy was directed at Hebrew education and youth work, and the results of all four were invariably acknowledged as impressive.

The background of the work in Rome was totally unlike anything yet encountered by the soldier-envoys. In Southern Italy, their work had targeted refugees from Yugoslavia or people who had crossed the border from Slovakia (with add-ons from Poland or Vienna) on their way to Palestine, and had run into mishap in a foundering boat near shores controlled by the Italian navy. In other words they were *displaced persons*, stumbling upon or brought to Italy where they were detained. Though they had no complaint about the treatment they received at the hands of Italian gaolers, they had their sights on leaving Italy, whether to Eretz-Israel or back to their country of origin or to another destination as immigrants.

Not so the Jews of Rome. Europe's oldest Jewish community, its continuous residence in the Italian capital predated the destruction of the Second Temple in Jerusalem. Rome's Jews (including the Zionists among them) were so deeply embedded in Italy and Italian society that, in terms of consciousness, language and culture, some of them were not merely assimilated but even members of the fascist party. Consequently, for the first time, the envoy had to deal with *Italian citizens who had not been uprooted from their country*. On the other hand, given Italy's alliance with Germany, they, as Jews, were subject to racial laws much like the Nazi laws. With the bursting of the bubble of Rome's immunity (based on the hope of Vatican protection and the city's demilitarization), and the faltering of Jewish self-confidence in the face of German-dictated realities

— Italy's Jews found themselves victims of the Holocaust, plain and simple. The vicious *akcja* against Rome's Jews in mid-October 1943 delivered a stunning blow to their self-image as Italians; a new option of identity was needed, particularly for educated Jewish youngsters. The Jewish soldiers' mission arrived at precisely the right moment, and was directed at these youngsters: to show them the way to the other, ancient homeland, and to the other, ancestral, biblical language that had been revived. The Zionist movement had actually functioned in Italy before the war, but the arousal of a new Zionist awakening, emanating from the horrors of the very recent past, was an immediate achievement of the mission of Eretz-Israeli soldiers. It infused the youth with a will for *aliya*, which no few put into practice; and it brandished the study of Hebrew not only as a means of communication for their future lives in Eretz-Israel, but as a cultural-ideological message. The envoys following the first emissary and his companions carried on the work, bolstering and spurring on the accomplishment of their earlier colleagues.

The other difference between Southern Italy and Rome, in terms of the activities of the Jewish units, was determined by geography and history. Not every envoy may have been conscious of this, but it was profoundly engraved on the soul of the first soldier-envoy, an advanced history student with a thorough knowledge of the history of both ancient Rome and modern Italy. He trained his eye to see beyond the sites, objects and landscapes as they appeared before him now, and to imagine them, with the help of book knowledge and intuition, as they had been in the past. Ferramonti had been an ancient bog with no history until it sheltered a Jewish camp that made history. Grumo had been a backwater village until the Rishonim farm was built there. Not so Rome. Ah, Rome! History incarnate!

Already on his very first evening in Rome, Ankori found himself enmeshed in the weft and warp of the internal squabbles within the Roman Jewish community. At all his previous posts, he had been careful to steer clear of the routine community disputes, and, in any case, the second thing on the agenda he had planned for the following day was to introduce himself to the community and to pay the rabbi a visit. (The first thing on the agenda of the historian in him was the tour he had promised himself of Rome's ancient Jewish quarter, Trastevere, "Transtiber, across the Tiber").

Much to his surprise, however, after reaching the Jewish Soldiers Club — where he was deposited when brought from Foggia and where he was to live while in Rome — he found five young Roman-Jewish activists waiting for him. They had learned of the envoy's arrival from Rabbi Urbach.

"Just call me Zvi" — he smiled after they introduced themselves formally one by one. He motioned to the Italian canteen worker to bring six bottles of soft drinks and pointed to a round side-table, surrounded by six chairs. The visitors responded with smiles that seemed forced and weary. They had obviously come here with something on their minds.

"Really" — he continued — "you shouldn't have bothered. I mean to be at the synagogue tomorrow morning to introduce myself to the community leaders and the rabbi, and we could have met there. I understand that the community institutions are admirably efficient, as much as is possible in wartime. I've heard only good things."

From the fixed, expressionless faces of the five young men, there was no question that he had unintentionally said the wrong thing. Did the respectable community façade conceal critical issues contrary to his innocent suppositions? The five exchanged a look and he understood that they were about to approach the subject that had led them to him. He felt uncomfortable. He had not envisaged this turn of events on his first night.

The first speaker introduced himself once more: Giorgio Pipperno. ("He's the serious member of the group" — the youth sitting on his right whispered to Zvi. "Since liberation, he has served as secretary of the Zionist Federation. He's in mourning. He lost both his parents in the *akcja* which you're bound to hear more about.")

"Surely, you know what's been happening, Zvi" — Giorgio

began, his friends listening with open respect as if for them, too, there was something new in the narrative that time had hewn on their lives with an iron chisel. "On September 8, 1943 the peace and quiet of our city came to an end upon Mussolini's ousting and imprisonment, and the surrender of Badoglio's government to the Allies. With the same blitz that the Nazis began this war, Rome and all the other cities that Montgomery hadn't conquered fell into their hands."

"The Jewish community leadership" — he grimaced in sharp resentment — "did not grasp the seriousness of the situation nor adapt its thinking to the new circumstances." He broke off, silent, whether because he was overcome with fury and personal pain or because he judged it improper to air all his complaints at their initial meeting. "You may be certain that in time you'll learn of all our gripes" — his stab at levity rang false.

But the others refused to hold back. It was, after all, a golden opportunity to lay bare before the Eretz-Israeli soldier, who had volunteered to become involved in their problems, matters that weighed on their hearts like a stone. And so, inadvertently, the opening monologue made way for multi-voiced criticism and complaints. "For two weeks — until the announcement that the Germans were demanding a ransom deposit of fifty kilograms of gold — our leaders did not tell the public what was really happening, but encouraged us to go about our daily lives as usual" — one of the group said — "and this, at a time that many of us might have fled the city or found protection in the homes of Christian friends or in one of the monasteries. The blatant evidence? On the fifth day of the German occupation, most of the community leaders vanished. Even the Chief Rabbi took shelter in a monastery for the entire period of Nazi rule, instead of shepherding his flock through those dark times."

Harsh words, but the young men were not being rough on the rabbi. They were aware of both the unfortunate circumstances surrounding his election to the high post after serving as the rabbi of Trieste for twenty years and of how high-handedly he had been treated by Rome's Jewish elite. The erudition of the former Eastern-Galician and the Italian suffix he had attached to his name — changing it from Zoller to Zolli — did not save the Yiddish-speaking Ostjude from prejudice and incessant sparring. In June 1944, neither the young welcoming committee nor the envoy they were welcoming could have foreseen the "big bang" that was to rock the Jewish community eight months later.

"Disaster came down on the Jews of Rome not only because their leaders failed to look for powerful allies who might have been able to influence the occupation government and thereby help. No, their assessment of the situation was wrong to begin with. They clung to old assumptions that had never been put to the test" — a third young man tried to explain the rationale of the community leaders. "Since Rome had been declared an open city, the leaders apparently assumed that it would not be attacked from the outside and that no harm would come to any sector of the population, seeing as that would be in breach of the demilitarized status. Moreover, the particular population in question did not endanger the contending powers or upset the balance of war one way or another; it had even paid the demanded ransom, on the understanding that it would be left alone. But all the understandings were worthless. On the day after the ransom was handed over, a group of Nazis burst into two synagogues while other Nazi formations separately plundered the two Hebrew libraries, the ancient community library and the Rabbinical Seminary library.

"Another naïve hope" — the fourth member of the group added — "was pinned on the Pope, who, in the first place is the Bishop of Rome. The community leaders believed that he would not let any harm come to the citizens of the city under his patronage, regardless of their religion. This assumption too, so tempting to the gullible, had never been put to the test and proved now groundless. The expectations nursed of the head of the Vatican — Roman Catholicism's absolute leader — has plainly been misguided. There was little reason to hope that the former Cardinal Pacelli, once the papal Nuncio in Germany and, as it transpired, sympathetic to the

Germans and their regime, would either change his views after being elected Pope Pius XII or warn Germany that the Church would not tolerate the spiraling evils against Jews."

"And so the unbelievable happened" — the last of the five summed up the indictment. "An *akcja*! It's one thing for atrocities to be committed in Central and Eastern Europe where they became a daily occurrence — but *here*? In Rome? The seat of the Jewish and Christian elites? To everyone's shock, at dawn on October 16, 1943, the Rome *akcja* became fact. More than a thousand of Rome's eight thousand Jews were hunted down, brutally loaded onto cattle cars and transported northward." Nobody tried to guess the train's destination. Nobody told the story of the additional thousand Jews who were caught and liquidated. Silence descended on the hall and on the occupants of the corner table. Zvi too was quiet. In any case he had decided just to listen, so as not to add to the pain in everyone's heart with words. He merely whispered, almost apologetically: "I didn't know. I hadn't heard. And I doubt that the people who sent me knew or heard."

The next morning Zvi bought a map and, en route to the Tiber, filled his lungs with the morning air of the city that, for years, he had dreamt of touring, knowing "everything" he had to see there. Back in the days that he had visited the home of Dr. Haim Vardi, his Italian teacher and guide to the love of Italy, he had paged through the albums of Rome scattered on Vardi's antique table, learning and absorbing "everything" he would be introduced to in the future, every thing of beauty he would delight in. Now, there was only one impediment: he didn't know his way around the city. He opened the map and perused it, memorizing every detail, until he felt that he had swallowed its topography whole, and now Rome dwelt inside him. Hereafter, he would be able to get to any part of town without difficulty, and soon, too, he would easily find his way to Trastevere.

Except that on the way, his eyes could not get their fill. The demon-instigator that took up permanent residence in his mind, set even now snares at his feet, splitting his personality painfully

Trastevere — woodcut, 1640 *(from the Jewish Encycopedia, 1905–09)*
Encircled: *Platea Judea* (left), *La Judea* (right)

and pleasurably at one and the same time. The right lobe rebuked him: "Shame on you! Here you are in Rome. You mean to turn your back on the Colosseum and the Forum? You won't even glance at the engraving on the triumphal Arch of Titus showing the Temple Menorah being carried off by laurel-wreathed Romans? And what about Michelangelo's 'Moses' — his fingers stroking an outsized beard and his head sprouting horns (originating in the mistranslation of the Hebrew *karan* (Exodus 34: 29 — for Moses' "beaming" face) — he does not deserve a greeting? Just as you recalled him when you stood face to face with Raamses' embalmed head? And the Vatican? Ah, San Pietro and the Bernini Square! Ah, the 'Pieta' and the Sistine Chapel! OK, so maybe you'll see them all in good time. But now — how can you skip Capitoline Hill and withhold an endearing glance from the she-wolf whose udders gave Rome the gift of life and grace, its riches and its beauties?"

The left lobe of his personality, however, censured him with the very same opening words: "Shame on you! Here you are in Rome — but you came neither as a sightseer nor as a history student. You came on a mission, a mission that's binding through every day and every hour. At Trastevere you are awaited by public figures and youth, Italian Jewish youth whom you are to 'turn into Hebrew-speaking youth; youngsters who have experienced the Holocaust and thirst for tidings of hope from Eretz-Israel. And your hands hold those tidings! No, you yourself *are* the tidings!!!"

And so, without his noticing or bothering to consult the map, his feet, of their own volition, conveyed him to Trastevere.

## II

But look — the work of the devil! — no "public figures" awaited him at Trastevere nor any girls or boys of the "youth", the "Italian Jewish youth", that he was to "turn into Hebrew-speaking youth". Worse still: No Jewish quarter awaited him at all! He had of course known that he would not find any traces of ancient Trastevere, where Jews had lived as early as the last century BCE and the first century CE and where the oldest synagogue ever built on European soil once stood. Jews had continued to settle in Trastevere later, too, according to the twelfth-century account of Benjamin of Tudela, though by then it was no longer the only Jewish neighborhood. In fact, for 1,500 years — i.e., throughout the classic period and the Middle Ages — none of Rome's neighborhoods had been set aside exclusively for Jews. In the capital of the Papal State, Jews had been free to live in other quarters too — free until the mid-sixteenth century. That was when the great change came, putting an end to Jewish residence in metropolitan Rome and confining the Jews to Trastevere, on the left bank of the Tiber river.

It had been Pope Paul IV who, in 1555, issued a series of edicts, primarily restricting Jewish residence in Rome. He had surrounded Trastevere with a wall and installed gates, enforcing the status of a ghetto on both the residents and the quarter. This status lasted for some 320 years during which time the quarter's physical plan, the spread of its streets and the style of its houses, remained virtually unaltered. And then came the festive year of 1870: it celebrated not only the defeat of the Papal State and the annexation of Rome to Italy; it was also a cause for joy for Roman Jewry, celebrating its release from the degradation of the ghetto. The wall was dismantled, opening the way for Jews to other residential neighborhoods. In 1901 a grand synagogue was demonstratively built on the *right* bank of the river — the irony of history! Exactly opposite the former ghetto. Back in his student years at the university, Zvi had read everything written about the ghetto and he had internalized its image. He surmised that the neighborhood was no longer as he knew it from the pages of scholarly works, of old woodcuts and traveler descriptions. Abandoned houses had no doubt crumbled, and the city of Rome had taken care to remove all traces of ignominy. Still, he was confident that he would be able to identify and locate the remains of the historic sites and compare the real Trastevere with the Trastevere he had learned about, studied and loved.

In vain! There was not a single recognizable shred of the past. Within fifty to sixty years, the entire area had become one hundred per cent Christian. Gone were the days when the Pope himself had ordered three churches removed from the neighborhood — whether to ease the terrible congestion and its accompanying stench; or to complete Christian-Jewish segregation and render it total and irreversible; or as a step towards further harassment of ghetto residents. Ah, where was the main gate's square, Platea Judea (or Piazza Giudea)? And where was the huge cross that stood in front of the San Angelo Church on the other side of the ghetto, with Jesus, his arms spread on the cross, fixing furious eyes on passers-by as if to torment the Jewish people with the words of Isaiah (65:2) that were inscribed above in large Latin and Hebrew letters:

*"I have spread out My hands all the day unto a rebellious people."*

And where were the lovely homes of the neighborhood's wealthy, along Via Rua and the parallel street, Strada di Pescaria? Or the huts of the destitute on the bank of the Tiber, their windows intentionally small so as to keep out the water in times of storm and flood? Oh, how the residents suffered from the river's flooding even when there was no storm, because the bank of the Tiber was low on this side and spewed out all the city's rubbish onto the shore. Is it any wonder that the ghetto was overhung by a reeking cloud that elicited malicious objections about "Jewish stench" — the recurrent slander voiced by anti-Semites down the generations? And where was the ghetto's loveliest building, the synagogue with the five separate synagogues that it harbored under its wing? Permission had been granted to build only one synagogue, yet there were five Jewish sections, each adhering to a distinct liturgy. Each thus occupied its own synagogue on one fifth of the allotted space, beneath a single roof. Nonetheless, it is told that by Jewish request, an additional gate had been opened in the ghetto for people coming from the direction of the Forum, so that they would not have to pass the Arch of Titus and repeatedly behold the Menorah's plunder. This may also have been the origin of the custom of having carved menorahs at the entrance to their homes. In any case, whether by ruse or request, the wall of the ghetto was moved even under the Papal regime and its area enlarged, enabling Jewish life to expand despite the edicts.

Of all these things, not a trace remained. Only in one corner of the quarter, barely touching the left bank but planted there nonetheless, did Zvi see an imposing modern building with an Italian inscription: "Scuola Elementare Israelitica Vittorio Polacco", and in Hebrew: "*Beit HaSefer HaIvri al-shem Vittorio Polacco*".

For the almost twenty years of its existence (the visitor was informed that it had been built in 1925), the Vittorio Polacco School turned out Jewish pupils at the elementary level with a knowledge of the rudiments of Jewish religion and the Jewish way of life. From here, the children went on to a state high school. The Germans shut down all — even non-Jewish — schools in the countries they occupied, from the elementary level through university. In so doing, the conquerors sought to crush all seeds of what Europeans call "the intelligentsia" for fear that education spawns revolution. On September 9, 1943, the day after the Germans seized Rome, the Jewish school was closed and so it remained until the Jewish soldier-envoy arrived in the liberated capital. 112 of its pupils — a memorial plaque on the school wall notes — had been rounded up, deported to death camps, and perished.

That morning, it was enough for the envoy to speak with two or three active community members to decide, that as a first step, the Jewish school would reopen the following day under his direction. Announcements to this effect were posted in the community. Zvi regarded his function as principal a trust, until such time as it could return to normal operations as an authorized, regular school in the hands of professional teachers, albeit with a supplemented curriculum of compulsory instruction of Hebrew. Until then, it

The Vittorio
Polacco School
(1944–45)

would serve as an "Ulpan"-like school of Hebrew and its teachers would be the soldiers dispatched to Rome by their units.

And so it was. The school was reopened the next morning at a festive assembly of all the pupils and soldier-teachers with a greeting, in Italian, by the community representative and a greeting, in Hebrew and in Italian emphasizing common Jewish destiny, delivered by the envoy-principal on behalf of the soldiers from Eretz-Israel. Everyone felt as if they were witnessing one historic revolution taking place within another: a revolution in the life of Rome as a whole, liberated from fascist tyranny and now awakening at an astonishing pace from a twenty-year-long political coma; and a revolution in the situation of Rome's Jews, saved from total extermination after the Nazi killing machine had managed to deport and slaughter a quarter of them with every intention of murdering the rest. Now, upon liberation, they pitched in to revive Jewish community and cultural life while, some, especially the youngsters, looked on Zionism as a feasible recourse in light of their encounter with Eretz-Israeli soldiers.

When Zvi walked into the classroom, he was happily surprised to spot one of the five young activists he had met at the Jewish Soldiers Club on his first evening in Rome — and whom he was now to teach Hebrew. From time to time in years to come, the ex-soldier would conjure up the picture of that meeting and hear, echoing in his ears, the grudge the young activists bore the community leaders for their conduct in the nine months of Nazi occupation, as if it had occurred only the day before. Another memory of that evening was the silence that had descended on the club and its occupants when one of the activists (who, two days later became his pupil) continued the tale of the atrocities and began to speak of the *akcja* of October 16, 1943; began, and broke off, out of consideration, perhaps, for another of the five, both of whose parents had been deported that day. They had not come back, and no one knew if the Nazi train that had carried off Rome's prey had embarked — much like hundreds of Nazi trains had carried off other Jewish prey from other countries in Europe — on a road of no return.

Zvi had never asked to hear the end of the story. Yet fifty years later, he received in the mail a monograph of a study conducted by his former pupil and written in a fine Hebrew that filled his teacher's heart with pride. He was especially glad that the then activist was in Israel now, devoting his energies to research on Italian Jewry. The article was well-constructed and well-documented, and the topic — incredibly — was "The Great Hunt-Down of Rome's Jews on 16 October 1943". The dedication read:

> *To my esteemed teacher, Prof. Zvi Ankori, who introduced me to the secrets of the Hebrew language (Rome, July 1944). Gratefully Michael Tagliacozzo*

Perusing the monograph, it struck the recipient that it was a continuation of the conversation that long-ago night, and that everything that had not been said then because the pain was too fresh and sharp, was now being bared in detail. Though both the methodology of the study and the distance of time dictated restraint — restraint on the part of the writer, yet not on the part of his reader. And the reader-teacher hardly knew if the tear that spilt from his eye and stained the printed page was for Rome's deportees alone or, perhaps, for the remembered parents and sister in a northern land, hundreds of miles away from Rome, who also perished in the Holocaust.

The *aliya* to Eretz-Israel of 300 families (about a thousand people) from Southern Italy in May 1944, and a comparable number in March 1945, emptied the Rishonim youth farm and the Dror agricultural training facility that succeeded it; and, the joy at realizing their dream notwithstanding, the young Italians felt —

so wrote the chronicler, Michael Tagliacozzo, in an anthology of memoirs of activists from those times — that the Hebrew soldiers' activity had come to a halt ("*una stasi nell'attivita dei sodati*"). The soldiers' work however had not stopped, despite the fears. Two centers soon arose in Rome "thanks to the interest of soldier Zvi Ankori of 178 and others" ("*grazie all'ineressamento del soldato Zwy Ankori della 178 Coy e da altri*").

The first action was the reopening of the Vittorio Polacco School. But Rome's youth were not content with formal Hebrew studies within a school framework. They were eager for the youth movement life they had heard of in tales of Ferramonti and the Rishonim farm — a youth movement in every sense, with its comradeship, ideological talks, singing and folk-dancing, aimed at *aliya* to Eretz-Israel and the pioneering way of life.

The young, who had lived through the painful period of Nazi rule and sought to recapture their youth, had their wish come true. A Zionist youth center did arise. The chronicler of the soldiers' work with Jewish youth recorded the establishment of a "Youth Center" with his usual reticence:

> "*A Roma, nei locall dell'"oratorio Di Castro" in via Balbo, sorse un Centro Giovanile sotto la guida di Zwy Ankori, gia sperimentato per attivita del genere nel Sud Italia.*"
>
> ("In Rome, in the rooms above the Di Castro Synagogue on Via Balbo, a Youth Center arose under the leadership of Zvi Ankori, who already had experience in activities of this nature in Southern Italy.")

The twenty-year hiatus of a free youth movement tradition (other than Fascist Youth) caused the Balbo group to be called simply "Youth Center" at first, unaffiliated to any Eretz-Israel movement or party. But it was not long before the Eretz-Israel spirit moved through the Balbo rooms and on the terrace, and the youngsters named the movement *Kadima* (Hebrew for "*Onward*"). Zvi does

Via Balbo Synagogue —
Youth activities took
place on the top floor
and on the terrace

אם תרצו אין זו אגדה.

Kadima Youth Movement on Via Balbo (1944)
Back row, center — Zvi Ankori

not remember whether the name sprang up spontaneously in the course of learning a song that contained the word, or whether he had suggested it. Either way, to this day the youngsters' parting gift to him rests on his desk: a silver box engraved with the words: "To Zvi — from Kadima".

The Kadima branch on Via Balbo boasted the kind of wide-ranging activities familiar to all the pre-war Zionist youth movements — in Poland, Rumania and, of course, Eretz-Israel. For Italy's Jewish youngsters, this sort of youth movement was a "revelation". They learned to sing Hebrew songs and sang them with fervor; they threw their energies into learning folk-dances and re-found their joy of life.

Zvi teaches an Eretz-Israel dance on the terrace at Via Balbo

Giorgio Piperno (or Yehuda, one of the five-man welcome committee greeting Zvi on his first evening in Rome and whose personal "Zionist revolution" inspired him, like quite a few others, to revert to their Hebrew names) — recounts in the Italian anthology of memoirs of the period that, after liberation and the appearance of Jewish soldiers from Eretz-Israel,

> "we immediately gathered around the Eretz-Israel soldiers. We met them on the very first days of June 1944, in the rooms next to the synagogue on Via Balbo…
>
> "In a short time, the street came to stand for Jewish youth activity. The Balbo Circle was a lodestone for a broad youth public, many of whom had previously been far removed from Jewish activity. The Nazi conquest made even the utterly aloof rethink their affiliation to Judaism…
>
> "Soon, an expanded periphery of a young public formed and was warmly embraced by dedicated counselors. Balbo took on a new meaning: more than a meeting place, more than a social pastime. The activity on Via Balbo reflected not only a decisive turning point in the personal lives of the participants, but a revolutionary stage in the life of Rome's Jewish youth as a whole. For the first time, a movement framework was formed. To describe it as a mass movement would be an exaggeration, but numerically, it grew to heretofore unknown dimensions."

This is how it was seen by Yehuda Piperno, who witnessed and participated in the activity from the day that the Balbo Circle was founded.

## III

Zvi's day in Rome was split in half, between the school and Via

Balbo. Every morning, a forty-five minute walk on the right bank of the Tiber brought him to the tall, protruding building of the New Synagogue, whose dome seemed to float above the treetops. Further on, the bank revealed an elongated islet alongside (Isola Tiberina); it was the Tiber River itself that bisected its own channel to embrace its daughter, Isola, with both arms.

Isola Tiberina: The bridge connecting the Synagogue area with the Hebrew School; on the left: the dome of the Great Synagogue.

At the tip of the islet, the two channels merge and a bridge crosses the river's reunited current. Twice a day, back and forth, the envoy crossed the bridge to the left bank and back again. On that bank, at the corner of Trastevere, it will be recalled, stood the three-storied building that was the destination of Zvi's walk: the Vitorio Polacco School. He was its first (temporary — he emphasizes) principal after liberation, and as one of the soldier-teachers, he taught Hebrew there, one class for beginners and another for advanced. The rest of his time until noon was given over to advising pupils and parents, and to talks with teachers on matters related to the work.

The school knew sad days. A child would suddenly burst out crying at the memory of a mother and father who had been snatched away on that dreadful autumn day. How were young, untrained teachers, with only a smattering of acquired Italian, to evoke words of comfort for an orphaned child? His classmates, also orphaned, wept as he did, and the entire classroom turned into a vale of tears.

On the other hand, the school knew amused and amusing days as well, sometimes embarrassingly so. The teachers would not forget the day that four packages of Hebrew textbooks arrived from Eretz-Israel. The books had been ordered some weeks earlier, but the mills of the military post and military censorship grind slowly. When they finally arrived, both pupils and teachers were gripped by excitement. Until then, there had been no printed text to follow. Lessons had been improvised, devoted to the Hebrew alphabet and the vowel system, to the joining of letters to form words and simple sentences, and write them on the blackboard. The first class held that morning was conducted by soldier-teacher Ze'ev who handed out a copy of the new books to every pupil. He told the class that the books had been sent from Eretz-Israel as a gift to the children of Rome. He then asked them to open the books on the first page, and instructed one of the pupils to read aloud. The improvised lessons proved to have been effective. The first boy started reading the first line with confidence, while the whole class followed the text on the page: "*Ani oleh hadash be-Eretz-Israel, shmi Avraham Katz.*" (I am a new immigrant in Eretz-Israel, my name is Abraham Katz). When the reader came to the last word in the line, he almost bit his lips in an effort to stem its utterance. The boys murmured, holding back a titter; the girls blushed, lowering their eyes. The same thing happened when the second pupil was asked to read. This time, the boys burst into open laughter. When a girl was asked to read the line, she simply refused.

Ze'ev acted wisely: he decided to skip the line and asked one of the pupils to go on with the next line. The embarrassment dissolved as one pupil after another went on with the reading. At the end of the lesson, Ze'ev collected all the textbooks and during recess, came by Zvi's office to deposit them. Quite upset, he related the incident, adding his conjecture that the first line must have contained a word that sounded like an Italian obscenity that was not said in decent society — and was there ever a society more "decent" than school? "Now, tell me, Zvi, after having wasted years learning Italian: what's the word that tripped us up?" Zvi read the line once and again and could find nothing wrong with it. "Yes, I've studied Italian. Ask me to quote you a passage from Dante's poetry or from the prose of Benedetto Croce and I'll give you an hour-long lecture in Italian. As for street slang, especially coarse language (which this apparently is), I'm an ignoramus in every language. You were right to collect the books. We won't hand them out in the other classrooms until we get to the root of the problem."

The inquiry bore out Ze'ev's conjecture, unearthing the problematic word. It was the name "Katz" at the end of the line, which resembled the Italian euphemism for the male genitals. (One might add that the 1940s were still relatively innocent, unlike the period sixty years later at the writing of the present book. Dirty words were not heard at school, certainly not in the presence of girls, and even more certainly, girls did not utter them. Moreover: in the preceding policed fascist atmosphere, natural innocence had been backed up by strict discipline.) There was nothing for it but to excise the suspect page from the book, and track down a press with Hebrew letters and a printer able to lay them out. After a good deal of running about, a small church press was located; it occasionally produced biblical chapters for a priesthood seminary. A generous hand and a fistful of cigarettes found the printer kindly disposed, and the page, minus the inelegance, was reprinted: exit "Katz", enter "Cohen". And rightly so, since (in Hebrew) "Katz" is an acronym for "Cohen Tzedek". Incidentally, no less paradoxical was the fact that the teacher's name — sh-h-h! Don't tell anyone! — was Ze'ev Katz!

Zvi asked the teachers to stay on in his office in the afternoon, to paste the corrected page into every book: "*Ani oleh hadash be-Eretz-Israel, shmi Avraham Cohen.*" The next morning, a "second edition" of the textbook awaited the pupils, their first Hebrew book, to be followed by others that were to belong to them in the future. "Yay! We're reading Hebrew!" Their enthusiasm spilled over. Hereafter, laughter and joy filled the stairway of the entrance, the corridors and the schoolyard, and their sense of accomplishment nearly wiped out the initial sadness.

In the afternoon, the soldier removed the robe of teacher and principal and turned into a youth counselor at Via Balbo. Before that, of course, there was a refreshing walk along the Tiber, a stop at the Jewish Soldiers Club, and a quick visit to the canteen to "grab" a sandwich and orange juice. On the way to the counter he would glance at the Eighth Army's English newspaper, not so much for news as for his daily date with the comics character of Jane, to check what additional article of clothing she was now shedding. Jane, the figment of a sick male imagination, a caricaturist "who knows what soldiers want", never let one down. True, if one compares what passed for daring then, in the department of women's garments or a lack thereof, with the comics of today, Jane was a veritable pious and demure virgin who, every morning, thanked God for "having created me according to His will", the blessing that orthodox Jewish women recite at the start of every new day.

In the canteen, Zvi chatted briefly with soldiers from other units about mundane matters, though he did not form any steady, personal ties. He enjoyed company and was able to contribute tunes and humor, and sometimes also a dose of gravity. But at that stage, his interest was totally taken up by the two sites of his mission and, after finishing work at the morning site, he set out for the second site where he was to remain until late in the evening. Via Balbo was in the opposite direction from his morning walk and the road to it was relatively short, all within a built-up area. It did pass near the monuments of classical Rome, but for the moment he did not succumb to the temptation to visit them. Four o'clock would find him at Balbo.

Working diligently at the two mission sites he set up, and devoting evenings to planning school programs and special events (on top of lessons), and preparing topics for discussion with Balbo's older members, he hardly noticed the passing of the six weeks (the maximum military furlough [i.e., "volunteering"]). Meanwhile, 178 sent word that the car fetching him back to his Unit would be delayed by two days — and he had already said his farewells and passed on the baton to other soldiers who had come to Rome from different units. There was no fear — Polacco and Balbo would continue to flourish on the foundations that he had laid, and he had to admit that he was a bit tired and Rome awaited his sightseeing.

The two free days he won, a drop in the ocean of sights to be seen, were like a gift from heaven. All his inner demon's early temptations in Rome had taken second place to the mission: he had quashed his inclinations and silenced the pest. Now the time had come to indulge himself. Free of his public and military work, he traversed the length and breadth of the town, gazed at monuments, visited museums, toured the Vatican and other churches or simply strolled at his leisure in parks, along boulevards, through squares. The socialist in him urged him to visit also the other Rome, the poor neighborhoods made even worse than ever by wartime poverty, but — to his shame — he elected to skip them. How could he have guessed that if he didn't go see poor Rome at his own initiative, it would come to him, embarrassing, paining and subduing him? In any case, he chose to acquaint himself with the excursionist's Rome. The demon now reversed his initial demands and summoning up the destruction that imperial Rome and the papal edicts had brought on the Jewish people, called on him to retaliate by ignoring Rome's beauty. But Zvi firmly shushed him.

Dazzled by the glamorous city, he wanted only to glide on the waves of time and relive in his mind the chain of events since the city's founding, "*ab urbe condita*", as the classical Roman historians put it. He breathed in Rome, intoxicated by its pleasing fragrance, absorbing it into every fiber. Amazingly, his high school Latin returned to sing within him: hexameters by Virgil, passages from Cicero, sentences from Tacitus' *Germania* — a different text which, unseen, he translated with flying colors at his matriculation exams, — *The Gallic War* by Julius Caesar and Livy's *History*. Overwhelmed and excited by the sights, and proud of the layers of Latin he remembered, he declared to the city and the world, "*Urbi et Orbi*", Bless you, Rome, "*Civitas Dei*" (City of God) — Bless you for ever and ever!

On his second and last free day, Ankori veered off the city's tourist route to scale Rome's hills for an overview. His head reran a verse of Psalms that seemed to fit the mood. Except that the original verse (Psalm 122) sang of Jerusalem and, he wondered, might its use, by way of a paraphrase for Rome, not be irreverent? Nevertheless, he etched the verse's twin on his heart and standing atop the hill, mouthed his version:

> "Our feet are standing on your hills,
> Rome, that art builded as a city
> that is compact together
> on seven hills…"

Janiculum Hill was green and lovely but too high to afford a comfortable view of the stunning scene opposite; the eye soon wearied and moved off to the mist-shrouded, distant horizon. Zvi had always preferred near landscapes to far ones, soft vistas to stunning ones, landscapes one could relate to and connect with humanly. Relative to Janiculum, Capitoline Hill was too low; the modern city closed in on it, it was bare of green, and the buildings left no room for fancy about the primordial region that had preceded Rome. Towards evening, the hill-climber reached Palatine Hill and pledged it his love at first sight. It was everything he had been searching for. And not only did it in itself bewitch him, but it stirred in him fond memories of another hill, another town, another time.

Climbing up Mt. Scopus in his student days, he was always excited anew at the hill's two faces, each of which gazed out in an opposite direction: the eastern slope overlooked the desert, the western slope — Jerusalem. Already then, he had imagined the hill as Janus, the two-faced Roman god. But the Janus metaphor was so much more apt for Janiculum (named after the god) and for Palatine Hill, especially as it was in this chain of hills that the Janus cult had sprouted: Palatine's one slope framed the Roman Forum while its opposite slope opened on an expanding patch of urban landscape, nearby (as the observer liked), its breath warm and its colors bright. It looked like a box of chocolates, a birthday present, beribboned by the Tiber before being presented. Presented to whom? To the soldier, of course. For the calendar had played a jest on him, making his last day in Rome coincide with his twenty-fourth birthday, on July 19. He had not told anyone, having learned in childhood from his mother to disdain such vapid celebrations to the point of refusing gifts, and this had been his practice ever since. Only Rome had guessed his secret, inserting this patch of itself into a chocolate box as a lover's gift from where it beheld him.

The last rays of the sun were getting entangled in the maze of streets, falling victim to the chaos between day and night. And it, the setting sun, an ostentatious red lipstick on its mouth, pressed a red pre-dusk kiss on both the Palatine Hill and the soldier-rover on its trails. The sun's place was now taken by city lights trying to wrap the treetops in a soft, mellow light, but the latter spurned the light and, having shed their green, wrapped their heads in a scarf of black — a hidden black, an arcane black, concealing the riddle of Rome's eternity and guarding the secret of its charms from generation to generation.

All at once, he felt a small, soft palm take hold of his left hand and not let go. "*Soljer*" — the little girl shook his hand with determination — "*Ciocolatta? Ciungum? Bonbon?*" It was an assault every soldier was prepared for. The present stroller, too, had the kind of goodies the child had asked for in his pocket, having bought them at the canteen before setting out. He now took out a handful and gave her some, leaving the rest for other children he might run into. "*Soljer*, a*nche per la mia sorella*" (also for my sister;) — the little child persisted, having apparently exhausted her English vocabulary. The soldier looked at her: Eight years old? Only six, perhaps? War matures children. She must have been worrying about a younger sister?

The teacher and educator in him suddenly woke up to find himself upset by the child's appearance at this late hour in this deserted place.

"How come you're about in the evening, on the hill, rather than at home, in town?"

"We have no home. Father beat my sister and threw her out, and I left with her."

"Beat and threw out your little sister?"

"You misunderstood. My sister isn't little. She's twenty-two. She also likes *ciungum*."

"Why did your father throw her out?"

"He talked about *onore* (honor). He's an old fascist. His Duce too used to scream '*Molti nemici, molto onore*'. Honor doesn't bring bread. The soldiers hand out candies. But for bread you have to pay. So my sister sacrifices herself. Bad people tell us, 'It's not nice, you are paid'. And I say: no, it's we who pay the heavy price!"

He was startled by the maturity and good sense of the six-or-eight-year-old, virtues she had not learned in any school (if she *had* attended school at all) but from life itself. Wise, sober, realistic, she felt that both she and her sister were untainted by sin. She was happy to talk to a stranger in her own language. Her story may have been authentic or not (he reflected). But the child was authentic. A child of war. He turned to leave after — contrary to his earlier decision — having emptied his pocket.

"*Buona notte*" — he wanted to be gone, but the sadness in her eyes held him back:

"*Soljer*" — she called after him. "Wait. Come with me. My sister saw you and likes you. She sent me to bring you. She is very pretty and you are handsome. We'll give you a discount."

He paled. The child was already a *madam*. Bringing her sister clients. She had learned all the tricks. To flatter, "you're handsome", "my sister wants you". Who knew — maybe, if their dearth grew any worse, she too would "sacrifice herself" like her sister. And all this took place on his dear Palatine Hill.

He was beside himself. Fury burst from his heart, his mind and his mouth, and from his inner depths he cried out: "Damn you Rome, *Civitas Diaboli* (city of the devil), look what you've done to your daughters!"

## IV

Ankori was pleased to return to 178 after his extended leave, and to feel the steering wheel responding to his every touch, yet Rome, blessed or damned, gave him no rest. Of course, the mission to Rome's Jews in their time of trouble lived on in his memory in full force and filled him with the sweet taste of satisfaction: the satisfaction of a job well-done and enjoyable, even if exhausting, in a field that he loved and valued, and the satisfaction of contributing to the community's recovery from the trauma of the Holocaust. But, as far as he was personally concerned, it was a closed book, to be carried forward by other able hands. In contrast to his sense of success regarding the Jewish community, the city of Rome continued to preoccupy him. Since his wonderful two-day "windfall", he had lived Rome, breathed Rome, thought Rome, dreamt Rome. The city turned his head and made his heart race. Whenever he recalled his sightseeing, he saw himself, in his mind's eyes, plucking the historic buildings and enchanted hilly landscape from photographs he had long known and finally planting them in the ground of reality. "Ah, divine Rome, when will I see you again?"

But Rome was far away, southwest of 178's base then, and 178's Movement Order pointed in the opposite direction: north, along the eastern Adriatic seacoast to Ancona, an important transit hub with a port and a railway system. Situated at the foot of the Apennines and richly irrigated by abundant waters running down the mountains, Ancona was endowed with lovely fruit gardens. Just then, it was the designated point for the Polish army-in-exile to rally anew, after having suffered heavy losses at Monte Cassino, and Ancona's streets were filled with numerous Poles. The army had been recruited from refugees in Siberia and transferred to Italy. During the Siberian enlistment, the number of would-be conscripts among Polish Jewish refugees had increased, though most had been turned away. Anti-Semitism?

178 was to be stationed at Ancona for some two months, servicing the eastern and central flanks of the front. The wheels of war were of course turned by HQ, but the wheels of the vehicles were turned by 178 drivers. Geographically and time-wise, the distances were shorter than in Southern Italy, nevertheless the months of August and September 1944 were eternally burnt on Ankori's memory because they bore two surprises, both — incredibly enough! — connected with Tarnów.

It was a hot, dry evening at the end of September. The base guard peered into Ankori's tent: "Listen, a corporal has just pulled up on a motorbike, British shoulder and arm tags, but I noticed that he came from the Polish base. Isn't that strange? Speaks a bit of Hebrew. Knows your name and asked about you. Should I let him in?"

"Wait. I'll come with you. The truth is I wasn't expecting anyone from another Company this evening."

There followed a whole night in which the two friends sat and talked: reminiscing about their Tarnów childhood and youth, remembering their army ramblings, as if willing the conversation never to end. Only the knowledge that in the morning, the Polish Company would be quitting the region forced the visitor to say his good-byes. A last embrace:

"We'll meet in Eretz-Israel after the war, Millek."

"*Dowidzenia* [see you], Hesiu" — he addressed Ankori by his childhood name. "Of my entire military service, this has been the most exciting day. We'll meet again. Let's promise each other that we'll meet again."

Millek Schiff, young and handsome, had been one of the best youth athletes of Jewish Tarnów. He was in the same grade as Hesiek, but at a different high school. Diligent, gifted, especially for languages, but moody. His love and excellence lay in sports. Not any sport — ping pong! Rung by rung, he started climbing up the ladder of success: first, he was his school's champion, then champion of all the high schools in town, then champion of the town of Tarnów with its four sports clubs. The carpet of success unrolled before him at an astonishing pace: champion of Poland. Champion of Europe. World champion!!

Sports newspapers and radio magazines adored him: photographers and newsreel journalists lurked for him in every corner; sports clubs around the world issued him invitations, pronouncing the champion's name in awe; girls were carried away, fainting at the sight of him and his game, their hearts beating to the hits of his racket. The name "Millek" passed through the sky of the Far East like a meteor and, in July 1939, its bearer was invited to Japan. He reached the Pacific by the Trans-Siberian train and from there took a boat to Japan. He was given a royal welcome.

Millek was wise enough not to let the glory go to his head, knowing that it came with a price tag: "This is the climax. Happy but sad. I haven't even finished high school yet. And from here — where next?"

On September 1, 1939 the Germans invaded Poland. War. When England and France entered the fray on the third, the conflict became a world war. Tarnów's 16th infantry regiment, deployed to defend the Silesian border, was pulverized on the first day of fighting. Tarnów itself was conquered on the seventh day. "There's nowhere to go back to" — Millek told himself. He stayed in Japan.

Japan had not yet become a side in the war against the Western states (its war exploits were concentrated on China), and life there was comfortable and very interesting. Millek's natural linguistic flair enriched him with an additional language. But when the clouds of war thickened in 1941, he understood that it was time to move and join the crowd of Polish refugees taking shelter in Central Asia. The refugees from forced labor camps were also on the move — they had been released, whether from Siberian gulags, from Vorkuta or Murmansk, for enlistment in the new Polish army — and they were making their way towards the Amu Darya River and the cities of Samarkand, Bukhara and Tashkent, where the main conscription efforts were apparently at hand. "That's where I must go" — Millek decided, taking advantage of any means of transportation he could find, including camels. "The last of the Radanites" — the remark escaped Ankori's mouth as he listened to the odyssey of a Jewish lad from Tarnów, who of course knew nothing about these predecessors of his, who had roamed the large continent a thousand years earlier. "What did you say?" — Millek asked. "Nothing. Go on with your story."

The road was longer than expected before Millek finally reached his destination. Conscription was in full swing, though there was none of the basic equipment that turned civilians into soldiers. British officers stood to the side, frustrated by their failed attempts to communicate in their own language. English was virtually unknown in pre-war Poland and was not taught in school. Millek approached the discomfited officers and, in splendid English, offered his assistance. One of them responded in astonishment: "Aren't you the famous ping pong champion? What are you doing here with the refugees?" The officer received the answer to his question in the jeep driving His Majesty's subjects to HQ in Teheran, with the lad from Tarnów at their side. His enlistment procedures were completed in three days. Millek signed a conscription order "for the duration [of the war]", swore allegiance, received his Soldier's Service and Pay Book, a British uniform, the tags of the HQ unit, and was sent on a crash course in marching drill and the rest of the "bullshit". When he came back, he was issued two corporal stripes and was appointed NCO liaison between the British and Polish HQs.

Thus, as the British spokesman to the Poles in Polish and the Polish spokesman before the British in English — Millek moved with the new Polish army from Iran to Iraq, from Iraq to Palestine and, ultimately, to Italy. After the brave battle fought by the Polish army at Monte Cassino and following its reorganization at Ancona, the British were to assign the Poles missions closer to home or, at their request, inside Poland itself. But the Red Army had advanced into Poland and with it, the Polish *Armia Ludowa* (Folk Army) — which, under Soviet command and subordinate to the Polish Communist Party, obstructed the Polish *Armia Krajowa* (Land Army) that took its orders from the Polish government-in-exile. Consequently, Britain apparently decided not to allow the Polish army posted in Italy to move northward. Instead, it returned it to the Middle East, including Palestine. The few Jews serving in the Polish army that was stationed in Eretz-Israel deserted, to settle there as immigrants. The Polish HQ didn't mind.

Since 178 did move northward, the two Tarnowians lost contact and the Polish army was not seen again in the vicinity where Eretz-Israel soldiers were stationed. Four years after their night-long conversation, Ankori (once more in khaki uniform, this time in besieged Jerusalem) learned that in March 1948, Millek, who lived in Tel Aviv, had committed suicide, leaving no letter or explanation for the deed. To this day, the former 178er can hear the hope in Millek's parting words at Ancona: "*Dowidzenia* [see you], Hesiu" — he addressed Ankori by his childhood name. "Of my entire military service, this has been the most exciting day. We'll meet again. Let's promise each other that we'll meet again."

They never met again…

The other surprise dropped into Ankori's hands unexpectedly, like an apple from a tree, on one of his short trips south of Ancona. The surprise had a name: Castelfidardo. The story went back to Rome and to Sergio, one of the local counselors at Balbo who had accompanied the folk dancing on his accordion. He was no mere accompanist but a born musician! Nor was his a mere accordion, but an instrument larger than life! When Sergio, wavelike, stretched the instrument wide open to its last fold, it seemed as if a mighty eagle had spread its wings and approached the dancers, approaching and receding, approaching and receding, or as if an undulating snake enthusiastically twisted right-left, up-down, its serpentine anatomy transmitting charmed tunes.

Zvi (as he was known in Rome) could not stop marveling at the sight of the accordion, not only because of its size and beauty but because its white keys awakened in him thoughts of the three pianos stolen from the house of his grandfather, the cantor-composer, in the First World War, after he had left his home and fled to Vienna for fear of the Cossacks overrunning Tarnów. Ever since, the pianos had taken on mythical proportions with the younger generation who knew about them only from hearsay. Nor had they known the grandfather who had passed away, brokenhearted at the loss. A wild idea flashed through the mind of the soldier-grandson: might the purchase of just such an accordion, its keys so similar to a piano's, soothe his grandfather's agonized soul in the afterworld? Wild ideas seem to come in pairs. Since it was unlikely that he, the grandson, would ever return to his former proficiency on the violin after the long war-imposed hiatus away from the string instrument, perhaps he would nonetheless return to music thanks to a formidable substitute — an accordion of this very sort. Wild ideas are not shared. Hidden in the heart, they simmer on a small flame. Sometimes the flame dies out, sometimes it bursts out more strongly.

Within days, the Rome envoy and former violinist decided to teach the youngsters the Arabic *debka*. On a piece of paper, he drew two rows of five lines each, the normal form of music notation, inserted the notes of the tune and handed the paper to Sergio: "This is the tune; the accompaniment you'll be able to improvise as you go along". To his astonishment, Sergio returned the piece of paper: "I don't read notes", he admitted unashamedly, "hum the tune for me and I'll pick it up at once. As for the accompaniment, with the accordion's 120 basses, that's no problem." Zvi complied and a mighty *debka* erupted from the throat of the snake, casting the entire terrace into dance, while the eagle with outspread wings, approached and receded, approached and receded, to Sergio's boisterous beat.

It was the start of an extraordinary friendship between an eighteen-year-old young man, a natural musician with perfect pitch, needing neither effort nor learning nor even note reading — merely his singular accordion obeying his fingers — and a twenty-four-year-old young man, a soldier-envoy, who also had a highly-developed musical sense but who had to work hard to conquer the violin that he played, his control of the instrument suffering from any interruption in practice, whatever the reason.

"Where can I get hold of such an accordion, Sergio?"

"Don't even dream of it. It's very expensive. And I bought it before the invasion."

"I've been saving for years, all the pay I've received from the army. I knew that I would need the money one day."

"I have no idea of course how much you've saved but it stands to reason that the British army — in fact, any army — doesn't pay its soldiers enormous sums. With all due respect, I must therefore assume that you don't have enough money to buy an accordion as fine as mine."

"Forgive my curiosity, but how could *you* afford such a large expense?"

"I got it at a 'bargain price', half the stated sum. You could get the same discount. After Ancona is liberated, go to the town of Castelfidaro, south of Ancona, and buy it there."

"What shop do I go to?"

"There are no shops in the town. It, and all the surrounding villages, are one large shop, or, in fact, one complete, factory. Go there. Maybe you'll manage to buy an instrument like mine."

Weeks after he returned from his Rome mission, Ankori found himself making his way with his Unit to Ancona, and the hope of visiting Castelfidardo took on life. It was a threefold experience: of discovery, of recollection, and of acquisition. Before his eyes, the visitor discovered an extraordinary production line for accordions, employing every town home and every village cabin in crafting accordion components, no doubt for a paltry daily sum. Town factories, in turn, buy up all the parts and assemble them into complete products, charging customers an inflated price. The home workhouse reminded Ankori of the hundreds of sewing machines click-clacking away day and night in Tarnów's Grabówka neighborhood: of the thousands of neighborhood poor in their overcrowded, dark shacks, their backs hunched over the machines making clothing bits, that were later assembled into elegant suits for export by the city's garment industrialists, who became magnates on the backs of Grabówka's toilers. The third aspect of the experience was the acquisition itself. As opposed to Tarnów's workers, an X or Y in Castelfidardo had learned to assemble the entire accordion himself from the parts that he made and, in quality and beauty, the instrument was as fine as any that the factories produced, though the cost was half. Ankori decided to buy one of the locally-made instruments. The socialist was embarrassed to haggle the price down, but he had no choice. For, without the discount he requested, he would have been unable to purchase it at all. Now, he could return to his Unit happy and well-disposed, the accordion hanging from his shoulder strap.

# V

A convoy of more than thirty transport trucks and of several other kinds of vehicles in the service of the 178 HQ and workshop, and boasting the Star of David on their doors, wended its way westward: it moved from ravine to hill, amid towns and cities, whose founders had inhaled the fragrance of olive trees, the intoxicating air of vineyards and the secret scent of cypress trees, deciding to cling to these hills forever. They built forts on the peaks and walls around their settlements. At their feet lay Tuscany, Italy's heart of hearts: always green, always young, always reinventing itself, always rebirthing itself anew — for this is the meaning of Renaissance, *Rinascimento* — as its great sons had felt seven hundred, six hundred and five hundred years earlier. And because Dante, Tuscany's celebrated son and exile, chose, from all of Italy's diverse districts and dialects, the dialect of Tuscany for the composition of his monumental work. Tuscany's dialect became the official language of Italy and its literature, and remains so to this day.

If Tuscany is Italy's heart, Florence is Tuscany's heart of hearts, and that was 178's destination. On the morning of November 9, 1944, the Unit reached the environs of Florence and the nearby site of Signa. The drivers complained about the wintry weather. Ankori saw no rain and felt no fog. From a few kilometers before their final stop, he already had been absorbed in fancy, imagining himself touring the city, thoroughly familiar with its sights, approaches and exits even though he had never been there. He greeted the cathedral and adjacent baptism site with warmth; ascended the Campanile tower; wandered through Signoria Square; surveyed at the Bargello Museum the statue of "Victory" by Michelangelo, on whom he had written a paper at the University; peeked into the Uffizi Gallery (a real visit required days) as well as the Palazzo Pitti across the Old Bridge over the Arno. But the statue of "David" at the Accademia Gallery could not be skipped: he stood entranced, assimilating the praises to the male figure that Michelangelo had sung in marble. Suddenly, the red back lights of the truck in front of him flashed across his eyes, causing him to slam his foot down on the brakes. "David" got a dose of his anger for nearly causing an accident, but also his thanks for saving him.

Only when he got down from the cabin, and rubbed his eyes to wipe away the illusive gossamer of the last few kilometers, did he feel the thinnest of rains splashing freshness and color onto his cheeks in advent of his date with the Princess of Art, Firenze, Florence. He had never even seen her, and he was already in love with her. What could Rome on the Tiber mean to him in comparison with Florence on the Arno?

The base — a wide-ranging, fenced-off area that took in all the vehicles and would house some 200 small, personal bivouac tents — leaned against the tall building of the former Nobel Company, whose profits, from the production of gunpowder, spawned the Nobel Prize, a virtue in compensation for a vice. Its upper floors had been destroyed by RAF bombing but the two lower floors were intact: the first, a large hall, was converted into the workshop; above it, the privileged had their quarters: the HQ and workshop crew. The "plebeians", i.e. two hundred drivers without whom there was no Company, no HQ and no workshop, were to erect half-a-meter high, three-sided structures from the piles of bricks and stones in the yard. This architectural feat, resembling in whole a Chalcolithic site, unearthed by archeologists armed with theories, was to support the small tents for protection from the rain. Sticklers would pave their self-appropriated estate grounds with bricks — a shield against the winter mud — and hang some sort of cloth screen over the open side of the entrance to fend off the wind and create the illusion of privacy. In the course of the construction, sergeants walked up and down — whether as inspectors or kibitzers, gushing with unsolicited advice. The guys had already proved their creativity with similar edifices in Libya, and they were more than willing to instruct the sergeants when their turn came to build themselves shelters.

Meanwhile, there had been personnel changes in the command. Major Aaron, a student of the British school and its conception that majors do not talk to privates, had completed his tour of duty. It amused Ankori that at the officers' conclave, Aaron had marveled at "the success of our envoy", yet he had never commended the envoy to his face. "Those in the know" whispered that he nursed hopes of adding two more transportation units to 178 when the

Jewish Brigade entered Italy, and that he would command all three at the rank of Lieutenant-Colonel. The proposal however was turned down. CSM Bankover returned to his kibbutz. The new CSM was Sergeant Miller, the same Miller that had treated Ankori to a nature lesson: "Why does a crab walk on its side? Because it has no brains." B Platoon also got a new sergeant.

Actually, it was clear to all that the new sergeant was close to retirement and that his transfer to 178 was his swan song in military service. A namby-pamby fatherly figure, he was with the platoon too short a time to leave a mark on the Company's life. His name was Shmulkeh. Shmuel? Shmuelevitz? Who cares?

"A 'pass', right now? It's only two o'clock!" he wasn't annoyed. He merely asked, like a father trying to understand his son.

"Sergeant" — Ankori replied, ostensibly not annoyed either, though the ground burnt beneath his feet and his desire to see the sights of Florence bordered on obsession. "Do come and see how I laid the brick floor, assembled the tent and tightened the ropes. I also swept all around and put my things in order. In short, I've finished. Now I am asking for a 'pass' to go to town."

"I don't have to check. You're a seasoned, orderly soldier and I'm sure you've done everything right." (Here it comes, Ankori thought with displeasure. After the compliment — a fatherly suggestion. He hadn't erred.) "Now, take a seat. Rest. After a wintry night of driving we're all tired. What's the rush? What have you got to do there? The cinemas don't open until five, you know."

Ankori was hard put to bite back the laughter rising up within. He knew the fatherly sergeant meant well, and he had no wish to hurt his feelings by being rude. He thus made do with a curt sentence, that seemed to him neutral and far from offensive: "I wasn't planning to go to the cinema, sergeant."

Shmulke considered for a moment. All at once, he released a staccato, "Oh-oh", as if the soldier's intent had suddenly dawned on him. He was not a preacher by nature, but now he reacted like a confessional priest: "If you are driven by an overpowering urge, put it off at least until tomorrow. We're screening a film on venereal diseases this evening and you really should watch it before you go there. Italy is Sodom and Gomorrah in this respect."

"I'm not going where you think. It's just that the museum closes at six and I'd like to get in a three-hour visit." The sergeant was totally confounded. Without showing a jot of empathy, he let out: "OK. All sorts of strange people want all sorts of strange things. You want a 'pass'? Here!"

The "pass" issue was repeated the next day too, which was Company maintenance day and ended with a thorough cleansing of the stains of grease and the odor of petrol and perspiration.

Work stopped at exactly two o'clock. On both days, the "pass" was already on hand but its issue, for some reason, was shrouded in silence, as if couched in some sort of "huff", apart from the recipient's smiling "thank you". What went through the sergeant's head on those days, and why he had resorted to a unilateral, self-imposed "fast of speech", as the Sages call it, God alone knows, just as God alone knows what caused him "to break the fast" on the fourth day.

"Well? Are you satisfied?" — he asked, his tone suggesting a warranted conclusion following on from a conversation they had conducted, each in his own mind and wordless. Not bothering to wait for an answer, he voiced an unexpected request. "At our first conversation (he said), you mentioned the word 'museum'. On my trips with the other unit, I occasionally saw the Italian word 'Museo' on an impressive building, but I didn't dare go inside. I've never been inside a church either. Out of fear, maybe, or because I was brought up to think that Jews shouldn't go there. But I understand that these are the most beautiful things there are in Florence. In short, if you agree, I would be pleased and interested in accompanying you wherever you plan to visit."

When Shmulke came to the end of his speech, he looked as if he had taken a load off his mind. He must have been kicking the idea around for the two days of his silence (the soldier thought). Such self-examination takes courage, courage to believe that it's not too late, courage to reach a decision and courage to ask for help.

The help, the soldier-cum-museum-lover was glad to extend, and he immediately drew up an itinerary for their joint touring. A few days later, the two new friends set out to explore Florence.

Meanwhile, something happened in the Unit that had not been anticipated — unless by Major Aaron, who may have proposed it: 178 was temporarily detached from the British Eighth Army and attached to the U.S. Fifth Army under General Clark. Major Aaron presented the development as a compliment, a mark of citation, a challenge, and proudly displayed the American tags that were to be pinned onto 178 uniforms.

The soldiers, including sergeants and petty officers, were very and visibly upset. Pride? A citation for the Company? A challenge? A compliment? Who needed American tags? What — ours weren't good enough?

Those who had a sick thirst for a pat on the shoulder from one or another *goy*, did view the measure as a compliment and a citation. But most of 178 saw it as a purely technical arrangement, and unjustified at that, especially as the Unit was soon to return to the Eighth Army and be incorporated into the Jewish Brigade. A challenge? Yes, a challenge it certainly was: to acquit themselves ably at work that the Americans performed with heavy, four-wheel drive Macs and three drivers per truck, when 178 had only light trucks that were good for desert conditions, not for the heavy mud of the Tuscany winter, and only one driver per truck. Nor was the British gear adequate. Oh, if only the Eretz-Israeli soldiers had been issued the kind of rubber boots that the Americans wore to scrabble through the petrol-and-grease-enriched mud, their lives would have been a whole lot easier.

The line plied by the Unit was Florence-Livorno Port (on the western coast), and the drivers were undeterred even by slides in the mud. But did the Americans really need 178? The Jewish soldiers did as they were ordered, they were however disgusted by the pretence of it being a glorious mission. The only cherry on the icing was the opportunity, when at leisure in-between missions, to visit nearby Pisa and climb up the Leaning Tower, or to delight in the gem known as Lucca and the belted wall hugging its hips and its lanes and squares.

A fresh breath of Eretz-Israel soldiering arrived in Florence one day, in the form of a Jewish Brigade troupe known as "*Me'ein Zeh* (Nigh Like" — a Hebraic imitation of the sound of the British ENSA [Entertainments National Service Association]). Since one of the troupe stars was Yossi Yadin (along with the well-known Hannah Maron) — and Yossi in 1937, together with Zvi Ankori, had founded the Gordonite Zionist youth movement branch in Jerusalem — the then-friend and now-soldier requested the job of being the troupe's driver. Thus, he not only served as their guide in Florence but attended their rehearsals. By the end of the evening, all of Jewish Florence was able to sing the song by Yitzhak Yitzhak and Zvi Ben-Yosef:

### Oh Titus, Titus

Titus Imperator,
Oh would that you had gazed
On whom goes real triumph,
Who deserves today all praise!
Having crushed Judean fighters
A triumphal arch you've raised,
Now come Eretz-Israeli heirs
To Judeans of ancient days.
  Beneath the arch 'twas built
  By order from above
  Stands a Hebrew soldierly two-some
  In uniform and love.

# VI

Oh Titus, Titus, oh would that you could see the 178 convoy in the first week of December 1944, the wheels of its vehicles plowing the soil of the *imperium*, yours and that of the grotesquely black-helmeted megalomaniac who, in the twentieth century, aspired to emulate you and the glories of the past! More than thirty trucks and additional HQ and workshop cars paved their way southwest from Florence and the Apennine slopes to the lowlands of the Tyrrhenian shore, some of the mountains wearing a fine lace of thin rain and winter mist, some gleaming white in their snow-capped peaks.

Look: the vehicles are entering the gates of Rome, your capital, Titus, with blue-and-white Stars of David on the sides of their doors, and driving through the streets on a journey the like of which history has never seen. They have come — in their uniforms, with their weapons and cars — not as conquerors nor as avengers but as liberators from the yoke of Germans, the same Germans whose forefathers and whose land you battled with, Titus, when you were young.

The passions that gripped the lads upon setting out on the long trek from Firenze and upon entering Rome stemmed not only from the memories of the past but from the prospects of the near future: the co-option of 178 as the transportation unit of "The Jewish Brigade Group", as it was formally called in English, or simply "*HaBrigadah*" in Hebrew. From now on, every soldier was to sport the blue-white-blue Brigade insignia beneath the upper sleeve seam, with a golden Star of David imprinted on it.

In Fiuggi, an hour's drive from Rome, the Brigade trained for battles that were to recapture the rest of Italy from the hands of its former ally and current conqueror, and advance from there to the heart of occupied Europe. It was the first time that a Jewish force, including 178, functioned under an independent Jewish command, a command headed by the Jewish Brigadier General, Levi Benjamin. When the call came, 178's drivers, this time with Major Shalit in charge, would drive Brigade soldiers to the lines, servicing the front efficiently and with the necessary mobility.

"Let me tell you something about the Brigade" — Tayyish began to tell the men one evening in Rome, when it seemed to him that quite a few of them were apprehensive and wondering "whether the 'match' between 178 and the Brigade would succeed."

To be sure, 178 knew joy and pride at having been chosen from all the Companies to become an organic part of the Brigade, but these could not totally dismiss the fears nursed by some serious members of the Unit about the possible changes ensuing from the Company's co-option.

Some lamented that the Company would lose the intimacy it had developed over four years of living together in desert heat and Apennine cold, in the fervor of the advance from el-Alamein and in the boredom of the months in Malta, in the work with liberated Jewish communities and with Holocaust refugee survivors, and the publication of *HaHayal HaIvri*, the Unit's independent newspaper; this intimacy had stood the test of years and deeds and had only deepened over time.

Some regretted that the autonomy of the small Company, which, as everyone acknowledged had done great things on its own, would be lost in the new large framework, and that its former actions would soon be forgotten or simplistically ascribed to the common denominator of "The Jewish Brigade", even though the latter had not even existed at the time.

(This did in fact happen, and goes on to this day, more than half a century after the war. The public is more eager to remember "the Brigade", surrounded by the aura of the upgraded Jewish force it represented, than to pick its way through the maze of three-digit numbers that the British army assigned the Hebrew units, in spite of their praiseworthy early achievements.)

The old-timers found it hard to accept the situation that new recruits would change the nature of the original volunteerism shown by 178 and its sister units: faithful to Labor Eretz-Israel, made up of numerous kibbutzniks, and obedient to the orders of the Haganah — such as transferring Italian weapons abandoned on the Libyan front to Eretz-Israel or directing refugees to sites from where they would clandestinely sail to Palestine. Brigade conscripts would no doubt continue the work that had been started, but in the larger framework, both the openness and the hominess would vanish.

"Let me tell you something about the Brigade" — Tayyish repeated his overture after managing to hush the noisy talk and wrangling about 178's future in the Brigade: "A few months ago, around the end of October, I was about to return from leave in Eretz-Israel when a friend told me that the 'buffs' were leaving for Italy. They added me, without any problem (rank *does* help) to the Brigade's three future regiments (which out of habit continued to be known as 'buffs') and we set out for Alexandria by train. On November 1, we all boarded a large passenger ship which, after a few days sailing on calm seas, anchored at Taranto Port. The trucks were already waiting on the docks to drive the regiments to Fiuggi, a name I hadn't yet heard. A British sergeant — RASC like ourselves — was in charge of the trucks and he told me that it was a resort town, south of Rome. In that season, it was empty of vacationers and the guys would be able to obtain excellent quarters. Then I was met by one of our own cars, which, to my surprise, drove me straight to Firenze. I hadn't known at home that you had already left Ancona. Anyway, the Brigade is here and I'm telling you: they're great guys! We'll get along just fine."

Meanwhile, until the Brigade got into the full swing of things, 178 enjoyed a quasi-vacation, thirstily drinking in all that Rome had to offer. Years later, they may have looked back on the Rome period as the richest in cultural fare of all the years of their service. At the same time, they performed short-distance driving duties, efficiently seeing to the Brigades' needs.

Ankori, who had been to Rome half a year before his Unit had the good fortune to reach it, systematically applied himself to filling in the gaps of what he had missed then, due to his obligations. Now, on his second Roman round, he paid almost-daily visits to the opera. For the first time in his life — since opera in Eretz-Israel, founded and directed by Golinkin, was still in its infancy — he had the privilege of watching and hearing the entire Italian operatic repertoire in top performances by the greatest of singers. In this way (he consoled himself), he atoned for his forced interruption in playing an instrument; true atonement, he expected, would come when he could diligently apply himself to the accordion in place of the unemployed violin. Ah, Verdi's stirring operas! Ah, the stormy choral "Dies Irae" in his "Requiem"! Ah, the dialogue of flute and soprano in Donizetti's "Lucia di Lammermoor"!

And blessed be the divine Maria Canniglia, the nightingale of Rome. Ankori also looked out for the renowned Tito Gobi whom he remembered from musical films, but he was told that the artist was banned because of his former appearances before Wehrmacht soldiers. All in all, it was a brutal period of wantonly settling political and patriotic accounts: women's heads were shaved, fascist jackboots were relentlessly hunted down, and the day was not far off that Mussolini and his mistress would hang by their feet, their heads swinging down.

Occasionally, as he sat in the auditorium of Rome's opera house, his fancy took flight: he saw himself sitting with his mother at the Vienna opera — her visits there being a frequent topic of the stories she told her children — the two of them applauding "Rigoletto", the performance of which had just ended on Rome's stage. Illusion and reality merged, the audience rose for a standing ovation, and the son couldn't tell whether he was clapping for Rome or for Vienna. Only one thing was clear to him: he would soon return home and, at his mother's request, he would play "La donna è mobile" on his violin, from the notes that she had bought him at Seiden's bookstore.

Still resounding with the previous night's arias, the auditorium turned into a political arena in the morning. It was interesting to watch the revival of democracy in Italy, a country that, for twenty years, had banned all political parties but the fascist one, had been ruled by dictatorship and muffled free speech. It was astonishing how quickly the parties reorganized and embraced the old-new political jargon. The Italian people awoke from a generation-long slumber and, in a twinkling, easily oriented itself in the maze of the world's political map.

As a socialist, Ankori was attracted by the speeches of Pietro Nenni, the socialist leader, and of Palmiro Togliatti, head of the Communist Party.

To his gratification, he found the two sitting together on the opera stage, both warmly cheered on by the audience. The drift towards creating a "united front" seemed to be a wise lesson learned from the tragic mistake of Germany, where the split of the Left had helped Hitler rise to power in 1933.

December! The last month on the Gregorian calendar of 1944, a month that marked the first anniversary of 178's landing in Italy and the first month of its incorporation into the Jewish Brigade. The Company could look back in satisfaction: apart from its military work, which had earned compliments from the British command, it had managed to do quite a bit on behalf of Diaspora Jewry, which, after all, was the main reason the Eretz-Israel soldiers had volunteered: the distribution of food, clothing and blankets to refugees; the Ferramonti mission; the Rishonim farm; the *aliya* of the Ferramontesi to Eretz-Israel; the Polacco School and Via Balbo youth group in Rome; and the many rescue missions, camouflaged by Movement Orders boasting the name of RASC TTG Company as the issuing authority, outsiders having no idea that the latter three letters, ostensibly British, were a secret code for a wily Arabic-Yiddish hybrid, *"Tilhas Tizi Gescheften"* — literally: kiss-my-ass business (ha-ha) — proof that even daring deeds taking place in the dark and away from headlines need not be devoid of humor.

December 25, then and now. Christmas 1943. The day after 178 reached Italy. What a meal! Stuffed turkey and free-flowing beer. After the glutting, a restorative sleep descended on the tableside feasters. Blessed sleep! Canceling the pointless speech forced on both the lecturer and the audience. Today's resolution: no such blowout banquet in 1944!!

Objective circumstances made it impossible to break the resolution. On Christmas Day 1944, 178 was already in Rome while the Brigade itself was a hundred kilometers away from its subordinate fleet of 178 trucks. The Company had no interest in whether or not a festive holiday repast was to be laid on for the Brigade as for all British units. It assumed that the Brigade had skipped it since, both officially and in name, it was Jewish. Instead of the denied banquet, some of 178's lads chose, along with tens of thousands of Catholic faithful and the merely curious, to stream to the papal midnight Mass at St. Peter's Basilica. Ankori also went. He, a Jew, brought along the Catholic canteen employee, a resident of Rome, who, wearing tattered clothes, had never dared cross the sanctuary threshold.

Tens of thousands of people who did not manage to get indoors stood outside the cathedral on the huge square framed by Bernini, a Baroque artist, in a semi-circle of pillars on the right and another semi-circle on the left, like two arms reaching out to the loins of the church. From time to time, a wave of excitement swept over the crowd at the sight of the cardinals in red, the priests in black and the nuns in white facing the gate. Cries of "*Viva il Papa*" soared up to the dome, designed by Michelangelo, and, sliding down from there, they made their way into the cathedral through the open gate. All eyes then turned to the doorpost as if waiting for a miracle. But there are no miracles in our times. There was only the grandeur of the square, flanked by Bernini's pillars and supporting an Egyptian obelisk in the center. Had God been there, he would have blocked his ears at the cries of "*Viva*" for his earthly stand-in, and diverted his eyes from the grandeur built in His name. But God was not at the square. The square was and is godless.

Inside, as well, God shrank into a corner. In the enormous shrine, built in the form of a cross, thousands of Rome's citizens, pilgrims from all ends of the earth, Catholic schools, choirs and so forth, crowded together. The first Christmas in liberated Rome! A murmur suddenly passed through the hall. Here he was, Pius XII, heir of the fisherman from the Sea of Galilee. Enveloped in purple and gold like a Byzantine emperor, he was borne in the portable papal throne on the shoulders of the Vatican's Swiss guard, dispensing the sign of the cross in all directions. His face was like a monk's in an el-Greco painting. Trumpeting cries — "*Viva il Papa*" — the papal throne circled the center so that its occupant could be seen from all sides, to magnify the *Papa*'s majesty. Finally the *Papa* was lowered before the altar.

The Mass commenced. In front of the altar, the Pope was awaited by his cardinals, enlisted to rescue God from the corner He had fled to and to bring him back, captive between two large, binding covers, inlaid with silver and precious stones. From this heavy tome of hundreds of hand-written sheets of parchment containing Christian liturgy, the Pontifex Maximus would assign passages to his priests for them to read in turn under the tutelage of the High Priest. But the reading of the Latin verses sounded to the audience like irksome mumbling, and even those who managed to hear bits of what was being said, found it hard to understand the text. Only at the end of the passages would the cardinals vary the monotonous reading with a few notes of scarcely refreshing melody.

Under the inspiration of the holiday and in true longing for spiritual elevation, the public heard the liturgy ostensibly pave its way from afar, from between the thick yellow altar candles; and whether or not they understood the reading, they all accepted the divine duty in love and listened in awe and holy reverence to the Pope's prayer.

Paradoxically, the foreign listener, a Jew, was one of the few people to be pleased by the Latin reading. It was a challenge to the faculty of his memory, pressing him to detect in the Christian parallels and borrowings in Latin the earlier layers of Hebrew prayer tradition. And just as the "*Sanctus-Sanctus-Sanctus*" is easily restored to the bosom of "*Kadosh-Kadosh-Kadosh*" (Holy, Holy, Holy), in Isaiah (6:3), and its incorporation in Hebrew liturgy is illustrated in the text of the "*Shmoneh-Essreh*" prayer, the same was true of most of the rhetoric hovering in the space of the Basilica. Thus listening to the text, the foreign witness harkened back to the fount from which the early Christians drew their inspiration — regarding themselves, for most of the first century CE, as Jews, and even rebuking Peter for eating heathen ("unclean") food in Caesarea.

All at once, unconnected to the altar prayer, eight members of the Swiss guard arranged themselves in a straight row along the front of the altar, their faces to the Pope, their backs to the audience and, as if in response to a hidden signal, they knelt as one and were about to sing. A hush fell. So complete was the silence that, despite the presence of thousands of people, wax could be heard dripping from the altar candles. The German-speaking Swiss chose the best-known, best-loved non-liturgical Christmas carol, "*Stille Nacht, Heilige Nacht*" ("Silent Night, Holy Night"). It was the joint composition of two rural teachers, organ musicians in small churches in the Salzburg region, Austria, in the first half of the nineteenth century — the one not really a poet, and the other a mediocre composer whose other works have mostly been forgotten.

The performance was opened by the Swiss guard in the middle of the row, performing in German a solo of the carol's first, so well-known words. He was then joined by his companion on the right and his companion on the left. After these came the turn of the remaining guards on the right and on the left, each extension of the ensemble raising the volume of the voices until, finally, it seemed that a choir was singing the song.

Silent night, holy night
All is calm, all is bright
Round yon virgin, mother and child
Holy infant so tender and mild
Sleep in heavenly peace
Sleep in heavenly peace

1. Stil - le Nacht, hei - li - ge Nacht!
Al - les schläft, ein - sam wacht nur das
trau - te, hoch - hei - li - ge Paar. Hol - der
Kna - be im lok - kigen Haar, schlaf in
himmlischer Ruh, schlaf in himmlischer Ruh.

What was it about the song (the foreigner wondered, as he watched and listened to the Swiss performance at St. Peter's at the height of the World War) — a carol written and composed by artists scarcely known in Austria itself and certainly not outside the country — that had made it take wing and conquer every land in which it was translated? Its tune was sung for more than a hundred and twenty years, and there is good reason to assume that it would continue to bloom for many generations still to come. Its popularity was not due to what the song contained, but rather what it did not. It contained nothing of the ancient pomp, warranting solemnity, nor of the ritualistically oppressive aura of church dignity; nor did its words carry a lofty message for man and society. Whatever the reason, the carol forever changed the aspect of Christmas, lending it a folk festiveness, a family character that embraced all generations, and true faith, free of unnecessary gravity and gloom.

The Swiss role came to an end. The carol continued to reverberate and flutter in the church air like birds of paradise, its humble composers, Mohr and Gruber, never having dreamt how successful it would be in future years. Even Pius XII forced his monastic facial features into something akin to a smile of satisfaction. Ankori guessed that, now, at the opening of the second part of the Mass, all the choirs that had accompanied the first part of the altar reading would rise and, in full formation and full force, deliver a joint finale with the song's translations into the languages of their home countries. As a musician, he felt that in a church venue, where applause was unseemly, such a choral gesture would be a fine mark of the audience's love of the carol and a fitting expression of appreciation for the performers.

However, to his surprise and disappointment, there was no such gesture. The altar did buzz with activity during the second, more ceremonial, part of the Mass. But the choirs did not reappear, as if they had succumbed to a self-imposed silence. At the end of the carol, the Jewish soldier-visitor looked around. The faces he saw were unreadable and, unlike at the start of the service, somber. He saw in some eyes a sense of insult. Something strange and unexpected had just happened here and now (he told himself), and that "something" had nothing to do with the quality of the carol's performance which had been moving to tears. It had to do with something else entirely. What that was he couldn't quite put his finger on at the moment, but, knowing that Italians were extroverts, he did not doubt that he would find out once they got outside.

For sure, at the end of the service, the crowd started pouring out of the cathedral, wave by wave, and mingling with the masses on the square. The soldier looked at the unreadable faces of before, and saw them open up to reveal amazement, disappointment, protest, anger and even a sense of betrayal:

"Why German? It's only seven months since we've got rid of them, and their language is back again, here?"

"Do you remember the SS officers sitting in the front row last year, with the blood of Rome's Jews on their hands, which they had spilt only ten weeks earlier? And now again, at this holy site — German?!"

"That's not fair. The Swiss speak German and the carol was originally composed in German!"

"So what? Is it a sacred text? Canonical? Goethe or Schiller? There are wonderful translations or paraphrases, including in Italian, that are lovelier than the original. Between us, the melody is beautiful, but the words are less than mediocre!"

The disagreement broke off momentarily — not for lack of arguments, but in anticipation of a first stone-thrower, daring to aim at the windowpane of the building acknowledged to be the seat of the real culprit:

"Friends, don't delude yourselves" — cried the first person bold enough to identify the true target — "nothing, whether small or big, happens in the Vatican without the Pope's review and approval. The problem is not the German carol, but the man sitting in the Vatican. Whether he calls himself Pius XII or the name he was given at birth, Eugenio Maria, he is Pacelli through and through, from start to finish!"

"For more than twenty years, he conducted Vatican diplomacy" — another completed the denunciation. For years he lived in Germany as the Nuncio of the Curia, fell in love with the country, its language and culture, signed a concordat with it after the First World War and, when Hitler came to power in 1933, rushed to sign a concordat with the Nazi regime too, making no attempt to condemn its brutality. He kept quiet. Germany had concentration camps before Auschwitz, and not just for Jews. Pacelli kept quiet, because he was sympathetic not only to Germany but to the Nazi ideology. He worshipped power and was resigned to tyranny.

"How dare you besmirch the name of the Holy Father?" — several women in the crowd crossed themselves, furious — "Everyone knows that he secretly helped. He kept quiet to protect Catholicism in Europe."

"Is that so?" — the first speaker taunted. "To protect Catholicism, ha-ha. Here is an interesting coincidence for you: Pacelli took the papal throne in 1939. The very year that Hitler invaded Poland, the most Catholic country in northern Europe, maybe even more Catholic than Italy, and ignited the world war. But Pacelli did nothing."

"He also kept quiet when the Wehrmacht overran Italy a year and a half ago, including our Rome" — another protested — "Thank God the Allies liberated us, but half of Italy is still groaning under occupation. And Pacelli keeps quiet."

"Communist!" — some people shouted, spotting the red star on the man's lapel. Expecting curiosity about a communist's presence at church, he preempted the question: "My father used to bring me here every Christmas when I was a child. Before he died, he made me promise that I would keep coming here *in his name* until my last day.

"This I've done, except for last year. I couldn't bear the sight of SS officers in church. I have no doubt that my father forgives me." A murmur of respect for the man passed through the crowd.

While the Italian Christian crowd wavered between condemning Pius XII for both his silence and inaction, and rejecting criticism of the Holy Father, Rome's Jewish citizens were unanimous in feeling that the Pope had betrayed them during the Nazi occupation and that their own community leaders had abandoned them, misleading them to trust that Pius XII would save them from all harm. Beyond the general criticism, that the Vatican had failed to denounce the Holocaust being committed in the lands of Europe, the Roman Jewish community could not forgive Pius XII for turning his back on the Jews of his own city; he had done nothing to rescind the extermination program devised by the SS command "right under his nose" and, tragically, a quarter of the program was carried out. True, people with connections to the Holy See, including the Chief Rabbi, had found shelter in monasteries. But ordinary Jews, for the eight months of Nazi rule in Rome, had lived in the terrifying atmosphere of a witch-hunt. Virtually the only one to defend Pius XII, whether in synagogue sermons or private conversations, and to laud his attitude toward the Jews, was none other than the Chief Rabbi of Rome's Jewish community, Israel Zolli.

"What's the big surprise?" — the cynics wondered. "On the fourth day of the conquest, September 12, 1943, Zolli was already gone, instead of standing beside his threatened congregation. A month after he fled, the *akcja* took place, but our sainted rabbi, under the patronage of the Holy Father, saved his soul. He returned from the monastery to his job only after Rome was liberated, without regret and without apology."

❖ ❖ ❖

Zolli's, was perhaps the sorriest episode in the history of Rome's Jews. It is not clear if the rabbi — an eminent Torah scholar, a native of Brod, eastern Galicia (which till the end of WWI was ruled by Austria), after two decades in the rabbinical seat of Trieste (also part of the Austrian-German cultural orbit before the First World War) — had been invited to the vacated seat of Rome's chief rabbinate. Or was he? Rather, he had put himself forward for the job — the jewel in the crown of the Italian rabbinate — regarding it as the realization of personal ambition. Either way, he was appointed despite the opposition of the Italian-Jewish elite, who had a hard time accepting the leadership of an Ashkenazi rabbi from Eastern Europe, no matter how great a scholar he was.

The undermining of the status of Rabbi Zoller (his original Ashkenazi name by which his opponents made sure to call him) did not stop with his appointment, but only grew worse with time. It was not difficult to find differences between Italian manners, the traditional form of the Italian sermon or Italian rules of leadership and the comportment of Zolli, the stranger, the "*Ostjude*".

Little wonder that, given the open and latent hostility, Zolli developed a persecution complex, espying foes on every side. Even the Eretz-Israeli soldiers in Rome and their military rabbis — among whom Zolli sought allies, but who resolved not to interfere in community affairs — were, in the end, suspect in his eyes as wishing him ill. The straw that broke the camel's back was the suggestion that he relinquish his rabbinate seat and direct the Rabbinical Seminary instead. It was obvious to him that he had reached the end of the road.

In early February 1945, Rome's Great Synagogue hosted a large celebration: the wedding of an Eretz-Israeli soldier and a daughter of Rome. Rabbi Zolli conducted the marriage service and both U.S. and British military rabbis were honored with a portion of the blessings. The singing and dancing continued into the night. Of course, no one really expected the elderly rabbi to stay until the end. Zolli, went out and entered his office, immediately followed by the bride's father. The rabbi received the customary honorarium for the ceremony and, without a word of farewell to the military rabbis, he donned his fur coat and left the building.

Two days later, one of the inside pages of the local newspaper carried the news beneath an inconspicuous headline:

*Rome's Chief Rabbi Converted to Christianity*

## CHAPTER FOUR
# The Story of Jewish Company 178
### D. With the Brigade

### I

THAT NIGHT — the night of February 27, 1945 — was the eve of the Purim holiday. Although the driving rain had stopped since the day before, the Italian winter does have up its sleeve other means of destruction designed to break the spirit of the average soldier; and that night, it gleefully pulled them from its arsenal: a wake-up call two-and-a-half hours after midnight into the mist-laden darkness, the cold and the wind — all this preliminary to the back-breaking drive from the southern region of the country at the Tyrrhenian seacoast in the west, via the snow-decked Apennine Mountains as far as the northern extension of the Adriatic shore in eastern Italy, and from there to the front line. But the men of the Jewish Brigade were no ordinary soldiers, and all the winter's tricks could not dampen their eagerness to face the Germans in battle. For the sake of this moment they had volunteered for the British army; this was what they had been training for these past months, and for this they had traveled to Italy, which had been conquered by the Nazis and whose northern part was still awaiting liberation. They looked forward to reaching the heart of Europe and taking part in the rescue effort for the survivors.

Purim morning broke in the skies of Rome as the Brigade's

motorcyclists entered the gates of the capital, leading the way for the convoy of more than four hundred vehicles of all types, Stars of David emblazoned on their doors. They had left Fiuggi at 4:30 A.M., while heavy darkness was still covering the highway. At the end of the fifty-mile journey, the convoy was now moving through the streets of Rome, advancing in a long and dense procession on its way north. The mist mercifully dispersed, leaving to the gray skies the act of hanging heavy rags of rain and storm clouds over the city — a warning as to what was yet to come. Locals who arose early for work stopped on the pavement, surprised at the sight of the impressive motorized force, and guessing with a satisfied smile where it was heading. When they identified the Stars of David on the doors of the vehicles, they clapped their hands or waved in greeting. Since it was an early morning hour, no Jewish crowds were seen streaming into the streets, as they had done before, when they had welcomed the 178 Company convoy moving through the streets of Rome for the first time to join the Brigade at Fiuggi. Only Jewish youth, who had been informed by envoys of other Eretz-Israel units about the expected journey of the Brigade, were waving hands and singing *Heiveinu Shalom Aleikhem* ("We bring greetings — *shalom* — to you"). Ankori joyously noted the presence of his youngsters from Balbo.

The convoy left Rome and went out onto the open highway. Ankori regretted that the last memory he was taking with him from Rome — the Rome he loved — was the Zolli affair. True, the Jewish units in Rome had decided, as was their custom in other communities where they had operated over the last years, not to interfere in the internal affairs of the Roman community. But disregarding the Zolli affair was impossible — both because there had never been such a miserable incident, and there had never been such pain, not since the exiles of Judea had settled in Rome two thousand years ago. An earthquake indeed! The chief rabbi converts to Christianity! What a disgrace! What a tragedy! The Zolli tragedy — and there can be no doubt that Zolli was a tragic figure — encompassed the entire community, and placing the blame on one person did not excuse the whole community's intolerable attitude towards the rabbi that had pushed him to this desperate step, which, although desperate, could have no atonement.

This last memory permeated the driver's consciousness and would not abate. Driving in the convoy in the solitude of the cabin inflamed his wrath even more. As a matter of fact, in the weeks prior to the Brigade's movement from the Rome area, all sorts of stories started to come out into the open; some of them genuine testimonies, which only served to sharpen the pain.

This is what transpired from conversations with the military rabbis who took part in that wedding: immediately after the story of the baptism spread wings, the two rabbis went to Zolli's house, hoping for a denial from his own mouth. However, the latter answered in an angry tone: "Indeed it's true. I am a convert out

Jewish Brigade convoy advancing in the streets of Rome,
on its way to the front.
(*From Niv A.h.i.m. soldiers' magazine*).

of spite!" The convert recounted his long-standing complaint that he had not been properly respected, that his status had been willfully undermined and that the community leaders had mercilessly humiliated him. The antagonists, who detected in this account a supportive attempt on behalf of the rabbis to "understand" the psychological breakdown of the man, claimed that the chief rabbi's step had certainly not come as an immediate reaction to any injustice, but had been a long time in the making. Nevertheless, the rabbi did not stop taking his paycheck from the community he had betrayed. On that tragic day, he collected his honorarium for conducting the wedding, and from there he went straight to the church to be baptized.

It was also reported that in the baptism ceremony, as was customary, the rabbi selected a new Christian name for himself. And what was the name he chose? Eugenio Maria — the name of none other than Pacelli, before the latter became Pius XII. It is self-evident, then, that Zolli's defense of the Pope in his sermons to the community was not an expression of a learned opinion, but an act that heralded his future personal step. In this connection, some accusers recalled that they saw the rabbi in the company of priests and monks who supposedly had come to him to learn the meaning of a Hebrew word or verse in the Bible. There were also others who claimed they had seen him bare-headed in their company. At the time, no one had paid any attention to this evidence. On the contrary, people had been proud of the papal establishment's admiration for their rabbi's learnedness. Now, however, everything assumed a different slant; it seemed that these things had not been innocent after all.

Some, relying on a source within the church, whispered about a supposed "deal". If there had been a "deal", clearly both parties guessed wrongly. Possibly the heads of the papal establishment presumed that the rabbi's conversion would lead to more conversions, but the reality was completely different. Anger at the rabbi's act united the people, and no one in the community abandoned the religion of his forefathers. On the other hand, if Zolli thought that in return for his conversion he would be given an important position in one of the academic institutions of the Vatican, he was in for a great disappointment. In the end he was forced to make do with teaching beginners' Hebrew to novice priests. Thus, paradoxically, he, the learned rabbi, who had considered the offer to give up the rabbinate and run the Rabbinical Seminary instead as an affront, lost his rabbinate by his conversion, and instead of teaching in a higher rabbinical academic institution, was introducing novice priests to the intricacies of the Hebrew alphabet.

Once the community had recovered from the blow, about a week before the soldiers from Eretz-Israel journeyed to the front, the presidents of all the Jewish institutions and organizations in Rome, as well as selected guests — the two military rabbis, the American Major Berman and the British Captain Hochman, and Dr. Nakhon (one of the former leaders of Italian Jewry and now on the staff of the Jewish Agency in Jerusalem) — were invited to an emergency meeting on February 18, 1945, in order to publicly condemn Zolli's conversion to Christianity, and try to decide how to heal the community's pain. With this the Zolli episode came to a close, as far as Ankori had been acquainted with it before he left Rome with the Brigade.

Only months later did he find out about the rest of Eugenio Maria Zolli's path after he converted. It turned out that Zolli himself — the Zolli "who was" — had understood the absurdity of the situation into which he had fallen. The scholar prodigy left the ridiculous position of teaching Biblical Hebrew for Beginners to novice priests, and donned the monastic cloak of a Franciscan. He went up to Assisi, capital of the order of St. Francis, and shut himself up in the monastery. Since then, none of his former acquaintances had taken any interest in his fate, and he, bearing his new Christian name like a wreath of thorns on his forehead, was lost in the abyss of oblivion.

The convoy continued moving northwest as planned, and, further along its journey, it entered the maze of Apennine ranges, their peaks covered with snow, while the sun coming out had added a gleam to their whiteness. The route that crosses the mountain chains is difficult for both driver and vehicle. But the view is breathtaking. In the end, after long hours of tiring, and sometimes dangerous, driving, the convoy proudly conquered most of the Apennine heights, and, as twilight fell, began carefully descending the eastern Apennine slope. Descending, the drivers were stunned by the far-off dark silhouette of the strip of settlements on the Adriatic shore. The sea was already enveloped in darkness and slumbering peacefully. Only the white foam forelocks of gentle waves — rising up and down as though they were the creatures of legend, rising up above the waters and dipping into them in rhythmic motions, rising and falling again — gave the night sea an appearance of movement. Ankori had to focus his weary gaze on the back of the truck in front of him, but could not contain himself and stole occasional furtive glances right and left in order to absorb a trace of the enchanted landscape that spun the coastal road from somewhere to someplace.

The drivers of 178 knew the settlements of the Adriatic Coast well, beginning with the heel of the Italian boot to as far as Ancona, and knew the extent of the destruction concealed by the darkness. But all this was history. This time the cars were bypassing Ancona from the north, and continuing to move for some distance on a road they had never previously traveled, a road that had apparently had its full measure of bombing from the air. Between Fano and Pesaro the motorcycle guides indicated the entrance to the night parking lot.

The drivers were tired, as were the soldier-"passengers" of the Brigade battallions, their bones aching from the crowding inside the trucks. After the hard journey — the officers announced — the next day will be designated a day of rest, and after that the long-awaited moment would arrive: the journey via Rimini to the front. The Brigade's three foot-battalions with their adjuncts would encamp in Cervia, Ravenna province, while 178 and its fleet of trucks would park in Faenza, at the rear of the Brigade. From there, its drivers would operate a continuous motorized connection with the foot regiments, in order to equip them with food, ammunition, clothing in place of what had been worn out in action, and emergency medical equipment. Those present at the evening call were all young, and obviously keen to go out to battle. No wonder, then, that at the beginning of the journey, when the officer mentioned Ravenna, he did not dare express in words that there might be casualties, heaven forbid, and that then the drivers of 178 would lead the victims to their eternal rest in the military cemetery next to Ravenna.

Ankori's heart missed a beat on hearing the names of the towns where the Jewish Brigade would be camping, ready for battle. Rimini! Ravenna! Those were the cities of Dante, the cities of his life and inspiration, and the entire province was his adopted country, after Florence, in her foolishness, exiled one of her greatest sons. "Fate did me a favor," felt the student-turned-soldier, admirer of the thirteenth and early fourteenth century poet, whose eternal verses, and most of all the verses of *The Inferno*, filled his memory while driving. "Fate did me a favor" — he repeated to himself — "the two ideals that ignited my spirit during these years while I was stationed in Italy and heard Italian around me have miraculously merged together: my military duty in Italy to liberate this land, and Dante's memory. I pray that just as in his poem he threw his enemies into the Inferno, so will he strengthen us spiritually to throw the Jews' greatest enemy into the same fire."

"Well, tomorrow we'll rest and the day after tomorrow we'll advance to the front via Rimini; most of the soldiers have never heard this name before. It may happen that we shall pass by Rimini, which is just a step away, and my colleagues will cast an apathetic eye over the ruin of the picturesque city whose wounds the sea cannot wash away. Possibly, one of them will add sin of scorn to sin of apathy. 'Big deal!' he'll say. 'You can find similar destruction in the other coastal settlements, too.' Then another soldier, one who insists on details, will ask himself who was responsible for this destruction — was it *our* Lancasters, when the Germans blocked here the only road through which the Eighth Army could advance? Or maybe it was *their* Stukas, which aimed at throwing us out of this strategic city, which is situated on the crossroads of the ancient Roman Via Emilia and Via Flaminia? Only Dante's reader will shout into space, "Oh, Francesca da Rimini, you pure adulteress! Do you still languish in the Inferno, where Dante met you, because your husband the murderer prevented you, by way of the murder, from atoning for your sins? But there is some consolation: you are in a comparatively high and comfortable region of the Inferno, while he, the assassin, has fallen into the depths of hell!"

Indeed, the public's knowledge of Rimini was not due to its own virtue as a city and harbor, but was thanks to Dante's story about Francesca, the daughter of one of the important personalities of Ravenna in the thirteenth century, and wife of the ruler of Rimini, Giovanni Malatesta. Francesca and Paolo, Giovanni's brother, had fallen in love, even though they were both married to other people. Were they both adulterers? Certainly. Were they to be condemned to hell? No doubt. Francesca's husband murdered the pair. Even in the Inferno, Francesca did not regret her sentiments and continued her invincible love. Dante, although a man of morality and faith, supported his generation's sympathy for Francesca. Generations to follow were also shocked by Malatesta's assassination of Francesca, and despite the adultery, were bewitched by her display of love.

Some say: an emotionally stirring story. Others add: remarkable for its period. In any case, Francesca's name overshadowed the name of her city, but, at the same time, brought Rimini into the consciousness of the world. Writers tried to add their own slant on the story of her love. Directors wanted to portray the drama. Tchaikovsky went one step further: he illustrated the act in a symphonic fantasy, which is no less exciting than the original story. And what a wondrous coincidence! Never dreaming that he would ever visit Rimini, Ankori, when in Rome, went to a concert in which Tchaikovsky's "Francesca da Rimini" was performed. More than any other artist, Tchaikovsky succeeded in demonstrating that this confession of love, which has no equal in all literature, takes place in hell.

The last day of the short month of February in 1945 was set aside for the Brigade's rest. But the Brigade soldiers' zeal to breathe the smell of the front convinced the commanders not to hold up the journey. After all, the distance from the units' nighttime stopping place to their final destination was not great. Hence, the following morning, the Brigade continued on its predetermined route north: indeed, it passed by Rimini, and in a short time reached the region of the Senio River, which would serve as the battleground, and, crossing it, would permit the Eighth Army a leap forward. The three battalions positioned themselves in Cervia. Road signs in Hebrew with the symbol of the Brigade were set up at the junctions, and the Brigade's MPs directed traffic. The Hebrew flag was raised to the top of a high flagpole, so that the German soldiers, entrenched on the other bank of the river, could see it with the naked eye. They expressed their feelings clearly with continuous bursts of fire from their Spandau guns. But the eyes of the twelve German POWs whom the battle patrol brought back from its tour, while flickering with the natural fear of a captive, openly reflected anxiety over anticipated "Jewish retribution". This of course did not take place, and their treatment was such as dictated by the laws of war.

178 Company set up camp a short distance behind the battalions, next to the city of Faenza on the ancient Via Emilia which descends to Rimini. The camp was situated in the shade of flowering almond trees. The feelings that these trees aroused in the young soldiers' memories, reminding them of the planting celebrations in the Tu-biShvat period, coinciding with the bloom of almond trees, remained hidden in their hearts, so as not to contradict the myth of the hardened Land of Israel soldier.

Faenza's world renown since the fifteenth century is due not to its orchards, however lovely and invigorating they may be, but to a special, high-quality type of ceramics made there. In France and while French was the international language of the West, this type of ceramics was called "faience" after the city. However, the name of Faenza as the camping site of 178 related not only to its being the departure point for driving missions in the service of the battalions, but the center of shared festive events for soldiers of the entire Brigade. Thus, on April 2, during the intermediate days of Passover, the soldiers of the three battalions joined 178 Company at the camp in order to listen to a speech by Moshe Shertok (later Moshe Sharett), "Foreign Minister" of the Jewish Agency, who had come to Italy on an official visit to the Eretz-Israeli units.

Also in Faenza, two days later they celebrated the unforgettable performance of Hannah Rovina, who bewitched the Brigade soldiers with a Soviet war ballad that had been translated from Russian to Hebrew, "Wait for me and I will return". She even taught the soldiers new tunes for texts of the Passover Haggadah, and the latest Land of Israel hits. Her erect, regal posture and warm attitude towards the Jewish soldier, whoever he might be, brought the Brigade a breath of the good old Land of Israel, the Land without uniform that kept on with its daily work and cultural life, thus lavishing serenity and security upon its sons who had donned uniforms, and wandered far from home in the service of the nation.

While these occasional highlights intermittently poured joy and satisfaction into body and mind, the daily routine of battle demanded the whole person, twenty-four hours a day without cease. Just four days had passed since the Brigade had arrived in Cervia. On March 5, the three battalions were already under fire, taking responsibility for the whole eastern zone of the line and being involved day and night in clashes with the enemy. The hardest battles were on March 18 and 19, in which the Brigade suffered heavy losses. It crossed the Senio at its upper end, establishing a bridgehead there from which it harassed the retreating enemy without mercy. Thus, on the eastern section of the line, conditions ripened for an all-out attack on April 9 across the Senio by the Eighth Army, while on April 16 the American Fifth Army joined in on the west. The goal was to take over the valley of the great river, Po, where the Germans had flooded the whole area with its waters in order to hinder the armies' progress. They understood that this was the crucial battle for control over Italy, and they put up a stiff fight. On April 12 and 13 the Brigade fought battle after battle, and the force suffered additional casualties until the Germans were finally pushed out of the area. The direct German resistance had completely collapsed, and the route to northern Italy was breached at two points, apart from several pockets of resistance which the Italian partisans wiped out.

Thus, alongside the advancing American force, the partisans liberated Milan in the northwest, second of Italy's cities in size and perhaps first in importance, and Genoa, the largest harbor on the Ligurian Sea. In the northeast, the partisans took advantage of the victory of the Eighth Army (and the Brigade), fighting to clear the university town of Padua of traces of the enemy, and to liberate the legendary Queen of the Adriatic Sea — Venice!

Distant some twenty kilometers from Cervia is Ravenna, ancient capital of the Western Roman Empire, after the city of Rome was deserted. Following the Byzantine conquest in the sixth century, Ravenna became second only to Constantinople in importance and beauty. The churches and historic monuments were encrusted with majestic mosaics, considered among the most beautiful in the world (including the mosaic wall with the image of Emperor Justinian and Empress Theodora). The city was conquered by the Canadian Corps around two months prior to the Brigade's arrival. But despite the Canadian conquest, the Brigade's soldiers were busy in daily confrontations with the German forces, as the Senio area was the last and most crucial battlefield. Consequently, the Brigade had no time to visit Ravenna's delightful treasures.

Yet, paradoxically, there was another aspect of Ravenna that attached the Brigade to it forever — the nearby military cemetery in Piangipane. The uniqueness of this burial place, in contrast to the big military cemeteries, was that only victims of the battles in the Senio area were interred there, mostly Canadians from the first stage of the fighting and Brigade victims from the last stage of crossing the Senio and the thrust forward. The bodies of thirty-three Brigade fighters remained in Italian soil, and the Stars of David rising over their resting place bore witness to the part of

Eretz-Israel in the war for the Senio. And now, where are you, Justinian, Christian Emperor of Constantinople, after you have passed so many laws against the Jews, objects of your hatred? From your golden image, encrusted in the mosaic in the Basilica of San Vitale in Ravenna, you surely see the forest of Stars of David, commemorating the Jews who fell in battle to liberate *your* Ravenna from the enemy, a common enemy — the irony of history! — *ours* and *yours*?

## II

For a while the area between the Senio and the Po was a Hebrew preserve — the blue-white-blue of the Brigade flew over the roads; the trucks of the 178 brought German soldiers to POW camps. The Eighth Army advanced, and the Brigade with it. Enemy resistance was minimal. The tantalizing scent of the end of war clung to everything — the cars, the petrol, the motor oil, the various kinds of ammunition, the POWs, even ourselves. When, oh when, had we inhaled the intoxicating aroma of the almond trees in the orchards of Faenza? A hundred years ago? Have we aged that much, serving in the Brigade on the front?

Friday afternoon. The Po is already behind us. We are advancing to the junction. The left-hand road leads west, to Padua, the famous city that competes with Bologna and Paris for the title of "the first university city in Europe". The right-hand road ascends northeast, near Venice, but bypasses the city, as it is impossible to enter it on wheels, only by boat on the Canal Grande, which divides the city in the form of a huge "S", and is the main artery for transportation — a kind of Venetian highway.

A British military policeman signaled the convoy: "Venice has been in the hands of the partisans for three days. For two days there was a curfew over the city in order to weed out Nazi collaborators. Starting today, the city is open." Now the 178 had an urgent job in store: to seek information about the fate of Venetian Jews. The decision was made to send Ankori on foot into town to investigate the situation. On Sunday a car would bring him from the same point on the highway back to the camp.

Ankori gazed at the retreating convoy and remained alone on the road. Without hesitation he decided to follow the coastline and within an hour he had arrived, as he had presumed, at the first stop of the municipal water transport, the *vaporetto*. There were hardly any people at the station. Pairs of partisans, red ribbons on their arms and guns on their backs, were patrolling the area. There was no enemy. Rather, the patrol was a show of power and control vis-à-vis the community. "Ciao" to the soldier. Brothers-in-arms. The soldier asks about the *vaporetto*. "Only the main line of the Canal Grande is working today, once an hour. The gondoliers have joined the partisans. Tomorrow all the lines will work. We are expecting many 'tourist'-soldiers. The shops will open, too."

The *vaporetto* arrived, sailing down the Canal Grande to the center of town. Ah, Venice! Ankori had never been here before, but it seemed to him that he had always known the dozens of beautiful buildings that graced the banks of the Canal. The town was exactly as he had imagined it to be. He had kept this image in his memory since childhood, its impression getting ever stronger as he grew up. The cityscape had come to him from his mother. She had never visited Venice either, but had clothed its image along the outlines she had put together from photographs and travel books. And it was Mother who had encouraged the son to dream that one day he would visit Marco Polo's city in her company.

But, alas, upon awaking to the reality of Jewish Tarnów in the difficult years of crisis in Poland after the First World War, both had understood, to their disappointment, that Venice was only a daydream, and that there was no chance that their journey would ever come to fruition. Never, not in their wildest dreams, did they imagine that one day the son, wearing a military uniform, would arrive here at the height of a war, cruise the waters, and see the splendor of which the two had dreamed.

The *vaporetto* stop adjoined the *Rialto* — the largest of the bridges in Venice. It looked like a saddle that had been strapped on the back of a giant water animal, which, hidden from view, bound the two banks of the Canal to its hips, ready to leap forward. The soldier-emissary climbs onto the bridge and looks at the water, empty of any movement. "There is no sadder sight than water orphaned of boats. We'll wait for tomorrow" — he comforts himself. "And now, straight to the ghetto! That's where my mission lies. There I will certainly meet Jews, brothers. It's the eve of the Sabbath, and it is natural that they will seek consolation in the synagogue."

The history student knew, of course, that the separation of Jewish neighborhoods from the living areas of the Christian urban community did not start with the establishment of the ghetto in Venice in the early sixteenth century. He knew the source of the term. The Jewish-Venetian neighborhood had been founded in the backyard of a metal-working factory, and the term "ghetto" was derived from an Italian verb that defines the work of casting. Still, he found it hard to understand how and why a word with such purely local background, so prosaic and completely lacking in emotion, "merited" adoption even in diasporas far from Venice,

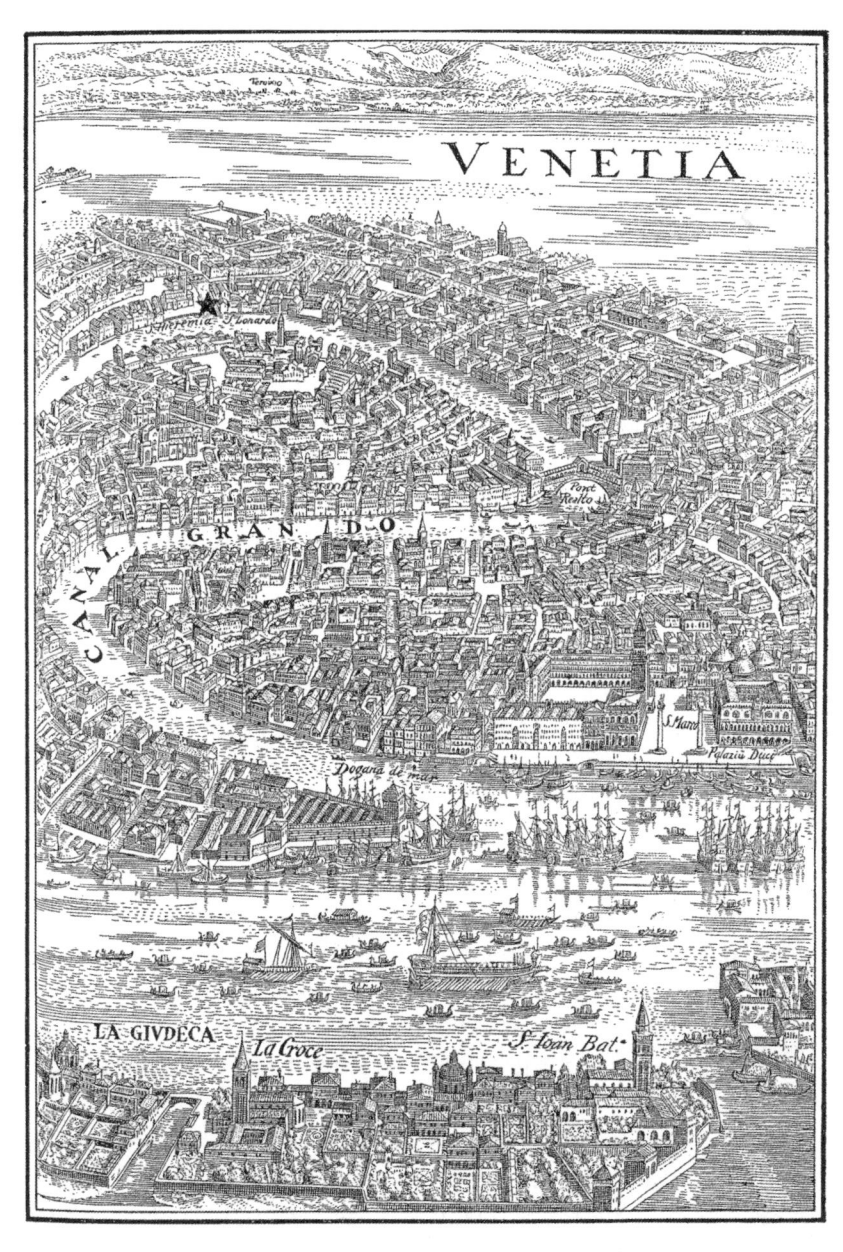

Venice: Wood carving from 1640. *From the Jewish Encyclopedia, 1905–09.*
(The Rialto bridge is in the center of the second bend of the Canal. The
star marks the location of the ghetto.)

and even caught on in the poorer non-Jewish neighborhoods of today.

Walking now to the original place where the patriarchs of Venetian Jewry had experienced the birth pangs of the ghetto, a tremor passed through Ankori's body. Here, in the place that his feet were treading for the first time — yes, here — decrees had been issued that had fashioned the Jewish inhabitants' way of life for centuries and served as models that affected scores of communities all over the medieval and early modern Jewish world. Here the living-area had been compressed into the size of an islet surrounded by water, until the only possible method of creating living space for children and grandchildren had been to build upwards. To this day, the top floors that had been added to the ghetto houses stand out from afar, small and miserable. Bowing his head at the arched entrance, which had a gate attached to it from the inside, the Jewish soldier felt that he was entering a place where holiness resided, a place that had been sanctified through the suffering of many generations.

The large synagogues in the ghetto, those with an oval-shaped interior, were still locked. Only one synagogue, the Levantine Synagogue, whose interior was rectangular, was open for Sabbath prayers and for the first gathering of the community after months of living in hiding. Upon its opening, hearts were also opened to the joy of renewed meeting of relatives and friends, and to tears upon discovering who was no longer there and would not return. Of two thousand Jewish families who lived in Venice before the outbreak of the war, only half had survived. Over the eight or so months of Nazi rule here — from the Allies' invasion of Sicily and South Italy to the last victories of the Eighth Army in which the Brigade had taken part — a thousand Venetian Jews, led by the rabbi of the community, had been sent to the extermination camps.

He who had not seen the joy and the tears of that Friday night could not imagine what liberation really means. Jewish soldiers had not yet reached this place, as it had been under curfew since its liberation by the partisans. The decision of the convoy command to let Ankori off to enter the town made him the first person to whom adults and youth alike clung because they saw the Brigade symbol sewn onto his sleeve and enjoyed hearing him speak Hebrew. At the end of the prayer service, the soldier-guest was asked to address the congregation. Excited on seeing the assembled survivors and grateful for being a witness to the Sabbath of liberation, the guest went up to the podium and brought to the redeemed brothers greetings from the Brigade in Hebrew and in Italian. The next day he also participated in the services, and was honored with being called up to the Torah. Word of the presence of a Jewish soldier from Eretz-Israel spread fast and also reached the Jews who had taken refuge in the homes of Christian friends during the Nazi occupation. Free now, they also came to the ghetto to join in the community's joy.

In the afternoon, the soldier debated whether to go into town and wander around San Marco and the Palace of the Doges, rulers of the maritime empire of Venice over generations, but he dismissed this thought out of hand. Would this not be like betraying his mission to the ghetto and its inhabitants? He had many visits ahead of him in future days in this legendary city. Thus he remained in the neighborhood the entire Sabbath, talking with scores of people, listening to the terrible stories from the period of the Nazi conquest, and being invited by several families to their homes. Already on the previous evening he had accepted a family's invitation to spend the night in the comfort of their home, and after the Sabbath he stayed the night with another family. He had been carrying some army food with him in a knapsack, and left it with the two families. The total experience of two nights and a day-and-a-half in the ghetto implanted in him a feeling of identification with the place, and hope that the inhabitants of the ghetto felt the same way towards him. In his mind, he had already completed his report, to be composed as after every mission and presented to the Brigade's "Diaspora Committee" that was overseeing all "Jewish activities".

The next day, Sunday morning, the soldier was about to return to the main road, where a car sent from his Unit would be waiting for him. But the arched opening through which he had entered the ghetto the day before yesterday was now choked with a battalion of photographers, led by the rabbi of the Brigade, Captain Gil. The *gabbai* (beadle) of the synagogue was waiting for him. An "Arc de Triomphe" was the only thing missing.

The reception begins.

The *gabbai* turns the iron key in the lock of the Levantine Synagogue, and the photographers take pictures.

Captain Gil wraps himself in a *tallith*, and the photographers take pictures.

Captain Gil opens the Holy Ark and the photographers take pictures.

Captain Gil hugs a Torah scroll and the photographers take pictures.

This was the finest hour of Captain Gil, who had liberated the ghetto.

"Photograph history in the making!" — he cried out to the camera-wielders.

In the 1960s, the ex-Brigade soldier was in Venice for long periods to do research in the historical archives of the colonial maritime state, and regularly visited the ghetto. He found that the large oval synagogues, which were locked on that first Sabbath after the liberation, had now opened their gates to worshippers and tourists. Yet, a veteran of the Second World War, in a forgivable outpouring of nostalgia, he asked to see the rectangular interior of the synagogue in which he had once enjoyed an unforgettable experience. Unfortunately, for some reason the Levantine Synagogue was always locked.

Until fifty years after those distant days that were forever etched in his mind, the unexpected occurred. On a trip to Italy that he and his wife, Ora, took with their granddaughters Yarden and Oran as a *bat-mitzvah* present, they included, of course, a tour of Venice and the Venetian ghetto. Wonder of wonders! The gate of the Levantine Synagogue was open, and from within came the voices of a group of American tourists and of the guide who accompanied them. Grandma and Grandpa Ankori and their granddaughters entered the hall and joined the group of tourists. The retired soldier looked around and a shiver ran through his body: yes, here is the rectangular wood ceiling; here are the railed steps ascending to the podium in front of the Holy Ark; here is the podium, from which he had delivered his speech to the congregation. The guide, whom the ex-soldier recognized immediately as the synagogue's *gabbai* of those days, finished recounting the horrors of the Nazi occupation, and went on to describe the first Friday night of the synagogue's liberation — the emotional meetings of the families that had been in hiding, the joy, and the tears. Then he added one more detail. A soldier from Eretz-Israel had come to the synagogue. He had been the first Jewish soldier to be seen in Venice, and had impressed all with his blue-white-blue symbol and his golden Star of David. Everyone had understood that this was the proud Jewish answer to the yellow Star of David that the Nazis had imposed on the Jews as a mark of shame. The soldier (the story went on) impressed the crowd even more with his speech from this podium, in Hebrew and Italian. Moved to tears, the worshippers had shaken hands with him, seeming to forget their troubles and suffering for a moment, because of the message and the messenger from Eretz-Israel.

"That soldier was I," called the man who had joined the tour late. All eyes turned toward him. Excitement gripped the tourists on seeing the subject of the story standing in front of their very eyes. The granddaughters clung proudly to their grandfather. True to the custom of those far-off days, he had never told them about that event, just as he had never shared the rest of his memories with them or anyone else. "Yes, I remember you," said the beadle, "and the ghetto inhabitants always used to mention you."

Thus it happened that the Levantine Synagogue of the ghetto became the scene of another unique emotional scene, just as that first excitement had been unique in those days. After the tourists left, the hero of the day asked the beadle," Do you have any photographs from then?"

"Certainly!" He hurried to the branch of the community office in the ghetto and returned with a large, thin file. "They only sent us five photos, but they are enlarged and we are planning to hang them up on the wall of the office as mementos. Here they are," — and he proffered the file to the veteran guest.

Ankori opened the file and pulled out photo after photo, reading the captions aloud and returning each photo back to the file without showing it to his companions:

"Captain Gil and the beadle opening the gate of the synagogue."

"Captain Gil going inside."

"Captain Gil wrapping himself in a *tallith*."

"Captain Gil opening the Holy Ark."

"Captain Gil taking the Torah scroll from the Ark and holding it in his arms."

"That's it?" asked Ankori. "And from that evening, the first Friday night after the liberation, there is no photo?"

"Of course not. Who had a camera then? Even if someone had run home to get a camera, he wouldn't have been able to take a picture. It was the Sabbath. Forbidden. Especially in a synagogue."

This was the latter of two defeats that the World War veteran suffered — this one a slight "ego" defeat fifty years later, unlike the first one, which came right at the end of the war and hit both body and soul.

## III

On May 2, 1945, the sun rising in the east over the Yugoslav border seemed to be deliberating where to send a celebratory beam of light in honor of the wonderful news that had been broadcast on the radio that morning: to the Italian Alps or to the Austrian ones? The official announcement said that Marshal Kesselring, commander of the southern front of the Wehrmacht, had signed an unconditional surrender in the office of the British General Alexander. At that moment all resistance ceased. Italy was free. Rejoicing and fireworks. But the Allies still had a lot of work cut out for them.

Truthfully, the cessation of activities mainly affected the Fifth American Army, which had battled the German rearguard in northwest Italy until May 2. Now that battle ended. This was not, however, the situation of the British Eighth Army and the Jewish Brigade, which were operating in the northeast. The German surrender brought no real change in their agenda or in their activities to clear the area of all German resistance. When Ankori returned from his visit to Venice, emotions churning without restraint, he found the driver of 178 company waiting for him on the road as prearranged. "You'll be surprised," the driver said with pride, as though boasting about something he had achieved himself. "This time I'll take you to the Austrian border itself. The day you left, the Brigade pushed through and spread out along the border on the Tarvisio line."

"That's really wonderful," marveled Ankori. "You'll see that *one of these days*, when we succeed in breaching the Austrian border, Tarvisio will become the natural gateway for en masse passage of refugees to Italy. Perhaps some of them will decide to remain and live here. That's their decision. But for most of them, Italy will be only an intermediate station for trying to get to Eretz-Israel "illegally", as the British saw it, or emigrating to other places of their choice. In short, the T.T.G. has a lot of work ahead, just when the war ends."

As he said this, Ankori did not envisage two things: that on returning to his unit on Sunday, the date he had defined as *"one of these days"* would fall before the end of that very week, and that the need for "breaching the Austrian border", as he thought, would be rendered unnecessary, as the Wehrmacht would surrender in Italy and southern Austria simultaneously.

There were other things he did not imagine — that he and two of his soldier-friends would be the first, yes, the first, to cross the border into Austria, the land in which Hitler, in 1938, had begun his aggressive annexations in Europe. Indeed, not more than an hour had passed since the historic broadcast was aired, when a truck from 178 set out full of food, blankets and clothing for distribution to the refugees, with three soldier-emissaries: Flaschmann, who had already performed the mission of emissary in the liberated Santa Maria camp in southern Italy; Ze'ev Katz, who in the past had taught Hebrew at the Pollacco school in Rome; and Ankori. As a "cover", they joined the military correspondent of the Eighth Army, Luria, who had received a staff car to cross the border on duty.

Scores of years had passed since that memorable journey on May 2, 1945, and still Ankori would lay on sleepless nights, his entire body and mind feeling what he had experienced on that day. A maddening experience — a combination of a road full of enemy soldiers and war equipment aplenty, with beautiful scenery of mountains and water on both sides of the road. It was a scene of such tranquility that were it not for what was happening on the highway, the war was all but erased from memory. The body longed to climb the Alps of Villach on the left of the road and pick from between the rocks the white, star-shaped edelweiss, which had erred in the calendar and were dreaming in warm May of snow past or snow to come. The eye yearned to reflect its blueness in the shiny blue mirror of Werther See, and take part, hypnotized, in the dialogue that the blue pond was carrying on with the blue of the sky. And when white clouds sailed across the sky, the eye would like to absorb and photograph their reflections and send them sailing, in parallel, in the calm waters of the lake.

As a matter of fact, there was no war here. The road that twisted between the scenery of mountains and of water was tidily smooth, with no trace of bombing or of tank chains mangling the virgin asphalt of the highway. Paradoxically, the war arrived here for the first time today, with the surrender. It came not as wars do — to conquer the enemy, but the opposite, with the Germans' shout to the British enemy: "Take us prisoner, quickly, and save us from Russian captivity!" Undoubtedly, this was Kesselring's consideration as well. When Hitler's suicide was publicized, and the red flag had cast its fear over Berlin, he took the urgent, independent step of separate surrender in the territories under his command — Italy and southern Austria. This he did not so much in order to save lives as to avoid falling into the hands of the Red Army, which already stood at the gates of Vienna, and the stories of its cruelty froze the blood in one's veins. Indeed, there still were, and would be, sporadic battles on the soil of the Nazi *Heimat*, but not far off, on May 8, the final defeat would arrive, and with it the victory holiday of liberated Europe.

Yes, there was no war here, and it came for the first time on this day, with the surrender — its sights, probably never recalled in military history and never to be forgotten by the four Brigade passengers of the staff car and truck. On both sides of the road, for kilometers, Wehrmacht soldiers in green uniforms and SS men in black uniforms, all armed to the teeth, waited for the British to disarm them and lead them, along with their weapons and transport, into captivity. But the British were not coming.

Apparently, faced with the suddenness of the declaration of surrender, the British were not ready to handle such a large number of prisoners. To transport them the British would even use the Germans' own vehicles, which were ready to start immediately, and were waiting for British motorcyclists to come and show them the way. The question of the availability of camps for absorbing the prisoners and of their preferred location — Italy or Austria? — had not yet been solved. Presumably, that morning the British military and state authorities were urgently checking into solutions. It is doubtful they remembered the departure of two solitary British vehicles of the Eighth Army, characterized by two different symbols on their doors — the staff car with the symbol of the Eighth Army, and behind it the truck with the Jewish symbol. Their drivers found themselves, to their surprise, within eye contact of an enemy corpus that had not been defeated but had surrendered voluntarily, and was properly organized and armed.

It is easy to guess what the Germans felt when they saw, from a distance, the British cars approaching. But it became clear to them, to their disappointment, that only two had come. They probably thought that these were the team of scouts that had come to examine the situation. In any case, from afar it was possible to determine the immediate bustle in the field, and how the soldiers in the first lines straightened up. What did the lone soldiers of the Brigade feel? "Oh, how exciting and dramatic it would be to recount," ruminates the author today, on writing these lines — "that I allowed the truck to advance slowly, by itself, as though moving in a slow-motion fantasy film, while I and my friends proudly showed off the golden Star of David and its blue-white-blue background with all their deeper meanings, casting spiteful, disparaging looks at the surprised Germans." But it was not so in reality. Without admitting it, anxiety gripped them on seeing the masses of the enemy, and many possible scenarios went through each and every mind, causing shivers: What if a nervous sniper who had been trained in the *Hitlerjugend* decided to shoot a last bullet in this lost war, as revenge against the Jews? What if a gang of Nazis approached the slow-moving car, pulled the driver from the cabin, and lynched him in revenge? No one would testify against his fellow, and the British investigating committee would never find the murderer. Even worse — it would check the dead man's papers and those of his friends, and discover that their movement permit had been issued by an anonymous TTG Coy, and then everyone would be in trouble. Without seeking advice from one another, the two vehicles began a dizzying race through what looked like a tunnel — its two walls being the two rows of soldiers — until they left the German forces behind.

Thus, what had been planned (in the envoys' fantasies) as a triumphant journey of the first soldiers of Eretz-Israel, brave and free of the fears and complexes of the Diaspora, into the depths of an enemy country, suddenly turned into an irrational, fearful flight, which would be forever remembered with a bashful blush and never mentioned to anyone (except here, for the first time). The hope, that once the nightmare ended, the rest of the way would be calm, is what helped the group to regain its composure, banish thoughts of failure and guilt, and continue adhering to their mission, with the confidence that it would be crowned with success.

When they burst into the light of the May sun from within the "tunnel" of uniforms and weapons of destruction that cast their threatening shadow from both sides, and when they saw the opening of the road, empty of all movement, the soldiers relaxed from the event. Almost exhausted, once again they looked to their left at the Alpine ranges of Villach, bearers of the edelweiss, which had so enchanted them at the beginning of the journey. With a glance at the scenery to the right of the road, they returned to sailing their thoughts on the blue waters of Werther Lake. After about half an hour, the first houses of Klagenfurt, the capital of the province, appeared in the distance. At that point, the three emissaries were hit by awareness of the fact that they had no sliver of information about the Jews who had lived in Villach and Klagenfurt before the war (if indeed they had lived there), or about their fate in the Holocaust. This was not like the immediate accessibility of the Jewish units to the communities of Italy or the refugee camps, or the initiative of the communities and the refugees on their part to create a connection with the soldiers of Eretz-Israel. So the first act of the soldiers, following their arrival in the region's government center had to be (so they decided) focusing on obtaining this vital information. The job was given to Ankori, while his two friends were to walk around the town square, so that the symbol of the Brigade on their sleeves or on the door of the truck might motivate some passerby to begin a conversation and identify himself as a Jew. Indeed, upon reaching the town square, with its impressive municipality building, and upon parking the truck, the soldiers acted as they had decided. Flaschmann and Katz walked beside the truck, while Ankori went up the staircase into the municipality offices. In answer to his inquiry, the town clerk pulled from the shelf a publication from May 1939, which listed twenty-nine people in Klagenfurt as "Jews according to the *Rasse*" (the Nazi racial laws), including eight "Jews by belief". Nowadays, he claimed, there were no Jews here or in Villach.

The investigating soldier left the municipality offices struck with doubts about the information he had been given. He leaned on the railing at the high entrance, which was the meeting point of two staircases, on the right and on the left, leading up to the building gate. From the balustrade one could look out over the city square. "This turnaround is maddeningly surrealistic," he mused. "Here I stand, a Jew from Eretz-Israel, when just yesterday a Nazi leader with the rank of at least a Gauleiter could have stood in my place, shouting slogans to the crowd that filled the square." The Jewish soldier closed his eyes. It seemed to him that he could see the throng — all with the same face, all of the same height, all wearing the same uniform, with the same hand-up Nazi salute, the same red ribbon with the same black swastika on the same arms, and the same roar, "*Sieg Heil! Sieg Heil!*" that everyone was shouting at the same pitch!

The imagined roar woke him and his eyes opened. Here was the same square, but it was quiet now, and there was a truck parked in it with a Star of David engraved on its door. Here was the raised balustrade: not the Nazi Gauleiter, but a Jewish soldier leaning on it, with the golden Star of David on his sleeve shining in the May sun. A few minutes ago they had informed the soldier that there were no Jews in this city. The soldier tried to compare the faces he had seen in his imagination, so similar to each other, with the faces of real people, in order to check whether those hundreds of faces were indeed from pure Aryan stock. But only a few people were walking in the square. Had all the inhabitants shut themselves in their houses, anxious as to what the end of the war would bring and what form the military regime of the conquerors would take?

Suddenly, the soldier's attention was riveted to the truck's surroundings. Next to the Star of David on the car stood his two fellow-soldiers, kibbutz members and veteran envoys of impeccable credentials. And — oh goodness! — they were calmly talking with two Aryan girls. How "Aryan"? Well, if an Aryan profile did actually exist, as that lunatic had claimed, then it was theirs. The soldier who had carried out his mission in the municipality refused to believe his eyes. "What?" his body was frozen in shock. "We haven't gone more than one hundred and fifty kilometers from our camp, and we've been in this accursed city less than an hour, but those soldiers are already flirting with German *shikses,* as though there was no Jewish moral directive against it, and as though even the British command had not explicitly decreed non-fraternization!"

The soldier shook himself out of his stupefaction and decided to act. The three soldiers were of equal rank, but he felt that if they had erred, it was his right to rebuke them. Still leaning on the railing, he started to send a series of harsh gestures toward those standing near the truck. The message was clear: "Have you lost your mind? Stop that nonsense immediately and send the *shikses* to hell!" However, instead of complying with his warnings, his friends sent back to him a series of urgent hand gestures of their own, saying, "Get down here right away! You're needed here!"

"We were standing next to the truck," related his friends when he went down to them, furious, "and these two *shikses* came up to us. The tall one stroked the symbol on the door, and the little one, bolder, stretched her hand out towards the tag on the sleeve. Just as the Jews in Italy did. But Aryans, of all people?

"We sent them packing, of course: '*Weg Schweine!*' (Get out of here, sows!) But they didn't move. The older one wouldn't take her hand off the Star of David: '*Wir sind auch…das*' (We are also… this…). It seemed to be difficult for her to articulate '*Juden*'. Maybe she was still afraid. The little one was braver: '*Wir sind Juden*' (We are Jews) — she declared, and related that they had been saved on Aryan papers as *Volksdeutsche* because of their Aryan appearance, just as were many others under similar circumstances."

"How did you get here?"

"Like the others, we were sent to work in German war factories."

"Where did you come from?"

"*Aus Polen.*" (From Poland).

"Ankori, speak Polish to them. These may be the first Jews we have met in Austria."

"*Skąd wy w Polsce?*" (Where are you from in Poland?)
"*Z koło Krakowa.*" (From near Kraków.)
"*Gdzie koło Krakowa?*" (Where near Kraków?), he shouted.
"*Z Tarnowa.*" (From Tarnów).
"*Z jakiej ulicy?*" (Which street?)

Ankori had already grasped her arms in his hands and was shaking her body as though he wanted to pour the information out from her, immediately. Suddenly the girl paled: "*Hesio?*" she whispered his Tarnów name. "*Is that you?*"

Thus on the first day of the war's end, in the enemy country, they stood in embrace: Hesiek Wróbel and Baśka, the younger of the Fabian sisters, close neighbors in Tarnów, who had not seen each other for eight years. She had then been a child of twelve, and he a youth of seventeen about to immigrate to *Palestyna*. Thus they stood in the center of Klagenfurt, embracing and crying.

## IV

After the return of the soldier-envoys and the military reporter from an unprecedented trip from Austria to Croatia:

— after they had entered Croatia, where they became involved, to their surprise, in a battle not their own, between Yugoslavs and Italians over the border region; when across from Italian *Trieste* Croatian slogans were shouting, "*Trst je naš*" (*Trst* is in our hands), and Gorizia became *Gorica* in Serbo-Croatian, and Fiume kept its original meaning, river, in the other language — *Rjeka*;

— after they met *all* the Jews of Trieste, an unforgettable meeting, in the cemetery, where the community members had sought sanctuary from the two warring parties;

— and after they had experienced the dreadful sight of the concentration camp Jasenowac (over which the Yugoslav refugees had wept back in Ferramonti), and had followed on the waters of the Sava the floating corpses of Jewish victims who had been thrown into the river, hands tied behind their backs; while at the same time the Ustaši, the Croatian fascists, had been lying in wait in the surrounding forests for Jews, and attacking stragglers of Tito's partisans;

— and after they had been deeply impressed by the enthusiasm of the Yugoslav revolution, and had listened in the central square of Zagreb to Tito's victory speech —

— an unusual driving mission was already waiting at the Company.

The Command had heard from Ankori several times that he was very eager, when the opportunity arose, to drive down to Taranto in his car and return from Puglia northward, plying his way along the entire Adriatic highway, including the zones he had not traveled with the Company because of his mission on the western coast, and to stop for one day in Ravenna before reaching Tarvisio. Luckily, the opportunity presented itself now. A British platoon had received a Movement Order in Germany to 178 Company, which would take care of its transportation to the port of Taranto, for the sake of sailing to serve in Egypt. Ankori, who had not yet rested from the previous journey, took this mission upon himself and was glad to set out.

The Company received the British platoon in 178's best tradition of hospitality: an excellent evening meal, in which the 178 chefs outdid themselves; communal singing in English with the addition of teaching them *"Heiveinu Shalom Aleikhem"* in Hebrew, led by the head of the Company choir (who had conducted it all the way from southern Egypt, via Libya as far as northern Italy); and comfortable sleeping arrangements. When Zvi Ankori was presented to the British as "your driver tomorrow", and they realized that it had been he who led the communal singing and taught them the Hebrew song, they all burst into applause; but it was hard for them to pronounce his first name correctly, and they preferred to call him "Curly".

Afterwards, when the British mingled with the men of 178 in a free chat, the guest-sergeant approached Ankori and a friendly conversation developed between the two on the subject of their musical training. Ankori told him about his violin, while the sergeant turned out to be an accordionist. Ankori told him that he had also been interested in this instrument and intended to learn to play it after his service, and therefore he had purchased a quality Italian accordion. However, the constant movement of the platoon made it difficult to care for the instrument and he had decided to sell it and buy another one when he finished his service.

"I have also been dreaming about purchasing an Italian accordion, but on this trip it's impossible. Not enough time to check it out. Could I see the accordion you bought?" Ankori went out and within ten minutes, brought the instrument to the tent. The sergeant saw it, and his eyes lit up. He had never come across such a beautiful instrument. He strummed some chords and whispered in wonder, "This is not an accordion, it's a complete orchestra. You said you're willing to sell it?" Ankori did not want to lose out or to make a profit. He quoted the exact price he had paid. The deal was struck, and the amount paid in pounds sterling. "Never mind," the sergeant consoled Ankori, who was standing as if he had been disinherited, "You'll buy another one!"

In the evening they reached Taranto. The ship was to sail at midnight. The passengers took leave of Curly amicably. The sergeant, accordion slung over his shoulder, hugged him and whispered "Thanks". Ankori parked his truck in the olive grove near the coast. "Oh, how much time has passed since we landed here from Malta! How many kilometers have we driven since then! How we have worked with the refugees and Jewish locals over this year and a half, from Christmas Eve 1943 until today! How the world situation has changed!" He lay down under the canvas of his truck, and, exhausted, fell asleep within a few minutes.

At nightfall he suddenly woke up, as though disturbed by a thought of regret. Half-asleep, he racked his brain to remember what he had said or done that he should regret. He touched the wad of pounds stuck in the buttoned pocket of his battledress, and in an instant he woke up completely. Yes, now he remembered. He had only told the sergeant half the truth. Transporting the accordion in 178's constant travel regime had constituted a hefty difficulty, and he had told the sergeant this openly and candidly. He had quoted the exact price he had paid. In this, too, he had stuck to the truth, as was his way. "But the second half of the problem, which is the most important part of the truth, you did not tell" — he thought, provoked by the little devil that for years had dared to serve as policeman for his conscience. "Admit it; you needed the money first and foremost in order to travel to Poland to search for your sister! This is why you decided to sell the accordion. Did you forget?"

Of course he had not forgotten. Now that the war was over, the matter had become more and more pressing. But the time had not yet come. He had not yet heard that repatriation had begun in western Galicia. Chaos still reigned in Europe. The final borders had not yet been determined and transportation was not yet resumed. There he would not have at his disposal a car from a Jewish unit that shared its soldiers' feelings. The matter was sensitive, complex, and he had to act with maximum astuteness and restraint. True, the Klagenfurt meeting with Baśka had lit another firebrand of hope. Ankori returned to the banknotes and wrapped them in his mother's Red Cross letter, in which Mala's address in Siberia was written. From now on, these two things would remain constantly on his person, until the day he found her, just as he and Baśka had found each other.

Does this take care of the "Did you forget?" No, for the British sergeant the "second half of the truth" was irrelevant. He was a product of the British army and this was enough for him, whereas we, like him, were performing our military duties, but we also poured into the British framework for which we had volunteered additional content, Jewish and personal. With all his goodwill, the Briton could never understand how and why a Jewish soldier in the British army would dream of getting to Poland. How would his Company command agree to it? Didn't our Sages use to say, "A foreigner could not understand this"? Could the Briton understand what "T.T.G." meant to us? Was it even worthwhile for us if he understood our codes? No, Ankori was not sorry. Aware of his responsibility, he had chosen his words carefully.

It was late. Tomorrow the long drive from the south to Ravenna awaited him. Oh, Ravenna! And with Ravenna in his heart, he fell asleep.

The road to Ravenna embraced the historic sites of the Adriatic Sea coast — beginning at those in Puglia, at the heel of the Italian boot — where the Spanish-Jewish traveler, Benjamin of Tudela, had traveled in the 1160s and recorded, among other things, facts about the Jewish communities whose names as Torah centers reached even far-off France — and on to Ancona, Fano, Pesaro, and Rimini, to Ravenna. The road in the Ravenna area was water-logged and difficult to drive on. During the battles, the Wehrmacht had flooded the area with the waters of the Po River in order to impede the progress of the Eighth Army. At that time, the flooded area was limited to the battleground alone. However, now the waters of the Po had risen up over the banks of the large delta, and the flooding included the Ravenna region, which adjoined the delta on the south. The area, which even in ordinary days was known as malaria-ridden, was now swarming with Anopheles mosquitoes. These wild emissaries of the Black Angel of Malaria rest from their work during the day, but with nightfall they go searching for prey, and attack all flesh without mercy. This means that they sting the victim's flesh and drink his blood, and as "compensation" for the suffering, they donate a generous dose of malaria.

The soldier-driver's luck got worse, and because of the difficulty of the road in the flooded area, he reached the Ravenna town center later than planned. In the darkness of the Po valley, the aforementioned accursed "Anopheles festival" was already at its height, and a female mosquito buzzed in her friend's ear: "New blood has arrived. We'll have a feast tonight!" (The bloodthirsty are always the female Anopheles, not due to inherent evil, but by obeying the command of nature that made their fertility process dependant on a constant supply of this red substance.) The accumulative fatigue of the soldier, from the days of Villach and Klagenfurt, Trst-Trieste and Jasenowac, Zagreb, and the Taranto trip both ways, overcame his fear of mosquito bites, and after parking his truck, which served as his home on the roads, next to the public garden, he climbed under the canvas and abandoned his body to sleep and to the bites of the female mosquitoes who lusted to fall pregnant with the help of the elixir drawn from his blood.

In the morning, bitten but refreshed, Ankori went forth in good spirits to bring his plan to fruition. After a cup of coffee, which was almost like the mud that the waters of the Po brought to the restaurant's entrance, he bought thirty-three red roses in the flower shop and traveled to the nearby military cemetery in Piangipane. There he placed one rose next to every Star of David, on the graves of each of the thirty-three casualties of the Brigade.

From there he returned to Ravenna and began walking around, part tourist and part student of Roman and Byzantine history, enthusiastic to validate the knowledge that he had acquired from books with the visual monuments that exist in the city to this day. In contrast to ancient Rome, Ravenna had not a bit of classical past. It had been built at the beginning of the fifth century, around a decade after the division of the Roman Empire in two: eastern, with Constantinople as its capital, and western, in which New Ravenna was founded in order to serve as capital. Thus Ravenna took the place of the ancient city of Rome that had been weakened and deserted by the emperors of the western half of the Empire. In the last five hundred years, however, the popes who returned to Rome to rule that city renovated and beautified it as the capital of Catholicism, and Ravenna, which became a small and insignificant town, was forgotten.

The five hours that Ankori devoted to intoxication from Ravenna's mosaics had no parallel for him before that visit, and during the long years thereafter of visiting and touring other ancient capitals, none of them in any way dimmed the original Ravenna experience. Three basilicas, two Christian baptismal fonts, a mausoleum in memory of the founding emperor's sister, who had shared the beautification process of the capital as well as having been her brother's co-ruler — all these shone in mosaics that were without peer in the art of the early Middle Ages.

It was hard for the enthusiastic student-tourist to detach himself from this embodiment of ancient beauty, but he had not yet executed the third stage (after Piangipane and the mosaics) he had planned for this visit, a stage that was completely different from the two experiences he had enjoyed so far: pilgrimage to the grave of Dante.

After having been expelled from Firenze, Dante moved to Verona, and finally found sanctuary in Ravenna, living and creating there to his dying day. For over four hundred years, the gravesite of Italy's greatest poet and one of the world's poetry geniuses had not been given a respectable monument. Only in 1780, when, with the rise of the European Enlightenment, interest in the first poet of the Renaissance had reawakened, did the city set up a modest mausoleum for its adopted son. Thus the Ankori Dantesque circle — the one that began with the little bust of Dante from his childhood in Tarnów, continued with his study of the poet's works in the original — closed in Ravenna and ended with the commemoration *in Hebrew* of his love for Dante in the memorial book beside his grave.

## V

The British army ambulance with the Red Cross sign stopped in front of 178 Company Headquarters. The sergeant of B Platoon, who was waiting for the Red Cross vehicle, climbed into the driver's compartment in order to direct him to the right tent. The large tents, called "Indian tents", stood row upon row, like houses made out of cloth — each with four cloth walls and a cloth roof. The tent could hold six soldiers in relative comfort. A wide path was left between the rows of tents, allowing a car to drive through when necessary. This time, too, it was convenient to park the ambulance right at the entrance to the tent. The other tent occupants had been ordered to leave, for fear of contagion, and only one bed was left in which the sick patient lay.

In the corner lay in all their glory those personal effects without which no soldier is complete: the kitbag, with the full "wardrobe" that the Quartermaster General put together for the soldiers of His Majesty the King; the backpack equipped with the necessary straps and the knapsack. The sick soldier's fellow tent dwellers packed all three of these for him. And, of course, they did not forget to put into the kitbag, right under the string that closes it (as this particular soldier used to do), the miniature Hebrew Old Testament, a gift from his father for his success in high school exams. "This book (his father had said) will strengthen your spirit, and reading its minute letters will strengthen your eyes. These two reinforcements will help you in your adult life to distinguish between good and evil, between friend and enemy." The soldier repeated his father's words numerous times to his colleagues, and sometimes he would read a chapter from that Bible at the beginning of the Company's Sabbath eve parties, which he conducted.

A few days after he returned from the Taranto trek, whose last stage was Ravenna-Tarvisio, Ankori fell ill, shivering with cold, and, simultaneously, with high fever. The ambulance driver, who was also a paramedic, entered the tent and looked at him. "Were you in the Po Valley recently?" he asked. When he was answered in the affirmative, he declared, "You've got malaria, and how! If I'm wrong, I'll treat your whole company to a bottle of beer." The paramedic was saved from spending his money on the beer. What's more, the halo of being an expert diagnostician shone above his beret, and even the sergeant, who was known to be very hard-hearted, melted in wonder and exclaimed, "A true doctor, indeed!"

The only one who could not participate in the praise was the patient himself, due to high temperature and the heavy sweat covering his entire body, alternating with chills and trembling from cold. "Malaria, and how!" — the paramedic repeated — "To the hospital, quickly." Preserving his self-esteem, Ankori declined the stretcher and climbed into the ambulance on his own, but once inside, he collapsed. The other paramedic, who was waiting for him inside the ambulance, lay him down on a stretcher, and when the kitbag and the two packs were placed inside, he pulled all three in and closed the door.

The warm May sun shone on Ankori's eyelids. He woke up, but remembered nothing after his helpless fall onto the ambulance floor. He knew that he was in an ambulance, which meant they were taking him to hospital. But when it had happened, what had developed afterwards, and where he was now was unclear to him.

"Woken up already?" asked a nurse in English as she passed by him. He knew this was a rhetorical question, reflecting no real interest and no desire for an answer. Like all nurses in all the hospitals of the world (as he remembered from the days of his appendix operation in Jerusalem), this anonymous nurse who worked here would hastily appear from somewhere in the back part of the ward, blustering like a storm to somewhere in the front part, with a rustling of her white uniform, starched and ironed to the last seam. But he decided not to let her get away with it this time.

"Nurse!" he grinned to himself. This was the first word he had uttered since his ride in the ambulance. Suddenly he felt his strength returning. She *had* to stop by him. She *had* to tell him in what town the hospital was located, how long he had been hospitalized, what was the state of his health, what medication he was receiving, when he had last seen a doctor, and what was the prognosis for his release from the hospital. Now that he had opened his eyes, he felt it was his right to see and know.

"Nurse!" There seemingly was a tone of command in his second call, because she stopped and came back to him. He thanked her and asked her all his questions. As soon as she started to answer he noticed that English was not her native language. It was neither British nor American. It was acquired. Too correct.

"*È italiana Lei?*" he shot a wild guess into the air. Her eyes lit up. She explained that this was an Italian army hospital near the town of Udine, situated about three hundred meters from the town's first houses. The Eighth Army had left the institution in Italian hands and it was run just as it used to be, with only one wing being reserved for sick and wounded British. The chief nurses in this wing were British, but three English-speaking Italian nurses had also been transferred to the wing. British and Italian doctors, all in uniform, worked together. Every morning two of them checked each patient. The service, kitchen and guard areas stayed in Italian hands.

After this basic information, she spoke of the patient's illness as well: "You were brought here in a bad shape, in fact in a critical state. You had an extremely aggressive type of malaria that could recur in another twenty-five years, and so one mustn't accept a blood donation from you. For three days you lay unconscious, and we had to open your mouth to give you quinine, which is the essential medicine for a sickness such as yours. You asked when you will be able to leave here. Well, usually, if everything goes according to plan, the period of hospitalization is about three weeks. You seem to me to be a strong man, so we will hope that from tomorrow you will feel better." She lingered unnecessarily for another few minutes, and it was obvious that she was happy for the opportunity to speak Italian. The happiness was two-way. He presumed that she would now ask the usual, "And where are you from?" but she did not ask. "It seems that she is only interested in my Italian and not in me", he faced the fact with slight disappointment. "Maybe tomorrow she will ask."

Suddenly he remembered something else. "Nurse, where are my personal effects?" She opened a small cupboard in the corner of the room, and the black of the kitbag and the khaki of the two backpacks waved to him in greeting. "What do you need them for? You get here everything that you need." It was as if he had insulted the institution. "There are two things that I need. First of all, for tomorrow morning I need my shaving kit. It's in my knapsack. Who knows how I look?" He told her about the British major in Tobruq who snapped at one poor soldier, unshaven after the last battle: "It is because of you that Tobruq has fallen!" "There is no need," she declared. "Tomorrow, and every other day, the hospital barber will give you a shave. And what is the second thing?" "In the black kitbag, right under the string that closes it, is my Bible." "*O Santa Maria!*" she crossed herself and clutched the cross hanging from her neck as she brought the Bible.

That very evening Ankori received a visit. In joy he thought that this was finally the visit he had waited for since he had regained consciousness. On that very first day of full consciousness, his forehead still burned with high fever, while waves of cold caused his whole body to shiver, and no matter how many blankets he pulled over his head he could not quiet them. Even then, one question kept cropping up to disturb his peace. How was it that no one from 178, neither officer nor fellow-soldier, had come to visit him and ask how he was? It is true that he had never been in Udine, but nevertheless he knew where it was situated on the area's map. The distances in northeastern Italy are not great, and to travel from any place to Udine would take no longer than an hour. Considering the wonderful camaraderie between all the levels in the Company — in fact, 178 Company functioned like a kibbutz at its best — such an oversight was unthinkable, unless some unknown event had prevented his friends from coming.

Ankori immediately realized his mistake in relating to the visiting soldier as a fellow 178er. This soldier was one of the last British-born Jewish recruits who had joined 178. With the establishment of the Jewish Brigade, young British Jews were given the choice to join a Palestinian Jewish unit instead of being in a standard British company. By serving in Hebrew units, they aimed, as Zionists, to internalize the Zionist standards of behavior and values of volunteer Zionist activity — standards and values which Eretz-Israel soldiers had formed during their service in this war, and beforehand in the Haganah and in the kibbutzim. Their fame had reached the European Diaspora, and especially the only free Jewry of Europe at the time, the Jews of England.

Johnny, the soldier who approached Ankori's bed, had indeed served in 178, but he did not come to visit on behalf of 178 Company, as the patient had expected. He himself had been hospitalized even before Ankori because of an infectious disease, but his sickness did not call for staying in bed during the day. And so the 178-greenhorn started visiting the 178-oldtimer on a regular basis. He was a short chap, with black curly hair — one whom everyone fondly called "snooper", because despite the fact that he was new in the Unit, he was able — no one understood how — to obtain information in every field, and happily let everyone know what he had found out. At the same time, he was by nature inclined to dependence, and in any time of trouble clung to a friend from Eretz-Israel, out of a mystic belief that an Eretz-Israeli would know how to manage and arrange everything. And so, as of this moment he clung to Ankori in the hospital. As a matter of fact, this clinging, which turned into true friendship, served them both.

Early in the morning, the hospital barber woke the patient and shaved him with a razor. This was something that had never touched Ankori's face stubble, and Montgomery's soldier — oh, the shame of it! — was somewhat frightened of the extremely sharp instrument. To be on the safe side, he did not tell the barber that he knew Italian, but kept quiet in order not to argue with a razor. The shaving operation ended safely, splashing not one drop of the contaminated blood in which the Anopheles mosquito had left its footprints.

Later in the morning two doctors appeared, a British captain and an Italian officer, who it seemed was of a rank similar to that of his British colleague, but it was difficult for a foreigner to be familiar with the Italian rank hierarchy. The British doctor checked Ankori in a seemingly thorough fashion and did not hide his dissatisfaction as to the state of the patient. He muttered something in the Italian doctor's ears. The latter repeated the examination and afterwards performed the same muttering, which must have been a formal summary of the examination. Both of them turned around to the two British nurses. The nurses had officers' ranks on their shoulders, and they themselves looked no less starched and ironed than their uniforms. Presumably they understood the doctors' mutterings, for they too turned around (in keeping with the hierarchical order) and said whatever they said to the Italian nurse, who held a pen and clipboard with the daily report, and wrote down whatever she wrote down. After advancing no more than two steps, the doctors returned to the patient, and the British one asked him if he had had a bowel movement. This was the one and only question that the patient was asked. His negative answer caused the officer-doctors to again turn around and mutter to the officer-nurses. Then the Italian nurse wrote down what the officers told her. The clipboard was hung on the front side of the bed. During all this time the Italian nurse did not even throw one glance in Ankori's direction.

"I apologize. You do understand that we have rules", said the Italian nurse in the afternoon when she brought the patient his quinine. "Of course I understand. Forget it." She looked at the miniature book that she had taken out of his kitbag yesterday, and that was now on his bedside cabinet. She did not stop wondering at how it could contain the complete Old Testament. She only knew the verses of the Old Testament that the priest quoted in his sermons, and presumed that the Bible could only be contained in a huge volume, similar to the one that lay on the priest's lectern. "May I open it?" she asked in awe, as though she felt it radiated rays of holiness.

She leafed through the small book, starting from the side that she presumed to be the beginning, namely from the left, and then from the other end, from the right, further from top to bottom and the other direction. Despairing of her efforts, she sighed:

"What is this? The letters are not only miniature, but they are not ours at all."

"Right. They are Hebrew letters, in which the original Bible was written."

"Hebrew? So you are *ebreo*?" She did not know how to react.

"Yes, I am a Jew. From *Terra Santa*. From the holy city *Gerusalemme!*"

"*O Dio Santo!*" she sobbed soundlessly, stupefied.

"It is possible that the priest did not tell you, but the Jewish

Brigade is the one that crossed the Senio and the Po, and, as part of the Eighth Army, liberated the region from the Nazi occupation. I came from a faraway land, strong and healthy, but when I reached the Po Valley to help you, I got malaria!"

"*O Dio!*" She held her head in her two hands and muttered endlessly, "*O Dio, O Dio!*"

"Calm down. Tomorrow, when you are calm, I will answer all your questions and tell you about my land and my city."

She did not come the next day, nor during the following days. Another Italian nurse took her place. She said that the previous one had requested three weeks' holiday in order to go to her sister's wedding in Milan. Was it the truth? Or perhaps only an excuse? Hadn't she said that the period of hospitalization would be three weeks? In any case, Ankori never saw her again.

A few days passed. Ankori started regaining strength. The medication did its job. The rest also played its part. His colleague, Johnny, visited him every day, and once Ankori could start walking around, they started going out into the hospital garden every morning after the doctors' visit. He would lean on his friend's arm and enjoy the fresh air and the pleasant May sunshine. The two soldiers became close to one another. They told each other about their totally different childhoods — one in Poland, the other in England. Two different worlds that had now become united into one. The Hebrew language united them. So did the hope to meet in Eretz-Israel, when his friend would immigrate as planned: they were united by love for their Unit, a Unit that had no equal, a Unit dominated by fighters' solidarity and sense of mission.

Until one day "the snooper" came to Ankori's bed, looking very disconsolate. What had happened?

The Brigade is no longer here — it has left Italy.

## VI

"What shall we do? What will become of us?" lamented the messenger. This was the first time Johnny was angry with himself for being a snooper. Even though he was proud of his "talent", this was information that he did not expect to pass on. "Shall we become MPs in some God-forsaken British depot, or scrub pots in some filthy military kitchen?"

Ankori "enjoyed" the lament. It proved that the youngster had become a true "one-seven-eight-nik". Only a 178-person would not resign himself to British Standing Orders in case of separation from one's unit, no matter what the reason. Standing Orders required separated soldiers to report to the nearest army depot and wait for reassignment or be given some odd jobs. What? Leave 178 now? When the main focus of our Jewish mission is finally reaching full momentum with the liberation of the concentration camps and with the streams of refugees returning from their places of exile? No way!

Ankori tried to calm his friend. "Don't worry. We'll rejoin our Unit. I vouch for that. We'll go back, by hook or by crook!"

"I'm with you, Zvi. You're not going to leave me."

"We'll do everything together. The main thing is to stay calm so that no one in the hospital will suspect that we are up to something. And secondly, we have to regain our strength. We have a long and difficult path in front of us. Better wait another few days, get stronger, eat well, and then — off we go."

"I'll do everything you tell me to do. You're from Eretz-Israel. You're the commander."

"We are both equal, two friends with the same purpose. Now go and rest. I'll lie down as well, and think."

When alone, the veteran "one-seven-eight-nik" reconstructed in his mind the approximate course of things from the start. It was bound to have happened! Someone in the higher echelons in Cairo or in Jerusalem had heard of the stream of refugees passing through Tarvisio, which was held by the Brigade. It was clear to the two soldier-friends that they had to get out of the hospital on their own accord, even though their recuperation was not yet complete and even though they had not received the official doctors' discharge letter as was customary.

The veteran explained the escape plan to Johnny. The best day to leave the place was Sunday, in other words, in four days' time. This was because most probably, on a Sunday the team worked on a half-holiday schedule, and the fact that fewer workers would be around would minimize the danger of discovery. Before they left they would have to tidy their beds in the usual manner — another talisman to help ensure that the soldiers' absence would not be discovered until the late evening hours. During the remaining days, at the end of the daily doctors' round, the soldiers openly swapped their hospital pajamas for the army uniform. They walked down the corridor and in the garden in uniform, but without the berets on their heads. In answer to the nurse's question, they claimed that it was more pleasant to sit in the garden in uniform. The argument was accepted.

The last problem was how to remove their personal effects from the building. The black kitbag was especially problematic, both because of its conspicuous color and its size. It was impossible to hide or camouflage a full kitbag on one's shoulder. Common sense said that this intensely black thing had to be completely emptied, then folded and hidden in the khaki bag. Two bags, one a backpack and one a carry-all, were filled to bursting. The Bible found refuge in the trouser pocket.

"I still have three pairs of underwear left, and the same number of undershirts, shirts and socks", moaned Johnny. "It is impossible to stuff any more in. What should I do, Zvi?"

"Wear them one on top of the other. You'll be too warm in this weather, but we can't leave anything behind us", declared the escape organizer. "I will do the same."

Ankori's guess was correct. Only the Italian doctor and the Italian nurse made the rounds on that Sunday morning. When the doctor and the nurse returned from the end of the wing to their office, the two conspirators took their khaki bags and khaki berets and quietly went to the stairs. Then each one put on his beret, and they marched straight to the gate with an air of total confidence.

Here too the guess regarding the Sunday work schedule turned out to be correct. Only one Italian guard was at the gate, as opposed to two on a regular workday. Ankori, a friendly smile on his face, raised his hand in greeting. "*Ciao!*" The guard greeted him back. The two soldiers suddenly found themselves in a Udine street.

"The hospital is situated near the town of Udine. The first of the town's houses are about three hundred meters from the gate", the Italian nurse had told the patient after he had regained consciousness and asked where he was. At the time, they both were unaware that this last detail, which she had unknowingly volunteered, would be engraved in the patient's memory and would one day play an important part. The two soldiers began walking along the street outside the gate. It declined slightly, then bore right. Indeed, after the right turn, a row of houses appeared on the left side of the street. The fact that they were now in a built-up area after their long days of confinement in the hospital gave the soldiers confidence, even though they did not know the town itself. Ankori followed the signposts that were written in Italian, and in one place he stopped and declared:

"This is it".

"This is what?"

"This is a restaurant that belongs to a Jew."

"How do you know? There is no name."

"There is no name of the restaurant's owner, but the restaurant itself has a name. *Vitello d'oro* — 'The Golden Calf'. The Christians in the small towns name their restaurants after male or female saints. 'Santo' this or that, or 'Santa' this or that. Only Jewish irony would use 'The Golden Calf' from the Torah. Apart from that, you noticed correctly that the name of the restaurant's owner does not appear here. The Christians are very particular about advertising their name on a sign. The Jew is sometimes inclined to hide his name for numerous reasons, and especially these days."

Johnny was not convinced. He wanted a clear sign.

"You know what? Let's go inside and check it out. We can always drink a cup of tea and go."

"How will we check it out? Ask?"

"God forbid. One doesn't ask such questions."

"So how?"

"We'll go inside and see."

Pressing the door handle caused a bell to ring. They entered. A man sitting by a table turned his chair around and stood up. He was a lean, middle-aged man, with all of Jewish history etched on his face. "Shalom!" — Ankori cried. In reply, an emotional scene was played out, one which repeated itself again and again in this war in Libya and in Italy. A Jew embraces an Eretz-Israel soldier. In embracing him he embraces the Land of Israel.

The name of the owner was Senegalia, a common Italian Jewish name. "Come and see soldiers from *Palestina*", he called to the children, a small boy and a girl about twelve years old or perhaps older. She introduced herself as "Sarah". "That's nice, my grandmother's name is also Sarah", Ankori contributed a personal touch to the opening conversation. "It is a name from the Bible." It seemed that she had heard that. Presumably it was her father who had told her and her brother Bible stories, for there was no Jewish educational institution there from which she could have acquired that information. And perhaps that was the name of her father's or grandfather's mother? In any case, she confessed, until now she had not given it any importance. From now on, she promised, she would be proud of the name.

The two children clung to the soldiers. They stroked the Brigade's emblem and received an explanation as to the meaning of its form and colors. They touched the soldiers' arms, as though wanting to prove to themselves that they were really made of flesh and blood. The house inhabitants called them *"i Palestinesi"* in the plural, and *"il Palestinese"* in the singular, without bothering to relate to their real names. Most of their communication — in Italian of course — was with Ankori, because Johnny, in the short period of time that he had been in Italy, had digested only a few Italian words. Johnny's friend regretted this deeply. He shared everything with Johnny, as he had said he would, but here, with no other choice, Johnny was mostly silent.

It turned out that the building served as an inn. On the entrance floor was a restaurant and café, and on the second floor were the bedrooms and bathrooms. The second floor was surrounded by a wooden banister, offering a view of the restaurant hall from above. "Just like the inn in the Ukraine in which my mother and grandmother were born" — a memory of the stories that his mother had told him flashed through Ankori's mind. Only the two rivers were missing, the Kropivnia and Korchick, as was the flock of white geese that would skim over the water in an arrow formation. And there was also something else missing — but that was for the better — the smell of strong drink and the other sickly smells of a tavern. Instead of these, the fresh scent of good Italian coffee wafted through.

The inn seemed to have had no clients at the time. Possibly, despite the end of the war, people were not yet taking pleasure trips, and merchants were also not traveling far from home, both due to insecurity in the area and the shortage of gasoline and merchandise. At any rate, the doors of all rooms on the second floor were open.

When he led them up to the second floor, Senegalia pointed to a back room flooded with sunshine overlooking the garden behind the building: "This is your room. You can stay here for as long as you like. I presume that you are eager to return to your Unit, but first of all you have to recuperate and regain your strength." He said it all before they told him their situation. Obviously, he understood that if they had passed by here, it meant they had left the nearby hospital. Their despondent and pale faces also testified to this. "No, not now. First we will eat and afterwards you will tell me everything. You will also eat your other meals here. Don't eat the junk food in town. I hope that you will be comfortable with us."

Their recitation of the story of the Jewish military unit grew longer and more colorful: from el-Alamein and Benghazi ("I served as an Italian soldier in Benghazi, but a long time before the war", Senegalia intervened with his memories.) Then to Malta, southern Italy, and Rome ("How that Zolli poured shame on us!") Then on to the Brigade's battle on the Senio and the Sabbath in Venice ("Yes, they told me about it. You must know that all the Jews from the small towns in this region, that is called Friuli-Venezia Giulia, are part of the Venetian community. So it was you who spoke in the synagogue? I'm honored to meet you.") The guest-soldier and now friend continued to reminisce about the pioneering trip to Austria and Croatia, absorption of the refugees in Tarvisio, and sending them to the Via Unione Center in Milan. In the end, he revealed how he had caught malaria in the Po Valley, been hospitalized, escaped from the hospital after the Brigade had left Italy, and decided to hitchhike through Europe and join the Brigade. The children listened as though hypnotized, and Senegalia did not try to hide his tears. "That is the Land of Israel, and those are the soldiers that it breeds," he summarized to himself, and perhaps to the children.

"I will contact a friend of mine, an Italian doctor, so that he will examine you." The friend agreed to receive them despite the Sunday holiday. After the examination he declared that Ankori still needed another week to return to himself, but his friend was fit to start the journey straightaway. Since the pharmacy was closed, the doctor gave Ankori ten portions of quinine from his cupboard, two per day. Together with this, he advised him to walk in the garden in the fresh air and even go up to the Castello. Sarah took on the job of tour guide, and straightaway, "like a big girl", explained that Udine developed around a hill crowned by a fortress, and that a boulevard surrounds the hill at its base. This gave rise to the boulevard's name Sottomonte. "The ascent to the ancient fort is not difficult. We'll climb it together." It was unclear whether she was encouraging them or commanding them. In any case, her seriousness evoked laughter.

After the May Sunday when they arrived at Vitello d'Oro, the four days that followed flowed like a quiet and calm stream, and the two soldiers flowed pleasantly along with it, as though they had come to a summer resort, one saving his body from the tribulations of the Anopheles mosquito, the other from the bacteria that had attacked him. Both of them enjoyed the sun and quiet beauty of the Venetian townlet ("Venice has ruled Udine since 1420"; Sarah was particular to be accurate with dates). The two soldiers decided between themselves that their original estimate as to their guide's age needed correction. In light of the seriousness with which she fulfilled her improvised job and the enormous amount of knowledge that she had displayed, they now considered her to be at least fifteen or sixteen. But they never asked her or her father about this point. (And have we mentioned her beauty?)

The highlight of the trips was the ascent to the fort. Even Ankori himself never guessed that when he saw the site, his memory would fly far off to his ascents of the Marcin Mountain together with his mother and sister in Tarnów, the town in western Galicia where he was born and grew up. But whereas only ruins remained of the fourteenth-century Tarnów fort, Udine's Castello, two hundred years younger than Fort Marcin, remained whole. In the past it was the residence of the Venetian governors, while nowadays it serves as a tourist destination. There were also two churches, one on each of the two hills. The wooden church had been built in the name of Saint Marcin, granting the saint's name to the whole mountain a thousand years previously, when Christianity was introduced in Poland. In contrast, the church of Santa Maria del Castello (Sarah recounted), was established three hundred years before the fort was built, taking the name "*del castello*" ('of the fort') only in the eighteenth century, when it also changed its façade to the baroque style. The mountain offers a view of the town of Udine as well as the hills of the entire Friuli region. The view resembles that of Tarnów and of the first chain of hills heralding the high Carpathian ranges.

When they returned to the inn in the evenings, Senagalia was already waiting for them with a hot supper (as opposed to the bags of sandwiches that they took with them on the trips, obeying the father's prohibition against consuming the "junk food in town"). At the end of the meal the five continued to sit around the table. As in Ferramonti and the "Rishonim" farm that he had managed in southern Italy, and as in Via Balbo in Rome, Ankori would begin describing the Land of Israel, its scenery, white Tel Aviv, the kibbutz, and Jerusalem. He would find a suitable Hebrew song for each topic. Thus the Land of Israel became the pivot around which life in the Senegalia house turned.

The warm friendship that instantly developed between the father and his two children and the two soldiers who had suddenly landed on their doorstep caused great joy. But the joint conversations, the shared morning and evening meals, and the enjoyable trips, were not enough to dispel two questions that the soldiers discussed between themselves in their room before bed. Where was the children's mother? They had not been introduced to her at the beginning, nor did they see her at meals or during conversations. Her actual existence had not been mentioned. Was she sick? Paralyzed? Or had she died, heaven forbid? And who was cooking and keeping the restaurant and the inn rooms clean? Perhaps Senegalia was divorced? The soldiers did not feel they could ask.

The last question was connected to a mysterious figure dressed in black, sitting with its back to the restaurant and its face toward the glassed-in balcony overlooking the garden. Was it a man? A woman? In truth, it was not clear if it was a live person at all, or a picture. The figure did not move or change position, but was always present when the soldiers sat with Senegalia and his children. Here too it was impossible to ask as to the identity of the mysterious figure.

On the fifth day of the week, and the fifth day since the soldiers' arrival at Senegalia's restaurant, things still carried on pleasantly, but it was very hot. The month of May had reached its end and the month of June was showing its signs. In the evening it was difficult to breathe inside the house — air conditioners were not yet known in those days — although Senegalia pulled out statistics from somewhere proving that such a heat wave had already occurred in the past. The soldiers refused to be comforted and decided to venture a stroll outside for a while and enjoy a breath of fresh air, whether real or imagined.

Suddenly, without them noticing, two angels of evil descended from heaven or perhaps rose up from the netherworld.

"Soldier, your pass", commanded the two British MPs (military policemen) in a tone that indicated a certain measure of enjoyment at the sight of two soldiers with a fifty percent chance of falling in their net. The silence of the two was understood correctly as one hundred percent success. The victims did not have a 'pass'. They had fallen into the army police net.

"Your Soldier's Service Book!" The policemen copied the names and army numbers and returned the booklets to the soldiers.

"Name of your unit?"

"178 Company RASC".

The policeman wrote down the unit number and the abbreviation of the transport corps. "Guilty of leaving the camp with no 'pass'" — they noted and signed the form, without asking where "the camp" was, and left to hunt down additional victims.

## VII

Months passed since the 'pass' incident, months that wound themselves on the scarlet thread of time and became years. Years piled one on top of another, and slowly a new picture of reality appeared that almost caused one to forget the sufferings of the World War and its upheavals, defeats and victories, fervor and despondency. The youths who had been enlisted by royal command, or who had voluntarily enlisted, like those from Eretz-Israel, grew up during the years of their service and matured, and became older, wiser and more sober. And nevertheless, despite Ankori's creative activity in academic research and teaching, which both exhausted and enriched the soul, the episode of the hasty departure from Senagalia's house in Udine in early June 1945 refused to succumb to oblivion, continually disturbing and allowing no rest.

It was clearly felt that the encounter with the MPs had suddenly violated the good spirit, comradeship and joy of hospitality that had fallen like heavenly favor on the two soldiers and the Senegalia household. Out of circumstantial necessity, the two who had escaped from the hospital in order to return to the Brigade were forced to escape for a second time, this time from the Senegalia home that had given them refuge. They had to escape without being able to express their thanks to the generous innkeeper — one of the legendary thirty-six righteous men — and to his adorable children, or to promise them everlasting friendship. The truth of the matter was that Senegalia himself had been the main promoter of haste. He remembered (so he said) the accepted procedure during his period of service in the Italian army before the war, and was worried that if his guests were caught a second time, they would be accused of desertion. Since in order to reach the Brigade in Holland one had to cross northern Italy and France, Senegalia stuffed into each soldier's pocket a fistful of Italian liras and French francs and persuaded the two of them not to delay but to set out at dawn.

The omission of proper leave-taking lay heavily on Ankori's heart and presumably also on Johnny's, though ever since their discharge from the army and Ankori's return to Eretz-Israel, while Johnny sailed back to England, the contact between the two ex-soldiers and friends has not been resumed. But all efforts by Ankori of communicating with Senegalia by post, whether directly to his address in Udine or indirectly via Venice, to whose Jewish community he belonged, were of no avail. Only in the 60s and 70s, when Ankori's academic research needs opened the gates to a series of visits to the Venetian archives for lengthy periods of time, was he able to address the Senegalia episode personally.

To his surprise, the community leaders, although they knew

him well, dismissed him with "go here" and "go there", and for some reason, avoided supplying him with the requested information. In the end, after pressuring them with continuous solicitations, they released a crumb of information: Senegalia was no longer alive; but they gave no details as to the date of death or place of burial. Is there a Jewish cemetery in Venice — he asked — other than that in the Lido? Silence. Frustrated, not knowing what to do, Ankori asked himself about the reason for their strange attitude, but he did not find an answer. The person who came to his help was the ex-beadle with whom Ankori renewed his acquaintance during that memorable tour of the Levantine synagogue. Commiserating with the by-now Israeli professor, the beadle whispered to him, "Here is a telephone number in Milan for you. Senegalia's son is there and he will tell you the rest."

Milan? Wonderful! That was where his friend Mekhek Bursztyn from Tarnów lived. Mekhek, because of his *"shaygetz"* Polish appearance, had survived the war on "Aryan papers", like the two sisters from Tarnów, and Ankori had discovered him as well on his first day in Austria. Mekhek had not remained in Klagenfurt but had settled in a holiday resort-village. The soldier went to visit him as soon as he discovered his address. Consequently, the Tarnovian friend was transferred to "The Refugee Center" in Milan. He decided to settle in the town, was successful in business, and married a woman from a distinguished Jewish Italian family. Mekhek and his wife Mara often visited Israel, and of course never missed dropping into the Ankori home in Jerusalem. In turn, Zvi and Ora, whenever they were in Milan, did not miss an opportunity to visit them.

The good news that it was possible to contact Senegalia's son in Milan and through him the rest of the family, after years of no contact, filled the ex-soldier's heart with both sadness and joy. Sadness — because he had not had the good luck of meeting Senegalia in times of peace. For if they had met, perhaps (this had been Ankori's secret hope) he would have managed to persuade him and his family to settle in the State of Israel that had come into being exactly three years after their meeting. "Perhaps it would be inappropriate to call a restaurant in Jerusalem 'The Golden Calf'", Ankori chuckled to himself, "but we can find another name". And joy — because it would at least be possible to renew the friendship with the younger generation, who in the meantime had presumably also established families. Ankori shared the details of the story with Mekhek over the telephone, and both decided that Zvi should come to Milan, and from there the two would continue with the necessary steps. Already the next morning, Ankori was seated on the train from Venice to Milan.

"*Pronto* (hello), *chi parla?*"

Ankori introduced himself. "Do you remember me?"

"Ah, *il Palestinese*! Of course I remember you. You brought light and joy to our house. The situation at home was quite difficult. We tried not to let you know. But now I can tell you. After all, you are like family. Perhaps even more than that!"

"Where is the family? How is Sarah? Can I visit her and the rest of the family?"

"In this heat everyone is at the seashore. They rented rooms east of Arenzzano. I will direct you how to get there. Sarah is there with her children. Her husband is a doctor and they live in Como."

"It's better that you direct my friend, he is the driver and knows the area. He speaks Italian."

"Have a successful journey."

Ankori was surprised that he was not invited to meet him. Later, after his return to Venice, the beadle told him that Senegalia's son had joined the Franciscans and wore a monk's habit. The father had died of grief.

In two days Mekhek finished his business concerns, and on Sunday he took his friend south by car, towards Arenzzano. Up to that point Mekhek knew the way well. He had traveled it dozens of times, from his apartment in Milan to his summer house on the seashore and back. His friend also knew the way from his visits to the Bursztyn summer house. But this time the destination was different. To his joy, his friend understood him and was prepared to accompany him wherever he went in order to locate the family, for which he had been searching relentlessly for years. This time it seemed there was a good chance that the mission would be successful. But how sad that Senegalia Senior was no longer with us!

They turned left on the shore road and drove slowly in order not to miss the house number. The road was raised, and in the spaces between the houses, they caught small glimpses of shore and sea. The shore was covered with droves and droves of people in various and strange positions, and in various stages of undress, frying themselves in the boiling sun and afterwards dipping in the sea that tolerantly gave them the kindness of a cool moment. The houses were not pretty. They had been hastily erected in order to immortalize the Milan summer slavery. This is the rule in August to this day: the entire city has to move to the seashore, and the *miserabili* who stay in town close themselves up behind shutters so that no one should see them in their disgrace.

"Here is the number of the house." Mekhek is even more excited than his friend. "It's just like a detective film." Ankori is thrilled by Mekhek's excitement. "Where to now?" — Mekhek waits for directions from the trip's instigator. "First let's go down to the beach. Maybe I'll recognize her?" The descent, worn by generations of bare feet soles, was steep and muddy. He knew that his hope of finding Sarah on the beach was complete nonsense. For Sarah had been a young girl when he knew her. Since then almost thirty years had passed. In other words, she was now in her forties, after so and so many births. How could he recognize her among the thousands of women and children sprawling on the sand? But he wanted to be sure that he had done everything possible.

"All right, so we did not succeed." The two detectives decided to climb back up and try knocking on the door of the apartment. Maybe not everyone had gone to the beach and there was someone inside. A wide-shouldered woman, tall and stocky, dressed in black, wordlessly opened the door in answer to his knock. Ankori's heart missed a beat. That back, that wide back covered in black — he remembers it fixed opposite the glassed-in balcony in Udine. It had not moved even a fraction, so much so that at the time he had thought for a moment that it was a picture, not flesh and blood, and had asked himself if she or he were paralyzed. And here she was, wordlessly opening the door. Dumb?

"Could we see Sarah?"

"Who are you?" (The dumb woman speaks.) "I know your voice. *Ah, certo, il Palestinese!*" She repeats the "*Palestinese*" several times as though she is playing with the word on her tongue like a piece of candy, enjoying its taste. "*Conosco la sua voce.* I know your voice from years ago."

"Who is the woman?" — Senegalia's one-time guest tries to make order out of the surprises. We might presume that she was a servant in the Senegalia house in Udine, who continues to work in their house in the Milan area and was brought to the summer resort in order to work here too in cleaning and cooking. She had not been introduced to the soldiers in Udine, because it is not customary to introduce a servant to guests. But out of curiosity as to what these strangers had to tell, she found a discreet place (obviously by permission), with her back to those present, and sat and listened to an unknown soldier's conversation and took note of his voice. And so, after thirty years (almost unbelievable!), the then-guest remembers an anonymous back and she remembers an anonymous voice, and here their anonymity ends. Up to this point the assumptions are reasonable and all is clear. All? Indeed?

"Would you like a drink? Cold or hot?"

"No, thank you. We'll wait for Sarah."

"My daughter and her children will soon come home from the beach."

*Her daughter*? The woman in black is Sarah's mother?? Oh, how eagerly had the two soldiers tried to work out why they had not been introduced to Mrs. Senegalia. Were the Senegalia children orphaned of their mother? Or perhaps their mother had been sick and confined to her bed? Paralyzed? Even so, it would have been appropriate to introduce the two Jewish soldiers to her. After all, a Jewish soldier from Eretz-Israel was not an everyday occurrence in the Second World War, and especially since the joy of meeting one another had instantly turned into a deep friendship between the two soldiers and the father and his children. So what could possibly be the reason for the estrangement or alienation of the mother? That was what the visiting soldiers had been debating in those days. The question remained sevenfold after the mother had appeared, healthy, active, and now a grandmother. It was clear that there was a secret here, one that extended over years, and they had no way of unraveling it.

Then came the turning point that revealed the secret. The woman asked about the life of the *Palestinese* in his land. "*E come sta Lei in Palestina*" ('And how are you managing in Palestine?'), she asked.

The blood drained from Ankori's face. Now he understood everything — the woman sitting with her back to the group, the fact that she was not introduced to her guests, the son's words that "Things at home were quite difficult", and certainly the evasiveness of the people in Venice. Ankori, highly agitated, whispered to Mekhek, "We're going". He got up and apologized that they could not wait any longer for Sarah. And they left.

Outside, Mekhek asked, "What happened? Why did you get so upset?" "Did you notice the question that she asked?" "Yes, she asked 'How's it going for you in Israel.'" 'No, she said in Palestine'. You see? Instinctively you erased the name that *she* used and inserted the name that *we* use. Thirty years after the State of Israel was established a Jew will not say 'Palestine' but 'Israel.'" "So what?" Detective Mekhek Bursztyn still did not reach a conclusion from these revelations. "There is only one explanation for it" — said his friend. "*She is not a Jew*."

Silence enveloped the two friends on the journey home. It is not clear what Mekhek thought. Obviously he participated in his friend's distress, and he too was disappointed that the thanks his friend had intended to extend to his past benefactors had been crushed in disappointment. Also, it is possible that he had learned a lesson, that one should not dig up the past or try to resurrect it in order to appease unfulfilled memories. The time has passed, the truth is irrelevant now, and the secret — and there is one in each family — should be left to rest in peace.

As opposed to Mekhek, the search's instigator was now troubled about the place of burial of Senegalia the father. It was clear that the Senegalia family had ceased to be Jewish. The mother was Christian from birth, the son was Franciscan by choice. The daughter was married to a Christian and whether she had converted or not, her children were obviously growing up as Christians. He recalled terrible incidents in Tarnów in which Christian wives, or children who had converted to Christianity, forced a Christian funeral on a Jewish husband or father who had died, and buried him in a Christian cemetery. He was worried that this was what they had done to the late Senegalia. And this must have been the reason why the community leaders in Venice had avoided an answer.

"How was it?" — the son asked, after the man from Eretz-Israel, as he remembered him, returned from the seashore. Ankori decided to tell him everything just as it had happened. There was a prolonged silence at the other end of the line.

"Now you know everything about us," the son returned the telephone receiver to his ear and his mouth.

"*Almost* everything!" — he added. "They say that Father died of grief at what I had done. Perhaps, but in any case I do not regret my deed. One thing I will tell you: when Father died — it was after my parents had moved to Milan in order to be close to my sister and the grandchildren — I received permission from the Father Superior of the monastery to bring my father to burial in our small cemetery. It is the only gravestone that does not have a cross on it. I engraved two Hebrew letters at its head, *peh* and *nun*, which I had seen on Hebrew gravestones, even though I don't know their meaning."

"*Qui é sepolto* ('Here lies')," Ankori inserted an explanation.

"Every day I go to pray next to the grave. And now, please do me a favor. I know how much you liked one another. Come, let's go to Father together."

The next day Mekhek brought his friend by car to the monastery gate. The son was already waiting for his guest. He led him to the monks' cemetery behind the building and pointed to the gravestone. There were long minutes of emotional silence. Then Ankori took out a skullcap that was always in his pocket and began, "*Yitgadal ve'yitkadash* ('Magnified and sanctified')". At the end of the Mourner's Prayer, the monk answered in a church-like melody, "Amen".

# VIII

The two soldiers were aware of the extent of the adventure. To travel from Udine to north Europe in the chaotic situation that reigned in the first few weeks after the war, when they had no independent mode of transportation and were unarmed, was no small thing. They knew that apart from great daring, without which no adventure is possible, they needed four conditions in order to achieve their aim. First of all, they needed information as to the whereabouts of the one and only, the beloved they were longing to join — 178 Company of the Brigade. Secondly, they had to enlist for the operation detailed and precise geographical knowledge of Western Europe. Thirdly, they needed the ability for fast orientation and navigation in unknown territory, and the intelligence to choose from the various unknown paths the most reasonable and promising unknown path. And last of all, they needed luck, barrels and barrels of luck!

Information: this was now Johnny's great moment, as well as a test of his talents as a "snooper". How and from where he drew this essential information remains a secret, a secret which even his friend was not privy to, despite Johnny's dependence on him. During the first few days after they had received the information that the Brigade had left, when the two soldiers were still in the hospital waiting for the safest and easiest time for their escape, the "snooper" put his feelers and nostrils into action in his best — and indeed, critical — "snoop". He learned that the Brigade had crossed Austria and western Bavaria, advanced along the right bank of the Rhine, crossed in the north to its left bank and distributed its units in Holland and Belgium.

Geographical information and navigational ability: after Johnny had fulfilled his mission, his partner's job began. The latter integrated the geographical knowledge he had acquired in his childhood from the atlas games he had played with his mother; the navigational ability he had specialized in when encircling all of Poland on his own at the age of fourteen; and the wisdom, apparently innate, to choose between possibilities. Independent life in Eretz-Israel since the age of seventeen, intensive university studies, and finally, military service had developed his knowledge and ability to make decisions. And so, he threw out the option of following in the Brigade's footsteps — one cannot compare hitchhiking to the massive trek of four hundred vehicles and thousands of armed Brigade fighters. Lone and unarmed soldiers wandering through a defeated land were prone to danger, especially since that land was no less anti-Semitic than before.

The above three factors — extensive geographical knowledge, orientation and navigational ability, and wisdom — dictated a path different from that of the Brigade. Rather, the two traveling soldiers had to encircle Austria and Germany from the west, in a wide arc that doubled and almost tripled the distance in comparison to the Brigade's direct path, and enter Belgium and Holland from northern France. Such a trek would take place from beginning to end in liberated and friendly territory, in which the soldiers could move around safely and with relative security. The leap west would not start in Udine, which was only a side path as far as long-distance transportation was concerned. Instead, they would first go down to Venice, a busy traffic junction, and from there start the journey, cutting across the breadth of northern Italy, passing over the French border, and continuing along the glamorous shore of the French Riviera as far as Nice. Here they would make a sharp change of direction. Whereas until now they had moved along the breadth of the continent, from now on they would go up its length and cross France from the Mediterranean Sea until they reached Paris. In Paris the chapter of hope would begin, hope that in one of the main boulevards of the capital a 178 vehicle would be seen, bringing a group of soldier-tourists from the Company for a holiday in Paris, and returning to Belgium with the previous group. This would be the final ride in the two soldiers' odyssey: return to the arms of 178 in a Company vehicle — and a peaceful end to the story.

But this was only a plan. Reasonable, exciting, but just a plan that had to be put into action. Now, with the crack of dawn, the two soldiers set out on their way just as their benefactor Senegalia had persuaded them. The historical Golden Calf would return to the pages of the Bible, and the redeemer from Udine would remain in Zvi and Johnny's hearts until their dying day as a memorable fact of the last days of the Second World War. This memory would be joined by that of the road from Venice to Nice, with all major and minor tribulations and difficulties, its comic situations, and even terrible disappointments that induced laughter the very next day, when a new hitched ride, obliging and long distance, erased any distress.

And have we already mentioned luck? The entire road was strewn with small pieces of luck and even smaller crumbs of luck that arrived, then disappeared as suddenly as they had come. But each one, however small, advanced the journey a bit, by one kilometer, by twenty kilometers, depending on the length of that stretch of the road. It seemed that the Angel of Luck understood who these travelers were and delayed the big bang until the right moment and the right people.

And then came the right moment and the right people. When Ankori and his friend stepped down from the train onto the platform at Nice station — and that was at the end of a series of hitched rides across all of northern Italy and a short trip by train from Menton, that is on the Italy-France border, via Monaco, to Nice — the bored Angel of Luck looked down from on high. And what a novelty — the travelers to whom he had thrown miserly crumbs of luck in Italy turned out to be a pair of Jewish soldiers with blue-white-blue badges on their crumpled uniforms. They were pale-faced and exhausted from hunger after who knows how many days and nights of sleepless wandering and insufficient nourishment. Sir Luck took pity on the two, especially as he divined that they were not in the best of health, but nevertheless had faced the hardships of the road, out of their own free will and initiative, in order to join their Unit so that they could continue to serve in the Jewish Brigade. He waved his hand, and look what happened: suddenly a train materialized on the railway tracks, and it had a sign on it that read Nice-Paris. It seemed to have been rented by the American army, for it was full of American soldiers who seemed to be going on leave to Paris, with not one man in civilian clothing.

Next to the stairs of the first carriage stood an officer and a sergeant, lists in hand. And a voice in Ankori's heart commanded him, "Go, speak". And he went and spoke. And the officer wrote down another two names on the page that was in his hand, and commanded the sergeant to let the two, clothed in British army uniform, enter the carriage, and to give to each five coupons for five days in the big hotel near the Opera building in Paris, in which his (American) soldiers would also spend the nights, as well as American K-rations for the way. Another wave of the hand, and the train moved off, at the command of the Archangel of Good Luck and a whistle of the engine. The two tired Brigade soldiers barely managed to sit on the carriage bench, when they fell into a deep slumber. Only the next morning's Paris sunshine woke them, to a breakfast from the K-rations that they had received. By the way, this was the first time they had tasted American army food. And so, rested and satiated, they got off onto the Paris platform.

Buses hired by the American army were parked in the square outside the large station, and all the soldiers, including the two in British uniform, got on and rode to the hotel on the corner of Opera square and the main boulevard. Registration and allocation of rooms took about an hour. Ankori and his friend took their bags to the room they were allotted, whose window overlooked the beautiful Palais Garnier housing the Opera. Then they went down to the street.

Paris! Oh, Paris!

"Do you get it, Johnny? Do you realize the situation we are in today after all our wanderings? For the first time since we escaped from the hospital we are our own masters. True, we were also free in Senegalia's house, but there was always an overhanging cloud of doubt as to whether or not we'd be caught before we succeeded in joining the Brigade. And that doubt was indeed realized, and descended upon us like lightning, and we had to escape again. True, we haven't yet found the Brigade, but we know it's nearby. Only a few hundred kilometers away. On the other hand, we are in Paris. Paris — do you get it? We have four complete days at our leisure to tour one of the most beautiful cities in the world!"

"That's all wonderful, but how will we get to the Brigade?"

"Don't worry. On Thursday we'll go out to the boulevard, with all our baggage — one bag on the back and one in hand — and we'll walk around in the street in 'ready' position, in case we meet soldiers from Eretz-Israel on holiday, or, even better, a 178 truck that brought the buddies on holiday to Paris and is taking the previous group back to the camp. And we'll go back with them as well — to 178."

"And what if this doesn't happen?"

"Then we'll go back to sleep a fifth night in our hotel — we have another coupon, don't we? — and on the sixth day we'll go out again to the boulevard with all our belongings, and I'm sure that we'll succeed. But for now, it's a shame to just stand around. It's better that we move. Let's go! As they say, 'Allons enfants de la patrie.'"

"Where do we go from here? First we need to get a map."

"We'll get by without a map. Here is the Opera. We'll cross the boulevard and continue straight down the road to Place Vendôme. We'll continue and turn right at Rivoli Street, on the other side of which are the Tuileries gardens. At the end of the street we'll go out into the main square, Place de la Concorde. Tomorrow we will start proper tours from that point, and we'll see all that Paris has to show to a tourist. Today we'll just get a feel for the city, walking along the boulevard and breathing the Paris air."

"When was the last time you were in Paris, that you remember every street? You couldn't have been here during the war years, so how? Did you come as a child or young man?"

"Neither. I have never been in Paris. My mother and I dreamt of visiting here one day. We were great travelers in our imagination and on the atlas pages. But with the poverty of the Jews in Poland, it was possible to learn things only from books — and to dream."

"Still, it's hard to believe. I come from an Anglo-Jewish home of means, but nevertheless we never traveled anywhere other than in Britain, and only now in the army am I seeing the outside world. Your background is so different from mine. Maybe it was the poverty that developed your dreams and the will to travel. I don't know whether to be jealous or embarrassed."

Excited by the wonderful tour that lasted four days and almost caused the two to forget the reason why they had come to Paris, Johnny again asked his guide-friend the same question he had asked on their first day. "Zvi, you've got to reveal to me the secret. How did you know Paris up and down, and especially in depth, without having ever visited here?"

"As far as in-depth is concerned, that is due to accumulated years of learning and interest in different fields that are not necessarily dependent on seeing the things themselves. But as to knowing Paris up and down, for that I have to thank Mme Badilac in the fourth-year French textbook, *Paris*. This book is a collection of conversations in which an imaginary lady with encyclopedic knowledge works as a guide in different regions of Paris, in the city streets and squares, in its gardens and cultural and artistic institutions — we only managed to visit some of these places in the four days we have had at our leisure. By reading the book over and over again, first as homework, later for pleasure, I took in every page and line, and I remember them as though the book was open in front of me today. By the way, you must have noticed that not only our trip on the first day, but also all the other trips, started from Place de la Concorde, and from there we set off for the places we wanted to visit. It seemed to me that you wondered at the fact that we were forever returning to that same square. Well, I was just following the mythical Madame Badilac, who started every trip from that square.

"Okay. Today it is Paris that says goodbye to us. Tomorrow we'll set off to the boulevard with our bags and try our luck. And if we succeed, this time it will be we who say goodbye and *au revoir* to Paris."

# IX

Ankori did not waste his time on the story of the adventure, even though the 178-soldiers of all ranks were keen to hear details after his return. True, the story was not on the same level as recapturing Tobruq or crossing the Senio, nor was it noted in the 178 Unit record as a personal initiative deserving a medal, but still, it was an experience worth recounting at the weekly Saturday eve gathering, and perhaps writing a ballad about.

Ankori declined both initiatives. Since he had reached Italian soil, he had not written a word, being too occupied with his missions. In view of his refusal, the Sabbath eve gathering nostalgically replayed his old ballads.

Just two days had passed since the two soldiers' return, when a charge sheet arrived from the Military Police regarding their leave without a 'pass'. Everyone — including Major Shalit, the new Company Commander, whose job, among other duties, was to judge offenders — knew well the background behind the lack of a 'pass', but the procedure had to be followed, and more importantly, had to be seen to be followed.

In accordance with the procedure, in which army tradition integrated signs of humiliation, the accused had to appear without beret and without army belt. Indeed, everything that took place outside, while awaiting the trial, was according to rules, as it should be. But once inside the Major's office, common sense reigned. Of course Ankori was absolved of any wrongdoing, as was Johnny, whose trial came immediately after that of his friend. Both were acquitted.

Nevertheless, despite his rank, and perhaps because of it, Shalit was alienated by the Haganah and TTG activists, who did not know "how to swallow this strange bird". They wondered "what he knows about our activities", and "if the fact of being a Jew and of having asked to be placed in the Jewish Brigade is enough for us to rely on him as 'one of us'". He was (or looked), from head to toe, like the epitome of a British officer: thin, upright and speaks through his nose as though he came straight out of Oxford!"

Slowly but surely the ice broke, and the one who broke it was Major Shalit, out of his own initiative. One day at dawn, two 178 truck drivers, together with a sergeant (sergeants usually took charge of an operation when more than one truck went on a mission) received a Movement Order to Germany. They were to transfer a British Company (it seems of the Engineering Corps) from Hanover to Essen in the Ruhr Basin. On the way back to the 178-base (which during that time had been moved from Tournai in Belgium to Breda in Holland, nearer the German border), the road passed by the liberated concentration camp Bergen-Belsen. This was a natural opportunity to fulfill diverse TTG missions in the camp. For, unfortunately, the Holocaust survivors still remained in the same camps the Nazis in their time had established for extermination purposes. It is true that the inmates were now free, but they had nothing to do and no hope, as a result of the British "White Paper" policy that fought against the rights of Jewish survivors to immigrate and begin new lives in the Land of Israel. The Jewish soldiers carried out their mission by bringing additional food and clothing, and assistance in immigration (called by the British "unlawful") to Eretz-Israel. British guard posts had been set up on the German border after the war, but on the most part, these checked the Movement Orders superficially and signaled the driver to pass. And yet, caution was still called for, because sometimes the check could be different, as Ankori was to experience on one of his trips to Germany, which included a mission to Bergen-Belsen.

That morning, the two drivers and the sergeant, charged to travel to Germany, were about to enter their cabins, when with no warning, as though out of nowhere, the Major suddenly appeared in front of them. The three soldiers jumped to "Attention", as was proper. Major Shalit seemed to be in a friendly mood, his nasal tone intensified when he joked. He immediately commanded them to stand "at ease", mentioned something about the weather, that according to the forecast was meant to be pleasant in the Rhine Valley and the Ruhr region, and ended with, "OK, to work chaps. Success in all that you do!" — and disappeared, as though he had vanished into thin air, leaving the boys open-mouthed and bewildered.

"Chaps"? "Success in *all* that you do"? Did he know or not? Shalit himself helped solve part of the riddle. While he did not discuss his background as a British officer, he did begin assisting the "Diaspora Committee" in all its operations, though he obviously kept understandable limits of discretion as required by his position. In view of this helping attitude, the whole camp's sympathy toward him increased, so much so that when he finished his tour of duty, the Company decided to inscribe him in the "Golden Book" of the Jewish National Fund.

Chance willed it, and over thirty years after the war, when Ankori and his family moved from Talpiyot to the rehabilitated Yemin Moshe neighborhood, one evening he met Shalit and his wife strolling on Hebron Street near their house in the Abu-Tor Quarter. Since then, in a sort of evening ritual, the Ankori couple would meet the Shalit couple for a chat in Hebron Street. After some time, Shalit gave Zvi, without saying a word, a number of photocopied sheets stapled into a booklet that contained an autobiographic sketch in English, probably written for a group of Anglo-Saxon immigrants. Only then, when he read the man's testimony about himself, did the Major's ex-subordinate learn two things. One — the Eastern European background of one who in his soldiers' eyes was the epitome of an English officer. Oh, what a pity that the soldiers of Eretz-Israel in those days did not know that their commander — the exemplary "British" officer — was Eastern European by birth, like the majority of the small Eretz-Israel population.

Shalit was born in Riga, Latvia (then under Russian rule). He and his parents had immigrated to England before the First World War. As a boy and young man, Shalit had become Anglicized in language and manners, but remained a Jew and warm Zionist and planned to immigrate to the Land of Israel in the future. Oh, how much anguish and unfounded suspicions would have been spared had all this been known previously. Only at a later stage — still without knowing his background, but thanks to his "Jewish" deeds — did Major Shalit earn the esteem due to him from the start.

The second thing that came out of his autobiography was doubly saddening: it turned out that until the end of his days, Shalit did not understand the lack of trust in him on the part of the inner Haganah nucleus of the camp. He had a natural love for England and the English and believed in their decency, and had not been witness to their colonial misdeeds in Palestine, for he had immigrated to the Jewish State after the English had left the Land. This was why he did not understand that the spirit of conspiracy characterizing the Haganah members and the other Eretz-Israeli resistance organizations was an inherent part of their way of life and their attitude to the English. Even one year before the end of the war, at a time when thirty thousand Eretz-Israeli volunteers were faithfully serving in His Majesty's army, other English soldiers, in the same uniform, carried out cruel searches for defense weapons in the kibbutzim. At that time, in his poetry Ankori expressed the pain of a Jewish soldier on hearing the news from the Land. Is it a wonder that distrust of England was the result? And how sad, oh, how sad it was that during all those years since he was appointed commander of 178 and until his dying day, this noble man carried in his heart an inerasable angry complaint against the distrust he suffered from his Company at first.

About three weeks after Ankori returned from Italy to his Unit, he was appointed sergeant. The sergeants were the basis of the military establishment, and they unquestionably merited the praiseworthy description as "the backbone of the British Army". Despite this, the new sergeant wore his stripes with mixed feelings. On the one hand, he was flattered by the congratulations of the soldiers and veteran officers with whom he had experienced the long course of four years of war, serving in Egypt, el-Alamein, all of Libya, Malta, and the whole length of Italy up to Germany, without injury. No injury, that is, apart from the last encounter, just at the end of the war, with the accursed Anopheles mosquito, the only enemy that beat him and knocked him down trembling and shivering with malaria. So as a soldier he had every reason to be proud of his record. As a Jew and Eretz-Israeli he was also allowed to look back on his activities on behalf of the refugees with justified satisfaction. And personally, he felt that these, as well as the fifth year before demobilization, were the best years of his young life, and the most meaningful in building his character and discovering his strengths and talents for the future. Similarly, it was an honor for him, as a veteran Haganah member, to bear a similar rank to that of well-known Haganah commanders who had joined 178 Unit, such as Levitza, his Haganah commander in Jerusalem, Eliyahu Cohen (later known as Colonel Ben Hur) and Yehiel Teiber. Nevertheless, he worried that the three sergeant stripes meant he would have to devote much time to administrative tasks rather than to field duties — and this was a time when field work was crucial. Not that administration was unimportant, but that was not what he had volunteered for. The World War had ended, but *our* "Jewish" war was just beginning, to rehabilitate those who had been pulled out from the fire and help them rebuild their lives in the Land of Israel.

Already in Tarvisio, when the survivors began streaming through that gate to Italy, Ankori had decided that when the fighting was over but the military service continued, he would focus on two goals: communal and personal. The communal would be expressed through operations in the liberated concentration camps. In Holland he learned that the camp nearest to the 178-base was Bergen-Belsen. On the other hand, the personal goal related to finding a way to reach Poland, to which Mala his sister would presumably come with those returning from Siberia as a result of the repatriation agreement between the Polish government-in-exile and the USSR. The trouble was that Poland and Eastern Europe were "out of bounds" to western forces and open only to the Red Army. But he, Ankori, had to get in there, no matter what! The letter with Mala's address that Mother had sent him via the Red Cross and which he had carried with him during all the war years burned his breast like fire and did not abate.

Ankori considered the communal goal as taking precedence, and his experience in carrying out such operations had been well-known for some time. The Company Command put him in charge of convoys. This arrangement enabled him to move survivors from Bergen-Belsen within the clandestine movement that was called simply, *Berihah* ("flight"). This name was repeated in a whisper on the lips of thousands in Europe. Whether it was because some command followed the increase in 178-trucks traveling to Germany, or whether someone informed about the vehicles' deviation from the path designated in the Movement Order and stopover in Bergen-Belsen, trouble did not delay in coming. One should presume that it was political, and came from Jerusalem or Cairo.

One morning, Sergeant Ankori's truck drivers passed the guard post in a routine superficial check on their way to unload cargo in Essen. On their way back they stopped in Bergen-Belsen and with twilight they continued on their way to the 178-camp in Breda. But this time, at the border post, the guard did not wave them on as usual. Instead he stopped the convoy and ordered the drivers to get out of the cabins. Sergeant Ankori immediately went into the office to find out the reason for the guard's action.

Meanwhile, the vehicles were checked by British sergeants,

whom Ankori had never seen before. They introduced themselves as serving in the Intelligence Corps. They found the last two trucks empty and returned them to Sergeant Ankori to decide what to do with them. He commanded their drivers to continue to the camp without him and report the incident. In his own truck the sergeants found five passengers in military uniform, but from their behavior it was immediately evident that they were not soldiers. Due to lack of a common language they were returned to Bergen-Belsen without interrogation, and were commanded to change their clothes and return the uniforms to the driver.

The Jewish sergeant remained in the office with his interrogators. The interrogation lasted until midnight. It was carried out fairly and with respect for the subject's rank, but with pressure. Questions were repeated again and again as to the details of his actions throughout the day, obviously in order to reveal gaps in his testimony. The sergeant's claim was that with nightfall, five soldiers had stopped him on the road and asked him in Hebrew if he was returning to the camp. It was clear to him that they belonged to the Unit, though not to his platoon, and he immediately answered, "Get in!" That was what anyone would do. It was not his duty to check hitchhikers' identities, as long as they were in army uniform. Throughout the interrogation, while facing constant questions from interrogators who were replaced every so often, the sergeant did not deviate even a little from his original story. He spoke with complete confidence and in English that was better than that of his interrogators. He was released at midnight, but was told that he would be interrogated again.

And indeed, beginning with that incident, a team of interrogators would come to Camp 178 every week and over long hours, repeatedly interrogate Sergeant Ankori as to the details of his movements on that day of the problematic journey. The interrogators' attitude continued to be fair and respectful, but the questions were increasingly designed to trip him up, whether in the hope that he would become exhausted and break down, or that with time he would fall into contradictions or deviations from the original story.

But nothing like this happened, and the interrogators understood that they were wasting their time and stopped coming.

There is a comic appendix to the end of the story. In the final report summary that the British Intelligence published in March 1946 on "illegal immigration" to Palestine (the document is filed in the Public Record Office in London), the author of the report lends Ankori the doubtful honor of mentioning him by name and rank as one who transported a female refugee in his cabin. The woman reported that the truck happened to cross her path as she went to visit her brother, who was serving in the Brigade's artillery. The report admits that the investigation did not bear fruit. Although there is some similarity between the two hitchhiking incidents, the mention of Ankori's name as somehow involved in the second incident was totally unfounded. Possibly, the two stories were mixed up in the file, and the one who summed them up in the report, knowing Ankori's name from the first investigation, implicated him in the second incident too.

After all, who can fathom the secret way of reporting by the Intelligence Services?

❖ ❖ ❖

Apart from these incidents, life in the unit in Holland during the first months after the war continued as usual. Unit 178 continued to be praised for the quality of its professional work and the high motivation of its soldiers, that increased for reasons obvious to the Eretz-Israelis but not to the army authorities, who were combating weakness and fatigue in units eagerly awaiting discharge. At the end of July, 178 moved its camp to Scheveningen, a charming summer resort near the Hague that overlooks the sea. Every morning one could see old Queen Wilhelmina riding a bicycle along paths in the woods with no escort. Juliana, her daughter, in line to the throne, also walked around without escort. On his visit to Leiden, the university city, Ankori spotted her participating in a students' rally. One who had not forgotten he was still a student was happy to visit the university library and even peep into its rich manuscripts division.

The Dutch roads were destroyed from the bombings of the two fighting sides. So were the ports and the bridges. On one journey to ruined Rotterdam, once the largest port in Northwest Europe, two trucks that were under Ankori's command failed to reach their destination. Their drivers, together with their sergeant, had to remove the remains of houses with their own hands in order to pave the way for their vehicle among the heaps of ruins. Nighttime driving was especially dangerous, because of the fog and steam rising from the rivers, apparently a typical phenomenon in the summer season.

One such evening, dark and drowning in its fog and steam, Ankori, alone in the driver's compartment, drove on a dark road leading to the bridge over the Schelde River. He could not see even one meter ahead of him. An inner voice whispered to him: Stop and check! When he got out, he saw that his vehicle was only centimeters away from the edge of an abyss created when the bridge was bombed.

If he had not stopped at the very last moment, this book would never have been written.

*CHAPTER FIVE*

# Each and All Took to the Road

## I

Each and all took to the road.

At the outset of war, when on September 1, 1939, the Wehrmacht burst through the western border of Poland, only a few dared take the first hesitant steps on an escape route they had never known before. They reached the sobering conclusion that the Polish army would not hold out against the German invader for more than a few weeks. In addition, the well-founded fear that the Nazis would immediately initiate persecutions against Polish Jewry, like Kristallnacht in Germany the year before, persuaded them to leave in order to save their souls. [The terms "Final Solution" and "Holocaust" were as yet unknown at the beginning of September 1939.] The flight was fraught with danger. Often the refugees were forced to step hurriedly off the road, which was in full view of the Messerschmitts, and take temporary shelter from the bombings in an incidental trench or nearby sewage pipe. German superiority reinforced the refugees' predictions regarding the approaching catastrophe and final defeat, inciting redoubled efforts to escape. Although Polish combat was not lacking in motivation and heroism, those qualities alone were not sufficient to stop the enemy. All of Europe was slow to respond to the Blitzkrieg and powerless to develop new tactics in battling the invader's unprecedented technique. Meanwhile, as in years past, Poland's military traditionalists prided themselves on their cavalry, as if shining swords and galloping horses were enough to force the enemy's tanks to bow their heads and silence their cannons.

Each and all took to the road.

After the daring few came the multitudes: without map or compass, guided like birds by a hidden sense of direction that was partner to the inborn instinct of survival, not knowing what awaited them at the end of the road: safe shores, or, God forbid, an abyss of destruction. Wave after wave they flowed, with only one goal in mind: to survive — to survive! Until the enemy was beaten and the storm of war abated.

The gray journey would take days and weeks, by foot and any available conveyances, on the roof of a freight train or by an exhausting grip on the edge of a passenger train car, under the wearying autumn sun by day and the cold moon by night. Feet dragging, September became October, October turned into November. Dusty autumn roads became covered with snow — a Russian snow to which nothing else in the world compares.

Geography dictated that Lwów be for the refugees of western Galicia the first stop in their wanderings. Before the outbreak of the Second World War, Lwów, as long as it was under Polish rule, had been the capital of Eastern Galicia. But on September 17, 1939, the Red Army invaded Poland and took control, by agreement with Germany, over the whole eastern part of the country. Thus Lwów, from now on Lvov, became the second-largest city in the Soviet Ukraine, after its capital, Kiev. Indeed, during the first few months, there was no better place to wait out the terrors of war and hope for the best, and the refugees deluded themselves that they could relax there until the fires dwindled.

But what geography dictated, history erased. The Soviets, and after them the Germans, who invaded the USSR in June 1941, turned Lvov into a dangerous trap, a marshy swamp crying out with poverty, despair, and worst of all, fear.

In order to reach Lwów, or as it was later called, Lvov, from western Galicia, one had first to traverse the San River. It separated two worlds: the world of Nazi occupation, where death peered from every crevice, and the unknown world of Eastern Europe, which had beckoned at the youth — mostly Jewish youth — for some twenty years as a Soviet Eden of justice and equality. But in Poland it was a forbidden fruit.

Each and all took to the road.

Their story will never be fully told. For this story is comprised of thousands of stories belonging to thousands of people. Each one has a name and a past that must not be erased. Each had a home and a family. Each dreamt of returning. Perhaps he will find the house he fled still standing, perhaps the family he left behind is still alive. And if all these no longer existed, at least the memories remained.

Only a few would have the passion to document their story with their own hand, recording it while they experienced it. If they did not document it while it happened, most would not have the strength to recount it after they returned, sometimes not even after many years had passed.

If indeed it is told, the story will be reconstructed only partially, skipping over painful details, whether intentionally or unintentionally. The teller chokes back a sigh that begs for release, stubbornly stifling the tears imprisoned within the inner reaches of the soul and memory, a choked and silent cry.

Of course, it is impossible to tell the stories of each of the hundreds and thousands of Tarnów natives who went to Lwów. We will thus draw a mere five or six drops from the depths of time, hoping that they are representative of all the young exiles who fled the invading army. They refused to surrender to the difficulties mounting in their paths daily and swore to hang on, no matter what.

Each one of these drops is a world unto itself, and redeeming it (as the Sages used to teach) speeds redemption for the world. Each drop is a personal story, personal despite representing a broad public. Although due to lack of documentation it may contain just a tiny amount of the experience, that little deserves to be engraved into memory in the chronicles of Humanity.

We have already recounted a little of Kresch, the Hebrew literature teacher at the Safah Berurah high school. He was a romantic who loved to travel. He documented his trips with photographs, and showed the slides to his students. Every summer he would tour a different country. A fervent Zionist, he concluded each trip with a visit to Eretz-Israel.

When the Nazi regime closed all schools in the town, Kresch, still a bachelor, returned to his mother in his hometown of Lesko, near the San River. There, in September 1939, he met his student Idek Biberberg, during Idek's flight eastward from the horrors of war. That night, teacher and student forded the river. They parted on the opposite bank, each heading toward Lwów. From now on, each would face his own fate and attempt to adapt to life in the new country.

Each and all took to the road.

Among the first to push eastward were Monek Leibel and his brother Henek. They left on September 5, 1939, before Kraków and Tarnów fell into enemy hands. Was it a premonition of military disaster that motivated them? Or a realistic evaluation of the situation?

Their father, a well-known Tarnów physician, was often called to the Wróbel home when one of the children was ill. This was an opportunity for the imps to make their first calculations in geometry: whose bald spot was larger in circumference, Father's or Dr. Leibel's? This amusing activity based on the bald spot sizes had the added value of distracting the child's mind from the pain and discomfort of the examination, and returning the smile to his face.

When the two Leibel brothers decided to flee the city in view of the imminent occupation, they went down Lwowska Street, the main street and the longest in east Tarnów. At the edge of the city, the street continues as an inter-city road leading east to Lwów — hence its name.

That day, only a few refugees wound their way down the road, pushing improvised carts loaded with hastily packed bundles. The pilots of the German Stuka fighter plane considered them an appropriate target for their machine guns. But a few days later, after Tarnów fell and they heard the news from the fronts, masses began to crowd the road in flight. The skies expanded for squadrons of bombers, and the Stukas made way, with due respect, for the Messerschmitts.

A ten-day march, interspersed with a constant game of hide-and-seek with the bombers and fighter planes, brought the youths to the San River. Polish army units were spread out along its two banks, unaware of the conspiracy being concocted behind their backs. As soon as the brothers forded the river on September 15 and began to walk eastward, one day and then another, they suddenly noticed a change that dominated the entire surroundings.

Giant signs in Cyrillic letters, mostly printed on red cloth, suddenly appeared, and red flags proliferated on the roofs and carpeted the windowsills. Groups of soldiers were scattered around, wearing uniforms different from those of the Polish army, but also different from the Wehrmacht uniforms. The two realized that something surprising, even historic, was taking place during their short advance on the soil of Eastern Galicia, but lacking a newspaper or radio, they had no idea what it was. Their progress remained unhindered until they reached Lwów, although the number of red flags increased. When they arrived at their destination, they realized that this was no longer the Lwów they had known in their youth, from school trips or visits with their parents for family celebrations. When they had first arrived here on the fast train, they had been taken by the beauty of the terminal. Along with the track, it had been built during the nineteenth century, when the Austro-

Hungarian Empire had ruled Galicia. It had made Lwów the capital of all Galicia, calling it Lemberg. The youths searched for the Latin sign that had appeared in large letters above the main entrance: *Leopolis semper fidelis*. Their father had explained: "Lwów is forever faithful". But the sign was gone. Lwów, now loyal to another side, had removed the sign from the entrance wall. Lwów was no longer Polish, it was Lvov. Ukrainian. Ruled by the Soviet Union.

Monek and Henek adapted to Lvov and to the poverty that dominated most of the refugee community and the rest of the city as well. They stood in line every morning to receive their daily ration of black bread. Their poverty was assuaged by Monek's work as a glazier. For a young man who would eventually become a doctor, his job was appropriate as a unique form of "healing": he healed "wounds" in thousands of windows in buildings in Polish Lwów that had been bombed during the early stages of the war. Monek's employer was Unger, a refugee from Tarnów and a family friend, who had been a glazier back in Tarnów and had found work in Lwów repairing the first damages of the war.

The two young refugees discovered that their father, an officer in the Polish medical corps, had moved along with the defeated Polish army units to Rumania and then to Hungary. After four months in Lwów, they decided to return to Tarnów in order to rescue their mother who had stayed behind alone, and take her to join their father in Hungary.

Although at first this plan seemed foolhardy, the rumors from Tarnów that reached the Lvov diaspora encouraged them to pursue it. These rumors indicated that after the first harsh events (such as the destruction of synagogues, the decree to wear the "Jewish ribbon," the closing of all schools, and the appointment of commissars for important businesses), life had entered a tolerable routine. The first fears that had caused many to flee hastily eastward did not materialize. It was not clear who spread these rumors or on what they were based; at any rate, a significant number of Tarnovians decided to return home.

Unlike the eastward crossing, the Leibel brothers very wisely did not ford the San westward together. Henek, the younger brother, went first. He forded the river safely and continued toward Tarnów. Monek was supposed to ford it a week later. As planned, he entered the border area at Szuwsko, a deserted site whose main feature was its anonymity. But conditions that night were not conducive to crossing. January on the San was harsh and stormy, and January 1940 was no less severe than its predecessors. Still, stormy weather could be a blessing, since it distracted the border patrol and eased the crossing to the western bank. But this time, the opposite happened: the guards heard even the faintest noise. Monek took cover in a nearby brick factory in order to warm up near the furnace. The warmth combined with his exhaustion from the walk made his eyelids droop, and he fell asleep at the very moment when vigilance was a matter of life or death.

We do not know whether someone informed the border patrol about the presence of a stranger in the area, although we cannot ignore this possibility. We might also reasonably assume that the border patrol discovered Monek by chance. Not only was the entrance of an unauthorized person into the border area a breach of Soviet law, but the authorities always treated such incidents with particular sensitivity: suspicion of spying was almost always the automatic reaction. At any rate, when Monek awoke to the guards shaking his body and suddenly saw two round military caps leaning over him and a flashlight shining into his eyes, he realized that he was in trouble. The guards did what they had been trained to do: silently, with a push or two, they signaled that he should stand up. Then they handcuffed him, and without asking his name or what he was doing there, sent him under guard to the nearby prison in Sieniawa.

Thus began Monek's odyssey, in innocence on his part, from prison to prison and interrogation to interrogation: from Sieniawa to Przemyśl; then he was deported from Galicia to Odessa, and from Odessa to Kuybishev. The accusation: spying. The sentence: three years incarceration. The relative ease of the sentence for such a serious crime proves that the judges were convinced of his innocence, but allowing him to go free with no penalty at all was inconceivable under the practice of Soviet justice. "How can my imprisonment," mocked Monek, examining the irony of his situation, "compare to the fate of the communist sympathizers who were so harshly oppressed in pre-war Poland? They were imprisoned because of the Polish government's hostility to the USSR, but now, when they arrive as refugees in the land of their dreams, they are thrown like me into prison and serve even harsher sentences than I do, although I never was a supporter of this regime. And how can my situation compare to that of the Soviet soldiers who fought in the Spanish civil war, and, having returned in late 1939 to their homeland, also 'merited' years of imprisonment? And have we already forgotten the horrors of the Moscow trials of 1937, including that of Karol Radek, a Tarnów native who became a leader in the USSR?"

Monek had no choice but to remain in jail, hoping for the success of his brother, who must surely have crossed the San, reached Tarnów, and been welcomed into their mother's arms with enough love for both boys. "Wait for me, *mamushka*," he thought, referring to her with the diminutive for "mother." "And wait, Henek. We'll go to Father together." But this script, starring the hopeful chance for a family reunion in Tarnów, was nothing but an illusion that Monek fabricated during the hours of maddening isolation and longing to return home, and alas, it was far from reality. The events that actually took place in Tarnów were utterly different from the rumors of the occupying army's moderation that had encouraged many refugees to return from exile in the Ukraine to their city. Monek had no idea that the returnees were murdered in cold blood even before the three fatal *akcja*s began in the city, and before the convoys of survivors of those *akcja*s were sent to the death camps. By the beginning of 1943, all the Jews of Tarnów had been exterminated, young and old, men and women, youth and children. Henek and his mother were among the last to be deported to the death camp in Płaszów, near Kraków. But they and their fellow sufferers never reached their destination. They choked to death on the way, sprayed with quicklime inside the train car, lying on top of the other occupants. In the meantime, it had been discovered that the father had died in Hungary. And thus the rescue adventure — the heroic idea of loving sons — came to its bitter end.

## II

A short time passed, and the refugees' sincere attempts to adapt to the way of life in their country of refuge failed, although not by their own fault. Apparently the authorities had plotted from the beginning to exploit this immense labor force that the circumstances of war had brought to their country. In July 1940 deportation orders rained down on the heads of the thousands who had hoped they had been rescued from the Nazis. Suddenly they realized that they were forsaken in the land of their salvation.

Each and all took to the road — again.

But this time they did not travel of their own will to a shared destination, as they had traveled full of hope to Lwów. This time they were exiled from Lvov by decree of the authorities and deported far beyond the Ural mountains, to the plains of Central Asia and the barren expanses of the Siberian taiga, and even to the Arctic Circle. They were scattered throughout hundreds of gulags, where they were ordered to build with their own hands forced labor camps for themselves. Even worse, the exiles no longer moved in large groups, each supporting the other as partners in destiny, but wound their way in sad isolation, individually or in small groups, each one to his predetermined place of exile and type of forced labor imposed on him.

For days and weeks they wandered until they reached their decreed destination. The clothes they had worn when they set out faded into rags. Their shoes did not survive the mud and snow. Their bodies shriveled from hunger, thirst, disease, and cold. Now that their fate was reversed, these refugees, who had fled German occupation and slaughter and were rescued by the USSR from the jaws of the Nazi death machine, became slaves in their land of refuge. The land they had seen from afar as a Garden of Eden became an enormous prison: the innocent prisoners were stripped of basic freedoms, chained to the sites where they were forced to perform slave labor, their arms tied into the straightjacket of futile slavery, their necks bent under the burden of a tyrannical regime that knew no mercy.

When each and all took to the road in July 1940, the deportation decree applied to Monek as well, despite his incarceration. He was not released, of course, but ordered to go north to forced labor. The muddy northern tundra in the Arctic Circle, which was sown with forced labor camps and soaked with the sweat and blood of forced laborers like himself, enjoyed only two months of a season that might be called summer. Monek and his partners-in-destiny labored at laying a railroad line from Kotlas to Vorkuta, to allow access to the coal mines, then planned for development. The nature of the work abrogated the need for the usual practice of establishing permanent camps. Rather, each section of rail was accompanied by temporary camps, which moved forward as each section of the rail was completed.

Monek began to keep a diary only after six months of toiling in the Arctic Circle. But at times, after he went to the south, the memory of the Arctic period filtered between the lines, and it is a fact that it was not the labor or the sweat that had caused him to tremble, not the hunger, or the kilometers he had to march daily back and forth between the tent and the rail. Those were repressed into the back of his mind. Rather, it was the cold.

The cold!

"There, in the Arctic Circle, on the banks of the Pieczora, Usa Ust-Usa, along the northern shoulders of the Urals, the winter was already at its height in September. The northern lights appeared. The tundra was covered with a thick coat of snow. The cold was about minus sixty degrees Celsius, and the *purga* (arctic blizzard) seemed to me like the end of the world."

Or on the banks of the Volga in Kuibishev:

"The winter was severe. The cold was minus fifty degrees Celsius. The snow reached the height of a man, and when the wind blew — Lord help us! But we prayed that the wind would intensify, for then we could stay 'home.' Indeed, we could not go out to work. We could barely take a few steps outside to get food.

Despite the beauty of the Arctic heavens, even the stars trembled with cold.

The heavens looked beautiful on the frozen nights. Each star was alive, trembling, jumping in place, as if wanting to warm up. Above every streetlamp, a gigantic pillar of light beamed upwards, so that the entire horizon was like a sanctuary, surrounded and supported by enormous pillars.

*(Extracts from the diary of Monek Leibel, translated from the Polish by Shulah Laviel)*

Monek Leibel in Vorkuta

However harsh Monek's imprisonment odyssey and the increasing physical exhaustion and mental pressure during the period of laying the railway line to Vorkuta in the Arctic cold, both jailers and jailed remained unaware that the succession of incarcerations and forced labor actually granted Monek the gift of life, making him the lone survivor of the fire that exterminated the entire Leibel family.

Idek Biberberg never spoke about what happened to him after he parted from his teacher Bezalel Kresch on the right bank of the San. There is no doubt that he reached Lwów like the other refugees. But how did he make a living? Where did he live, or at least find shelter? Was he imprisoned for a short or a long time, just as Monek Leibel and most of the other youngsters were imprisoned for varying periods of time? We only know that when the deportation order arrived, he was sent to a forced labor camp close to Murmansk, far off in the Arctic Circle, one Tarnovian laborer among tens of thousands who had been exiled to the northern frontier to construct an enormous aluminum and nickel factory, and next to it a power station for the factory. Just like Monek Leibel, Idek Biberberg left behind no written description of how he suffered from the Arctic cold and from the forced hard labor in the Murmansk region. But while Monek in the relevant parts of his later diary gives random hints as to the locations of his imprisonment and his suffering from the cold during his labor, Idek refused to discuss that chapter of his life.

In a series of private meetings (until Idek's death in Haifa a few years ago), the author of this book tried, in vain, to encourage Idek to talk about that dark period of his life. It was as though Idek had closed off those experiences in a forgotten corner of his mind and made a conscious decision never to visit it again. Or perhaps he managed to put the memories of that period behind him and erase them completely. He was only willing to talk about his schooldays, the years when he shared the bench with Hesiek Wróbel in the Hebrew high school. The school friend had the impression that during the period of his forced labor, Idek must have used the recollection of those school days as a defence mechanism. During the sleepless, cold Arctic nights, he would recall those happy days at the Hebrew high school, sights he had seen during school trips, experiences with the Zionist youth movement, books he had read, and lectures that had impressed him. The memories bolstered him against despondency and loss of hope in the liberation that was so long in coming, and would perhaps never come.

But suddenly a hint of the liberation appeared. In the beginning it was just a feeling based on a change in the behavior of the guards towards the prisoners, and their willingness to tell them the news that came from the war front.

In October 1941, that feeling turned into real information.

Like a fire in a field of weeds it spread throughout the gulag network to the Murmansk district — an end to the suffering has arrived. Following the German invasion of the Soviet Union in June that year, an agreement was signed between the Soviet government and the Polish government-in-exile that led to the release of all prisoners of Polish origin, including the Jews, from the work camps.

They called this act of government a "general amnesty". Amnesty? For whom? For which criminals? For what crime? None of the prisoners amongst the forced laborers had committed any crime. If someone had, it was the Soviet government — a crime against humanity. It must be stated loudly and clearly, for the sake of humanity and history, that the extravagant construction projects the Soviet Union implemented to the admiration of its supporters were no better than pyramids built by slaves.

The only factor that alleviates the Soviet blame is that the lives of the laborers were saved by the fact that they were located in the Asian region of the Soviet Union. A moderating factor, yes, but it cannot cancel the accusation that hundreds of thousands of free people, through no fault of their own, suffered forced labor at the hands of the Soviets who exploited them as an unpaid workforce.

## III

Each and all took to the road.

They set out for the third time. The first time they left home as free people searching for refuge. The second time they turned into evacuees from their safe haven in Lvov and were sent as forced laborers to the harshest regions of that enormous land. Now they were moving for the third time, as freed slaves whose prison gates had been opened. October, November, December 1941 — a Russian winter. Wandering across the snowy plains, abandoned to hunger and cold — but this time they are marching to their freedom. They are still in exile, yes, they are exiled from their homes, which perhaps no longer exist, and from their land, to which they will never return. But they are freed from imprisonment and forced labor. They are called '*Grajdanin*'s, free people.

They took to the road — but where to?

In addition to the ongoing struggle for survival, two goals charted the wanderers' way in this wilderness of people — two aims that led them like the biblical pillar of smoke and pillar of fire, not knowing which of the two roads that the refugee might choose would lead him to life. One way was to start moving west, toward home — either as a soldier in a Polish or Red Army tank, or as a partisan stealing along the forest paths, or as a wayfarer making his way in his ragged clothes. It was good, in fact, that the return home was still several years away, for it left time for dreaming. Alas, on their return home, they would often find that their home either no longer existed, or had been taken over by the non-Jews who had previously been their neighbors. Or even worse, they would discover that their homeland, even though it too had suffered severely in war, remained indifferent to their pain and ignored their tragedy. Sometimes, their country was as openly hostile to

Jews as was the German invader whom they and the Allies had stubbornly fought to defeat.

The alternative was to break through south along the Allied supply route in the Persian Gulf toward Iran and the Middle East, a direction that offered a breath of hope for a new beginning in Eretz-Israel. The tension between the two roads was intolerable, the struggle to decide exhausting. For no matter what choice was made, it would always involve an element of chance. Any solution was final and irreversible. This was a game of life or death.

Some of the liberated youngsters joined the Polish army that had been formed under the command of General Anders and whose purpose was to participate in the Allies' last war effort on the Western front. The others temporarily settled in the Asian regions in the south of the USSR. What paradox! In the European section of the Soviet Union the Wehrmacht continued to devour the flesh of Russia and the Ukraine piece by piece, and did not stop until its progress was checked in Stalingrad. After the Wannsee Conference, the wheels of the Nazi destruction machine turned ever faster, working at full speed and cruelty against the European Jews. Yet here in Soviet Asia, the liberated camp inmates began the march to freedom. There was nothing like it since the Israelites' Exodus from Egypt. Being the descendants of the refugees from famine in ancient Canaan, who had first found refuge in Egypt but eventually became slaves to Pharaoh, their liberation was a modern exodus.

At that time, Monek Leibel was liberated from Vorkuta. When he left the tundra to freedom, he turned south, deciding to finish his exile as a fighter in the Polish army that was then forming in Central Asia.

Monek Leibel, now known as Dr. Amos Laviel, a resident of Haifa and a respected ophthalmologist, recounts that his journey took weeks — weeks of cold and hunger in a creeping freight train, during which the liberated slave ate whatever came to hand. That might be a slice of bread grabbed from a friend who had two, or a piece of wild vegetable picked at the edge of the railroad track.

Finally he crossed the black sands of the Turkmen desert (Kara Kum) and reached the Amu-Daria River on the western border of Uzbekistan. Over the course of history, that river had witnessed countless invasions and waves of refugees.

Idek Biberberg also began his march south to long-awaited freedom from slavery in the Murmansk camp network. For two and a half months he wandered, finally crossing the Kara Kum and reaching the west bank of the Amu-Daria in January 1942.

The two Tarnovian partners-in-destiny met on the riverbank. After spending a few days in heart-to-heart conversation, they separated, each following his chosen path. Monek joined the Polish army and eventually reached Palestine. Unlike him, Idek, crossed the river to the east and entered the gates of Bukhara.

## IV

Uzbekistan, historically called Bukhara, is embraced by two arms of water — the Syr-Daria and the Amu-Daria. Nowadays, the name refers to the city of Bukhara alone, which is still the diamond in the Uzbek crown. As the two rivers cascade down the northern slopes of the Afghan mountains, they flow around the Kizil-Kum, the Red Sands of the Uzbekistan desert, forming wide deltas as they seek refuge in the Aral Sea. Jews lived there for centuries, and some of them came to the Holy Land in the late nineteenth century. Full of religious fervor, they arrived at the same time as the First Aliyah, but had no conscious connection to the Hibbat Zion movement. They settled in Jerusalem, building the neighborhood that is still called "Bukharian", no matter what the origin of its present residents.

Then — wonder of wonders! — in 1941–42, amid a mixture of Muslim-Turkic Uzbeks and Tajiks, Kirgizis and Kazakhs, in the shadow of both the ancient minarets and the modern red flags, there sprung up a small Ashkenazi-Jewish Tarnów group of refugees, war survivors, and liberated slaves from the labor camps. This new Asian diaspora spread to three cities — Bukhara, Samarqand, and Tashkent.

Bukhara. Did it ever occur to the war exiles from Tarnów, searching at the beginning of 1940 for refuge in this land until the situation stabilized, that one thousand or twelve hundred years previously, some of their ancestors had already been there and had played a historic role in regional and world trade? Had they ever heard of the "Radanites" — merchants originating from Near Eastern Jewish communities, who, due to favorable international circumstances, had for more than two hundred years enjoyed a quasi-monopoly on international trade from Europe on the famous Silk Road to China? But even if they had heard of their Jewish predecessors, they were hardly interested in them. The sole focus of them all was survival.

The prisoners' exodus from the gulags and arrival in Bukhara was an exciting, historic drama. But among the refugees were also some natives of Tarnów who reached Bukhara straight from the West, having suffered neither the misery of Siberia nor the pain of the forced labor camps. One who followed that particular path was Rachela Spinrad of the Tarnów orphanage, who had been a schoolmate of Hesiek in primary school. And blessed be the guardian angel of Jewish orphans, who whispered to Rachela that she and her younger sister Fella should flee far to the East, before the ground of Lvov, overflowing with refugees, began to burn beneath their feet. Their early flight saved the two young women from the deportations of 1940 and the imprisonments in labor camps. Instead of map and compass, Rachela relied on geographical place-names in Soviet literature of the 1920s and '30s that was popular with members of the Zionist left-wing youth movements. In this manner she managed to navigate safely across the vast Russian continent.

Following Sienkiewicz's *By Fire and By Sword*, the only Polish book she carried with her that was written before the Bolshevik Revolution, she crossed the Ukrainian plains and rivers and moved along the sites of Gladkov's masterpiece *Cement* and the Donbass coal mines. From there she went on to Stalingrad and took a boat on the Volga to Astrakhan — as in the title of Pilniak's book, *The Volga Flows into the Caspian Sea*. She continued south along the eastern shore of the sea until the port of Krasnovodsk, and then crossed the Black Sands of Turkmenistan, finally reaching Samarqand, Bukhara and *Tashkent, City of Bread*, following the title of Nievyarov's book.

Thus, advancing along memory lane, the two sisters made their way to Uzbekistan — hungry, but free; hurt, but free; and often, on the verge of despondency, but free; not knowing what the next day would bring, but free. Free!

At the end of 1942, after two years there, the two sisters joined the youth counselors accompanying the "Tehran Children", a Youth Aliyah project that brought one thousand Jewish children from Poland to Eretz-Israel. Most of these children were orphans that survived in Central Asia and were gathered under international auspices in the capital of Iran to await departure for Eretz-Israel. Finally, in February 1943, at the end of a long journey over mainland and sea, the two sisters, together with their charges, embarked on the last leg of their wandering and arrived in Palestine, two or three years before the other Tarnów exiles, inmates of forced labor camps, also reached the Promised Land.

The Tarnów refugees in Bukhara were not a homogeneous lot, even though most of them knew one another to some degree. As in any group of displaced persons, deep economic gaps soon appeared. Business skill was an individual's main source of security, and the accumulation of money or goods with financial worth on the black market guaranteed a person's freedom of movement. But for those who had not been blessed with financial acumen, or who refused to participate in such activities because of ethical inhibitions, survival depended on the kindness of others. Idek did not know many people. But in the Bukhara bath house, he discovered both those who found it difficult to support themselves and those who traded in gold and foreign currency and had achieved relative affluence. A place that requires one to peel off his clothes in front of others also encourages the disrobing of the soul. Thus it was in the local bath house that Idek discovered that another person from the Safah Berurah Hebrew high school was living in Bukhara. It was none other than Kresch!

"Kresch? Bezalel Kresch?" cried Idek. He did not know what made him happier — the fact that Kresch was all right, for he had heard nothing of him since they had separated on the bank of the San; or the fact that Kresch was in Bukhara, which meant that teacher and pupil could meet as in former times.

"If you want to see him, surely you will find him at the 'Planty'," some others said, pointing to the public garden and calling it by the name they had used back home in Tarnów and in Kraków.

"He stays at the 'Planty' day and night", Idek's companions repeated. "Look for him there, and you are bound to find him."

But Idek returned to the bath house a few days later and told them of his failure to find Kresch.

The Tarnów acquaintances were surprised: "The man who sells homemade candies in the garden could not have just left the place and vanished", they argued.

"Kresch has a claim on a certain corner in the 'Planty'", they explained. "He stands there all the time, and since he has no home, at night he curls up on the nearby bench. Every morning he brings candies from an old lady that makes them for him. We don't know whether he is selling them for her. In any case, many of us saw him in his corner over the past few days."

"Did you say the candy-seller? I saw him and walked past him several times. But that is not Kresch!"

Were they mistaken? And if not, why did he not recognize his teacher? After all, only two years and a quarter had passed since they forded the San together. Was it possible that in such a short time, a person could change beyond recognition, due to unbearable suffering?

Indeed, there was no mistake. It was Bezalel Kresch.

Chronic hunger had turned his face black and wrinkled, and his dimmed eyes were hidden under heavy eyelids. "He is becoming more and more like his father, the shoemaker", said two people from Lesko, his birthplace, who had known his father before the war. "He was a poor, hungry shoemaker. Out of pity, people called him 'Reb' Alter, even though he could hardly read from the prayer book." Yet apparently Bezalel's father was, so to speak, better off than the son. For while the father was born in poverty and ignorance, he had a useful trade, though not one that sufficiently provided for his needs. In this situation, his ignorance mercifully protected him from the true test of reality. But that was not the case with the shoemaker's son, whose livelihood was based on his education. Even though, in exile, the son had reverted to his childhood state of poverty, his education had erased the innocence of ignorance that was a the natural twin of poverty. As his knowledge increased, not only did it add to his suffering, but, as the Bible says of Adam and Eve when they ate from the Tree of Knowledge, Kresch also acquired a sense of shame. Affluent people from Tarnów remembered him as an intellectual and were willing to assist him, but he was too embarrassed to ask, too ashamed to receive. Did his sensitivity put them off, or were they really ignoring his need?

"For months I haven't had a piece of bread to bite into, so my teeth have become loose in my gums. I only manage to prepare a watery soup from the grasses that grow around here" — Kresch told Idek when they finally met on his sleeping bench for their second meeting during the war.

For a moment it seemed to Idek that Kresch was crying. In fact, his voice broke for only a split second, and immediately regained its calm. Idek did not know if the calm was a sign of renewed emotional strength or resignation to the weak, helpless state of his teacher's body. In an otherworldly, monotonous tone, Kresch kept on speaking, speaking, speaking, ceaselessly, as though reading a story in which the main character was not himself, but rather a stranger who happened to get stuck in Bukhara.

The last rays of Buchara sunset gently glided over the green tiles of the minaret of Kalan mosque, as if refusing to continue west, fixated on the surrealistic scene of two lost souls that did not belong to this place and landscape — a teacher and pupil from faraway Tarnów. They had unexpectedly found each other in the shadow of the mosque of the mighty King Timor (Tamerlain), who had inspired fear in all of Europe, and whose name is revered in Uzbekistan until this very day.

Kresch closed his eyes, perhaps to block out the mosque and travel in his imagination far back to his hometown on the edge of the Carpathian Mountains overlooking the San valley. The forests gave the place its name: Lesko in Polish, Lisku in Ukrainian, both meaning "grove". Of three thousand inhabitants, one-third was Ukrainian while the majority was Jewish. Even the mayor of the town was a Jew. The community was proud of its affluence and high level of education, as well as the large number of Hebrew speakers.

"But only a few enjoyed wealth and education", Kresch sighed deeply, as though describing a situation that still existed, as though he had not heard that the community had been completely wiped out in the war.

"The wealthy ignored the pockets of poverty and ignorance that persisted. *Into one of those sad pockets, I was born.*"

Kresch was not complaining about his father, the poor shoemaker, who made him go out to work at a very young age, and thus forced him to give up school despite his talents and thirst for knowledge. As the eldest of eight children, he understood that he had to forego his desires for the sake of providing the family's needs. "Luckily", he said, as if speaking to himself and forgetting Idek, "my troubles were my salvation."

Completely illiterate, young Bezalel was employed as a porter in the Fleischer family bookshop — the Fleischer family's educated sons and mother were well-known in town. The boy's efforts to decipher book titles impressed the educated shop owner, and she decided to teach him reading and writing. She even lent him some books from her shop.

When he grew up, townspeople supported his studies at the Rabbinical Seminary in Vienna, which in those days was the highest institution for Jewish studies in Europe. Drily, Kresch explained that the education he acquired at the Rabbinical Seminary did not make him an observant Jew, nor awaken in him any desire to become a practicing rabbi. For a moment Idek thought he recognized the Kresch of yesteryear, when a hint of a sarcastic smile took over the corners of the teacher's mouth. The thirst for knowledge he experienced in his youth made the teaching profession his ideal, and over the years this remained his sacred ambition. When he finished his studies in Vienna, he was accepted to his first and only job — teaching in the Hebrew high school in Tarnów.

Kresch stopped talking, but his eyes remained closed. Idek felt uneasy. The teacher's silence, his limited movements, swollen eyelids, and mainly his pale, closed face were such a contrast to the enthusiasm of his long-ago lessons. He looked dangerously ill. Idek had seen such a state of disconnection from reality only in Murmansk prisoners, those called "hunger-burnt" who did not have long to live. "Criminals!" Idek cried out voicelessly from the bottom of his heart. "Oh, you wicked Tarnovians, you heartless people! How could you stand by and allow this man to reach his present state? How could you bring a saint like Kresch to the brink of death?!"

Suddenly Kresch regained his power of speech. He told of his last days in Eretz-Israel, of the Agnon books he had managed to purchase, and how he had left Haifa on the last sailing of the *Polonia* in order to reach his teaching position on time. These last words contained not a hint of regret, nor did his voice or facial expression. When again he stopped talking, his face no longer resembled his own, nor did it look like his father's face of poverty. This was the face of death, and his words were those of one who had already crossed to the dark side of the moon.

Each and all took to the road. To Bukhara.

Bukhara. Many of those alive today owe a debt of gratitude to this blessed piece of earth, for it saved their lives. But there is also an outstanding debt owed by those who died. Many refugees who reached their threshold of suffering or died in the plague found their last resting place here. Since the local Jewish Burial Society did not know the refugees by name, their graves are unmarked, nor are their names listed in the Registry of Deaths. So the burial sites of many of these refugees remain unknown.

Bukhara. At the end of the twentieth century, the author of this book, together with his wife Ora, visited the ancient Jewish cemetery in Bukhara. He did not delude himself that he would find a gravestone of one of the "Radanites" who did not bear the difficulties of the journey and was buried there. Even if such a gravestone were erected, surely it would have disintegrated over the thousand years that have passed since then. Today, whether by chance or design, the cemetery is divided into two sections. The first section holds the gravestones of members of the Buchara community. Some of these gravestones are outstanding in their beauty, and the hyssop that clings to the stones lends them a quasi-patina of centuries on end. The back area contains tombstones sunk into the ground. These have no writing on them, and are obviously the graves of the Ashkenazi refugees who died and were buried here. The two visitors wanted to lay a rose on Kresch's grave, but finding no name on any of the stones, they placed the flower on the gate in memory of all the deceased.

The magical twilight hour in Bukhara does not match the atmosphere in the cemetery. The visitors stood silently at the gate that closed on the dead of an unpredicted eastbound Ashkenazi migration. The storm of war of the 1940s had flung the migrants into the awesome expanses of Asia, and anonymous slabs of stone remain to this day the only testimony to their fate.

## V

Each and all long to take to the road for the fourth time — this time to finally return home.

But the path was still blocked and they would have to wait another year or two until the Red Army reached the gates of Berlin. Its victory at Stalingrad changed the situation in Eastern Europe. With powerful strides and relentless fighting, the Red Army restored to the Russian and Ukrainian people region after region, that had been their home for centuries, and after the German invasion in June 1941, the Wehrmacht and SS had transformed them into valleys of death. Galloping towards the enemy land, and with the help of its protégée, the AL (*Armia Ludowa*) — the Polish People's Communist Army — the Red Army pushed back Hitler's forces from the eastern half of Poland and reached the right, that is, eastern bank of the Wisła River, in the heart of occupied Poland.

And then the unbelievable happened — unbelievable and frustrating to tears. The Red Army, standing on the Wisła opposite Warsaw that lies on the other bank, has only to cross the bridge and enter the capital. But before the eyes of the Polish people, the army stands motionless. No movement to cross the river can be seen in the camp. Warsaw is an inferno. The capital is bleeding to death. The Germans are cruelly crushing the rebellion that broke out under the initiative of the AK (*Armia Krajowa*), the National Polish Army. The AK claimed exclusive legitimacy and obeyed the orders of the Polish government-in-exile in London. Relations between the two Polish factions were hostile and the Soviet Union was suspicious of the Allies. Still, the AK hoped that the Red Army will respect the common goal of defeating the Germans, and immediately send its full force into the city and support the rebellion, or at least save the inhabitants from massacre. But no, the Reds continue to stand on the waterline east of Warsaw. They see the slaughter but do nothing about it. Political considerations took precedence over fraternal ties and fighting alliances. The Warsaw rebels were abandoned, and the same thing happened down south, in Polish (that is, western) Galicia. The Red Army occupied Jarosław in early July 1944, and three weeks later, on July 31, 1944, entered Rzeszów [read: Zheshoov], inspiring high hopes for a western breakthrough. But the expectations are dashed. The Red Army doesn't move towards

Tarnów, Kraków, Auschwitz. Till as late as January 1945, Rzeszów remains the westernmost liberated town in Polish Galicia.

Rumors spread through Bukhara that the Red Army had entered Poland (but not that it had stopped dead in its tracks), causing hearts to tremble with hope and a light to be kindled in the refugees' eyes. Every morning, the veteran refugees would meet near the synagogue in Centralnaya Street for an update on events at the front. Some went inside to pray, others stood outside in groups in excited conversation. In the late hours of the morning, all listened attentively to the seven o'clock news broadcast on Radio Moscow, heard only then due to the time difference. A daily street symposium conducted by Centralnaya strategists who supplemented the radio coverage with prolific "advice" for Zhukov and Koniev. But the generals, like all generals, "concealed" the "advice" of the anonymous street experts and grabbed all the praise for themselves.

After the tumult of the veterans' daily symposium subsided, the novice refugees, standing at the edge of the road, also listened to the news. Lonely and in dire poverty, they had just arrived from the camps after an arduous journey. They kept their thoughts to themselves, calculating the distance between the last position of the Red Army and their former home, debating whether or not to begin the march back west in the army's footsteps.

In contrast to these recent arrivals, the veterans who had reached Bukhara four years ago and had all the time on their hands to organize in preparation for the day of return, to collect information about road conditions, and even save money for the journey —

— and unlike the youth groups, who had joined the Polish army in Tashkent, and being fortified by their enlistment, could move with the army to the Middle East bases (including Palestine) and from there to the Italian front to join the British army and take part on behalf of their former homeland in the defeat of Nazi Germany —

— the solitary ex-gulag-inmates, who had thrown off the shackles of slavery and arrived in Bukhara on their own, remained alone and without the means to finance the fourth odyssey. Nevertheless, they resolved to move westwards on the path paved heroically by the victorious army. And — wonder of wonders! — once they had made that decision, their bodies, bent by the forced labor, the hunger and the cold, emaciated with typhus, pneumonia and tuberculosis, suddenly gained strength to stand erect. Their heads, bowed in humiliating surrender to their fate, suddenly looked up. They rubbed their eyes and realized that not everything looked black. The forest, which until then they had viewed as a place for back-breaking labor, seemed blossoming, afresh with greenery. The trees, previously destined to be cut down, now lifted their crowns until they knocked on heaven's gates. Indeed, there is still hope; yes, there is still hope at the end of the day. Each one, though not part of a supportive group, stood taller and stronger, believing in his ability to take fate into his own hands.

Rzeszów! The chance that this city, situated midway between Lvov and Kraków, would be the point where the westbound breakthrough of the Red Army would take place, excited the refugees in Bukhara, both the organized veterans and the solitary ones who had just recently joined the refugee community. But more than the others, the new hope excited the Jews back home, who failed to flee the invader in time or whose flight eastward had not succeeded. Helpless, they remained in Galicia and survived the massacres of 1942 by luck, finding hiding places from the Nazis in various villages.

Before the war, the Jewish industrialists of Tarnów had turned the city into the capital of Poland's ready-made clothing industry. In wintertime, when the farmers in surrounding villages could not work in the fields, the Jewish manufacturers used to give the villagers work they could do inside their huts. The men did the cutting and sewing, while the women did the washing and ironing. The "hut worker" system [*chałupnictwo* in Polish] was also implemented in Tarnów proper. Jewish workers of the proletarian Grabówka neighborhood were employed in their huts throughout the year — to the benefit of both sides, but there was enough work for villagers too. Through years of proximity to the villagers, the Jews had formed close relationships with them — employing them, doing commerce with them on market days, granting farm loans during droughts, giving them gifts on their holy days, and sending a Jewish doctor and midwife to the village when necessary. These ties, thanks to the fair, egalitarian, and unpretentious treatment on the part of the Jewish employers, often proved even stronger than the villagers' contacts with the arrogant non-Jewish townspeople, and stood the test in times of peace despite the anti-Semitic incitement. That was not the case in this horrible war. Not all Polish acquaintances agreed to hide Jews from the Nazis in barns, pigsties, or attics at the risk of endangering their own families and themselves. Most were frightened that a neighbor would inform on them in order to receive a reward. Unfortunately, there were also some who, unable to resist temptation, turned in a Jewish refugee hiding in the village to the Gestapo, in exchange for a cone of sugar or a couple of bottles of vodka.

One Jewish Tarnów family that was saved by Christian villagers was the Kellers, who had been friendly for years with the Wróbel family. Father Hayyim made sure that when his two sons, Nasiek and Henek, friends of Hesiek Wróbel, returned from high school, they supplemented their general studies with Jewish topics, under the tutelage of Reb Aazik Wróbel. Rutka, the daughter, was a student at the Hebrew high school, and together with her mother, Liebche, often visited Golda Wróbel to discuss embroidery. The Kellers lived at 1 Goldhammera, next door to the Aberdam family, bankers who owned the building. The other floors were occupied by the family of wealthy Yitzhak Brandstätter and the well-known Zoldinger Hotel that hosted the Ahavat Zion Conference in 1897 — (details appear in *Chestnuts of Yesteryear*, published by this author in 2003). Miraculously, the building's inhabitants were saved from the first *akcja* in June 1942, even though drunken hooligans invaded the neighboring houses.

On June 19, 1942, at the end of a terrible week of massacre, the Jewish neighborhood was declared a ghetto. The Kellers and their neighbors were driven out of the beautiful Aberdam building. They moved to Staro-Dąbrowska Street, which was lined with small houses and wooden huts. The part of the street that was close to the Jewish cemetery was included in the ghetto, but the street continued outside the city on the old road to the small town of Dąbrowa, hence the street's name. This location made it easier for *schmuggler*s [border smugglers], hired by the head of the family, to take the five Kellers, dressed in Wehrmacht uniforms, out of the ghetto to the village. A friend in the village arranged a hiding place, while another villager obtained Aryan identity cards for each member of the family. In this way, the parents became Jan and Maria Boyan, the boys continued to be brothers, Mieczyslaw and Roman Dąbrowski, and the daughter became a second Emilia Sobol. For three and a half years, the Kellers lived with this false identity. After the war, when they settled in Vienna, they returned to their original identity, except for Nasiek, who retained the name Dąbrowski — perhaps because the name reminded him of the hut in the Staro-Dąbrowska ghetto. As he had developed financial connections in Vienna and signed contracts in his false name, he may not have wanted to complicate his business affairs by returning to a name he had given up in order to protect himself from a death-threatening reality.

Now that the wonderful red news illuminated the darkness of the Jewish hiding places in the villages, the Jews lost their fear of the Germans who had retreated under the pressure of the Red Army. A large number of Jews, including the Kellers, began to leave the villages. They left in secret so that the villagers would not be tempted to steal their effects or even murder them. They settled in liberated Rzeszów, in houses vacated by the Germans and their Ukrainian collaborators. Paradoxically, despite having themselves suffered under the German occupation, the Poles internalized a great deal of their oppressors' anti-Semitism. They added it to the historical Polish anti-Semitism that had existed alongside massive immigration of Jews driven out of Western Europe in the Middle

Ages. The Jewish immigrants had brought with them into the new refuge their own language, Yiddish, and created a closed culture of their own, completely separate from that of the host country. There were other reasons for the renewed post-war anti-Semitic hostility of the Poles. They were worried that the Jews who came back from their refuges would demand return of the property that the Polish neighbors had appropriated during the war and made their own. They also felt hatred toward the Soviet Union and feared that a Polish "People's" Communist government would arise. After all, it was supposedly a "well-known fact" that the Jews were fervent followers of atheist, Communist ideology and would be only too happy to enforce it on Catholic Poland.

The hostility grew along with the growing stream of returnees, especially since reaching Jarosław, the Red Army took its time until it arrived in Rzeszów, possibly due to supply problems following the extension of lines of communication. During the interim period of no government, after the Germans had fled and before the liberation and establishment of Polish "People's" Communist rule, anarchy reared its ugly head. Hostility toward the Jews increased and reached the killing point. Ten Jews who returned to Rzeszów were murdered in full daylight. The nationalist militia did not even bother to make a show of justice and released the murderers in exchange for the proverbial bottle of vodka.

No matter what their original hometown, the Jewish returnees, from now on Rzeszowians, were in shock, mourning the ten Rzeszów victims of anarchy and anti-Semitism. Their shock was not only at the horrible deed — after all, the last four years of atrocities had blunted their sense of horror — but at the circumstance of the murder. How terrible! These people had managed to hold out in their hiding places all those awful years, and now, having survived the lethal Nazi hunt, they returned home in good spirits, only to be murdered by the residents of their own city!

The Tarnów group of refugees, who temporarily settled in Rzeszów, suffered a double shock when one day, a Góral (one of the mountain people) came down from the ridge north of town, that was part of the Carpathian mountain range, holding the body of another Góral in his arms. Both men, the living and the dead, were dressed in traditional Góral clothes and wore black Góral hats. The stranger placed the body on the ground, and people stood around at a distance, too frightened to approach the anonymous body. The Góral spoke a Góral dialect of Polish that is impossible to replicate. "We knew he was a Jew, and we gave him refuge. But when he heard that people from his town of Tarnów were in Rzeszów, he wanted to meet them and see who had survived. One of our tribe volunteered to show him the safe path over the mountain, but instead of taking at some point the turn down to Rzeszów, as I did, he continued going up, crossed the front line, and fell into the hands of the Germans. Apparently, the guide was frightened, and to save himself told them he had come to turn in a Jew who had disguised himself as a Góral. Straight away, a German guard shot the Jew. The Góral guide carried the body on his back to the path that goes down to Rzeszów. There he met us and related the story that I have just recounted to you. We will investigate to see whether he really made a navigational error or intended to turn in our Jewish friend, and we will judge him according to the laws of our fathers."

The Jews stood petrified. Although the August sun poured heat on their heads, they stayed in place, trembling, but not from cold. The deceased's body seemed to radiate a mysterious, accusatory message, freezing the onlookers despite the noon heat. For several long minutes those present stood with their eyes closed, as if hoping that when they opened them they would discover that all this had never happened, and only a memory of the nightmare would remain. The very experience of listening to a Góral converse about humane matters against the background of the war was new to them. It was totally different from the usual contact between townspeople and Górals, which involved haggling over the price of a climbing staff with a handle like a Góral ax, or renting a Góral carriage in a mountain holiday hamlet. Two youngsters took the body, which was covered with a dark Góral cloth. Someone with a beard and skullcap chanted the *kaddish*, and when his voice broke the silence, it seemed to awaken the bystanders, and they dutifully responded in the appropriate place, "May His great Name be sanctified…" and "Blessed be He", and "Amen".

The self-appointed prayer leader began the *El Male Rahamim* prayer ("Oh God full of mercy") in a heartrending Ashkenazi melody. But when he reached the words "the soul of…", an embarrassed silence hit the crowd, for no one knew the name of the person who "had gone to his resting place" as is required by the text. One of the Tarnów old-timers plucked up the courage to approach the body, and removed the cloth from the face. The cry that escaped his lips echoed from mountaintop to mountaintop, along the entire range of the Carpathian Mountains — from the Dunajec River in the west to the Czeremosz in the east, and perhaps even from the Wisła to the Dniestr.

"*Oh my God!*" the man exclaimed. "*It's Noyekh (Noah)! Noyekh Wald!*"

# VI

In August 1944, at a distance of only a few hundred meters from the Rzeszów front, a Nazi gun put an end to Noyekh's life. The Red Army had stopped at that line for the same reason it refrained from coming to Warsaw's aid during the uprising. The Soviet advancement westward was renewed only toward the end of January 1945. If it had not been for the freezing of the front line in August, it is possible that Noyekh would have enjoyed a longer life.

The tragedy of Noyekh Wald, one of the most prominent young Zionists of Tarnów before the Second World War, began three decades prior to the unfortunate encounter at the mountainside German post overlooking Rzeszów. Hayyim Yoysif Wald had five sons and two daughters. He was a modest trader of skins, and a follower of the Dzikiver Rebbe. At the beginning of the twentieth century, the Rebbe moved his court from Dzików, a hamlet on the bank of the Wisła, to Tarnów, but the name of his hassidic group remained as before — "Dzikiver". Hayyim Yoysif had suffered considerably, but he never complained. Once, Polish nationalist fanatics attacked him on the train and brutally pulled out his beard, hair by hair. At the other end of the spectrum, anti-Zionist religious extremists from the *Great Kloyz* in Tarnów insulted him and threw him out of the synagogue because two of his sons immigrated to Eretz-Israel, and one of his daughters was tried in a Polish court for joining the Communist Party, then illegal in Poland. Hayyim Yoysif suffered more than enough to make the hairs that grew back in his beard turn white.

One by one, the Walds left Tarnów and immigrated to Eretz-Israel. One by one, for each immigrant had to obtain an individual immigration certificate for Palestine by the ruling British Mandate, and these were distributed in small quantities. Moshe Wald, the youngest son, was a friend of this author and shared details about the family. He and his parents were the last of the family to emigrate, reaching Eretz-Israel in 1935. Like the others, he Hebraized his name to Ya'ari. The Ya'ari family settled in Eretz-Israel, except for two — the daughter, who was a communist and chose to join the Communist Party in France; and the son Noyekh, who out of no wish of his own, stayed in Poland, abandoned there by his parents due to a disability. Thus Noyekh's tragedy began. Possibly, it began even earlier when he was a defective fetus in his mother's womb, or when he became ill after his birth.

Moshe Ya'ari did not know whether the disability — his right arm hung paralysed from the shoulder down and was supported by a cloth brace — was from birth or whether he had had polio in his childhood. Medical knowledge of the matter was negligible in those days, and because the child did not complain of pain and managed without his right arm, his parents stopped worrying. Noyekh learned to do everything with his left arm, and wore his brace unselfconsciously. "It wasn't him but my parents who were ashamed of his situation," said Moshe indignantly.

Noyekh's vitality aroused admiration and made people forget his disability. Endowed with theatrical talent, acute hearing and a phenomenal memory, he could learn any song quickly and by ear, without written notes, and play it on the harmonica (mouth organ), holding it to his lips with his left hand. At the Hebrew parties at Safah Berurah hall, he was king. An unstoppable *horah* dancer, his singing and dancing was the driving force behind any Zionist party, school play at the Hebrew school, or reception for guests from Eretz-Israel. When the writer and emissary Bystritzki came to visit, the *horah* dance Noyekh led, chanting "Long live Bystritzki with the *horah*!", spun everyone round until they could no longer stand up straight. The Tarnów Zionists have never forgotten it. Noyekh must have imbibed the *hislahavis* (hassidic fervor) of Dzików Hassidism in whose midst he grew up, translating it freely into the mode of *kvutzah*, kibbutz and "the Eretz-Israel of Labor".

His audience viewed Noyekh's dancing and Hebrew singing as stage shows whose main purpose was entertainment for eyes and ears, arms and legs; but this was not Noyekh's view or expectation. True, his performances were designed in the best taste, his dances choreographed with the aim of inspiring a sense of unity. But he was saddened at the realization that, for the most part, his audience did not understand the message that he wove between each song and dance. This message was "*Aliyah* — immigration to Eretz-Israel". Immigration now, immediately, before it was too late! In his heart he was proud that his family was fulfilling his message and that the Walds were becoming Ya'aris in Eretz-Israel. Soon it would be his turn; *he too would immigrate to Eretz-Israel and become Noah Ya'ari.*

Indeed, his turn arrived and there was no end to his happiness. He was the most Zionist of all Zionists, those who talked but did not put their words into action; the most Eretz-Israeli of all Eretz-Israelis before his foot ever trod on the Land of Israel. But suddenly he received a slap in the face that was an insult as well as an end to his dreams. The family decided to leave him in Tarnów. "The realization of Zionism depends on working hands", they explained to their stunned son. This was also how the pioneering movements purged their ranks of those who wanted to pursue academic studies. The Zionist ethos of the 1920s and '30s was one-track minded, mercilessly fanatical, and demanded submission to the ideology of manual labor, with no exceptions.

Noyekh's parents paid no heed to what might happen to their handicapped son, ignoring the fact that Hitler had already been in power in the neighboring country for two years. A few days after they closed the gates of Eretz-Israel in their son's face because he would never be a *halutz* (pioneer), Noyekh disappeared without taking leave of them. He would never see them or his elder brothers again. But he did have a heart-to-heart talk one night with his youngest brother Moshe, who was about to set sail with his parents for Eretz-Israel. He told Moshe of his pain, and explained to him his plans: no more Zionist parties, no more Hebrew songs and no more *horah*. He continued to feel warmly toward the Tarnów Jews who had shown him much love over the years. But the Zionism he had believed in as a way of life, a vision for the future, no longer existed for him. As far as he was concerned, it was dead. From now on he would join an ethnic group that had aroused his curiosity on a trip to the Tatra ranges of the Carpathian Mountains — the *Górals*.

While during the nineteenth century and at the beginning of the twentieth century, all Górals lived within the borders of the Austrian-Hungarian Empire, after the First World War the tribe was divided between Poland, Slovakia, and Hungary,. What united the Górals and preserved their individuality — and their poverty — were the Carpathian Mountains, their true homeland. Polish writers, poets and composers discovered the Góral people at the end of the nineteenth century. They not only fell in love with the Tatra, the highest range of the Carpathian Mountains, and with its scenery, but they decided to actually settle in this primeval world. They turned a forsaken village, Zakopane, into a center for tourism and winter sports and the cultural capital of the Carpathians.

Most artists came because they were captivated by the landscape, but Michał Bałucki was the first to show an interest in the Góral mountain *men* as individuals. He looked into the Górals' soul, understood their love of the mountains, and commiserated with them when poverty forced them to go down from their beloved mountains into the valley, to find work in the villages and the marketplaces in order to feed their families.

Noyekh was enchanted by the ridges of the Carpathians and fell in love with the Góral population. He put on Góral clothes in the mountain villages, making the villagers smile at this expression of identification with them. With his acute hearing he was able to learn their special pronunciation of Polish, their style of speech, proverbs and unique modes of expression that townspeople could not understand. He even planned to write a dictionary of Góral phrases, and collected Góral songs, legends, and history. The Górals accepted him and considered him one of their own.

During his rare trips down to Tarnów to obtain supplies and meet like-minded friends, Noyekh would remove his Góral clothes so that he would not look like a fraud, and exchange them for city clothes. On those rare occasions, he felt how much he actually loved his city, his birthplace. He loved its streets, the "Planty", the Jewish quarter, the Great and Old synagogues, the *kloyz*es and the *shtibbelakh*, and especially his childhood Dzikiver *kloyz*. He always paid a visit to Mt. Marcin, though it was no more than a speck of sand compared to the Tatra. He stayed away from two places — the *Grand Kloyz*, where they insulted his father, and the Safah Berurah hall, where his singing and dancing still resounded from wall to wall.

Friends who remembered his youthful Zionist days exhorted him to organize a party like in old times, not necessarily a Zionist one. Why not in Góral style? The idea piqued his interest. He promised to have a party on his next visit, for both Jews and non-Jews, in the auditorium of the Second State High School (non-Hebrew, of course, but with a predominantly Jewish student body).

He began the party with communal singing — Bałucki's emotional song that was familiar to all.

> Góralu, czyż ci nie żal
> Odchodzić od stron ojczystych?
> Świerkowych lasów i hal
> I tych potoków przejrzystych?
>
>> Góralu, czyż ci nie żal?
>> Góralu, wróć się do hal!
>
> A Góral na góry spoziera
> I łzy rękawem ociera:
> I góry opuścić trzeba
> Za chleba, Panie, za chleba!
>
>> I góry opuścić trzeba
>> Za chleba, Panie, za chleba!

> Oh Góral, are you not sad and sorry,
> To leave mountaintops and forests you call home?
> To part with your ancestors' lifestyle and glory,
> And wander instead and in strange places roam?
>
>> Oh Góral, we hear you bitterly sigh —
>> Turn back, turn back, climb home up high!
>
> The Góral looks up, weeping and sad,
> And shyly wipes away the tears with his sleeve:
> Alas, my beloved mountains, too, I am forced to leave
> For bread's sake, dear sir, for bread…
>
>> Alas, also mountains I'm forced now to leave
>> For bread's sake, dear sir, for bread…

Afterwards Noyekh taught the young audience to dance the *kołomyjka* — a dance of the so-called Huculs (Hutzuls), i.e. the Górals of the East Carpathian mountains. He liked to wander there, recalling that the Baal Shem Tov used to seclude himself in this region with his Maker and allow the birds to teach him the art of song. Noyekh accompanied the dance with his harmonica, which he held between his upper and lower teeth, freeing his one healthy hand to direct the dancers or wave a handkerchief over their heads as dance leaders do. The tune was familiar, but only a few knew a line or two of the lyrics. Noyekh sat the dancers down to teach them the song in full, lyrics and tune together:

> Czerwony pas, za pasem broń
> I topór co błyszczy z dala;
> Wesoła myśl, swobodna dłoń —
> To strój, to życie
> Górala.

> Tu szum Prutu, Czeremoszu
> Huculom przygrywa,
> A ochoczo 'Kołomyjka'
> Do tańca porywa.

> Dla Hucuła niema życia
> Jak na Połoninie —
> Gdy go losy w doły rzucą
> Wnet z tęsknoty zginie.

> > In his red sash a sharp dagger nests
> > The gleaming hatchet's ready for strife;
> > The mood is joyful, but the hand never rests —
> > That's the dress,
> > That's the life
> > Of the Góral.

> > The roar of Czeremosz and Prut
> > Is music to the Hutzul's ear,
> > He keeps stamping, boot by boot,
> > The *kołomyjka* to high gear.

> There's no life for Hutzul's taste,
> Except on mountaintop up high —
> Should fate hurl him down in haste,
> Of sheer longing he would die.

At the audience's request, after the song had been joyously performed by all, the crowd returned to the dancing area, this time to do the *kołomyjka* with both mighty singing and boot-stamping dancing.

Wiping their brows, the dancers calmed down and seated themselves on benches in a half-circle. Now the time had come for Góral stories. With his flair for the theatrical, Noyekh knew not only how to tell a story but how to make it come alive. He would leave the most thrilling part for the end: the story of Janosik (read: Yanoshik), a Góral hero from the Austrian period. He was a kind of Robin Hood, a noble bandit, who used to rob and smuggle his loot over borders, but then gave it all away to the poor of the mountains. Paradoxically, he was as much at home in the palaces of the Polish nobles as he was in the huts of the simplest Górals. Everyone in the audience listened with bated breath to how Janosik evaded for years the suspenseful chase of the Austrian police. At last, the authorities managed to catch him with the oldest (and most efficient) ruse in history:

> Co sie stało w borze
> Na liptowskim dworze?
> Ułapili Janosika
> Z dziwcynom w komorze.
>
> Jencom góry, jencom
> I sumi osika —
> Ej, ze nigdy nie zaginie
> Imie Janosika.

> What had happened to our bandit
> In the Liptow wood? Alas,
> They captured Janosik, caught him red-handed,
> Hugging and kissing in a storeroom a lass.
>
> Mountain to mountain sends sorry sigh,
> Tears make the pines and the tall poplars wet —
> There's no one like him down the vale or up high,
> The name of Janosik we'll never forget!

(To the Polish reader: the unorthodox Polish spelling in the verses above reflects the Góral dialect prevailing in the Eastern Carpathians.)

When the war broke out, worrying for Noyekh's personal safety as a Jew, his Góral friends of the Tatra advised him to leave toward the East Carpathian Mountains, to the land of the Hutzuls, which was less exposed to traffic and to tourism. This would make it easier for him to avoid the SS, as opposed to Zakopane, which was crawling with SS and German soldiers on leave. Noyekh took their advice, but never imagined that he would stay there six years. Although he carried out an anthropologic and linguistic field study during this time, he missed the West Carpathians and Tarnów.

And then — a surprise! At the beginning of August 1944, a radio broadcast announced that the Red Army had been in control of Rzeszów for two days already. It is unknown on what ground Noyekh surmised that many Tarnów natives had congregated in the liberated city of Rzeszów and were waiting for the most opportune moment to move, this time, finally, back to Tarnów. If this rumor was correct, then Noyekh Wald from Tarnów would also want to be one of those who would take to the road, even though he no longer had a home there. In the remote Hutzuł village, where the solitary radio broadcasted only official announcements, no one knew that the front line had been frozen. Noyekh left with high hopes.

We have no information about the results of the internal Hutzuł inquiry into the circumstances of Noyekh's death. The murdered man was alone, and anyway no one even asked about his whereabouts. Furthermore, the Hutzuls did not usually publicize their internal affairs. The general opinion of the refugees was that there was some kind of treachery involved on the Hutzuls' part. That is what Moshe told his friend many years later. He did not blame the Górals. His rage was directed against his parents and older brothers who sacrificed one of their own kin for an ideology that had no basis in natural justice, and that, thank God, has passed from the world.

In January 1945, the Red Army began, at long last, to move west.
On January 18, Tarnów was liberated almost bloodlessly.
On January 19, the Red Army entered Kraków.
In short order, all of Galicia was liberated.
The Red Army reached the gates of Auschwitz.

Each and all of the Galician people took to the road.

Home! The Tarnów refugees who had been sitting impatiently and fearfully in Rzeszów began the act of return. On arrival, they saw with their own eyes the tragic scope of the Holocaust in their town. The home no longer existed.

Noyekh did not have the chance to take to the road with them. He lost the opportunity to see Jewish Tarnów in its destruction. He was not there to mourn it.

# VII

The murder of the ten Jews of Rzeszów — and more than that, the murderers walking free — shook the town's Jewish community. Anarchy ran rampant. Jews felt they had better move to save themselves! But where should they go? Forward? The Germans had indeed fled the town, fearing the Red Army. For political reasons, the Red Army was taking its time, and even though it had entered the town, it had not yet moved the front line. This meant that the Germans were a mere kilometer or two away, and their proximity could be deadly — as proved by Noyekh's case. Their presence in the area continued to provide a dangerous example. After more than four years of practical schooling in the government's institutionalized methods of murder, the Polish and Ukrainian hooligans, who had collaborated with the Nazis in the extermination of the Jews, saw no reason, all of a sudden, to stop doing what they had become experts at under the guidance of the master practitioners. The very air still had Nazi undertones, laden with echoes of a past that had not yet passed. The streets breathed anti-Semitism, and the Jew, by virtue of being a Jew, was still considered an open target (in German, *vogelfrei* — vulnerable as a bird to the shots of every passing hunter). The release of the murderers only served to reinforce this impression of a complete absence of law and order. Such was the atmosphere in Rzeszów.

Hence, the Jewish apartment buildings went on the defensive, closed up under lock and key. From the lookout post on the second floor, manned day and night, anyone who knocked on the door could be identified. Perhaps he was a fellow refugee who had just arrived, in which case he was welcome, as the apartments were spacious, and more inhabitants meant more security. Or he might be one of the wild mob, who would hide behind the bushes, and as soon as the door was opened, would attack as in the past.

Indeed, refugees kept arriving, in the hope that the decisive attack would begin from Rzeszów. One day in the street in Rzeszów, Nasiek Keller (Dąbrowski) met an old friend, Hesiek Schmidt. His father, Itchileh, and his younger brother, Ziga, managed to cross the San and find refuge on the Russian side. Later, a faithful gentile woman brought his mother over as well. However, the German invasion of the Soviet Union forced them to hide inside a cellar. One day, Hesiek went out to get some food, and on returning to the hideout, found it empty. Alone and heartbroken, he wandered the area already liberated by the Red Army until he reached Rzeszów, where he joined the Kellers. Guilt at separation from his family continues to gnaw at his heart even today.

The refugees kept streaming in, as though a clandestine communication network had sent coded messages of the kind that only refugees, whatever their origin, would be able to decipher and respond to, thanks to some kind of genetic coding. Some had been considered hopeless cases, as they had shown no sign of life since fleeing the Nazi army in early September 1939. They had disappeared from the face of the earth, only to surface upon hearing the call of Rzeszów, when they took to the road.

One autumn evening, a nervous knock was heard on the locked iron gate of the Kellers' living quarters. Anxiety gripped the residents and a pall of silence fell over them. Who or what could it be at this late hour, when the streets were empty due to the curfew? Did the breathless knock mean that the person had been running, perhaps to escape the curfew supervisors? The knocks continued, increasing in intensity. Nasiek Keller and Hesiek Schmidt went up to reinforce the lookout on the second floor. They signaled quietly that the person knocking on the gate was standing there alone, so he was not a gang member. The man looked somewhat like a refugee, but not quite, since he was older and wore glasses.

"I'm opening the door," announced Rutkah decisively — "before the curfew supervisors catch him." This first sentence, spoken out loud after long minutes of careful silence, loosened everyone's tongues. Henek Keller, to be on the safe side, placed himself behind his sister on standby. Slowly they turned the keys in the locks and opened the gate.

"Good God! It's *Adolph Seiden*!" She wanted to fall on his neck from happiness, remembering how all of Jewish Tarnów had mourned him since they had had no word of him, and how whoever came back from Lvov to Tarnów had testified that Seiden had not been sighted among the refugees. Many had interpreted his disappearance as suicide, considering the feeling of loss that had eaten away at him after his son was killed on the first day of the invasion, and in view of the collapse of his belief in assimilation after the Poles abandoned the Seiden family in its mourning. Seiden didn't allow Rutkah near him: "Be careful! I'm full of lice and anything else that's enjoying my flesh!" "At least they didn't eat your sense of humor!" He laughed out loud, maybe his first laugh in many years.

Nasiek and Hesiek led Seiden to the primitive bath — a tub, like in most of the Jewish apartments in Tarnów, including the Kellers, the Schmidts, and the Wróbels, which they filled with water heated in pots. (The autumn had been cold that year, and that meant heating the grate day and night. The pots were continually on the fire.) The two young men took Seiden's clothes and sentenced them to fire in the grate together with all the tiny creatures that had been using his clothes as their own. While Seiden was paddling around in the water, Hayyim Keller, the head of the family, came in holding freshly ironed clothing and a suit. Seiden became a new man, beginning to resemble what he used to look like before the war, apart from the furrows that time had carved into his face.

When he entered the room, glowing from the bath, all rushed to pull him into a hug. But again he stopped them with a wave of his hand, and asked Hayyim Keller for a *tallith*, a skullcap, and a prayer book open at the *HaGomel* blessing, recited when someone is rescued from danger. They all realized that it was a different Seiden standing before them. Apparently, his latter years of exile had awakened him to seek deeper answers to the problem of his Jewish identity, purifying him of any semblance of assimilation. When everyone answered *Amen* after he recited the blessing, it was time for hugs and kisses, sighs and laughter. Naturally everyone wanted to know where Seiden had been all those years, but he deflected their questions, deciding that he would never mention that last chapter — and hopefully never remember it. On his part, he asked nothing, not even about the fate of his wife, Regina, or that of Giza, his daughter. In the evenings he told stories about his childhood in Rzeszów, but, pushing away the past, he was only prepared to relate to the present or to dream of the future.

Seiden asked why the house was locked during the day. He was told about the ten Jews who were killed during the anarchy, and about the death of Noyekh by a German bullet in front of his friend (informer?), the Hutzuł. "And what happened?" "The murderers were caught, and the militia released them. The Hutzułs promised to investigate." "Then what did you do?" A general silence, partly out of embarrassment, and partly out of helplessness, served as the answer. "Let's swear to God that those were our last victims," declared Seiden, like a prophet delivering exhortations to the crowd. "We haven't suffered for nothing. We will not be afraid. We will defend ourselves and will never again be fair game." Suddenly all present felt a sense of spiritual elation. Their eyes began to shine, and their hearts swelled with hope. *They are no longer alone. The end to hiding in the face of terror! A leader has arisen.*

"Come with me to town, Henek. The rest of you — don't worry about us if we don't come home tonight. We might be away for several days." None of those sitting around the table dared to ask where the two were going and why. The question wasn't asked, nor did Seiden offer an answer. "Out of necessity, we will postpone the story of my childhood in Rzeszów to a later evening. I'm sure we'll have many evenings together," he added with a smile. But no one returned the smile — smiles do not erase worry. A roaring silence was the response. The anxiety in the air was palpable, suspended over them head-down like a bat.

It was Seiden who felt he must break the silence. "Hesiek," he turned to Schmidt, "Could you lend me the short wind-breaker you were wearing yesterday, the one that looks like a cross between a coat and a jacket? The suit you gave me, Hayyim," he said, addressing Keller Senior, "is too elegant for these days. I don't want to look bourgeois. After all, we are now under a 'People's Regime.'"

"No problem," Schmidt answered eagerly. "I'll bring it to you this very minute. But you should know that you look bourgeois even when you're not wearing any clothes at all. Nasiek will confirm it." The memory of Seiden's bath made everyone laugh, and the tension dissipated.

Five days had passed since Seiden left, dressed in Schmidt's jacket and accompanied by Henek, their destination unknown. The house carried on as usual — the gate remained locked, the topics of conversation around the table were the same. They said nothing out loud, trying not to speculate about Seiden and Henek's activities or location, but the subject gnawed at them all. The lookout from the second floor continued its watch, and reported back on what was going on in the street. Several times, it followed groups of young people who passed by the house. Some of these sprayed swastikas on the gate, or wrote in Polish, not *Żydzi*, which is the correct form, but *Żydy*, which has an obvious anti-Semitic implication. But the groups went on their way, and the inhabitants of the house did not consider their actions as demanding a response.

On the sixth evening after Seiden and Henek had left, the screech of a car's brakes was suddenly heard outside. The lookout signaled that a black car from the U.B. (*Urząd Bezpieczeństwa*, the Polish Office of Internal Security, equivalent to the Russian N.K.W.D.) had stopped at the front of the house.

The very sight of the black U.B. cars cast fear into everyone's hearts. They normally predicated an arrest, or, at least, an order to present oneself for interrogation. Wondering at the reason for a U.B. car appearing in their street, the Kellers and Schmidt fantasized that the car had stopped preparing to ambush someone around the corner. Clearly, it had nothing to do with them. Hardly had they managed to turn the thoughts racing in their heads into words, when an additional sign came from the lookout — two Polish officers had exited their car and were approaching the gate. Their knock sounded most authoritative. There was no time for an emergency consultation, but they all knew one could not, on principle, refuse to open the gate to army officers, whatever their intention.

Again it was Rutkah who took the task upon herself. This time Nasiek took Henek's usual place behind his sister in order to protect her. It was lucky he was standing there, as when she pushed open the gate, Rutkah took one look at the officers and fell backwards in a faint, straight into Nasiek's arms. One of the officers strode forward, lifted Rutkah from her confused brother's arms and brought the girl, as if he knew the way, straight into her room. While Nasiek, uncomprehending, attended to his sister, the officer returned to the living room and sat down quietly next to the table, followed by his companion. The two removed the army hats, whose visors had shaded their eyes. Then it was the family's turn to sit down, in total shock. In front of them sat two U.B. lieutenants in Polish uniforms — *Adolph Seiden in an everyday uniform and Henek Dąbrowski (Keller) in shining officer's attire.*

"Adolph, I'm going out for a minute to park the car in the courtyard. It's not a good idea to leave it out in the street. There are too many hooligans around waiting for a good opportunity." After he returned to the apartment, he locked the gate and returned to his chair. Silence reigned in the room, either due to shock or amazement at the miraculous sight. Finally they all regained their senses, and rising from their chairs, hugged the "officers". Rutkah awoke from her faint, and came into the room with Nasiek. Everyone approached Henek and Seiden, and patted their uniforms: "Let's toast the occasion with a drink *lehayyim* ('to life!') "— said Keller Senior —" and then you will tell us everything."

When Seiden and Henek had left town five days previously, it never occurred to Seiden that he might render any service at all to an organization of the state. Surely, he would never join the ranks of Internal Security, especially since the Soviets had warped its original character and turned it into a tool of repression. Instead, Seiden set a limited, one-time goal for himself and Henek — to investigate and reveal the identity of the murderers of the ten Jews, and uncover their location.

Seiden had no prior experience in trailing criminals, and apart from occasional leafing through detective literature, had only common sense at his disposal. "I think", he explained to Henek, "that people who commit showcase crimes in an encouraging environment behave differently from the common criminal. The latter evade the law by taking advantage of their anonymity. Not so the former. These openly brag about their deeds and expect to win appropriate publicity. The market is the best forum for this. I suggest we go there." The work of the amateur detective turned out to be easier than they had thought. Three of the murderers had made a name for themselves as heroes: the butcher, the baker and the peddler of dried mushroom strings. In the market, rumor of two additional partners-in-crime ran rampant. They lived in another neighborhood, and Seiden and Henek could not locate them. "Never mind," Seiden calmed his friend. "In their investigation the criminals we hold will be sure to incriminate each other, and we'll get the missing ones, too. Let's go to the U.B. and report our findings so that they can proceed accordingly."

"I thank you for the initiative and effort" said the U.B. major. "Based on your testimony, I promise that all the pogrom instigators will be interrogated tomorrow. By the way, when my aide comes in, I will tell him to make sleeping arrangements for you so that you'll be nearby if we need you. In the meantime I will wish to have your advice on another matter that has been bothering me since yesterday. It may develop into something even more serious than the previous case, and I am determined to do everything in order to avoid the danger."

The major looked very agitated. He paced from one end of the room to the other, lighting cigarette after cigarette. Only when he came close to the point did Seiden realize that the major had been searching for the right words so as not to offend his Jewish visitors. It transpired that a Polish man had raped a Polish girl. Perhaps because she had struggled, he had strangled her to death and thrown her body into the yard of a Jewish house. Historically, this was a proven recipe for a blood libel.

The major took Seiden's advice in its entirety. This included the unprecedented wording of the mourning notices, emphasizing the rape and that the rapist was Polish. A police force under the personal supervision of the major surrounded the mortuary and patrolled the streets of the Jewish neighborhood. These measures took the wind out of the sails of those plotting to harm the Jews, and the fear of another pogrom dissipated (unlike the Kielce pogrom a year after the war, in which a similar trick had preceded it, but no immediate steps to prevent the pogrom were taken).

At the end of the operation, the major turned to the strange duo of amateur detectives — one older and more level-headed, the other younger, smiling, with the air of an adventurer. He asked them to join the U.B. officers, with all the accompanying rights and obligations. "We need an *Uczony Jevrej* ('a learned Jew') like you, Adolph. Your free and creative thinking will refresh our service's routine, which is continually under threat of decay, like all other routines. I would like to add something else that I shouldn't really be saying: in two days, you have managed to help your community twice, and this doesn't seem to be the end of the dangers, which means more operations like this one will be called for. I will leave you now, and you can talk it over among yourselves and decide. You are under no obligation to agree. Personally, I would be pleased if you would join us." The major got up, waited a second, then spoke again: "By the way, my mother is Russian, but my father was a Polish Jew. On the day the Germans invaded Poland, he escaped to the Soviet Union and volunteered for the Red Army. He died a hero in the battle of Kursk". The major turned sharply toward the door, leaving his listeners open-mouthed.

The next day, satisfied with their positive answer, the major sent them in his car to military headquarters in Jarosław to swear allegiance, receive their officers' rank, uniforms, and a two-hour accelerated course in procedure and paperwork. Afterwards, Henek passed a driving test (he had already been driving in Tarnów), and in the end he was given a black car. The major welcomed them with open arms, yet from then on, they made sure to salute him, as was required.

The Kellers and Schmidt listened to Henek's story until the wee hours of the morning. Finally, Seiden recited the Jewish blessing for a gentile ruler, "Blessed be He, who gave of His honor to mortals".

## VIII

A gust of Carpathian wind swept the autumn leaves and covered the orphaned trees and the ground under them with a shiny layer of snow. During the month of November, this layer grew ever deeper, especially when the January 1945 snows outstripped those of December 1944.

The heightened activity of the Red Army signaled that the time had come to renew the pursuit of the enemy — this time it would be the last. Indeed, enormous forces along the whole frontline, from the Baltic Sea in the north down to the Carpathian Mountains in the south, began to move westwards. While the central bloc had set its sights on Berlin, the central nerve system of the Third Reich, the Western Galician bloc hungered for Kraków and vowed to break open the gates of horror at Auschwitz.

According to Soviet military procedure, the N.K.W.D. used to enter together with, or immediately after, the front military force, thus acquiring control over the conquered city. The Polish "People's" U.B. in Galicia followed the same procedure: after the attacking army raced forward, the U.B. received orders to advance at once.

Seiden and Henek hastily parted from their families, and promised that once they found suitable accommodations, the car would come back for them. It was clear to everyone that Tarnów was no longer and would never again be their city.

Where is this Tarnów that had once been their town? It seems that out of shame it has been hiding behind the proverbial "Mountains of Darkness". Maybe the true darkness is not caused by true mountains, but rather by the refugees' memories. When, traveling now in that direction, the town finally appears and they breathe its air. Will they remember their childhood and their life there? What will they feel when they pass the main streets of the town, Lwowska, Wałowa, and Krakowska, on the way to Kraków?

Henek was behind the wheel and Seiden in the seat next to him, when after a journey of two hours they reached Rzędzin, the village flanking the eastern border of Tarnów. On the border the large cross was still standing. Here the village women, returning home from a day at the city market, would cross themselves, giving thanks for the sizeable profit they had made from selling their wares. They crossed themselves to the crucified, but their lips mumbled the Polish Ave Maria, *Zdrowaś Maryjo*, in homage to the one they worshipped as the Mother of God. After the cross, the eastern part of the town spread out. No. This used to be the eastern city, but it is no longer. All of the former Grabówka area, which had been densely carpeted with cabins of hard-working laborers, was now covered with white snow. The remains of the ruins stabbed up through the snowy shroud, as though trying to rend it asunder, and protest on behalf of life and justice.

The car, heading for Kraków via Tarnów, does not stop. Seiden's eyes track the remains of the landmarks of Grabówka hiding under the snow — the synagogue, the *remiza* at the last stop of the electric train. But in vain. It is impossible to identify anything. Along with the inhabitants of the neighborhoods, the Germans destroyed their houses down to the foundations, turning the neighborhood into a pile of debris. Henek, on his part, was engrossed in his driving, trying to locate Lwowska Street under the snow. Most of the snow removal work had already been done by Soviet military vehicles galloping west. They had dug a black line of road, framed on both sides by the white snow. But the snow continued to fall, covering what had been exposed a moment before. After a few kilometers, they began to see two- and three-story buildings on both sides of the road. These, as well as most of the buildings in the center of town, were a throwback to the Austrian era (the nineteenth century), when the Jews had established industries in Tarnów and erected stone buildings, inside which not a trace of a Jew remains today. Some of the houses were confiscated by the Germans for their officers; the Poles took over the scores that remained.

Lwowska Street, after ascending continuously to the historic hill of Tarnów, turns right and changes its name to Wałowa. Here Henek, too, began to look around — at the corner of Wałowa and Goldhammera was the Aberdam house, where he and his brother and sister were born. This was where he had spent his childhood and youth, and experienced the anxiety of the Nazi *akcja*, which luckily had passed by his house. From there he had been expelled to Staro-Dąbrowska, to the ghetto that had been established after the first of the three bloody *akcja*s. Henek checked himself — no, the house did not move him at all; it was as though he did not recognize it. He felt a stronger emotional pull to the small house on Staro-Dąbrowska. No wonder he and his brother (but not the other family members) called themselves "Dąbrowski". He tried to share his feelings with Seiden and asked him whether it was possible that, while in exile, a young man could lose the human sense of love for his childhood home.

But Seiden does not listen. He is completely engrossed in his own thoughts. He is aware that in another minute or two, the car will reach the most important site of his life, and he will face memories that are still powerful despite the long years of exile. This is the bookstore that he had established on Wałowa, a unique place that had been both a shop and cultural center for the whole city.

Right here, in 1912, on Wałowa Street, opposite the elegant pink building of the Savings Fund, he and Regina, just married, had stood on their first day in Tarnów. Here the two lovebirds had decided to settle, to build their home and fulfill their dream.

Their dream embraced the whole world. He remembers it clearly, as though thirty-three years had not gone by, two world wars not intervened. The two lovers had left the Ministry of Culture in Vienna, arm in arm, holding an unusual business license for the establishment in Tarnów of an agency that would bring the best concerts, plays, dances and entertainers to the entire Galician community. The agency would be run from a bookstore that would specialize in both Polish and world literature and in a wide variety of sheet music.

The car moves slowly, clinging to the sight of the shop that the young Seiden couple had opened and that had had a formative influence on the city's culture. The door, through which Seiden had passed thousands of times when the shop had been a living entity, is now blocked up. The shop is devoid of life. But wonder of wonders, its lifeless body remains standing almost upright, resistant to the laws of nature, although its innards and sinews have been ripped out. In contradiction to the law of gravity, the sign that Regina had hung up before the shop's opening is still flying: "A giant black sign above the gate," she had suggested then."It will say in gold letters KSIĘGARNIA SEIDENA — Seiden's Bookshop." Seiden cannot recall when and why they had decided to change the wording: leave only KSIĘGARNIA on the top line, in large gold letters, and under it, "A.J. Seidena" in smaller letters. What was the meaning of "A.J."? Adolph Joachim? Maybe Avruhm Yitzhak, as he had been known as a boy? And another wonder — it seems to Seiden that the shop window still holds books with picture-portraits above them. Are they the very books that he used to switch in the shop window twice a month? Could a book have a life after death, unlike people?

The car has moved on already, but Seiden is still living the past. What was left of the theater agency? "Oh, where are you, Rubinstein and Kreisler, Morini and Millstein, Brailowski, Sigetti, Imreh Ungar and Kubelik? Do you remember how we hosted you

The Seider Bookstore *(after the Wehrmacht occupied Tarnów, 1939)*

in our residence, and how hard I worked to fill the 'Marzenie' hall with music, the likes of which Tarnów had never heard before I came along? The Dresden quartet that appeared several times? And Beethoven's Ninth Symphony, with which I opened the agency, and for which I engaged the Vienna Symphony and the Kraków Choir. Oh, those were the days!"

Wałowa Street is coming to an end, after circling the northern half of the historic hill of Tarnów. At this point a wide street descends from the mount, allowing for greater speed. But Seiden still asks Henek to drive slowly so that he can at least take a look at Santa Anna Street, which runs down from the left, and at the two buildings at the bottom end of the street. But one of the buildings he has expected to identify on the left side of the street has disappeared! A large hole, empty and black, gapes between the two buildings that stand on either side. The black hole can be seen from the top end of the street. Ah, this is the Temple. No, it *was* the Temple, and this hole is all that was left of it. Undoubtedly the evil German pilots had destroyed and burnt it. That same air force had plucked Millek from the flowerbed of life, although as a doctor, he and his patients were supposed to be protected by the Red Cross whose giant symbol had appeared on the infirmary tent.

Seiden used to come to the Temple with his wife, Regina, only twice a year: on the Jewish New Year, and on Yom Kippur, for *Kol Nidrei* and the memorial service for the dead. "That was also too much for her," he laughs to himself, "an incurable atheist!" Contrary to her views, on those two holidays — only these two! — he made sure that his shop was shut down. The ideological and spiritual changes he had experienced during the war made him now contemptuous of his "daring effort" to keep his shop open on the Jewish Sabbath. "Against whom was I trying to protest? God, or the Jews?" On the opposite corner he identified a building that was still standing. "That was our home for thirty years!" he murmurs listlessly. "What difference does it make to me if that building is ruined or if it still exists under Polish control? We will never go back to live here!"

Wałowa Street does now the same thing that Lwowska Street had done to Wałowa — it turns right and changes its name to Krakowska. The descent from the historic hill just begins and the car is free to speed up, as there is nothing on this road to awaken memories. There is no reason to slow down after they leave the town. There is no public transportation, and the Red Army has leveled a road to Kraków and beyond. In this war, Kraków had been declared a protected city, in order to preserve its historic sites, and is hardly damaged; it is certainly as lovely as Seiden and Henek remember it from before the war. Now they drive rapidly, impatient to see it again.

The U.B. office was established in the center of town. Henek quickly located an apartment close by. As promised, he returned in his car to Rzeszów to pick up the Kellers as well as Schmidt, so that here, too, they would all live together. The joyful slogan on everyone's tongue and the subject of every conversation was *"repatriation"*, going back. "But going back to where?" asked the returnees. "To a world that had been destroyed? To Polish anti-Semitism, an anti-Semitism without Jews, no less harsh than that of defeated Germany?" Despite the despairing questions, the "repatriation" slogan expressed renewed energy and hope that someone was still alive and would return — a family member, a friend, or someone from the youth movement. If alive, he would probably be dreaming of locating family members and friends, and the natural place to meet was the hometown or place of residence before the war. Or maybe this would be Kraków, the large city that was saved from destruction, a magnet in those days for those yearning to return things to their previous state. Thus people started coming back to Kraków, and to Tarnów, too, remembering the past, crying over the present, and hoping for an unlikely and impossible future.

Yet, when Seiden took up his U.B. position in Kraków, he was not satisfied with the routine work of the organization. He decided to design his own mission, under U.B. auspices of course, but a *Jewish* one. The small groups of survivors who had begun to return to their towns, whether to try to settle back there or merely to seek relatives, had set up representative committees to contact the government, to obtain what they needed for rehabilitation and, above all, protection. The blood libel of June 1946 in Kielce and the ensuing pogrom convinced the returnees of their vulnerability. Soon, a rumor began spreading among the committee heads, that "one of us" was quietly serving as an informal liaison between the Jewish community and the authorities in Kraków. That man, they whispered, was Seiden from Tarnów. Hayyim Schiffer rose after liberation as the leader and committee head of the handful of Jews who returned to Tarnów. Decades after the war, Schiffer would relive the situation in conversations with this author, who traveled to visit him in his new home in America. Enthusiastically, he recalled that "Seiden, of his own initiative, became the ultimate address for us. He, or someone working on his behalf, would answer all pleas for help swiftly and efficiently, especially complaints about hooligans who fought the Jews' return and threatened their personal safety. True, Seiden refused to visit Tarnów in person, and justifiably so. But what would we have done without him?"

"Oh, Millek, Millek," sighed Seiden. "If only you could see your *Partia* (Party) friends today, after defeating the old regime as you had dreamed. Everyone rushed to Kraków as though to a fair for high offices. Some changed their names, adding the noble-sounding ending '-ski' to their new Polish name. I harbor no resentment toward them on attaining positions of power. But why, oh why, after the terrible tragedy that befell our people, do they have to ignore the plight of their brethren, and sometimes, after tasting power, harass them unmercifully?"

On hearing these terrible accusations of Jews harassing other Jews, and also because he thought his late son, a communist, would have been pleased with his initiative, Seiden began contacting communist Jews from Tarnów of Millek's age and welcome them in his office. Seiden would encourage them to tell him about the *Partia* in Tarnów. They admitted that there had never been more than forty or fifty activists, but, apart from the "salon communists", most of the activists had been "top quality material", fire-spitting ideologues who had joined the *Partia* as high school students in the early 1930s. Most of them members of HaShomer HaTza'ir at first, they had no qualms about preaching communism clandestinely, or working in one of the "official" institutions that served as a front for their propaganda. Such was the *Peretz Verein*, which held Friday eve Yiddish gatherings, and the *Mendele Moikher Sforim Kultur Klub*, where literacy was taught. Well-meaning people joined this mission. Naïve souls! They believed that the *Klub* was truly battling ignorance. But the Polish police thought differently. Many members were sentenced and thrown into jail. They were released at the beginning of the war.

Unusual admiration was reserved for the young communist women. Legends arose about their self-defense during their trials, and about their distinguished backgrounds. One *Partia* member was the daughter of the religious Hebrew writer Yosef Umanski, the head of a Zionist family that immigrated to the Land of Israel in the 1930s — all except the communist daughter, and the son, Janek. The latter became friendly with another well-known communist woman, Rivtcheh Unger, daughter of the Zhabner Rebbe residing in Tarnów and sister of the American Yiddish writer, Menashe Unger, and of the Polish writer Adolph Rudnicki. When Janek became an anarchist, Rivtcheh left him; he was sentenced to four years in prison. Another young woman who served time in jail for communism was the sister of several well-known figures (whose former name was changed to Ya'ari): Eretz-Israel novelist Yehuda Ya'ari, librarian Avraham Ya'ari, youth *aliya* activist Moshe Ya'ari, and Noyekh, the wanderer in the Carpathian Mountains. She had also refused to immigrate to Eretz-Israel, when by 1935, almost the entire family (with the exception of Noyekh) had built a new home there.

But the one female communist who won the highest praise in Tarnów communist mythology as the Jewish Mata Hari was Hanka Sakhwald. Her father was a simple butcher in the "Burek" market at the base of the historic hill. He had made great efforts to give her the best enlightened education. She began as a member of HaShomer HaTza'ir, then joined the *Partia* while a student in the girls' high school, known as "Hayderek". Her father sent her to Paris for higher education. Upon her arrival, however, she volunteered to spy for the Soviet Union, being endowed with all the necessary credentials — youth, brilliance, beauty and willingness to sacrifice herself for an ideal. Apparently the French police received advance warning about her from Poland, and after a long stake-out, they arrested her. With luck, her end was unlike that of the real Mata

Hari: before the Second World War broke out she was included in the treaty of spy exchange between France and the Soviet Union. It seems that her contribution to the communist state was highly appreciated, and she lived peacefully in Russia for many years.

The Soviet Union also welcomed Shulim Bikkel, a Tarnów Jewish communist who had been imprisoned in a Polish jail for nine years because of a bloody confrontation with a drunken Pole. He was released when the prisons were emptied in 1939, at the beginning of the war. Like each and all, he too, took to the road, fleeing the German invasion, and all trace of him had disappeared. But when the Red Army entered Kraków in January 1945, Bikkel reappeared, marching along with the Red Army in the uniform of a Soviet colonel encrusted with medals. When he died, the army gave him a splendid official funeral, as befitting his rank and deeds.

Seiden attentively listened to the story of the *Partia*, but his special interest was anchored in the Strammer family, the best-known Jewish communist family in Tarnów. Moreover, he had discovered that Millek had spent much time in the company of the Strammers, and it is they who had recruited him to the *Partia*. The Strammer father was a traveling agent, and his four sons and two daughters were all communists.

Often Seiden would sit until after midnight in an enlightening conversation with Rudek, the eldest of the Strammers and the nearest in age to Seiden. Seiden was impressed with Rudek's practicality, a refreshing change from the usual verbosity of most *Partia* members. "Their tendency to long-windedness could be a reaction to the cautiousness of the underground that imposed silence in previous years," Rudek said, trying to find a justification for their garrulousness. Rudek himself had never been in prison, unlike his wife who had been sentenced in Tarnów before the war. When the war broke out, and each and all took to the road, he, too, went east with his brother Salek. "Unfortunately, Salek died in Russia, a heavy loss for the whole *Partia* as well as for myself. A philosopher, a theoretician of communism and the Comintern, he was incarcerated in a Polish jail for four years. I have no doubt that if he were alive today, he would definitely be a member of the Politburo, or in the government service."

The story of the third brother, Hesiek, is a typical Soviet scenario of the late 1930s. All of Tarnów, supporters and enemies alike, and Seiden as well, spoke of it with sadness. Hesiek was a personal friend of Tarnów native Karol Radek, and married his sister. Everything was going well, and Radek, a high-ranking Soviet leader, even managed to fit in a visit to Tarnów to his parents, the Sobelsohns, on the occasion of a Soviet state visit to Poland in 1934. But after the "Moscow trials", the couple broke up. Did Hesiek get a hint from a higher authority that his relationship with Radek's sister was not to Stalin's liking, since her brother was under indictment and Hesiek could consequently be harmed? Or maybe it was Hesiek's sister who decided on the divorce, as it was hard for her to bear what they had done to her brother, and this was her reaction to what had been going on in the Soviet Union during those years? No one asked why. This is also part and parcel of the Soviet story — no one ever asked questions. At any rate, Hesiek came back from Russia a colonel, and was appointed the director of the Polish "People's" Radio.

In the meantime, the Polish spring sailed on into the month of May 1945, heralding the end of the war in Europe. Survivors flowed from the Soviet gulags and the liberated German Lagers, each and all eager to go home, but no home was left standing. One lovely Krakowian evening, the two Strammer sisters, Salla and Wella, went for a walk in the "Planty". Suddenly, they were startled to see a woman in rags curled up on a bench. They carefully approached the bench and looked at her, then cried out together, "*Boże mój!* (Good God!) *It's Giza Seiden!*"

## IX

It has been decided that Giza will stay with the Strammer family in Kraków under the care of Salla and Wella as long as necessary, until she regains her health. It has also been decided, out of concern that the shock of an immediate meeting with her father might have a detrimental effect on her precarious health, that not before she recuperates completely will they tell Giza that her father is still alive, and is within walking distance of her. In any case — and this was harder because of the daily contact with the U.B. offices, and with the Kellers and Seiden himself — they would hide from Seiden the fact that his daughter has returned.

It is possible that the Strammer sisters were no more than what was derided as "gray communists", insofar as their understanding the intricacies of ideology was concerned. But there is no argument about their expertise in the complex matter of how to return color to a woman's cheeks, eyes, hair and clothing, and how to put a smile on her face after she had undergone so much sadness and despair over so many years. That expertise had become known back in the old days in Tarnów, when the two sisters were asked to take care of female communist friends who had returned from prolonged imprisonment. There were also matters of secret relations that were topics for gossip. As this book does not lower itself to gossip, it will borrow an idea from the ideological lexicon of pre-war left-wing circles: collectivism. Possibly, Salla Strammer, "gray communist" that she was, mistakenly expanded the scope of the idea of collectivism to include the collective use of another woman's husband. To hell with gossipmongers!

The beginning of Giza's care regimen was similar to what Seiden had received in Rzeszów. The lice-ridden clothing was sentenced to the fire, of course. There followed a series of hot baths, and new undergarments and dresses, the softness of which she had not felt for three years. The only complication was in purging the hair of all the undesirable creatures that insisted on making their home there. Unlike Seiden's hair, which consisted of a few strands combed over his scalp, thus offering the pretence of a lice-less full head, it took a long time until the invaders of Giza's hair were defeated. A final visit to a hairdresser's shop completed the victory. Thus, a month later, Giza was ready for the great moment — the mutual discovery of father and daughter, alive and residing in stunning proximity.

The morning began typically. Henek, who sat across from Seiden every day, entered the office as usual. There Seiden, again as usual, had been working since early morning at his desk. But unlike the usual pattern, Henek did not approach his desk immediately. Still standing, he bid Seiden his daily *dzień dobry* (good morning), and said, straining to keep his voice natural, "Adolph, there's a visitor to see you." This in itself was nothing new — visitors to the office were an integral part of the work. "Bring him in," (Seiden used the masculine form, as most of the U.B.'s visitors were men). Henek went out to the hallway, where Giza was waiting, certain that he was inviting her into his own office. Using his best Polish manners, he opened the door for her with a broad smile, but stopped on the outer threshold. She entered, and he closed the door behind her as though shutting her into the office alone. For a moment his hand remained on the doorknob, fearing that Giza would turn around, and on seeing that Henek was not following in her footsteps, reach out and open the door.

Out of security concerns, the walls of the U.B. offices were soundproof, and the "oh"s and "ah"s expected in such a situation were not heard in the hall. Father and daughter were as if cut off from the world. There were only he and she, and nothing else existed. In such isolation, there could be no photograph to document this private meeting between father and daughter, and no written account to record their words. Did the father tell his daughter what he had never told anyone else — where he wandered while each and all took to the road in 1939; how and under what conditions he survived for nearly five years; and how he knew to turn back with each and all toward Rzeszów in 1944? Did his childhood memories summon him to his birthplace, after the real world and the imagined one he had built for himself in his adolescence had collapsed around him? And did the daughter tell him what her mother and she had experienced after they were left alone in Tarnów, and how she discovered that her mother had perished in the exposed bunker? Did she tell her father what she had kept to herself — how she had arrived at Ravensbrück concentration camp in 1942, and how she had survived there until the gate was breached? And how, with a sense of navigation she never knew she had possessed, she had dragged herself all the way to Kraków? Or how she had fallen there, completely exhausted, onto a merciful bench, not knowing where it was or how it had sprung up? She only knew this — she had wanted to die. Indeed, what father told his daughter, and what the daughter told her father and nobody else, forged a new connection between the two sole survivors of the family, and a resolve that they must never, ever lose each other again!

The two remained in the room the entire day. The tea urn and box of pastries, regular fare in the office, made them forget the meals awaiting them in vain at home. Toward evening, in the enchanted Kraków twilight, the father and daughter went for a stroll in the "Planty". Time seemed to turn back past the six years of the war to those far-off days thirty years ago when father would take his daughter by train to Kraków. They would walk then around the central square, wait for the *hejnał* trumpet blast, and vie for who would be the first to glimpse the gleaming trumpet held by the trumpeter in the open window at the top of the Marian Church. Several times the two had gone up to the "Wawel" (read: Vahvel), descended into the legendary monster's cave, and approached the bank of the Wisła. On another trip, they had visited the Jagielonian University. Father had told her about this university, Poland's first, and explained the meaning of its name. He had repeated, "Look, Giziu, when you grow up you'll study here, and your father, who hadn't studied in Kraków, but who studied in Vienna, will be proud of you." At the end of each trip, both tired, they had strolled around the "Planty" and relaxed on the familiar bench of her childhood.

They arrived at the same bench this time, too, on their first promenade in the "Planty" after the war. "Do you remember, Giziu, how we used to sit on this bench?" Giza did not answer. Through a hazy mist, she saw the very bench she had reached with her last vestiges of strength, after a month-long march from Ravensbrück. Dressed in rags, itching all over from lice, she had curled up in an army coat that she had stolen from the camp's warehouse. Hungry, thirsty, and on the verge of passing out, she woke up from her faint, saw two pairs of eyes over her, and fainted again. The rest was well-known to all, although her father was still ignorant of those events. Now, sitting next to him, overjoyed that they had found each other, she asked herself a different question than the one her father was asking, still sunk in the memory of those far-off days. Could it be — she pondered — that her marvelous sense of direction had led her to Kraków, not only as a general destination, but specifically to the beloved bench that fate had preserved for her?

"Tato (Daddy), let's go home," she whispered, head spinning with the thought that the bench she was sitting on at this moment was the same bench of her salvation. "Let's go, father. They are surely waiting for us, and maybe even worrying about us."

The next day, Father invited daughter to the office to show her his work and his plans for the coming months. The U.B. missions were confidential, of course, but Seiden spoke with satisfaction about the "Jewish missions" he had voluntarily initiated. He told her about the repeated complaints of the survivors' committees in the various towns against municipalities that because of the Holocaust were no longer familiar with Jews. They were making it difficult for the survivors to set up a community center in one of the empty Jewish houses. Thanks to Seiden's intervention, the Jews of Tarnów got back Aberdam House, on the corner of Wałowa and Goldhammera Streets, and set up the committee's offices there. There is also a small meeting hall, rooms for temporary living quarters for people looking for their relatives, and even a small synagogue, and an apartment for the synagogue's guard.

"So that my official role as a U.B. officer won't be compromised," Father explained, "I come to the office at dawn and work on our issues until nine, when the government offices open. Then I dedicate myself to my security role. The U.B. office closes at four, like the other government offices, and then I go back to my Jewish projects and work on them until midnight. Beyond giving practical help and psychological support to the many needy, I feel I am fulfilling a mission. Personally, I feel I am atoning for the many years that I preached the delusion of assimilation, and was antagonistic towards Judaism and the Jewish community, even though I never denied my heritage."

"It's really important work, Tato. But when do you think it will be over?" asked Giza.

"If the situation doesn't get worse, there's at least another year's work here."

"We'll live that whole year in Poland, which didn't mourn Millek and let them murder Mother?"

Seiden was silent. A painful chasm opened between the newly-reunited father and daughter.

"I suggest we think about moving. A few days ago I saw a newspaper at Rudek's. It said that New Zealand will accept Holocaust survivors with skills. The visas will be given out at the New Zealand embassy in Paris. It would be an excellent solution for us."

"They need me here, Giziu. This is where I am making my contribution. This is where I am valuable. No one needs me there."

"I need you there, and any other place we'll go. Didn't we decide that we'll never separate again?"

Father had no response to his daughter's words. "As a first discussion about our future, I think that's enough," thought Giza, and remained silent.

Their conversation came to a close for the time being. Seiden went back to the unusual case that was worrying him. Giza continued the conversation within her own mind:

"The seed has been planted, and I have to give it time to sprout. Not too much time though, as the situation will surely worsen. The problems that Father is trying to solve are insoluble. They will never be solved. Father is naïve! Just as his assimilation was naïve, so is his experiment to revive Polish Jewry. Poland is one big graveyard today, and there is no life in a graveyard. Even those who believe in resurrection don't believe it will happen soon. Our generation knows only destruction.

"I, on the other hand, am the only one who has absolutely lost that naiveté. Just as in occupied Tarnów, I was the one who performed the role of grown-up at home and led Mother by the hand as if she were a little girl until she woke up, so it is with Father. He's still dreaming that he is leading a little girl by the hand, as in olden times. Life will never be as it was before. The quicker Father wakes up to reality, the better for him and for both of us.

"The Strammers and the Jewish communists will sober up, too. If they don't do so on their own, someone else will open their eyes and kick them out. There is no pity in their world. I don't care whether Roman Malinowski, the king of Lodz — Motek Leibel from Tarnów — gets blown away with the changing wind, as he has no compassion. But I pity Rudek Strammer — an honest, clever person, happy to live under this regime and build his home in communist Poland. When the time comes, he will also understand that there is no room for Jews here, whatever the regime.

"And we — where shall we go? Anywhere, but not to Europe, that blood-soaked continent (Giza decides). Palestine? That's already Asia, but under the rule of a European empire. I always was a Zionist. But the gates are locked, and after all that I've been through, I have no strength to be battered around in a flimsy boat and wind up in a British jail. I'm not sure that Father will be able to withstand it after the hell he's been through. Then where to? As far away from Europe as possible! To the end of the world. To New Zealand!"

Giza gazed into the distance. Her eyes reflected the beautiful views she had once seen in a travel brochure. They seemed to have awakened, pulling her with ropes of enchantment. "It's impossible to get any farther away than that!"

Seiden was very tense during the next few days, due to the unusual case he was working on. He feared there was no alternative but to involve the U.B. and the police. Giza came by every morning to wish him a *dzień dobry* and to exchange a few words with him, but they could not hold a proper conversation. Seiden showed no sign that he was thinking about the journey his daughter had mentioned several days before. It was but natural to explain away his silence not as ignoring the subject, but as a result of the difficult case that was demanding all his attention, as well as that of the official bodies. While Seiden and others were occupied with the special case, Henek was put in charge of routine office activities.

Giza, on her part, continued to work on the emigration issue. On her own initiative, she sent a letter to the New Zealand embassy in Paris. In her letter she gave details about her father and herself, and requested that their names be added to the list of the candidates for an immigration permit. Moreover, she concluded that as long as her father was so busy with public affairs that he had no time to consider their own future, she would do something no one else could: she would return to the teacher in Tarnów to collect her father's bibliophile collection, which she had placed in his hands for custody back then ("BT", she called the "back then"). She remembered that Sunday. The churches in town had been full of worshippers. The German commissar was sitting in the officers' club, enjoying the Bavarian beer sent to him straight from Munich. She recalled having walked down Ogrodowa Street (after removing the "Jewish ribbon" from her sleeve), two suitcases in her hands. She had crossed the Gestapo junction, heart pounding but head held high, relying on her Slavic appearance to get her through safely. Finally she had arrived at the teacher's gate. That was then. But today the situation was different. The Germans were no longer here. Poland was free. She would bring her father his collection standing tall and fearless, heart calm. She imagined how the teacher would receive her: "Ah, you have returned, Giziu. Happily, Ciołkosz's information was wrong after all. You look wonderful, like nothing ever happened. Sit down, please, while I bring your suitcases down from their hiding place." He would give her the two full suitcases: "Just like they were when you brought them, except maybe for a little dust." She would laugh and thank the teacher for guarding the treasure during the war years, and bring him her father's thanks for the noble act he had done for his old friend.

## X

"So, we journey to Tarnów. But how? Henek will be glad to take me. But on second thought, should I do that to my honorable teacher? I'll point out the house, and the car will stop. Henek will get out of the car in his officer's uniform, and pull the bell on the gate. In the first-floor window looking out onto the street, the brocade curtain will be pulled aside a little, and the man behind the curtain will see a black U.B. car and an officer at the gate. Even though he is a peaceful, law-abiding citizen with nothing to be afraid of, nonetheless he will be uncomfortable. He will press the button. The gate will open. Who will enter, to his astonishment? I will! What is this? A cruel joke? No, I will not do this to him!

"So I will go by train. It's an hour and a half to Tarnów, and the house is only about a twenty-minute walk from the train station. It's very simple. It is also simple in Kraków. You walk along the "Planty", past the Barbacan fortress, and continue to the station."

The train is already standing on the platform. The crowding is unbearable. Throngs push each other, battling to place their foot on the steps of the cars. Suddenly people, wagons, track and signs spin around and around in her head. Half-fainting, Giza collapses onto a bench on the platform. Eyes shut, she re-experiences the nightmare of the station as it was years ago:

> The storm-troopers push wildly with their rifle butts, screeching orders at the deportees, men, women and children, inside the station gate. A living wall of SS personnel fences them in on all sides, preventing any attempt at escape. The screams of the troopers mingle with the heart-rending cries of refugees separated from each other in the crowding. Husbands call to their wives, mothers to

their weeping children. Dazed, Giza gives in to the crowding and unwittingly moves toward the gate, pushed from behind by the weight of the crowd. All of a sudden she finds herself on a platform teeming with deportees.

On the platform two cattle trains are waiting. First the guards push the tortured people into the wagons of the right-hand train. When it begins to overflow, they seal the openings and begin to squeeze the rest into the second train. Giza remains standing on the platform as though made of stone, despite her Aryan papers. "*Warum stehst du dort, du dumme?*" An SS man notices her, lifts her up in arms of steel and throws her like a sack of potatoes into the last wagon. They lock the wagon. The locomotive whistles. The wheels begin to turn west. To where?

To Płaszów extermination camp?

To Auschwitz?

After several wagons are unloaded in Płaszów, and most of the remainder in Auschwitz, two wagons of women prisoners are reorganized. Somebody recognizes the track and whispers — Ravensbrück.

No, she would never board a train again, however comfortable and elegant it might be. Aside from that, the crowding on the platform in Kraków was hopeless. So against her will, Giza returned to Henek. She would travel with him to Tarnów, but on arriving at Ogrodowa, she would ask him to park in the lane around the corner and wait for her in the car. That way the blackness of the car and the officer's shiny uniform would not frighten the teacher, who often looked out of his window at the street. She would walk to the gate alone, ring the bell, and be welcomed. And that is what she did.

In response to her ringing, the gate opens with an automatic click. Giza recalls her fear during her visit over three years ago, when the click had symbolized not only the opening, but also the closing of the gate, meaning she had no control over the exit. Yet this time all her fears dissipate, and she goes up cheerfully to the first floor. The door is open in response to the ringing, as it had been then, and the shadow of a person is framed in the door, waiting to identify the guest.

That morning on her first visit, he had recognized her immediately, from the end of the long, dark hallway. He had come to greet her with a hearty *dzień dobry* and shaken her hand warmly. To her amazement, this time the shadow does not move. Pale and frozen, it looks as though it is seeing a ghost rising from purgatory and invading his peaceful world. Now it is Giza's turn to smile a *dzień dobry*, and fearing that the man has dementia, she takes pains to explain slowly and clearly who she is: "I'm Giza, your ex-pupil, the daughter of Regina and Adolph Seiden. You used to enjoy visiting them at their home and bookshop. Unfortunately Mother was killed, but Father came back, healthy and active as ever. As you can see, I have also returned, and after convalescence, I am also well."

Recovering his power of speech, the teacher is impatient and nervous. "No need to explain, I remember you well. Your return is not merely a surprise but a real shock. I didn't believe that you would survive. It seems that the vitality of your people is superior to that of others. Even Hitler underestimated you. I relied on Ciołkosz and acted accordingly."

"What do you mean, 'you acted accordingly'?"

"I sold the collection."

"You did what?! You s-o-l-d i-t?" The syllables refused to unite; they came out as separate units, shouting. Several seconds passed before Giza could control the words and allow them to express the fullness of their anger.

"You sold something that wasn't yours! You betrayed my trust in you, and you stole — yes, stole — my father's collection! To think that you were a lecturer of ethics at the high school, and we, stupid girls, believed your every word as the God-given truth. There is no forgiveness for what you have done, you pitiful pretense of an intellectual. There is no forgiveness, and there never will be!"

Only then did she notice that she had not been invited to sit down, and she had been standing this whole time, gripping the back of the chair with all her might so that she would not fall into a faint. For a moment, she decided to leave the room. Her eyes searched for the button that controlled the gate. She would push it and escape. But soon she recovered. She sat down, without the chair being offered as part of Polish manners, and decided to deepen her queries and bring the full truth to light. Who was the nameless individual who had acquired the collection? Where was he now? What could be done in order to return the collection to its rightful owners?

"That collection is worth tens of thousands of złotys," she began her inquiry with a stern look. "What Pole had that kind of money during the war?"

"You're right. I didn't find any Polish customers. I sold the material to a German."

"To a German? You removed such a cultural treasure from the country?'

'The man is a very intelligent officer, older than the combat officers, definitely not one of the murderers. He is a man of books, and understands the value of masterpieces and first editions. He has a book-and-antique shop in his hometown, Munich." So thrilled was the teacher to enumerate the officer's qualities, he did not notice that on hearing his words, Giza had slipped from her chair to the wax-polished floor and, fainting, was lying there motionless. The mask of indifference fell away from the teacher's face, and he bent over the young woman lying between the sofa and the chair.

"What happened, Giziu? Come, Gizienku, I'll pick you up and put you on the sofa, and I'll bring you water right away."

He rushed to the kitchen and brought a pitcher of water, a glass and a wet towel. Raising Giza's head and supporting it with his arm, he gave her drops of water to drink until she could take full swallows. Then he gently wiped her forehead and eyes. Giza slowly awoke from her faint and looked around in shock. How long had she been lying on the sofa in this house? How long had her head been leaning on this man's arm? She jumped from the sofa as though bitten by a snake, her strength returning to her in a flash. She stood as before behind the sofa, in a position of height and control, while the teacher sat on his chair bent over in complete wretchedness.

"I thank you for your concern about me. However, we haven't yet finished the matter of my father's collection. You said that you sold it to a German officer. Did you at least get a full price for it?"

The teacher stuttered. "There was no monetary deal. The officer said the authorities had confiscated all the books from the Jewish shop. He took for himself the books in German and the music books his own shop did not have. All that has already been sent to Munich. The officer wasn't interested in the books in Polish, so he removed them to a warehouse whose key was in his pocket. After I gave him the collection, he took me to the warehouse, and I returned in his car with around two hundred Polish books. Here they are." A new bookcase stood beside the old one, and on its shelves stood the stolen goods in all their dubious glory.

"I sense that you have not yet understood the depth of your baseness. Even if I ignore your treachery in betraying Father's trust, this deal between two thieves is unbelievable. You stole from Seiden a unique collection that he had built up for over forty years, and you dared to give it in exchange for the contents of the unique shop that Seiden built up ever since he settled in Tarnów thirty years ago. In other words, Seiden paid with his own property for what you stole from Seiden, and Seiden also paid with his own property for what the officer stole from Seiden. Not even Satan has ever invented such a deal! My curse will hound you both until the end of your days. Satan never made a daughter's curse such as this either! That's what you're going to get, damn you!"

"Just don't faint again," Giza repeated to herself. "You're not finished with him." The teacher raised his hand as though about to speak in his defense. But Giza nipped his attempt in the bud. "The respect of a pupil for her teacher is dead. You murdered it. Now you will listen to *me*!"

"Let me begin with a declaration of love. I love Poland. I was born in this country, I grew up here, and I was educated here. I love its scenery. I love Tarnów and Kraków, the mountains and the rivers, from the Carpathian Range to the Baltic Sea. But you do not represent the *land* of Poland, you represent its *people*. You consider yourself as belonging to the Polish elite. I have no qualms about declaring here that I hate the Poles, I hate their pseudo-elite and you as their representative. You said before that even Hitler underestimated us and our power of vitality — and I'll complete the sentence. Even more: he correctly, yes, correctly appraised the Poles. He understood that only here could he cover the entire country with innumerable concentration camps for the annihilation of Jews, without fearing that the Poles would arise against the massacre. He preferred to bring them here in the thousands, trainloads of Jews from France, Holland, Hungary and the other countries, rather than having to face their populations. Instead, he turned Poland into a central slaughterhouse, knowing full well that this people, steeped for generations in anti-Semitism, would not object to this crime. The situation today is proof: three million Jews are no longer alive — murdered — and still, hatred of Jews prevails, even though no Jews exist in the country. The day will come when this beautiful country will vomit you out, just as it vomited you out from its eastern half. Then what will you be left with? With Mickiewicz, who wrote in Polish but was a Lithuanian, according to his own declaration? With the three great poets of our generation — Tuwim, Słonimski, and Witlin — who are either Jews or of Jewish descent? Or with the modern Polish composer, Karol Szymanowski, a descendant of Frankist Jews? No, you Poles will remain behind with your horses and cavalry, with which you intended to face tanks and planes of modern warfare, but you were defeated ignominiously!"

The teacher got out of his chair. "Enough, Giziu. I was wrong. Let's make up. Every sin has its forgiveness. I will compensate you any way you want. Only don't reject me in anger." He held out his hand to Giza, but she had already turned her back on him, pressed the button and run out to the gate. "I must leave Poland! I must leave quickly! I can't breathe the air here!"

She raced as quickly as she could to Henek who was waiting in the car on the corner as agreed. "What happened?" Henek worried, seeing her face flaming with anger and her eyes flooded with tears. "To Kraków, Henku. Please, to Kraków, to Father!"

❖ ❖ ❖

About fifty years later, in the early stages of writing this book, the author received an envelope by registered mail. It was a yellow office envelope, too large and full for a letter, too small for a parcel. At first touch, the object inside gave the impression of a hard cover. A book? A bound collection of documents? No novelty or reason for surprise there. Books and documents are the inseparable tools of a professional historian. But the name of the sender and her return address were totally unexpected: *"Giza Bend, Wellington, New Zealand"* — née Giza Seiden, of course!

Giza and Ankori met each other in Tarnów, when a high school student and "promising" violinist, then named Hesiek Wróbel, used to visit her father's store. Giza was already a student at the University of Kraków, and on her vacations would return to Tarnów and help her father organize the annual concerts of Professor Bau's pupils. She was lavish in her praise of young Wróbel's playing. Several times the youth saw her at his house, when she came with her mother to purchase new embroidery patterns and threads of different colors in Golda Wróbel's home shop.

Since his *aliya* in 1937, Ankori and Seiden had fallen out of touch. The young man's life entered several stages after his immigration: first came integration into Eretz-Israel and an MA degree at the Hebrew University. Then followed the Second World War; five years of service in a Hebrew "Palestinian" Unit and the Jewish Brigade, both within the British Eighth Army; and his work for the Holocaust survivors in Africa and Europe. During the War of Independence and the founding of the State of Israel, he served in the Israel Defense Forces. He set up a family, then obtained his doctorate at the University of Columbia in New York. He spent the next forty years teaching in universities in Israel and abroad, and publishing books and articles. All this diverted his attention from the bookshop that no longer existed and from its owners, whose fate he did not know. But then he began to gather material on the epic of the Jews of Tarnów. While his previous book focused on the various branches of Hassidism and on early Zionism in Tarnów, one of the subjects of this book is the opposing ideology — assimilation — and eventually, the victory of Zionism. During this research, Ankori realized the importance of renewing ties with Giza Seiden in New Zealand, and the information from extended telephone conversations with her enriched the book immeasurably.

Each and all took to the road.

The Seidens' road back from exile led them to New Zealand. "Leaving Europe was like the Exodus from Egypt," Seiden labeled the act. "It was an Exodus from an accursed bloody continent", so dubbed it Giza, rooted in the present, not in memories of biblical proportions.

They waited for their immigration visas in Paris. While waiting, Seiden exchanged one Jewish mission for another. In Paris, he could not continue defending live Jews, but he could perpetuate the memories of the Holocaust victims. Thus he and Dr. Chomet, the last leader of the Jewish community and the Zionist Federation in Tarnów, then also in Paris, decided to write a book commemorating the town's Jewish population and Jewish life. For various reasons, the Tarnów Memorial Book did not materialize in Paris but was published belatedly, in Tel Aviv in 1954. Chomet, who went to live in Israel, was the sole editor. On the eve of their departure for New Zealand, Seiden and his daughter had the good fortune of participating in the joy that engulfed all the Jews of Paris with the tidings of the establishment of the State of Israel on May 15, 1948.

As something of a penance for not coming to live in Israel, Seiden returned to the Hebrew of his youth, that of the prayer book and the Bible as his grandfather had taught him. The pinnacle of Seiden and Giza's expectations was to go to Israel, at least for a visit. Giza's marriage and the birth of her daughter put off the visit for thirteen years. In the winter of 1961, Seiden, his daughter Giza and son-in-law Leon Bend, and their daughter (Seiden's granddaughter), finally tread the ground of Israel.

Seiden and family plant a tree in the Balfour Forest in Israel.

For the elderly Seiden, the month in Israel afforded an impressive and comprehensive trip as well as an opportunity to meet long-lost friends. It signified the closing of a circle from the days of the Hebrew-religious education that he received from his grandfather, to the modern Hebrew he heard ringing in the mouths of Israeli youths.

That Jerusalem morning, an oversized envelope was dropped into his mailbox. Excitedly, Zvi opened the envelope. What did this unexpected delivery mean? His telephone conversations with Giza had been exhaustive. She had offered information willingly, knowing that he intended to include it in the book — apart from details that Giza had given him but requested not to reveal to the readers (such as the name of the teacher, and the name of the person who had broken down under torture and delivered information about the secret bunker where Giza's mother had hid). The author honored her request, and these names will never be revealed. In any case, their last conversation had taken place a long time ago. If anyone had an obligation to send anything, it was the author. But, unfortunately, his book was not yet ready for print.

Out of the open envelope came a homemade volume, with more than 150 handwritten pages in German. Each page was accompanied by illustrations, original photographs taken by Seiden's son-in-law, Leon Bend, postcards and cuttings from tourist brochures and newspapers. It was a comprehensive survey of the trip from New Zealand to Israel, arranged in December 1961 into a proper book, typical of a professional bookseller, with title, table of contents, page numbers, place of "publication", and date. On the other side of the title page was a dedication: "To my children, Giza and Leon, and my granddaughter, Helen Renée".

On reading the dedication, the recipient of the unexpected delivery was shocked and called Giza immediately. No, he could not accept the transfer of the manuscript to his hands. This was a Seiden family possession, and that is what its author intended. The diary had to be preserved in the hands of the family for generations. The tremendous work that Seiden had invested in the manuscript, its editing and illustration, demanded honoring the will of the hand that had written all this and dedicated the masterpiece to the Seiden family.

Silence reigned on the other end of the line, a silence that the instigator of the conversation was not sure how to interpret. Was Giza persuaded by his words? Was she looking for the right words in order to tell him what had led to the delivery?

"Zvi," she said, breaking the silence. "Father passed away at the age of eighty-three. My husband has also died. Our daughter married out of the fold, and has no interest in this. And you know — she added, laughingly — how old I am. In short — the Seiden tribe has all but disappeared. Please take the book in custody, and through you the memory of the Seiden house will be preserved."

"Nach meiner Geburtsurkunde war ich Oesterreicher, hernach Pole, jetzt infolge Naturalisation, New-Zealander — aber dem Herzen nach, bin ich und bleibe Jude."

Seiden's handwritten creed in German.

Her distant interlocutor had no answer to this. He turned another page, and found the leitmotif of the entire manuscript:

> "According to my place of birth, I was an Austrian.
> Then I became Polish. Now I am a New Zealander
> through naturalization,
>
> BUT IN MY HEART, I AM, AND WILL FOREVER REMAIN,
>
> A JEW."

## CHAPTER SIX
# Mala

### I

THE LUCK OF Mala Wróbel, this author's sister, took a turn for the worse when, in the summer of 1939, she left Jerusalem for Tarnów to visit her parents and her younger sister, whom she missed terribly, but the war that broke out turned her trip into a nightmare.

In October 1937, the sister and brother had made *aliya* to Eretz-Israel to study at the Hebrew University, which was founded in 1918 but did not begin regular instruction until 1925. The two young people rented a room in Kerem Avraham, in those days a neighborhood full of students; they both registered for literature, history, and philosophy; and together they used to take the No. 9 bus to Mount Scopus. Already when they were walking the deck of the *Polonia* — the ship specially hired by Hebrew University to bring a joyful group of students from Poland, after obtaining special *aliya* permits for them — the sister and brother decided that from the moment they entered Eretz-Israel, they would talk between themselves only in Hebrew. The brother even Hebraized his first and last names, and from then on Hesiek Wróbel was known as Zvi Ankori, and even Mala, though it sounded forced at first, called him "Zvi". For the brother, the Hebraization of his name was a confirmation of full acclimatization to Eretz-Israel and an irreversible integration into the heritage of previous generations for which Hebrew was the Holy Tongue. At the same time, it was a vow of final separation from the land of his birth.

When the parents suggested to son and daughter in the summer of 1939 that they come home for vacation, the son refused, pledging never to return to the Diaspora. In contrast to the brother's practical and ideological rift with his old country, Mala had no ideological inhibitions. The brother's vow did not apply to her. She knew that the journey itself would be difficult: from Haifa to Constanza on the Black Sea, from there by a sealed Rumanian train to the Polish border, and thence, by a regular Polish train to Tarnów — a ten-day journey in each direction. But she lovingly accepted the forecast of hardship, even though she had to travel to Tarnów alone, without the usual support of her brother. In fact, this was the first time that Mala decided on a course that was entirely independent. No matter how difficult, what mainly enthralled her was the anticipation of the visit itself: to embrace the city of her childhood and young adulthood, and above all, to reunite with her mother, father, and sister Gunia, after a separation of almost two years.

Mala had not yet readjusted to her city of birth when the war broke out, playing havoc with all plans and hopes. The seven weeks of vacation she had expected to be a holiday for her and her family grew into seven years of suffering and struggle to stay alive. Taking a stroll on September 7, 1939, she saw the motorcyclists of the German advance force entering the city. She hid in the gate of a house, but after an hour or so decided to return home by a much longer and circuitous route. On arrival, she heard the frightening news that the German advance units had burst into the Rynek and begun to take over the large Jewish edifices in the historic square in order to house army officers. The homeowners were allotted half an hour to leave their buildings and were directed to the Jewish neighborhood. Indeed, at home she found Eltchi Baron, a friend and former employer of her father and a wealthy owner of oil wells in the Eastern Carpathians, who had also been expelled from his beautiful house in the Rynek. Golda and Aazik welcomed him warmly and gave him the back room, the bedroom, thinking they would improvise their own beds in the front room. Shaul Spitz was also banished from his home in the Rynek. Shaul, Aazik's study partner, was the son of Leibtchi, Aazik's patron and supporter at the end of the *kloyz* period, who died before the war. Aazik remembered father and son fondly, and offered shelter in his small apartment to Shaul as well.

Confronting this situation, Mala decided to return immediately to Constanza, the Rumanian harbor where the *Polonia* was docked. "On that ship I will return to Eretz-Israel." She verified that she had the return ticket in her pocket, and received from Baron generous advice, addresses of his Rumanian business partners, and a pocketful of Rumanian bills. Poor Mala! Did she not understand that when the country of Poland fell, its fleet, including the *Polonia*, had also ceased to exist? A ten-day march brought her to the San. She forded the river on the exact day on which, by agreement with the Third Reich, the Red Army was about to position itself on the eastern bank, after capturing Eastern Galicia from Poland. Beginning on that day, September 17, 1939, Mala found herself in the territory of the USSR. Undaunted, she deviated from the path of the refugees marching toward Lwów, and turned southeast in the direction of the Rumanian border, hoping naively that the Polish boat awaited her. But when she reached the Czeremosz — behold, on the other side was Rumania, Constanza, Eretz-Israel! — and studied the river, searching for a safe crossing point, suddenly, reflected in the water was the figure of a man in uniform, whose footsteps she had not heard as he approached the riverbank. With the same suddenness, the figure that had previously been reflected in the water stood before her on the ground — no vision, as she had imagined at first, but armed flesh and blood: a Ukrainian border guard. For a moment, she was shocked, but quickly relaxed at the sight of his unkempt uniform that was unlike that of a policeman in the regular force.

"What are you doing here? This is a border area." The man, middle-aged and with a pleasant, almost fatherly, face, was apparently a part-civilian guard. He began speaking in Ukrainian and switched to Polish for her sake, as did the Ukrainians until two weeks previously, when they were still part of Poland. For the time being, no one had found fault in this twin usage. Two sister languages, after all. But would the ascendant Ukrainian nationalism accept it in the future? "What is your name?" — the guard asked again, as before — "and what are you doing here?"

Upon sensing the guard's kindness, Mala recovered her natural self-confidence. "My name is Mala Wróblówna" — she declared loudly, as was her way in conversation — indeed, rather louder — intentionally emphasizing the Polishness of the name. "I had a date with my boyfriend for a stroll along the river, but look, he's not here. Now, *you* tell me, please, can we girls trust you men?" They both laughed, and his laugh indicated to her that she was out of danger and that her words sounded honest and acceptable.

At that moment, something out of a children's fairy tale occurred. Out from behind the curve of bushes appeared not the good fairy, but a young man: "Mala! Mala, where have you been? I've been waiting for you for more than an hour." He waved at the dumbfounded guard, wrapped his arm around Mala's shoulders, and disappeared with her behind the curve of bushes.

Mala was even more shocked than the guard, and like him, lost her power of speech. The only one who behaved logically and with the necessary haste was the young man. He continued leading Mala down the path: "I heard how you stated your name and invented a story that you had a date here with a boy. Clever excuse, but let's face it, you wanted to ford the river, didn't you? That's the only reason why refugees come here. Many have succeeded, and consequently the authorities brought a guard, and because of him your plan failed. But I also knew that if your story was not accepted as reliable, you would be in trouble. I decided to act; I would never let Ukrainians try a Polish woman. Now, look: as long as you are here, the danger has not passed. You must flee this place at once. Here, we've reached the highway. (He glanced at his wristwatch.) A direct bus to Lvov is supposed to pass by right now. That's where you want to go, isn't it? Do you have rubles? (She opened her wallet.) No, that's Rumanian money. Save it for another time. (He stuffed a handful of ruble notes into her wallet.) Now you're all set. The bus will arrive soon. Here it comes, in fact. Get on and go. Now listen to me (he added in a commanding voice): never come back here!" — and disappeared.

Not before she sat down on the bus did she recover her thinking ability. "Who could that have been?" — she asked herself. She wrinkled her forehead but could not come up with an answer. "Maybe it was the prince of dreams, about whom the young girls love to read fairy tales and nurture rosy fantasies that one day he will arrive?" — she giggled to herself. "Or maybe he was a *lamedvavnik*, one of the legendary thirty-six righteous Jews? Or perhaps Elijah the Prophet in all his glory came down to save a young Jewish refugee who got into trouble?"

She regained her practicality: "Enough! Three silly ideas suffice for one day!" She recalled that she had not asked her rescuer for his name, nor had she thanked him. How would she return the money he had given her? "Maybe I will spot him one day among the refugees in Lvov." For days and nights on end, she obsessively repeated her wish: to meet him! Suddenly she felt ashamed: was she also awaiting a prince, like those silly teenagers? She determined: "No, I will never take another step to meet him!"

## II

Lvov welcomed Mala with a smile. She remembered by heart the address of Yokhtche Weissmann, her classmate at Safah Berurah high school, with whom she had corresponded ever since the

Weissmanns moved to Lwów when it was still part of Poland. Their well-being had visibly improved. Compared to their home in Tarnów, their apartment in Lvov was large and well-appointed. No less than Yokhtche, his parents were also pleased to accept Mala in their spacious apartment and gave her a room of her own. Parents of one son, they now received the gift of a daughter.

Her days in Lvov compensated Mala for the vacation days she had hoped to enjoy in Tarnów. She read copiously and toured all the city's neighborhoods, historic sites, and cultural institutions. In the wake of Franz Werfel's book, she was especially interested in the Armenians and the Armenian Quarter. She found great resemblance between the Armenian fate and dispersion, and the fate of her own people. And what of her personal fate, as a daughter of her people? A heavy cloud lay over the horizon, disturbing her and the other refugees. Rumors and whispers hinted at hidden future plans of the Soviets against them. The lack of any formal identifying document in her hand, such as a passport, caused Mala additional worry. She wrote to her parents, but they failed to locate the passport at home. Could she have taken it with her and lost it in her wanderings?

At her request, her brother obtained a new Polish passport for her at the Polish consulate in Jerusalem, and sent it to Mala as quickly as possible, paying double the insurance in order to guarantee delivery. But this did not help. Mala waited for the desired document in vain. In spite of her distress, she may have found some consolation in the likely assumption that, at any rate, the Soviet government would not have honored a Polish passport as a recognized, acceptable document, since the USSR had for some time ceased to recognize Poland's sovereignty. Thus, presentation of the passport would not have changed Mala's legal status even one iota.

The signs of approaching calamity prophesied truthfully. In July 1940, deportation decrees were issued to the tens of thousands of refugees from Polish western Galicia, who had found shelter in what had become for these past ten months the Soviet western Ukraine, with Lvov as its capital.

Mala was sentenced to forced labor in the forest of Omsk province in Siberia. From the moment of exile, the deportees' status was defined as prisoners, confined under guard to Vyerkhneye Baraki, the camp that the prisoners were commanded to erect with their own hands along the banks of the Irtish River. Their job, of both men and women, was to cut down trees and saw off their branches, in order to process the tree trunks into railroad crossties and use the branches for heating. This work demanded physical strength, skill, and great caution, but the city people gathered there had no experience whatsoever in this type of labor, and the careless dropping of a tree could cause disaster.

This was exactly what happened to Mala: a tree chopped down by a team that worked beside hers fell on her back and pinned her to the ground. Long, precious minutes passed until her companions-in-fate were able to free her from its weight. Meanwhile, under her shoulder a painful swelling appeared, which was neglected due to the absence of proper medical services at the camp. And yet, despite her pain, Mala was forced to continue daily the forest labor, carrying on her back beams and heavy branches and dropping them in a pile at the side of the road. When the pile grew, the cutting work would stop for a while and everyone was recruited to load the branches onto carts. The repeated movement of lifting the branches and placing them in the cart intensified the pain. The back wound hardened into a rough growth, like a hump. Thus, the lovely young woman turned into a hunchback.

The exhausting labor, the meager and unbalanced diet, the cold, and the lack of sleep depleted the prisoners' strength and exposed them to a wide range of diseases. In time, a typhus epidemic broke out in the area, killing many prisoners. The plague left Mala alive, but claimed her hair and teeth.

The brave decision to conquer pain on a daily basis and the infectious optimism that Mala radiated served as an example to her companions-in-fate, and also signaled to them that they must not allow the "plagues of Siberia" to conquer their spirit. In the long string of "plagues", two were intolerable: the Arctic cold and the marshy Siberian mud, which was covered with snow in autumn but remained swampy underneath, or, alternatively, the snow that turned into mud. There was no way to vanquish the plague of cold, or, in other words, to fight the maliciousness of the climate. The small consolation it brought was that the guards suffered from it no less than the prisoners. As opposed to the cold, the mud and snow had a cure: boots that withstood the damp and cold. But such a treasure was distributed only to the guards.

Mala was exiled from Lvov in late July 1940, wearing light summer sandals. Snow fell in the Omsk region as early as September, and her toes froze from cold and damp during her labor in the forest. "Don't give up!" — she said to herself, and wrapped her feet with rags she found in the area and with a layer of straw. This temporary arrangement solved the problem for one day only; the next day she had to repeat it. But when the snows of autumn and winter began to fall with vengeance, the rags froze on her feet and were covered with a layer of frost that made them stick to the skin, causing severe wounds when she unwrapped them in the evening. All this in addition to the sharp pain in the hump, and the lingering exhaustion from typhus. In pain to the point of despair, Mala, despite her innate optimism, wished that death would come to her rescue.

The pact between the USSR and Nazi Germany enabled the exchange of letters between inhabitants of the USSR (including those exiled to Siberia) and their families in countries under Nazi occupation; thus, Mala was able to correspond with her parents. Usually she was careful not to complain in her letters about her situation, both because of the censorship and so as not to worry her parents. But when her situation worsened and became intolerable, she poured out her heart in a letter, without inhibition, come what may!

Possibly the censor empathized with her feelings and let the letter pass. At any rate, it is a fact that one month later, when at the end of the workday the incoming mail was distributed, a package — unbelievable! — arrived for Mala from Tarnów. The first package since her exile to Siberia! Mala opened it with excitement, and, to her joyous surprise, it did not contain, as surmised, cookies lovingly baked by Mother, but a pair of felt-lined boots, boots almost mythological, known to her since childhood. Mala did not try to restrain her tears, this time tears of pleasure. Could there be a warmer greeting (*warmer* in both senses of the word) than this? It seemed to her that twenty-five years after her father had worn them at the end of the First World War, these boots which she used to polish regularly, had felt from afar her distress and volunteered to help her survive the Second World War and the Siberian exile. She put on one boot, and then the other, in slow motion, as if wanting the soft felt to slowly caress her feet with its warmth, feet that had already forgotten the feeling of warmth and softness.

Mala rechecked the box in which the boots rested. She searched for a letter from her mother, since Mother was the one who had been punctilious about keeping up a regular stream of correspondence. This time, Mother surprised her daughter by refraining from attaching a personal letter of her own. Undoubtedly, she felt that this was Father's fête, and one must not mix one celebration with another. And indeed, in the corner of the box, Mala found a small one-sentence note in Father's flowery handwriting:

"Come home in my boots, strong and healthy."

That night, Mala did not go to bed, so as not to take off the boots. Sitting propped in a chair, swathed in her blanket, she felt the cold of her feet gradually thawing inside the boots, making room for her natural body warmth to rise up to her knees and above, and from there seep into all her limbs. The warmth, whose pleasantness she had not known since her exile to Siberia, transported her in a bubble of half-sleep to an evening crowning the end of the Sabbath in her parents' home in Tarnów, when after the *havdalah* concluding ceremony, the children, including herself, would beg their father to tell the story of the boots once more.

Due to the many weekly repetitions, the children were well acquainted with all points of the tale. The cruel World War. The frontal Russian attack against the Austrian army in Galicia (then part of the Austrian Empire). Their future father forcibly recruited into an Austrian artillery regiment and sent to the front. In a surprise attack, the Austrian regiment, along with its cannons, is taken prisoner by the Russians, and the man who is to become their father is also among the captives. The Austrian prisoners are sent to exile in the forest of Moldavia. There they take shelter in abandoned shacks, and according to the custom of the time, they receive their food from the inhabitants of the nearby town in exchange for various services. Among the town's inhabitants are well-off Jews, tree and fur merchants. Everyone knows the brawny P.O.W. water-carrier, whose muscles burst the worn-out rags on his body. His tattered shoes are wrapped in a layer of straw against the cold. Everyone knows that he is a Jew, since he comes to the synagogue on Sabbath eves, but his humble standing in a corner due to his worn clothing earns him the reputation of an ignorant simpleton.

But that was not the end of the story that the children have heard dozens of times. Now they wait for the icing on the cake. They know the closing part, too, from countless recitations, but they beg to hear it again and again. One day (the story continues), the water-carrier brought, as usual, water to a Jewish home, and saw that a rabbi and his students were sitting around the table over their books of Talmud, struggling to understand the topic. The water-man approached the table, looked at the page, and, in the tune of Galician scholars, he explained the wording, added the Rashi, Tosafot, and other early and late authorities, and, having finished his explanation, went on without another word, buckets in hand, to do his daily work. The rumor spread through all the nearby communities, and they competed with each other to have him for their rabbi. But Reb Aazik (as they called him from then on) wanted only one thing: to return to his wife. His will was honored. He was equipped with clothing, money, a watch, and most importantly, boots for the long route.

In October 1941, something extraordinary happened. When the Germans violated the 1939 pact with the Soviets and invaded the Soviet Union in June 1941, an agreement was reached between the Soviets and the Polish government-in-exile regarding the release of the deported Polish nationals (including Polish Jews) from the gulags. Mala was also liberated, but she did not join the many deportees who went south. Instead, she chose to remain in Omsk province, although not in the camp itself. She decided that, in her condition of health, she must not allow the strain of the journey to erode the last of her strength, and must not be tempted to make the trip to Uzbekistan and Iran, even though at the end of that route shone the sun of Eretz-Israel. She thus planned to settle, a free woman, in the charming town close to the former camp and wait for the breakthrough west.

The news of the opening of the gulags and Mala's liberation reached her brother in the Brigade, but despite his inquiries, he could not ascertain the name of the town where she was living. After that, he heard nothing more of her.

## III

"Each and all are returning home, but you, Mala, my sister, are not among them. Where are you, Mala? Where?"

"The war has ended. Repatriation is now beginning. The roads are full of refugees. A few deportees have returned to Tarnów as well, although only a small number, you could count them on one hand. But there is no sign of life from you. None of the returnees has met you in the wave of those going back west. No one has heard from friends that they saw you traveling, on foot or in a chance conveyance, in the one and only direction both of us can imagine: home. The last *information given to me by our friends in Degania (they received it from deportees who returned from Tashkent about two months ago) is undoubtedly outdated — from almost three years ago: the period when you were released from the camp and were about to settle in the nearby village, but they did not know its name. Even had they known it, I doubt my letter would have arrived there. Whether you are still in that same anonymous town, or whether you have begun to march, like most of the refugees, toward Poland, your address in Vyerkhneye Baraki, which Mother sent to me in early 1941 through the Red Cross, and which I have carried with me for five years, is no longer valid. So where are you, Mala? Where? Give a sign of life! And know that you are not alone."*

This imaginary letter, which Ankori repeatedly wrote and signed each night in his dreams, was never sent, due to the lack of an address. But one night, a thought flashed in his brain, disturbing and yet redeeming, and he wondered how it had not occurred to him until then: just as he had been trying ceaselessly to contact Mala, Mala herself, with her meager means, was probably searching for him, too, but she did not know his address. In fact, she had not known it ever since he enlisted in the British Army, and possibly she did not know that he was a soldier. In short, there were no addresses, nor would there be. The one and only possible meeting point was in Tarnów proper. Eastern Europe was Soviet territory, out of bounds for soldiers of the West. Despite the military alliance, no 'Western' soldier had gone there until now. Until now? "Yes, until just now, and Stalin should know that your brother will reach Tarnów, no matter what and no matter how!"

Once he understood that there was no point in waiting for a miraculous contact with his sister, he resolutely decided to go to Tarnów, and look from there for a strategy to bring his message to her. The deliberations and doubts that preceded the decision were dismissed, and the time came to organize this unprecedented journey to Poland. Objective reasons mandated urgency: with the end of the war began the process of demobilization of the drafted soldiers, since their recruitment had been "for the duration", in other words, as long as the war lasted. It was important, therefore, to hurry and use the advantages granted by a uniform in the postwar chaos. He took his decisions one step further: even if it did not work out and he did not find his sister in the coming year, at the end of which he would probably be discharged from His Majesty's army, then he would remain in Europe and accept the proposal to join the *Beriha* organization, in which he had been partially active even while in uniform, assisting refugees to move clandestinely to Palestine. This is what he would do, until he was lucky enough to find his sister. He would not return to Jerusalem without her!

From now on, the preparations progress methodically, step by step. He receives a month-and-a-half of leave (the maximum allowed by law) from the Unit, with Major Shalit's best wishes for success. He was already well-acquainted with the geography of the countries through which he was to pass; now he learns the network of European railroads and their estimated times of departure, since from now on the train will serve as his main mode of transportation. He decides to leave his kitbag in the Unit, in the hope that he will find it upon his return. He stuffs all his clothes and belongings into the backpack and knapsack, in order to ease his movement. His rifle is returned to the armory. He has money: the pounds sterling that he received in exchange for the accordion. On the way, he would exchange amounts into local currency as needed. (In light of the situation in Europe — he chuckled to himself — he would surely turn a profit.) And last but not least: he gets two official Movement Orders. The first one to move from Paris to Prague (in actuality, Pilsen, west of Prague, was the farthest eastern outpost of the Americans). Up to this point, everything is clear. From here on, God would help. The second official Movement Order was for the return route: Vienna-Paris. Aside from these, he hid in the bottom of his pack spare TTG orders that he himself would complete. Finally, comes the only sad part of the whole procedure. Heavyhearted, he unravels the threads and removes from his battledress the badge of the Star of David on the blue-white-blue background, and the inscription identifying his unit as "The Jewish Brigade". The Jewish survivors in Poland would surely be excited to see this badge on the sleeve of an Eretz-Israeli soldier, but he could not wear it there. On the road and in every public place, he will have to be a model British sergeant. This he was, in fact. Only among Jews could he reveal that he was from Eretz-Israel and belonged to the Jewish Brigade of the British army.

September 1945. A radiant Parisian autumn. Fallen leaves carpet the boulevards with gold. If there had been a war, in Paris it left no trace. Cheerfulness, movement of people, and play of light and shadow gusting through the space of the train station. No wonder an Impressionist artist painted a train station, still a novelty in the nineteenth century, to display a "trainscape" on the canvas. People rush to the ticket office, hurrying to the platform, ambushing the free seats in the cars. Have they read Shalom Aleikhem's assertion (Ankori chuckles to himself) that one does not walk to a train, but run?

He checks the board. The direct line to Prague has not yet been renewed. He buys a combined ticket. He will change trains and cross the three Occupied Zones of West Germany: British, French, and American. In each area, MP's will check the Movement Order. The fourth zone, the eastern one, and the countries beyond it, are a taboo he is about to violate: not in East Germany itself, which is under the strict rule of the Red Army, but in the two countries, Czechoslovakia and Poland, which are still living in the twilight stage, at the end of which they would become full-fledged communist satellites of the Soviet Union.

The train arrives in Prague the next day. Despite the unavoidable changes of trains during the night and the tiredness, the "Benjamin of Tudela" in his heart does not allow him to skip a tour in the city of the well-known rabbinic scholar known by the acronym Maharal and of Kafka. At the same time, he does not miss the opportunity to contact communist students of Prague University. Thrilled by his story, they promise to contact the Party in order to obtain his sister's address from the Soviet population registry. Two days of hope. The young communists are still deluding themselves that they have some sort of influence. End of delusion — disappointment. The soldier-tourist continues his tour. Going up to the Hradčin Palace, seat of the government, he unexpectedly sees the successor of Tomáš Masaryk, Edvard Beneš, who this very year (1945) returned from his Second World War exile and was appointed prime minister; one year later he would again become president. Beneš leaves the building and gets into his car. No guards, no ceremony. People who know what time he leaves his office wait for him in admiration and applaud. Years later, when Ankori recalls those few minutes when he saw Beneš, he blesses his luck, that, unrelated to the goal of his journey, he had the chance to see with his own eyes the resurrection of a last remnant of the Masarykian democracy. A few years later, the communist revolution of 1948 would abolish Beneš's presidency; Masaryk's son, minister of foreign affairs, falls (was pushed to his death?) from his office window. "Defenestration" was even centuries earlier a characteristically Czech method of getting rid of a political adversary.

When evening falls, the train enters a region that, until the end of the First World War, was the duchy of Teschen under the Austro-Hungarian Empire, and at its center the city the Czechs call Tešin, while to the Poles it is Cieszyn. The Olza River crosses the city in its center. With the fall of the Empire and the rise of nationalist states, each one of the two countries, Poland and Czechoslovakia, which gained independence in 1918, demands ownership of the entire city for itself. The Olza seperates Polish Cieszyn in the north from Czech Tešin on the south bank. For the next twenty years the city and the surrounding district continue to be a point of conflict between the two states. When the Allies sacrificed Czechoslovakia's freedom to Hitler in autumn 1938 in exchange for the illusion of peace, partly fascist Poland thought this was the right time to demand the pound of flesh from its neighbor, the bleeding Czech democracy. While the Czech president Beneš leaves for exile in 1938, in Poland patriotic demonstrations intensify in support of Edward Śmigły-Rydz, who succeeded Józef Piłsudski: "*Wodzu, prowadź nas na Czechy!*" ("Our marshal, lead us against Czechoslovakia!") Indeed, on October 2, 1938, the Polish army crosses the river and takes control over the southern half of Cieszyn (as the united city would be called) and of the district in whose mines Poles labored, and whose name from now on was Zaolzie ("Trans-Olza").

Nemesis of history! Only eleven months passed, and on September 1, 1939, the Wehrmacht invades Poland in a pincer movement, with one arm passing through "united" Cieszyn, and begins a second world war. The victory in 1945 returns the situation to its previous state: in the middle of the bridge over the Olza, a white line is again painted, indicating the border between Cieszyn and Tešin, as well as between Poland and Czechoslovakia.

The threatening darkness of the Czech night shrouds the two parts of the city (now once again two separate entities) in an atmosphere of gloomy fear. The moon has not yet risen. No star appears above. Not one light flickers in the windows of the houses or in the streets on either side of the river; only the bridge is lit from all angles and in the center. From a small hill, Ankori looks at the bridge: "Here is my entrance exam. As soon as I succeed in crossing the white line in the middle of the bridge I will be in Poland, the first Eretz-Israeli soldier to tear the curtain of darkness that has descended for the past six years on Poland and its Jews. End of the road? Or a new beginning?"

He stifles his emotion, and fearlessly, with full self-confidence, strides over the bridge. As he walks, he checks the pockets of the battledress uniform. In the left pocket, his Soldier's Service Book, from which it is forbidden to part; in the right pocket the Movement Order. Not the official one, Paris-Prague, which had gotten him this far, but the TTG one, Paris-Prague-Kraków, which he had prepared in his hotel. He had attached a photograph to the Order and marked it with a stamp, having prepared both before his departure. He also stuffs into the pocket a few British pound notes, just in case. In general he is careful not to carry any other papers with his effects, so as to prevent confusion of the documents. Thus, level-headed, cautious, but calm, he mounts the bridge.

The crossing from Tešin to Cieszyn and back is not the main route for entering Poland or Czechoslovakia or for leaving these two countries. Its main patrons are Polish miners, returning home to the Polish city or reappearing for work on the Czech side. The counter of the Czech border clerk, who after some waiting became available for Ankori, is located next to the Polish counter, with only the white line separating them. The clerk carefully reads the Movement Order — refreshing proof that he knows English. He admits that he has already heard of the RASC that is mentioned in the Order, since his brother who immigrated to England also served in the transport corps. But the TTG arouses his curiosity, and Ankori, castigating himself for not preparing an answer in advance, shoots straight from the hip: Territorial Transport Group. Referring to the brother who lives in London, the Czech thrusts an envelope into the "British" palm and asks to send it to his brother's address. Ankori knows from personal experience how important it is for someone to nurture a connection with a brother or sister and takes the mission upon himself, despite the vast difference between this incident with the Czech, who is asking for a favor solely for convenience's sake, and the problem of Mala, whose whereabouts and welfare are unknown.

Having completed the checkout at the Czech desk, Ankori crosses the white line, goes to the Polish clerk's counter, and finally finds himself, literally and metaphorically, in Poland. He presents the Movement Order. The clerk asks something in Polish, and the "Englishman" signals (as he would always do in Poland) that he does not understand. The clerk is satisfied with comparing the photograph on the Movement Order to the facial features of the foreigner. But when the foreigner imagines that the matter is closed and hurries to fold the order and place it inside the pocket of the battledress, the Pole begins, in harsh Polish, to give him an official warning, whose main thrust is a strict prohibition against bringing any letter or message from the Czech to the Polish side; violators would be guilty of treason, for which the punishment in the "People's" Poland was death.

Ankori, pretending he didn't understand the warning, is plainly afraid. Is it possible that the Pole had seen the Czech slipping a letter into the foreigner's palm? Would he, the foreigner, have to pay the debt of the hostility between Czechs and Poles? The letter to England burned in his trouser pocket. But in order not to reveal the secret of his knowledge of Polish, he must pretend as if he is listening, and only signals with his hands and face that he understands nothing. Discouraged, the Pole asks his Czech colleague to translate the warning into English. The man in the British uniform continues standing with an inscrutable expression, listening to the translation, even though he knows quite well what is being said in the original. And it is a good thing that he listened, because to his astonishment, the Czech does not translate the Polish at all, but rather vilifies Poland in English, under cover of translation, and does not relate to the warning at all.

The soldier, who understands every word, is furious deep inside, and wants to fling the letter in the face of the Czech. Should he endanger himself and his entrance into Poland by helping this trickster? But every move on his side would reveal his pretence. Therefore, he waves goodbye to the two border clerks and proceeds right to the end of the bridge. While he walks, he turns his head around: the Pole is speaking on the telephone. With whom? About the letter? The descent from the bridge onto Polish soil takes place in total darkness, especially after the strong light on the bridge. The moon has not yet risen. Perhaps he should memorize the address, destroy the letter, and send a personal letter to the brother, explaining what had happened? But he cannot read the address in the opaque darkness of the night. Consequently, he goes over to the underbrush on the side of the road, tears the envelope into small pieces, and scatters them in the brush. He has barely finished, when "*Stój! Kto idzie?*" (Stop! Who's there?) "English/ England / Britannia," he says, identifying himself fearlessly, although this may be the last sentence he will utter in his life. Three rifles point at his chest, and a flashlight blinds him. "This is a Polish welcome," he chuckles wryly to himself, despite the mortal danger.

"*Papiery!*" (Identification papers!) The Movement Order is unhesitatingly pulled out of the pocket. The militia commander cannot read it, of course, but using the flashlight he checks the photograph and verifies that it corresponds to the Englishman's face. He is satisfied, yet signals to the militia to carry out a search. Luckily he has destroyed the letter. Search. Soldier's Service Book. The money in the pocket? "English," he explains. "*Na stację* (To the station)?" they guess correctly. They point for him: "*Tam*" (It's there), and disappear in the darkness. The soldier goes up "there", and is swallowed into the Polish Cieszyn station.

In a medium-sized hall, which served as a temporary waiting room until Poland would build a station worthy of the name, about one hundred people, all Poles, sat, leaned against the wall, rested their heads on their suitcases, or sprawled on the floor in various positions, waiting for the train that was supposed to leave in the morning. The soldier, still in shock from the rifles pointed at his chest, found a spot next to the wall, and, completely alert, began to study the crowd — for the first time a crowd without Jews. The night shrouded the people in a fitful sleep; some lay down, eyes staring at the ceiling, but without seeing a thing. Fatigue. The soldier tried to comprehend the source of the Polish fatigue spread before him. Was it the ordinary fatigue of night, which would disappear when the train sets out? Or the accumulated fatigue of six years of war, which had ended a mere four months ago? But didn't the end of war call for joy as well? Perhaps the border changes imposed on the state with the armistice left its citizens feeling disoriented? Suddenly, he felt that from the opposite wall, eyes were staring at him, drilling a channel from wall to wall and sending their look through it, toward his eyes. But these eyes were different from those of the Polish crowd. These were Jewish eyes! The eyes of the first Jew Ankori had the occasion to see on the eve of his entrance into post-Holocaust Poland.

The eyes opposite embrace him from afar and murmur: "We understood who you were at once. From Eretz-Israel, a member of the Eretz-Israel Labor Party, a pioneer, a kibbutznik, a Jewish soldier. He-whose-eyes-we-are also belongs to your camp. We have decided to get to the Land of Israel by way of *Ha'apalah* (immigration the British considered illegal) and once in Eretz-Israel, we'll look like your eyes. This hope is the only thing that saved us from the inferno." And the owner of the communicating eyes complements their sparkle with wordless body language: "Allow me to approach you, friend, to shake your hand. In you I meet Eretz-Israel for the first time."

The eyes of the man from Eretz-Israel, the member of the movement, the pioneer, the kibbutznik, the Brigade soldier, reply: "We also recognized at once that you are a Jew, and we embrace you. But so as not to reveal our true identity to the gentiles, we'll postpone any contact until our meeting in the Land of Israel. Until then, go in peace! Gird yourself with courage!"

Sixty years have passed since then, and the meeting that the eyes planned, without name or address, has still not taken place. "Friend, I remember our meeting/non-meeting at Cieszyn station, in September 1945, on my first night in post-war Poland, and the secret dialogue of our eyes. I remember this as one of the most precious moments of my life. If you come across this book, you will recognize yourself in it. You know my name from the title page of the book, but I do not know yours. Please contact me, and we will meet."

## IV

With a pounding heart, the soldier ascended the next morning the three steps of the train car that will take him from Cieszyn to Kraków, and from there on a different train, to the meeting with the city of his birth. A traumatic meeting it would be, after eight years of absence, and after he had decided that not only was he permitted to break the vow he had taken when making *aliya* to Eretz-Israel — that he would never, ever return to the Diaspora — but rather, in the horrifying circumstances of the bloody Holocaust, which no one could imagine then, he must return. Yes, he must take leave of destroyed Jewish Tarnów, embrace the stones of the neighborhood that no longer existed, and cry at his parents' grave which also did not exist. Only a mass grave without marker or name made the ground of the local cemetery tremble. He already dedicated several pages to this meeting in his previous book. He wrote those pages with bleeding heart and weeping eyes, and the tears come back to haunt him and demand that he relive now that experience and etch it deeply into his memory and into this book as well.

This was not the soldier's first glimpse of the sights of the Holocaust or of the survivors. For, concomitant with his military role, he had spent most of the years of his service in the British army doing volunteer work among refugees and camp prisoners. But even though this welfare and rescue work demanded immeasurable stores of emotional strength, devotion, understanding and courage, it could not prepare him for his final personal confrontation, a confrontation that he — as son, brother and friend — simultaneously longed for and dreaded: the confrontation with himself in the face of the Holocaust of his city and the destruction of his parents' home.

Countless times, in an anxious procession of images, the young man tried to envision what he would see, how he would feel, how he would rage, cry, wail, upon his return to his place of birth, which had meanwhile become a valley of death — but, when he did come, in autumn 1945, none of this happened. Mechanically, like a numb robot, he looked around him unseeingly; and in the noon hours of an autumn day he found himself, an alienated stranger, sitting on the train from Kraków to Tarnów, a leaden soldier in the uniform of a British sergeant. And, mechanically, numbly, unseeing, the robot alighted from the train, a programmed mechanism, hidden somewhere inside him, moving his limbs as he began to stalk the streets that had been — was it a million years ago? — a living part of his childhood.

The robot had been well-programmed. From the moment he left the square in front of the Tarnów train station, he transmitted messages from his memory disk, which he himself obeyed with predictable responses:

* Advance in a straight line from the railroad station. Turn right onto Krakowska Street and walk up the street to the end…

/continue/

* On the right — the lit-up ads on the wall of Duke Sanguszko's beer factory…

/continue/

* On the left — the twin red spires of the Missionaries Church…

/continue/

* On the right — The small *bis-medrish* where Father Aazik taught Hesiek Talmud in the mornings…

/continue/

* On the floor above — Auber, the second of Hesiek's three violin teachers…

/continue/

* On the left — Mash Bakery. M-m-m… Hot buns for Father and son on their way to the early morning Talmud lesson. Next to it, the Baum building. The residents are Father's students; they all made *aliya* to Haifa…

/continue/

* On the right — Mroczkowski, the photographer. Childhood photos. The classroom tableau in the photographer's window in May 1937, before matriculation exams. The flat of Beirysz Bursztyn, classmate and fellow youth movement member, and his brother, Mekhek. Their older brother, Romek, one of the first Gordonia members to immigrate from Tarnów to Eretz-Israel to repair the ruins of Hulda after the riots of 1929…

/continue/

* On the right — the residence of Dr. Feig, physician of the Hebrew school and Shulah Laviel's father. The toy store where the kind

doctor bought Hesiek a ball of many colors. Home of the teacher Weinberg. The Weg sisters. The whole town rushed to see the banister, bent by Mother Weg's fall…

/continue/

* The studio of photographer Hutter, the socialist, liked even by his opponents…

/continue/

* The Silberpfenig home: the apartment of the Hebrew high school's first principal and of his sister, the teacher, Henda. The home of Janek Borgenicht and Idek Biberberg, Hesiek's friends…

/continue to junction/

* On the right — the *Urszulanki* girls: the St. Ursula Convent high school, focus of wet dreams and boasts of conquests by adolescent boys…

/continue/

* On the left — turn to the Apollo Cinema. On the next street: the Marzenie Cinema, which doubled as a concert and lecture hall. Oh, the first silent movies! Oh, the concerts Hesiek heard there with his mother! Oh, Dr. Schützer's lectures!

/continue/

* On the right — *Gelati Italiani*. M-m-m, Italian ice cream. Café Secesja…

/continue/

* On the left — the Skolimowski Café. On the square, the salute stand for May 3 and November 11 parades. Eternal participant: an old man in blue uniform recognized as the Tarnów last survivor of Poland's January Revolt of 1863. "1863" on his cap. Site of the disastrous end of "International Brigade" streetplay.

/continue/

* On the right — the *Starostwo* (District Ministries). First passports, issued to Hesiek and Mala in anticipation of *aliya*!

/continue and stop at the junction: two streets go down to the right/

* The nearest street: 3 Santa Anna Street — the Safah Berurah Hebrew school. The Dr. Spann lending library. Eva Leibel, the beautiful librarian. Mietek, the *shaygitz* (gentile boy), the terror of the whole street, stoning Safah Berurah pupils…

/continue/

* The Temple, where Weinberg officiates as cantor — a prayer house avoided by Orthodox Jews, who wouldn't even walk near it…

/continue/

* The other street: Targowa Street — to the Burek Market and to *tashlikh*, i.e., throwing all the year's accumulated sins into the Wątok. Haber's Tavern. How happy the town was when his Communist son escaped from prison!

/continue/

* Across the junction — the shot rabbit, hanging at the entrance of Paluch's *goyish* shop…

/continue/

* Kazimir Square. The Mickiewicz monument. Adler's pharmacy with the angel. May First. The red of flags. Ciołkosz, the socialist leader, addressing the crowd in both Polish and Yiddish. Hesiek plays hooky to attend the rally. Detectives mix with the demonstrators. Fear… Like a true revolutionary, Hesiek raises a fist in socialist salute and sings the "International". Fear… In a moment a detective will come to arrest him. Fear… What's this? The detective doesn't care? Despair!…

/continue/

* From there to the Rynek, the Central Square. The cathedral and the Town Hall. The grocery owned by Hannah, whose grandson, Buziek, is in Hesiek's class and youth movement group. The Baron and Spitz homes — three generations of connection to

Father. The Wald store, where Witos, leader of the Peasant Party, buys leather for his boots...

/continue/

* To Żydowska Street. The "Old Synagogue". Dudek Schiff, Hesiek's classmate, but not in the same youth movement; Father teaches him Talmud, and his brother and Hesiek both take part. After the lesson, a violin-piano duet by Hesiek and their sister, Gusta: "the Caucasian Suite"...

/continue — turn left from Krakowska onto Wałowa Street/

* On the right — the Hebrew bookstore of Tony Kanner and Abraham Weinberg...

/continue/

* The stationery store owned by the parents of Hesiek Schmidt, Father's pupil, and of Zyga, the younger brother, who is Hesiek's classmate...

/continue/

* Books and sheet music, at Adolph Seiden's, impresario for the city's cultural performances. Tickets to concerts and plays. Portraits of famous composers in the shop window...

/continue/

* The bookstore of Fenichel, the Zionist sports functionary. Used textbooks and banned "help" books for Latin. Fenichel's bald spot is bigger than Father's...

/continue/

* The Berglas stationery. Above the shop, the home of Siańka, Mala's friend...

/continue/

* Pani Gelbowa, the embroideress. Proud of her son, a professor at an American university...

/continue/

* Maschler's home. Luśka Maschler. Luśka. Lusiu. Lu...

/continue/

* On the left — the Savings Bank and a concert hall above it. Annual recitals by Professor Bau's pupils. First violinists: Hesiek Wróbel and Artek Schanzer. At the piano, Bau's red-headed daughter. Bold Schanzer makes eyes at her...

/continue/

* The street going down to the First High School and the Seminary for novices of the Catholic priesthood (mocked as *biskupyaks*). Disgusting acne on their faces...

/continue/

* To the Eternal Flame for the Unknown Soldier. To Piłsudski Street and the municipal park...

/continue on Wałowa Street/

* On the left — Legionnaires Street. To the Sokół theater and sports auditorium. The home of widow Regina Fluhr, whose son, Nolek, is tutored by Hesiek. The flat of Dr. Schützer, director of the Jewish hospital and an outstanding orator. The residence of old Mordkhe Duvid Brandstetter, one of the latter fathers of Hebrew Enlightenment literature in Galicia...

* On the right — *City*, Weiss' Hotel and Restaurant. Lauber Senior, father of Millek, Hesick's friend, works as a waiter there...

* On the left — the home of Dr. Spann, the city's elder Zionist. His children all have Hebrew names: Yehudit, Naomi and Zvi. Dr. Goldberg's flat. Reśka Goldberg. Resiu...

/continue/

* The Metzger confectionary and its cream cakes, competing with Krumholz's cakes across the street...

/continue/

* Police station and city fire station...

/continue/

* On the left — turn off to Brodziński Street. To Niuśka Feld. Oh,

Niuśka... To Koenig, the old teacher, and to his daughter, Róża, Hesiek's First Grade teacher...

/continue/

* To Ciechanowski, classmate and youth movement peer. How everyone envied him when he made *aliya* to Ben Shemen! To the Sobelsohns, Karol Radek's family. To Monek Leibel and the Second High School, which he attended. His father, a doctor, with a large bald spot...

/continue/

* At the corner of Wałowa and Brodziński — Wilhelm Spiro's paper store. His son, Szajek — one of the founders of Gordonia and among Father's students — a violinist. Szajek's younger brother — a pianist...

/continue, and stop at the corner/

* At the corner — up three steps, Izraelowicz's candy shop, Eder's cosmetics store. The *Eskontowy Bank* of the wealthy Aberdam family. Widow Jortner's *trafika* (kiosk). Stamps and post cards. The mail box...

/continue/

* To the right of the junction — *Rybna* (Fish Street), leading to *Fischplatz* (Fish Square), the "Old Synagogue" and the large *bismedrish*...

/continue/

* The glassware shop owned by the parents of Dora Wakspress, Mala's friend. Blatt, the baker. His daughter, Dora, made *aliya* to Kibbutz Deganya, along with Idek Sprung and Mendl Wax, Gordonia counselors. How proud everyone was that they were to be part of the collective in which the great A.D. Gordon was active...

/continue/

* Across the junction — Wałowa Street continues to Pilzno Gate. Wachtel's restaurant. From there, to the left, to the end

of Lwowska Street. To Grabówka. Oh, the strolls with Father in proletarian Grabówka. The sound of hundreds of Singer sewing machines...

/continue/

* To the left of the junction — Goldhammera Street: Dr. Saltz, father of *Ahavat Zion* and *Mahanayim*, and one of Herzl's deputies at the First Zionist Congress...

/continue/

* The Soldinger Hotel. To Rutka Keller and Nasiek and Henek, her brothers, Father's students...

/continue/

* Also on Goldhammera: to Wolf Getzler, head of *Mizrahi*, whose sons study with Father. To the "Planty". First violin lessons with Rausch. Opposite, Professor Bau's Music School. The HaShomer HaTza'ir center. The barracks, and a little way from there, Roh'ka Baiczer's squalid apartment...

/continue/

* Turn right — to the Sanz *Kloyz*. The "Great Synagogue". The *mikveh* (ritual bath)...

/continue/

* Now turn left to Bóżnic Street. Number 9 Bóżnic — no, the number's been changed to 5...

/Come on, turn left already, LEFT, to No. 5 — HOME!/

It was already late in the evening — the first evening of the Jewish soldier in the city in which his cradle stood years ago — when the gathering organized in his honor by the committee of survivors, the saddest gathering at which he had ever spoken, came to an end. Twenty-five thousand Jews lived in Tarnów before the war. One room was enough that evening to assemble all those who survived and returned — some fifty people — and most of these, too, were from the vicinity, rather than from Tarnów proper. Rumor spread through the town and everyone gathered to see and hear the soldier, son of Tarnów, come from the free world, from Eretz-Israel.

Until the middle of the night the guest interrogated each one of those present regarding Mala, yet to his distress and that of everyone else, his efforts were in vain. But the gathering not only expressed sadness, but also brotherhood, the fellowship of a people that despite orphanhood and grief was celebrating its continued existence and belief in the future. Such fraternity — although in an atmosphere opposite to the one of that night — he had felt only in the company of his fellows-in-arms at el-Alamein and when besieged Tobruq was liberated and the order was given to move to the Libyan desert. And such fellowship he was to experience two years after the evening in Tarnów, on the night when all Eretz-Israelis would dance in the streets, drunk with joy, locking arms and hearts, upon hearing the news of November 29, 1947, when the UN would vote for the establishment of a sovereign Jewish state.

The next morning in Tarnów, the joy was relocated to the train station, as the escorts maintained eye contact from a distance, so as not to betray the Eretz-Israel origin of the "Englishman". From the window of the train car, the eyes of the soldier kissed his brothers': "See you in Eretz-Israel!" "See you in Eretz-Israel!" roared fifty throats when the platform inspector raised his green flag. The engine whistled and the wheels of the train began to move toward Kraków.

# V

To his amazement, the view from the train car on the journey from Tarnów to Kraków and back awakens in him no emotion. Instead of looking at the view, as he used to in his youth on trips to Kraków with his mother, he closes his eyes, sitting in the corner of the train car, and plans his stay in Kraków. Surely he would stay there longer than he had stayed in Tarnów. Despite the gestures of friendship toward him in Tarnów by the handful of friends from back then, and from people he had just met after the gathering, the atmosphere in Tarnów was grim to the extent of stifling. Even his outing to Mt. Marcin, sown with a host of memories from his childhood, was not able to restore his love for the mountain, or for the image of the city of Tarnów as viewed from its peak. When it became clear to him that he had exhausted every source of information, he decided to breathe different air in the charming historic capital that he loved. He also hoped that there he would meet returnees from exile in Siberia who might shed additional light on the mystery of Mala. Moreover, he had the feeling — just a feeling — that new experiences were awaiting him in Kraków, experiences unique in their newness, although he had no idea what experiences he could expect.

The feeling came true. Just half an hour after he left the station in Kraków and went to the address given to him by a corporal from the Brigade in order to pass along greetings to his sister, Ankori had an experience that was difficult but also encouraging, and in any event, unexpected. The corporal had not prepared him for the visit, he himself not knowing much, except for the fact that his sister had returned home from Auschwitz. The address was correct and the house was undamaged on the exterior (Kraków was an unwalled city), and, wonder of wonders, untouched inside by thieves. But it was empty. Empty, for apparently they had all died in Auschwitz, and only the daughter had survived. Had she survived due to her labor in the German war factory next to Auschwitz? Or had she been saved by a miracle?

In those days, visits to the camp were not permitted, and although it was infamous as a death factory, the survivors did not tell and people did not ask. The corporal's sister was the first survivor of Auschwitz that Ankori met during his stay in Poland. The encouraging part of the experience was the sister's external rehabilitation in the four months since the Red Army's conquest of Auschwitz. The guest, who had not seen her condition prior to her liberation from the camp, could only imagine the change in her: her back had straightened after the daily forced labor that had apparently demanded long hours of bending; her black hair had recovered its luster; her refined makeup complimented her face; and her clear voice was losing its hoarseness. Still, to Ankori's astonishment, the story of her brother and the Brigade's operations, which he had hoped would excite her, produced only a hint of a smile in her eyes, a thin smile, disconnected from mind and spirit. The difficult aspect that weighed on the onlooker was her meager speech. In addition, she told nothing of her whereabouts in those dark days, but remained closed inside herself and refused to open up to any other topic — even her brother. But there was one thing the woman did not withhold from her guest: her singing. In fact, she recounted everything in song. And she sang and sang without end; in other words, she narrated and narrated incessantly. Listening to her song made the listener shiver, and became a coercive, binding experience. These were Polish songs that the prisoners had written by and for themselves, telling of their pain, and mainly of their fears. Particularly shocking was a song about fear of the crematoria at nearby Birkenau, whose smoke was visible in the camp from half a mile away. Each stanza ended with the cry, "*To Birkenau!*" (This is Birkenau), as if at that very moment she was seeing the flames creeping toward her body and the smoke filling the room.

Leaving his hotel the next morning, Ankori began an exhausting tour of the refugee aid centers and interrogated those who had returned from Siberia. The questioning was useless. In the evening, he returned to the home of "the silent singer" (so he called her to himself), in order to escort her, at her request, to a dance hall.

"Yes, ballroom dancing" — she replied to his surprise, which had a touch of disgust.

"Do you mean those bourgeois brush-ups that I preached against as a socialist youth-group counselor, encouraging only folk-dancing? And the 'People's' regime agrees with this deviation?"

"On the contrary! It's the most popular entertainment the regime sponsors." Later, Ankori would discover this phenomenon in his journeys through the communist countries: in the evenings, restaurants would become dance halls.

"But I have no experience with this kind of dancing" — the guest tried truthfully to evade it.

"Neither do I. That's why there's a balcony, we'll just sit and enjoy watching others perform."

"That's the most absurd thing I've ever heard!" — he replied impatiently, and immediately apologized.

In answer, he received a discourse that was the longest he had heard until then from the reticent woman:

"After everything I went through, and especially after the terrible feeling of isolation that gnawed at me despite the thousands of people who surrounded me in the camp, I find peace and quiet not when I sing of Birkenau, but when an anonymous singer pours out her longings for love. I repeat: after all that I went through, I derive pleasure and happiness from watching people enjoy each other, she with he and he with she, and in their embrace, I feel like I am the one who is once again embracing the world, embracing a humanity that has recovered its humaneness, embracing the memory of the life I lost and that will never return. I'll enjoy sitting in the spectators' balcony, a few steps above the dance floor, and I'll watch the couples without jealousy, without envy. In this way, as I watch them, happiness is rekindled within me."

They entered the hall, and five steps led them up to the comfortable seats in the spectators' balcony, as the orchestra ceaselessly belted out tango after tango, waltz after waltz, over and over again. On the dance floor below, dozens of couples danced to the beat, as if instinct was commanding them to add, along with the orchestra, tangos and waltzes of one kind or another. Ankori was astonished at the woman sitting beside him as if hypnotized: "I'm sure that she'll quickly go back to living a normal life. And just as she vanquished that earthly Auschwitz, she will vanquish the Auschwitz that is entrenched in her memory and doesn't let go."

Then one of those unexpected things happened, the kind that overtake you at an unexpected moment and in an unexpected place, leaving you wondering whether you fell asleep for a moment and are still dreaming, or whether this is reality. From off the dance floor jumped a young officer, undoubtedly the dream prince of more than a few of the high school girls in the city: groomed as Polish officers loved to groom themselves (each officer had his own soldier-groom); back straight as a ruler, thanks to the girdle under his uniform: on his head a four-cornered hat, the metal that framed its visor gleaming as if made of gold; and the stiff brown leather, which enveloped the calf of each leg separately from the boot, shining as if cast of copper, and seemingly cocked to jump on a horse or to turn the head of a young woman in a stormy dance.

The officer skipped up the five stairs of the balcony in two jumps, and to the astonished eyes of all present, wrapped his arms around the British sergeant, and as he did so, whispered in his ear, "Hesiek, I'm Henek Keller"; and Ankori returned the whisper, "I'm in the Jewish Brigade in the West, but here I'm a British sergeant who doesn't know Polish. I'm afraid a long conversation in public would betray me." "I'm glad to see you." "Me, too. A real miracle. My greetings to everyone."

When Henek returned to the dance floor, Ankori urged his neighbor to get up and leave. Realizing that there was some basis to his request, she got up at once. On the way, their roles were reversed: she did not ask, and he did not tell. Only at the gate, when they were about to part, did he attempt to share with her the excitement he had enjoyed that evening. She listened, but as with the story of her brother, did not display particular interest. He was not hurt by her indifference, since he was aware of her condition. After all, the unexpected experience belonged entirely to him and to Henek. He was leaving Kraków the next day — he told her — and thanked her for everything. She invited him to come in for a cup of tea. "I really enjoyed this evening, and I thank you for taking me to that hall. I did not think it would be so lovely." That was the second time he saw a smile on her face.

He took advantage of the moment of grace to explain the evening's event. "That officer is a Jew from Tarnów. He studied at the

Hebrew high school and with my father. I don't know what his connection is with the Polish army. At any rate, the meeting was very exciting." "I could see that" — the reticent woman surprised him. "So you're leaving tomorrow. (Again she surprised him.) Have a good trip." As he left the street, it seemed to him that he heard her singing.

## VI

"Zvi, is that you?"

A battered car stopped next to the sidewalk, while the soldier, deciding there was no more reason to stay in the city, walked to the train station with his army pack on his back and the belt of his knapsack crossing from left shoulder down to right hip. Kraków, although it had not supplemented the information about his sister as he had hoped, had been generous in experiences he would never forget. In contrast to the period he had spent in Tarnów, where the sight of the city had weighed on him painfully, Kraków, as beautiful as ever, took its leave with a smile.

He peeked into the open window of the car: "Ah!" The passenger hushed him immediately. "Call me 'Shimek'. That's my name in the *Beriha*. Get inside and ride with us." The soldier got in without asking where they were going. He trusted Isser Ben-Zvi, whom he had befriended seven years earlier when the latter was sent from his kibbutz to join Ankori in conducting the activities of the Gordonia group in Jerusalem, after Yossi Sukenik moved to Tel Aviv to the Cameri Theater that was being established in those days. According to the confidentiality procedure of an organization like the *Beriha*, the four passengers and the driver did not introduce themselves by name. Years later, when a photograph of Israel Barzilai appeared in the newspapers after he was appointed minister of health in the Israeli government, Ankori recognized his black hairstyle as belonging to one of the men who had then been sitting in the car.

The Kraków airport was almost empty. The travelers — the four, Shimek, and the soldier — were taken to a small single-engine airplane, apparently purchased by the organization from remainders of the first fighter planes now considered junk. It had no seats, only benches attached to each side. For balance, they sat three on each side, across from each other, and took their lives in their hands. Perhaps someone mumbled the Wayfarer's Prayer; anyway God was not listening, as He was busy holding the piece of junk up in the air. Even without the prayer, a miracle took place: the plane landed in Warsaw, modest and conscious of its wretchedness alongside the kings of the airfield, the Russian Aeroflots. Only then did a "late spark" lit up in Ankori's brain: "This is the first time I've ever flown" — his face green with nausea. He recalled one Sabbath in Tarnów when he was still a youth: an airplane like that one had fallen on Lwowska Street. The whole city had rushed to view the wonder — even the ultra-Orthodox, who had come out of the *kloyz*, prayer shawls over their shoulders and Sabbath *shtreimels* on their heads.

A taxi brought them to the Polonia Hotel — the only hotel (as the soldier was told) left standing, while everything around it had been destroyed when the Germans suppressed the rebellion of the AK, the Polish Home Army, in 1944. "I arranged a room for you" — said Shimek — "Now come and let's chat over a cup of coffee. I have half an hour until my next item of business, for which we came to Warsaw. By the way, I heard about your deeds in Italy, and lately on the Dutch-German border, and I thought it would be very useful if you would choose to join us when you are released from service, and especially since you were already in touch with us when you were still a soldier. A few discharged soldiers of the Brigade have already entered the organization. There's plenty of work, and it will only increase as the stream of freed camp prisoners grows. Think about it, Zvi, seriously."

After the story of Mala was told to Shimek in detail, he was not surprised that joining the *Beriha* had indeed occurred to his Jerusalemite friend several times — most recently, just a few days ago — after finding no new information in Tarnów or Kraków. Shimek promised to raise the subject in his meetings with the refugees. Therefore, they agreed that if the brother did not succeed in finding his sister while still in uniform, he would remain in Europe even after removing his uniform and join the *Beriha* operation, in the hope that while fulfilling his role, he would come across conclusive information about Mala.

"I suppose you'll go to see the destroyed ghetto," said Shimek when they rose to part.

"Of course. The Jewish cemetery, too. As a student of history, I want to honor the memory of Meir Balaban, whose books I studied in high school. I know he died back in 1942, before the destruction of the ghetto, and had the honor of being buried in the Warsaw cemetery."

"Still, you should remember" — Shimek continued to instruct Ankori — "that the main Jewish institutions — like the Jewish Historical Institute, which you will certainly want to visit — have temporarily moved to Łódź (Lodz in Yiddish), which was not severely damaged like Warsaw."

"I did intend to travel to Łódź tomorrow. When I was still in Kraków, I was invited to speak about the Brigade at the PSP (Partisans-Soldiers-Pioneers Center) in Łódź."

"Too bad I won't be able to hear your summary because of my duties" — and they parted with an embrace.

Since then, the Jerusalemite friend encountered Shimek's activities many times, but did not have the opportunity to meet him again.

More than by the overwhelming sight of the destruction of the ghetto, Ankori felt oppressed by the silence that breathed from the enormous area — a real breath, like the breath of a dying man — haunted, choked, struggling with its remaining strength for a portion of air. No one could be seen for half a mile away, maybe more, so much so that it seemed to the Eretz-Israeli youth that he was the only person who had survived in this world of devastation. He sat down on the corner of a smashed house and was glad to feel in the flesh of his thighs the spiky projections, broken bricks, and glass shards that protruded from the corner. He wanted to run from one corner of the wreckage to another, to sit on all of them and intensify the pain. It seemed to him that through the physical pain, he was experiencing what had happened here. For what was destruction of houses if not testimony to the true ravage, the ravage of human beings, in their thousands and tens of thousands. And what was ravage of human beings if not testimony to the ruin of an entire civilization. The devastation had choked the Jewish creativity of past generations, and all the more so would it stifle the creativity that might begin here in the future, but no — it could never rise again. Never.

Evening came and the mourner managed to sit on the corners of only ten or so destroyed houses, and there was no chance that he would reach all of them. He would not visit the historic cemetery of Warsaw, as he had planned. There was no cemetery like the cemetery in which he stood at that moment, and there were no tombstones like the mounds of wreckage that surrounded him here. Yes, he will remain here. Here he will sob together with the sobbing silence, scream along with the screaming silence. And be silent, silent, silent with the silent hush.

On his way back to the hotel, he passed the only synagogue that escaped destruction in Warsaw, called the Nożyk Synagogue. About ten worshippers were there at that hour, the time for the evening service. Inside, he was told that even a few communists made a point to come there regularly in order to make up a prayer quorum of ten, all murmuring what they had murmured before the destruction, what they had murmured at the time of the destruction, and what they would murmur the next day and in the days to come as well. Some would say: this is proof of the strength of the people, the strength of the heritage.

"Why don't you throw the 'heritage' into the garbage can of history and invent new prayers, rebellious ones, shouting, hurling accusations on high, unforgiving, unreconciled?" — Ankori said to himself. But he did not have the courage to speak his thoughts out loud.

## VII

He reached Łódź on the morning of the next day, as planned. Dr. Phillip Friedmann, a historian who had published important research on the history of Galician Jewry and the Jews of Łódź, welcomed him with open arms. He had heard of Ankori from the teachers at Hebrew University and was pleased to present to him his plans regarding the direction of the work of the Jewish Historical Institute that had just opened in Łódź. At that time, Friedmann was working there alone. Most of the pre-war Jewish historians of Eastern Europe had been killed in the Holocaust or had died; some had made *aliya* and some had immigrated to America. Thus the Łódź Institute was now empty of researchers and of research material. But its director believed that it had a future. Although Friedmann's own research went back only until the 1860s, it was clear to him that he and the Institute would focus on Holocaust research. For this purpose he would try to gather public and private materials as a basis for research worthy of the name. When Jewish life in Warsaw revived, the Institute would move there, and especially since the beautiful old building of the Jewish Studies Institute had not been damaged in the war. The conversation on historical research served the former student as a refreshing intermezzo between searching for private information about his sister and military activity. At that time, Friedmann could not predict, nor could Ankori guess, that eleven years later, the student from Jerusalem, who received a fellowship for doctoral studies at Columbia University in New York, would defend his dissertation there. And, wonder of wonders: the examining committee of judges would include Professor Friedmann, who would emigrate from Łódź to the United States.

In the afternoon, members of the Partisans-Soldiers-Pioneers

(PSP) group gathered to hear the Eretz-Israeli sergeant survey the aims, activities, and accomplishments of the Jewish Brigade. This was the first meeting of its kind: of Eastern European fighters, whether partisans or regular soldiers of the Red or the Polish People's Army, with a Jewish brother-volunteer from Eretz-Israel who talked about what those present had never heard of before — Hebrew-speaking units in the British army, under their blue and white flag. Everyone was proud of military achievements, but only the Eretz-Israel soldier could talk about another aspect: educational and welfare activities among refugees during the war. Still, it was for good reason that the partisans and Jewish soldiers of Eastern Europe had added the name "Pioneers", *halutzim*, to the title of their organization. Despite their suffering, they saw themselves as potential *halutzim*, potential *ma'apilim* (immigrants to Eretz-Israel considered illegal by the British), and potential kibbutzniks, and they were expecting the chance to use their military experience in order to protect Eretz-Israel, their country. The meeting concluded with "See you in Eretz-Israel", and with a feeling of Jewish brotherhood.

Many of the participants remained after the meeting for group singing (of partisan songs in Yiddish and Red Army songs in Russian), and in order to have a personal conversation with a brother-in-arms from Eretz-Israel. On his part, the soldier took advantage of the opportunity, and when those who introduced themselves as survivors of Siberia appeared, he asked them whether they had known a woman refugee from Tarnów residing in the Omsk district. Since her release from the gulag (he recounted), he did not know where she was. Even though the war had ended and the refugees had begun to return to their homes, there had been no sign of life from his sister. The friends shared in his distress, but unfortunately, not one among them had been sentenced to forced labor in the Omsk forest.

From then on, the tables were turned. When Ankori finished interrogating them, they interrogated him: "You asked if in Siberia we had met a woman-refugee from Tarnów, your sister. That means you must also be from Tarnów."

"Yes, but I left eight years ago, two years before the war, when I was seventeen."

"At any rate, you knew Tarnovians and you remember them today."

"Of course, particularly those who were about my age, high school students."

"So surely you must know Roman Malinowski well. He looks around your age."

"Malinowski? There wasn't anyone of that name in our community. That's not a Jewish name."

"It was changed to a Polish name. Many people did that in order to save themselves."

"Who is this man, and why are you interested in him? Does he live in Łódź now?"

"Unfortunately, he not only lives here, he rules the city. He is an important member of the Party, and forgets that we are Holocaust survivors or war veterans, and that he must be considerate and ease the burden after what we went through. Instead, he carries out his ideological experiments on our flesh."

"I'm curious to know who is the man you are talking about, and whether I really know him. What was his original name?"

Embarrassment prevailed; they did not know. When the man was sent to Łódź, he was already known by his Polish name.

"You said he was around my age, that means we went to high school at the same time. There was a boy in our high school who was a known communist. What color is Malinowski's hair?"

"He's a redhead."

"If so, we've solved the riddle. He must be Motek Leibel from Tarnów."

"You say his name is now Malinowski? Surely he was saved from the Nazis on Aryan papers. That trick saved thousands of Jews, and there's nothing wrong with it as long as it doesn't hurt others. Why is he sticking to his borrowed name now? That's between him and his conscience. Shame on him."

"They say that he saved his entire family and his wife's."

"Wonderful. I wish that had happened to me. I have only the sister, for whom I am searching."

"Tell us more about him."

"He was one class above me, in the same one as my sister. He's about two years older than I am, maybe three. In those days, the age and class difference seemed significant. So there wasn't any real basis for friendship between us. But we knew each other, and I'm sure he remembers me as well. I think he was a very good student. After the matriculation exams, I heard he went to study at the Polytechnic in Lwów. But I don't know any details about that, since in the meantime I made *aliya* to Eretz-Israel.

"I'm still wondering why we're talking about him so much and why you want to know about this man's past. I'm listening to your problems, but it seems that you are interested in something beyond my listening. Enlighten me if I can be of any help."

"Possibly, your acquaintance with Malinowski might convince him to be more considerate with regard to us and moderate his harassments. If you would be willing to speak with him — here is his address, he's at home right now."

In those days, most private houses did not have telephones; for sure, there was one in the Malinowski home, but the number was confidential. Thus you could not inform someone that you wanted to visit him unless you had discussed it in advance. If not, it was acceptable to simply knock on the door, at a reasonable hour of course, and wait for it to be opened. "Funny (Ankori chuckled to himself, riding in a fiacre to the indicated address), instead of preparing for my mission, I'm as tense as a blushing youth of those days: will the lovely Lutka open the door? Did they get married, after going together throughout high school?" He knocked on the door. "Lutka! Lovely as always!" "Hesio! What a surprise! And in uniform as well! Come in, please!"

After several minutes of polite conversation, the kind of conversation one can have anywhere and anytime and with anyone, Lutka understood, on her own, that there was no point in continuing fond remembrances of Safah Berurah that was and is no longer, and that they should not delay the real conversation for which the unexpected guest had surely come to her home. The guest did not ask, and it was Lutka herself who commented, "Motek is ill — apparently a little cold — and he's lying down in the next room. But I'm sure he'll receive you willingly, despite his illness." When Ankori entered the room, he had the feeling that Motek was not surprised at his appearance, whether because the voices from the conversation with Lutka had reached him, or because Fela, Lutka's younger sister who had not sat down with the two at the table, went in to him and told him about the arrival of the friend from high school.

# VIII

It immediately became clear, after non-committal introductory sentences, that Motek was being careful not to get into a conversation about what was happening in Łódź or his role in Łódź industry. Apparently, he had guessed with whom the messenger had spoken and in whose name he would be speaking here. Thus Motek was satisfied with a general declaration that a new socialist society was being built here, and that everyone had to work on its behalf. Naturally, its economy was directed by Marxist doctrine, and "it was unwise to disparage the doctrine that the regime supported." The threat was clear. The mission on behalf of the Jews of Łódź was nipped in the bud.

An enthusiastic debater, this time as well, Motek was eager to polemicize on lofty universal issues. He seemed to listen attentively to the story his guest told him of the Jewish Yishuv in Eretz-Israel volunteering for the British army, and of the establishment of the Jewish Brigade with the blue and white flag. "The sergeant sitting before you is one of thirty thousand volunteers who went with Montgomery from the battle of el-Alamein to Germany. Let's hope that after the slaughter of millions of our brothers, and considering our part in the victory, the free world will be good to us in solving 'the Jewish problem.'" He intentionally used the Polish expression *kwestia żydowska*, which in the years before the war had been a bone of contention between Zionists and anti-Zionists, such as the Bund and communists of Motek's ilk.

"You expect the world to solve the *kwestia żydowska*? Ha, ha. What's left to solve? 'The Jewish problem' has already been solved. It no longer exists!"

Motek knew how shocking his words were, and that a provocative statement such as this could not pass without an angry retort from a nationalist Jew, especially an Eretz-Israeli soldier. "You said, 'The Jewish problem has already been solved'?" Ankori's blood reached the boiling point. "Who do you think solved it, and how? Hitler, maybe? With his Final Solution? It's all right for you. You saved your family and your wife's family, and I'm truly happy that you did. But what about the millions of bereaved, orphans, and displaced persons, millions of whose relatives were slaughtered? What about me, whose mother and father, whom you knew, and my little sister who studied at Safah Berurah like you, were murdered in the Rynek Square that you knew from your boyhood? Go to the displaced persons' camps in Germany, that we, the Jewish soldiers, are supporting and aiding in all kinds of ways — go and tell them that 'the Jewish problem' has been solved, and listen to what they answer you. Go to your Jewish workers in Łódź, whom you harass because they ask for humane treatment and consideration after everything they went through because they were Jewish, explicitly because they were Jewish, and tell them that 'the Jewish problem' has been solved — go and listen closely to their reaction!"

Ankori sank, agitated, into the upholstery of the chair, furious at himself for allowing the provocation artist to push him off balance. But because it had already happened, at least he would hurl everything in his heart at him:

"Or perhaps you did not mean the problem of the entire people, but that it would be enough to find a solution for the Malinowskis and their ilk: just as they hid their identity from the Germans with Aryan papers, so they hide with a borrowed identity from history and reality, and what's more, they hold the power and authority to do so?"

Motek did not respond. He continued to lay in silence, and it was impossible to decipher his thoughts. After several long minutes, he rose to a sitting position, and suddenly, a voice was heard. It was not clear where the voice came from — from the mouth of Motek himself or from that of some hidden ghost, concealing itself, like him, behind a mask — and the voice completely ignored the topic of the previous conversation, and erased everything that had previously been said, and seemed to start a new page, whose content was unexpected and among whose words obviously lay a trap:

"Incidentally, Hesiek: as far as I noticed, you are the first British soldier I have seen on Polish soil. Tell me, please, how did you manage to get here?"

Ankori regained his control within a moment. He realized that the rules of the game had been changed without warning. Until then, this had been an ideological battle between equals, provocative on one side, emotional on the other, but all on one general topic, that of "the Jewish problem" after the war. The debaters argued, but they themselves were not part of the issue. From the moment the last question was thrown into the ring, equality was obsolete. Not only was the friendly tone of the conversation stifled, but the topic of the conversation was changed. It was no longer "the Jewish problem", but rather the personal legal status of the soldier partner in debate, and the legality of his being found on Polish soil. There was a hint of threat in the words. The Pole on the bridge considered smuggling a letter as betrayal, not to mention the smuggling of a foreigner into the country. As a member of the establishment, Motek knew that a Western soldier could not enter the Soviet region. But now, hearing things he did not enjoy, he appointed himself judge: if the answer satisfied him, fine; if not — he would act in accordance with the law.

"Attack is the best defense" — Ankori had internalized this basic military precept until it flashed in his mind instinctively when needed, without delay. This was how he now responded to Motek's provocative question. He rose slowly to his feet, and not only was he fearless, but he drew back his bow smugly, nonchalantly, with a smile that became more brazen with each second, and shot a poisoned arrow strait to the center of the target: "Motek, neither of us are stupid. Did you really think I would answer that question? No matter what I tell you, **you will inform on me and turn me in!**"

"Now, really, Hesiek — would I do something like that? To you? We've known each other since childhood." He extended his hand for a handshake, but there was no longer any hand nearby to shake. Hesiek either heard or did not hear, saw or did not see the reaction; either way, the fire of spite and contempt blazed in his eyes. Quickly he opened the door of the main room, waved his hand without a word to the surprised Lutka, and left the apartment. Luckily for him, a fiacre passed by that took him to the hotel and was willing to wait. Ankori locked himself in his room, pulled from the bottom of the pack a Movement Order form, photograph, and stamp, and filled in the form: TTG, Łódź-Katowice-Vienna. Then, packs in his hands, Movement Order in his pocket, he paid for the room and hurried out into the street. "*Na stację!* (To the station!)" he called to the driver. "For security's sake," he thought to himself, "better to flee Poland and trouble at once!"

Years and historical events, which engraved their impression on the heart of Poland and Eastern Europe after the war, transformed the "certificate of resolution and death" that Malinowski had granted the "Jewish problem" into a document carved in ice. "The Jewish problem" dissolved every corner. Although we must assume that the die-hard communist said "Amen" on November 29, 1947, after the UN voted in favor of establishing a Jewish state, not because it thrilled him but in obedience to the Soviet foreign minister, Gromyko, who declared that the Soviet Union sided with this solution of "the Jewish problem". On the other hand, we can assume that he, again as a die-hard communist, also said "Amen" when the Soviet Union changed its mind and amended its *realpolitik*, meaning it embraced Abdul Nasser and turned its back on Israel. Still, in his ideological conservatism Malinowski apparently continued to hold the view that Israel was a product of the interests of world powers as an excuse for a solution to "the Jewish problem". After all (in his view), that problem was dead and would never live again.

Eleven years had passed since the angry encounter in Łódź, and Malinowski bore witness to his dire portent that "the Jewish problem" was still alive and kicking, even in the communist paradise for which he had helped establish a satellite in Poland. The crisis of 1956–57 that shook the entire communist world due to the Hungarian revolt and the reverberations of the revolt against Soviet dictatorship in Poland and Czechoslovakia, and the shock that reigned after Khrushchev's speech, corresponded with the rise of Władysław Gomułka to the leadership of the Communist Polish *Partia*. The agitation continued. An opposing faction pulled from the ancient treasury the anti-Semitic ruse that had proved its efficacy under all governments: distraction from internal complaints by transferring the anger to the Jews — when it was claimed that their number in the *Partia* leadership was too great, and one must "Get rid of the Abramowiczs!" Indeed, in 1956 Jakób Berman, one of the *Partia*'s great ideologues, was dismissed, and the minister of industry, Hilary Mintz, resigned (or was forced to resign) — both Jews, as their names indicate. Further, Jews in lower positions also resigned or were dismissed, and some left Poland. This was still not the great exodus of 1968, in which anti-Semitic propaganda after the Six-Day War would revile Jewish communists as "Zionist traitors". But the Mintz affair signaled to Malinowski, who was subordinate to the minister, that if not in '56, then in '57, his time would come as well, and "the Jewish problem" would catch up with him, and, following the lessons of history, as a Jew he would be

forced to leave Poland for another Diaspora. Another Diaspora? Why? From now on, the Jew has a land of his own!
The Jewish State!

## IX

The fourth day after the soldier's return from Łódź finds the British sergeant again in a train car. This time he is leaving Poland and Czechoslovakia to Vienna and beyond. Oh, what a week it was! A week of mission? Pleasure? Fear? Or surprising adventure? The first visit of an Eretz-Israeli soldier in post-war Poland. All the sights and experiences, the conversations and emotions that were Ankori's lot in the days he had spent in Poland, and his experiences during the three days of travel there and back, now pass through his mind like a moving picture, as he sits with eyes closed in the corner of the train car on his way from Vienna to Paris.

Indeed, a great week, which would leave its impression for many years, perhaps until the end of his life. But what about the goal for which he had undertaken the journey? The answer is short: failure. The journey brought him not one step closer to his sister. Was, then, his journey to Poland a complete waste of effort and energy, money and emotion? Was it all, all, all for nothing?

"No!" Eyes closed as before, the traveler refuses to succumb to pessimism. He admits: the main goal still has not been achieved (emphasis on "still"), for the repatriation is only at its inception. The various improvised modes of transport are limited in the number of refugees they are capable of carrying. But the pace would increase. The train service would be fully restored. Then one in a thousand would happen to appear, and on his lips the news that he had seen Mala and remembered her address. "Oh, let it be!"

Despite his temporary failure in dissipating the bank of fog that had descended on Mala's location and on her welfare, and despite his prayer that the messenger would not tarry and arrive quickly with the stream of returnees, it seemed to him that the journey itself was far from a waste. Major and minor experiences, all unique, accompanied him during his stay in Poland. And their memory would remain engraved in his mind forever.

His arrival in Tarnów, and following it the emotional meeting with the survivors of the Jewish community, was undoubtedly the jewel in the crown of all his experiences. These were preceded by the drama on the bridge over the Olza, his descent onto the *terra firma* of Poland, and just after this, the remarkable experience he had after the encounter with the guard, when he entered the temporary train station in Cieszyn.

Ankori opened his eyes. In a moment, he knew where he was. A crazy idea flashed through his mind. Really crazy, such that he did not dare speak it out loud, and he turned his head right and left, fearing that one of the people sitting in the carriage was reading his thoughts. Strange, the rhythmic noise of the train wheels brought serenity to his spirit. No, no one had discovered his secret. Chuckling up his sleeve, he saw himself placing his idea in an imaginary box and burying it in the depths of memory. Perhaps, in spite of everything, its time would come? Perhaps the day was not far off…?

The station loudspeaker silenced his thoughts: "Paree! Paris!" If so, here in Paris was the end of the road. Where would he turn from here in the search for his sister?

He goes out to the station square, awash with the autumn sun. He decides to walk the entire way to the home of his two friends in the Latin Quarter, despite the two packs on him and despite the distance. He wants Madame Jeanne and her pretty young protégé Erna, who had supported his efforts to reach his sister, to be the first to share the story of his experiences in Poland.

The boulevard is crowded with people. The fuel shortage has limited the movement of vehicles, so that people are walking freely on the avenue proper, adding a last pre-autumn glow to their suntanned cheeks. Are they trying to extend the holiday — the first one since the war — by annexing this warm September to the group of summer months, despite its golden fall? The fallen leaves (so it was when he had come here a week ago to begin his journey) carpet the wonderful boulevards of Paris in gold and copper. "Oh, how wonderful it is to breathe the Paris air!" Suddenly, he stops. "Could it be? Just four days ago, I breathed the air of the grieving ghetto of Warsaw and embraced its ruins, and a day later suffered the despicable encounter in Łódź!"

This year, the autumn in Poland was also like summer in its warmth. Yet, during his stay there, Ankori had not taken time for trips, but had rushed from meeting to meeting, from one inquiry to another, from one group of refugees to another, or listened to the click-clack of the hooves of the horse harnessed to the fiacre that took him not only to the nearby local address but also to the distant territories of his childhood. As he walks, he rubs his eyes, and the sights he thought he had pushed aside in Poland since he was so occupied with the mission he had taken upon himself, now suddenly awaken, as if by themselves, from the deep sleep he had imposed on them there, and they pursue him as far as the outskirts of Paris. And instead of the City of Lights in which he now walks, standing before him are the houses of Tarnów and Kraków, the ruins of Warsaw and Łódź.

He reaches the bridge over the Seine. Crossing it will bring him to the Left Bank of the river, to the entrance of the Latin Quarter. The Seine? he argues with himself. No, this is not the Seine, this is the Olza that separates Polish Cieszyn from Czech Těšín. He steps onto the bridge. A white line divides it in the middle. Remember! When you cross the line, you have left Czechoslovakia and entered Poland!

"I'm in Poland. After eight years of absence, I have returned — to post-Holocaust Poland."

The next morning he left the Latin Quarter, going toward the boulevard in front of the Opera, where the drivers of 178 usually deposited the soldiers going on leave and boarded the returning group. 178, which at that time was encamped in the holiday village of Scheveningen near the Hague, received the fellow who had "come home from over there" with mixed emotions: joy and sadness. Joy — that their comrade had returned from the unknown world untouched, and that he had succeeded in breaking the evil taboo, engrained in their consciousness, of a country arbitrarily closed to the Allies from the west, including the Jewish soldiers, although for many of them it was their homeland, the land of their childhood and youth, from which they had been separated when they had made *aliya* to Eretz-Israel. Alas, they remained connected to it forever, a connection of orphanhood and bereavement and Holocaust that had descended upon their parents homes. And alongside the joy was sadness, for the failure of the mission that had motivated their friend's journey to Poland. Alas, he had added not one crumb of information as to his sister's fate.

In the meantime, changes had taken place in the Unit — in the command, in the operational duties, and in the special Jewish mission, both open and clandestine, for the sake of the liberated camp prisoners and refugees. To the Jewish units these were "brothers"; in the British military lexicon they were known with the sterile and completely non-empathetic abbreviation of "DP's" (Displaced Persons). Unit 178 had a long history of aiding refugees, but the climate in which the activity took place now and the attitude of the British authorities became ever more suspicious after the war, in contrast to the heyday of activity in Libya and Italy.

In addition to all these, the atmosphere that now hovered above the soldiers was unknown in the previous chapters of their service: an atmosphere of impending discharge from uniform and return to Eretz-Israel. The Command was aware of the fact that many young soldiers had been recruited before learning a profession, or that they had no regular source of income. The remaining months before discharge must therefore be utilized in order to train them in a profession of their choice. Ankori was appointed to manage the project. He went all over Holland searching for individuals or civilian factories that would agree to train a soldier or two in their profession. A Christian farmer in Gouda, known for producing cheeses for export, took in soldiers, housed them, and taught them the secrets of production. Soldiers were also placed at Asher's, the well-known Jewish diamond factory in Amsterdam. "I know," said the manager with a smile, "that the day will come when Tel Aviv will compete with me. But for Jewish soldiers, I will yield and forgive."

The year 1945 began to roll along, without stopping, to its end. Six months had already passed since the victory in Europe — the rejoicing that was then, the celebration, the flags! The Hague, Amsterdam, Paris! De Gaulle and his generals lifted copiously decorated chests: it is *we* who liberated France! Generous-lipped young women climbed onto the tanks — partners, if not in the victory, then of the victors. Who would remember daring, bravery, and death on the coasts of Normandy? Only the bereaved families would ache in the distance: in the United States, England, Canada, Australia, and New Zealand.

Christmas is coming, the first one after the war. Here it rejoices and spreads its wings. They are already decorating the streets and the stores; the Christmas trees in the display windows bow under the weight of tempting items. Paris! Surely a holiday will be declared in the army, as is usual during the season. After all, the war is over, and the command is generous in granting leaves to the soldiers and organizing trips.

Ankori was not in the mood for trips, but he gave in to the pressure and could not avoid guiding his comrades in Paris, a city he knew and loved well. He avoided holidays and Sabbaths and other vacation days that imposed chaos on his soul; they invited sad thoughts on questions that were central to him personally, and for which he had no answer: "What else can I do about Mala that I haven't done already? Where to turn? From whom to ask advice?" Madame Jeanne, a strong personality with influence and good connections as an activist in the Jewish Agency, proposed that he meet with well-known Yiddish-speaking intellectuals, members of the French communist party — perhaps they could obtain the information? — and convinced an author to introduce him to these people. Ankori would do as she said, only in order to be certain that he had not disregarded any advice, although he did not believe this attempt would bear fruit. These old-timers lived in a world of illusion, and they enjoyed recalling the early days of the movement, when they were listened to in revolutionary and Third International circles. But it was doubtful that their former influence would pass the test today.

## X

In his new position, Ankori found some escape from the disturbing and conscience-wracking thoughts that he had not succeeded in reaching Mala or saving her. The job required collecting information, creativity, and understanding people, whether the aiding or the aided, recipients or givers. The lesson would accompany him for many years, but it contained no solution to his deliberations at the moment. "Oh, help me, Mala!"

The first snows of 1946 gradually thickened, endowing the problem of Mala with a feeling of urgency. Another terrible Russian winter?! Hadn't she suffered enough? Fear for the sister's welfare led the brother to put an end to his wanderings in the maze of searches and advice, and to make a bold and independent decision. The urgency was derived not only from fear for the welfare of the sister and her health, but also from worry about the obstruction of possibilities for action, considering events in the Brigade. The scent of closure wafted from every order and mission. According to the pace of the discharge process, the logical forecast for his turn was the summer of that year, in other words, in five or six months. Time was thus pressing. He must tarry no longer. This was the time to pull out the ultimate secret proposal for a solution, which had come to him as a brainstorm during the train ride from Vienna, and was deposited in the imaginary box in which it had been hiding throughout these months.

For a full day, Ankori sat and wrote, and rewrote, and tore the page, and wrote again the story of Mala's tragedy and of her brother who searched for her. "It must be no longer than one page" — he repeated to himself the governing rule of every office. Therefore, he erased certain parts and shortened other parts, and went over the corrected text carefully — one page exactly! Then he rushed to the Company office and asked permission to use the English Remington after working hours. "I don't trust anyone" — so, with a mischievous smile and thanks, he explained why he refused the assistance of the office clerk, who was willing to type the composition for him. "What's one page for me? I'll finish it in two minutes!" said his friend, incredulous. But the author of the composition insisted: "True, I type slowly and with only two fingers. But in return, I get a page free of mistakes." All the buddies in the office burst out laughing, never imagining that their friend's refusal was motivated by the wish to keep the contents of the letter and the identity of the addressee a secret. To the page typed on the old and tired Remington, Ankori added half a page in his handwriting, a Polish version of the imaginary letter he used to write every night to his sister in his dreams.

The next day, the page in English and the half-page in Polish in hand (which, lacking the Polish diacritical marks on the Remington, had been typed for him in the nearby Polish unit), he requested a meeting with the Unit commander. The Major, Avraham Silberstein, was no *homo novus* in the Company. Unlike the earlier majors brought from outside to command the Company, he rose from within the Unit, first as responsible for the workshop. He had arrived in the Unit in Egypt as a young officer, shortly after Ankori had arrived straight from basic training, when the old 5MT fell apart, and 178 RASC took its place.

Silberstein and Ankori were among the few who had gone with this Unit from its founding in Qena in Upper Egypt to its end in Holland. Their story was the story of the Company's changing mood, beginning with the spirit of defeat that the old-timers of 5MT, witnesses to the first defeat of the British in Libya and the retreat all the way to a mere sixty miles from Alexandria, bequeathed to the young members of 178; through the recovery that the Eighth Army under Montgomery instilled in the entire army; accomplishing the historic breakthrough from el-Alamein and occupation of Libya; the long wait in Malta and finally, the landing in southern Italy; the advance to the north of the Italian boot; joining the Brigade and the battle on the Senio; the passage to Belgium-Holland and missions over the western border of Germany. And have we already mentioned the praiseworthy "Jewish" activity in Libya and in Europe?

Major and sergeant (who brought the pages with him) met together for about two hours in the spartan Company Headquarters office. All at once, barriers of rank and age fell. The commander tried to create a comfortable atmosphere for conversation, although he did not know as yet what the sergeant wished to discuss: "I enjoyed the Sabbath parties you organized and the songs you wrote — important contributions to creating the Unit's team spirit as it has endured to this day." They both smiled.

When Ankori left the Major's office, his hands were empty. The English page and the Polish half-page were locked in the Company Commander's safe. After implementation of the friendly plan of action that was reached in the meeting, the waiting period shared by these two only would begin, and no one in the camp would know that they carried a secret in their hearts. Aside from that, the world carried on as usual: the snow enveloped the camp and the roads with a shroud of white. The driving missions were carried out as always, without regard for the threatening weather. Each week the trucks received a by-the-book maintenance check. The workshop tried to restore a youthful blush to the vehicles — exhausted workhorses — groaning from the aches of old age and knowing that they would wait in vain for a new, younger generation of vehicles to replace them. The Sabbath parties took place as usual, and although the end-of-war discharge from the army diminished the number of attendees, those who remained were more punctilious than before about participation, and although Ankori was not in the mood to compose new songs, they nostalgically took pleasure in the songs of the past. Major and sergeant maintained the appearance of formality, but they had a special code of communication. When the sergeant stood, in the course of duty, before the Company Commander, he looked up and asked with his eyes, "Anything?" and the Commander's eyes answered, "Nothing." End of "conversation". And so, January made way for February, and March took the latter's place. "Anything?…" "Nothing…."

The last week of March 1946 spread clear signs that winter's end was approaching. Still, the ocean was covered in a contemplative grayness, as if unsure whether the signs had not hurried too much, for a damp chill still reigned in the air. But the snow stopped and the wind and scattered rains tried to sweep away the layers of fog that hid the horizon.

Joy was reflected on the soldiers' faces, for not only was winter coming to an end, but their service was as well. As long as the warfare had continued, and with it, the advance toward enemy territory, motivation was high and the final goal overshadowed the path of hardship that led to it. But now that final goal — victory — had been achieved and replaced by another final goal: home! Also the method of "discharge" was made easier, and all its stages until final release from service were known to all. In parallel, the motivation to act among and on behalf of the refugees did not subside. Except that lately, civilian emissaries had begun to arrive from Eretz-Israel — each one undoubtedly dedicated, but enthusiastic to sell the merchandise from his own political party's store — and the soldier-emissaries, who had consciously worked to hide their differences of view and at the outset wove a mask of unity that transcended parties, saw their praiseworthy work gradually buried under a wave of propaganda that took the place of education and welfare.

Nevertheless, Ankori's face was also full of joy, obvious but restrained, diluted with anticipation. But every passing day gnawed at the anticipation and added a strip of gray shade to the suntan of his face — suntan that had been nourished by the intensity of the desert sun in Libya and by the more moderate summers of *la bella Italia*.

## XI

"Ankori! They're calling you to headquarters!"

The sergeant went into Major Silberstein's office and saluted smartly. But as his saluting palm rose above his eyebrows and approached his right temple, his eyes repeated the regular question that had put them to the test of patience for almost three months: "Anything?"

The Commander broke the code that had enveloped the two men in a cloak of secret and cried, "Zvi, there is something!" Silence. What does "something" mean?

"You've won, Zvi."

"No. If it's victory, then it belongs to both of us!"

"But it was your idea. It would never have crossed my mind to ask the British Military Mission in Moscow to contact the Soviet authorities in order to locate your sister."

"I began to turn this idea over in my mind while sitting on the train that brought me back from Poland, realizing that the methods I had tried were doomed to failure. There was no one outside the Soviet government who could bring my sister to me. She disappeared in that enormous country, as if the earth had swallowed her, and only an official system could find her. Because I have no legal status in relation to the Soviet regime, I thought that with my status as a British subject, the way it's stamped in my passport, and as one of the veteran volunteers in the British army in this war, and because of my sister's status as a subject of the British government before the war, a status that was not ended by her will but by an enemy that Britain fought against, it was legitimate for me to ask the Military Mission representing the British army in Moscow for this humanitarian assistance."

"I agreed with you (said the Major), and thought you should write Mala's story, including dates and the name of the gulag where she was held until her liberation — not more than one page — and emphasize that she does not know English and that contact with her must be in Russian or Polish, better Polish. Surely the Mission employed a translator who could do the job."

The difficulty had been in communication with the Mission in Moscow. According to military procedure, soldiers, even of high rank, were not allowed to contact other military bodies except through what were called "proper channels". Such a non-security-related telegram was certain to get stuck at one of the levels of bureaucracy, or to get lost altogether. Here was where Major Silberstein's daring came in, for which Ankori would be indebted to him for the rest of his life. While his subordinate deliberated whether to attempt another step, on his own initiative the Commander telegraphed the sergeant's letter directly to the British Mission in Moscow, adding warm words of recommendation. Here was where the worried wait began: was the telegram received? Did the Mission Commander complain about this violation of procedure? Or did it arouse his empathy for the brother and sister, the only ones of the whole family to survive, and thus he took steps to carry out the request?

The Moscow telegram exceeded all expectations and everything they could possibly imagine.

In reply, the telegram did not detail the steps taken by the British Mission in order to obtain the information. It only summarized the results of the investigation. And so, thanks to the British in Moscow, for the first time the brother was informed of the location of his exiled sister after she had been liberated from the forest gulag near Omsk. On her way west from Siberia, Mala had reached the Ukraine, and apparently, due to her husband's illness (his name was not given and it was not clear whether he was a Jew, a Pole, or a Russian), she settled in the town of Barwienkowo in the Kharkov district, and thus lost her right to repatriation to Poland (because she was too late? or because her husband was Russian?) After her husband died, Mala was left alone in the town. Her request for restoration of her right to return to Poland was denied, but was renewed due to the redemptive intervention of the British Mission. The telegram did not mention financial support, but detailed the arrangements for Mala's journey to Tarnów and estimated that in May, she would reach her city. And consider: at that very time, in Eretz-Israel tension prevailed between the British Mandate Government and the Jewish Yishuv, while here the assistance was overwhelming in its generosity!

The British Mission performed another kindness for the brother and sister. Major Silberstein added to the telegram, sent from 178 Company, the Polish text of Ankori's letter to Mala. The Mission sent a copy of the letter to the sister, and she was invited to reply to her brother, and her letter was attached to the reply telegram. This was the first time (just that once) in seven years that an exchange of letters was established between the brother and sister.

Relying on the British prediction that May would be the date of Mala's arrival in Tarnów, Ankori left for Poland for the second time, accompanied by the good wishes of Major Silberstein and the rank and file of 178. He knew that this time, he would have to extend his stay in Poland for a longer period, because of the arrangements required for Mala's transportation to Paris, as the first stage of her return to Eretz-Israel, and because perhaps she would need medical care due to the state of her health. He telephoned the Tarnów committee of survivors and discovered that Mala had indeed arrived a week earlier, and had at once become involved in community activity. The destruction on every corner energized her to act, together with the sculptor David Becker, to create a memorial for the victims of the massacre.

This was not the reaction of the brother. The thought of a second visit to destroyed Tarnów made him tremble. He thus remained in Kraków and telephoned Mala to come there. The next day, at the appointed hour, he was waiting at the train station. An old friend waved to him. Beside her stood a bent woman. It was lucky that the friend had come:

the brother did not recognize his sister.

## XII

The delay in recognition lasted only a second or two, but Mala felt it. Apparently, it had often happened that her acquaintances from the past had difficulty recognizing her. The mirror did not lie each morning — to such an extent had life in the camp, the hunger, the hump from the injury of the tree-trunk, and the effects of typhus left their mark on her face. But the fact that even the brother was nonplused for a moment in recognizing his sister hurt her deeply. She did not mention anything about it, not at the time, nor years later. The brother, on his part, could not forgive himself the incident: still, he thought that words of apology might hurt more. Better to let time obliterate it. Indeed, the topic did not arise at all in conversation, and seemed to be forgotten. Until at a party that Mala's daughters held to celebrate fifty years since her return from exile in Siberia, Mala was asked to recount her experiences during the first days of her meeting with her brother after a seven-year separation. Suddenly, she stopped her story and laughingly addressed the brother, who was present at the party together with his wife: "You should know, Zvi (that, and not Hesiek, was what she returned to calling him, as she had done in the good old days in Eretz-Israel) — I sensed that you did not recognize me at our first meeting in Kraków. It didn't surprise me. I really did look terrible then. Good thing you didn't have a camera. But you cared for me devotedly, and after a year I slowly began to resemble the Mala whom you knew from before. Do you remember how I held your hand at the doctors'? That was the only way I stopped being afraid."

In Kraków, the two were invited to stay at the home of Mrs. Rosenbusch, widow of the last principal of the Hebrew high school Safah Berurah, one of the first group of Tarnów's educated, Jews and non-Jews, who were sent to Auschwitz as part of the Nazi plot to liquidate the local intelligentsia in every location, out of fear that rebellious elements would seek out their leaders. The oldest daughter, Zvitka, survived along with the mother. They both, together with the youngest daughter, had hidden in the cupboards of the righteous gentile, the Pole Dr. Horbacki, superintendent of high schools in Kraków district, in whose area of supervision the Tarnów Hebrew high school was included. But one day the Nazis invaded the neighborhood, although only Poles lived there. Unfortunately, they discovered one of the hiding places (some say, through an informer), dragged from it the younger sister, and murdered her.

For some reason, it was difficult to get Mala to talk when they sat around the table on the afternoon of that day. She barely touched her food, although in Poland lunch was the main meal of the day, and Mrs. Rosenbusch had tried to make it especially tasty. At a loss, Zvi proposed that just the two of them, he and Mala, take a walk in the "Planty", hoping that a conversation would develop that might atone for seven years of silence and lack of contact between brother and sister. In those clear sunny days of May 1946, the brother tried to revive a handful of memories from similar days in their childhood, when they toured Kraków with their mother, who loved the city dearly and tried to transmit that love to her children — but he found that he was talking to himself. He therefore decided to change direction, and leave the "Planty" toward the central Rynek, where crowds were enjoying a stroll and "having a good time". Indeed, Mala's expression cleared somewhat at the sight of the cheerful throng in the square. Excited, the two stopped in the middle of the square in order to listen to the lone trumpeter, sending from the taller of the two towers of St. Mary's church the chilling notes of the ancient *hejnał*, four times every hour, on the hour.

The brother was pleased that the successful visit to the Rynek had improved his sister's mood, and hoped that it had also brought back her appetite; for food had not entered her mouth since morning. They returned to the "Planty", and after crossing it, they went out to a quiet part of the city with streets bearing common names from the days of old Kraków, such as Szewska ("Shoemakers' Street"). Here and there, they saw small restaurants and several stores, prosaic in appearance and function. Zvi suggested they go into a restaurant, but Mala recoiled and refused. The brother did not pressure her. They continued to walk down the street, and unintentionally passed by a simple grocery store. In the dusty window near the entrance, two loaves of bread, apparently leftover from that morning, lay together intimately. "That's what I want" — said Mala, pointing to the bread. These were the first words she said of her own initiative, not in reply to a question. The brother now understood that walking beside him was a deportee from Siberia, and many days would pass until she would readopt habits common to all people around. From now on, he would not initiate purchases, but would only respond to her desires. Still, he asked Zvitka to go with her the next day to buy a dress, skirt, blouses, underwear, sandals, and a new toothbrush, among other items; but he would warn her not to pressure, not to convince. He purchased the two loaves in the store. To the astonishment of those present, Mala devoured an entire loaf while still in the store. "The second one will be for this evening" — and Zvi wrapped it in paper. They both smiled, happy and in good spirits.

When that same evening, Mala rejected the idea of making the next day a shopping day, Zvi cancelled his original plan to stay in Kraków another day in order to outfit his sister with new items of clothing, and decided they would leave the next day on the morning train to Warsaw. After all, who knew how long they would have to wait there until they received the documents? Mala looked as if she did not understand the difficulty her brother feared. She was in Poland thanks to the repatriation, and so what if it had been restored due to British intervention? The document had been taken from her when the train crossed the Russian-Polish border, and she was again left without identification papers, but she did not consider this of any importance either. She did not internalize that a year had passed since the end of the war, the chaos at the borders had ended, and 1946 was not like 1945 when Zvi had first come here. The period of free crossing of borders by refugees had ended. There was no more traveling in Europe without passports or visas. As a Polish citizen, if she wanted to leave Poland in order to return to Eretz-Israel, she had to equip herself with a Polish passport, and the passport had to be stamped with all the visas for the rest of the journey.

Zvi went to Warsaw, worried. A surprising highlight was making friends on the train with Grisha, a pilot in the Russian air force. Their friendship sparked suddenly, seemingly without introduction, the British sergeant's basic Russian — from six months of self-instruction — although sometimes amusing, nevertheless enabled an acceptable level of communication. The pair's friendship was sealed at parting with a handshake (and the pilot's unlisted telephone number) and a warm invitation to fly in his airplane from his base in Warsaw to one of the destinations of the Russian air force: often Berlin, and once every two weeks, Paris. Zvi memorized the number, for he had his reasons.

Aside from wisecracks with Grisha, the journey was long and exhausting. But ten times longer and more exhausting were the queues Zvi was astonished to see the next morning when he walked around the office district — lines that snaked around the building of the Polish Ministry of Foreign Affairs and crowded the entrances of the American, British, and French consulates. His instinctive thought at this sight was whether and how he could bypass the packed human chain and get in without standing in line. But he was immediately ashamed at the selfishness of this idea: everyone standing in line is there because of trouble, and who could determine whose distress was greater and demanded a more urgent solution?

Despite these doubts, Zvi justified the urgency of his mission, even at the price of bypassing the lines. As a soldier, he had only a few days at his disposal to arrange the documents for his sister, and after that he had to report to his Unit, at a distance of so many kilometers and so many borders from Warsaw. Could he leave his sister here, when he had finally found her after seven years without contact? She had no home and no one besides him, and she was unable, physically and emotionally, to carry out the mission after the travails she had undergone. Without pangs of conscience, then, and as quickly as possible, he must obtain the documents that would enable his sister to leave with him to the West.

He returned to the hotel for lunch at the restaurant. This time as well, Mala refused to join in the meal and preferred to go up to her room. There she kept busy with bite after bite from the mythological loaf of bread that remained from the day before and had traveled the whole way from Kraków to Warsaw. The brother also went up to the room, angry and desperate. Where to turn? He closed his eyes, and suddenly envisioned a building with a respectable façade and brass sign beside the entrance. He had never seen the building with flesh-and-blood eyes, did not know the name of the street, and could not make out the words engraved on the brass. But he sensed — more, he knew without doubt — that this was the place he was looking for and this was where he had to go the next day to ask for help: "British Military Mission" in Warsaw — was that what the brass plate in the vision had foreseen?

Two factors combined to help him obtain at the Polish foreign ministry, in just two days, a passport for his sister, by way of bypassing the queues. One — and this was the most significant, since for the brother it broke a way straight through into the consular section — was the letter from the commander of the British Military Mission to the Polish Foreign Ministry, in English (which no one understood) and in French (the language of diplomacy in those days). The letter was given with obvious unwillingness ("Are you out of your mind? Under the present political situation, there is no correspondence between us and the Foreign Ministry. You should know that this letter will go straight into the bin!" "I'll take that chance, sir.") The second factor — the secretaries: the letter began to travel from secretary to secretary, and to another secretary and a fourth and a fifth, as the soldier continued "not to understand Polish" and joked with them only in French. So the Polish women, imprisoned in the East, discovered a "British" man from the legendary West, and they unrestrainedly stroked every decoration on his chest. The next day, practically fainting with excitement, they parted from their dream-prince by presenting him with a gift: a passport.

Passport in hand, Zvi returned to the office of the Military Mission: "Here is the result of your letter, sir" (and he showed the document to the Mission Commander). "Now please be so kind as to give me three similar letters to the American, British, and French consulates to obtain transit visas for the three military zones of West Germany and for entry into France itself." This time, the Commander saw no reason to hesitate. As the saying goes, "Nothing succeeds like success" — and he instructed his bureau chief to issue the letters. One day later, the visas were already stamped into Mala's new passport.

Zvi phoned the confidential number of his friend Grisha, the Russian pilot, to check if and when there was a flight to Paris, and if the invitation was valid for two. "Next Monday I'm leaving at eight A.M. on a flight to Paris" — a friendly reply in Russian was heard on the other end of the line. "Of course the invitation still stands, and it is valid for two. It's important to get there early and be at the airport in Mokotów, near Warsaw, about twenty minutes before eight A.M. Every taxi driver knows the way. Take into account a drive of about half an hour. I'll wait for you."

This was great news. Zvi rushed to share his joy with Mala, and was surprised that his happiness was not met with similar emotion. "Don't you get it, Mala? We're flying in another few days. Aren't you excited? We'll leave in the morning, and in the afternoon or early evening we'll be in Paris already. In Paris, Mala, the most beautiful city in the world! Do you remember my French fourth grade schoolbook about Paris? You didn't want to learn French, but you loved looking at the pictures and asked me to explain to you what they were. There was a photograph on almost every page. Remember? So just think that we'll be seeing those sights with our very own eyes! And all that on the way back to Eretz-Israel!" Mala was silent. "What's wrong, Mala? Why are you so quiet?"

"I don't want to fly. I am afraid."

## XIII

The train arrived at the Gare du Nord. A blue-pink twilight clung to the roofs of Paris. "*Au Quartier Latin* — to the Latin Quarter!" The taxi drove along the same route that Zvi had walked over half a year earlier when he had returned from his first trip to Poland.

This time, his mood was uplifted. Not only because he was again staying in Paris, a city that, aside from Jerusalem, he loved more than any other, even more than Kraków, but also because he saw in his mind's eye that his plan to bring Mala back to Eretz-Israel was becoming a reality. He would still need the assistance of Major Silberstein and the 178 Command, and the aid of the Jewish Agency for Eretz-Israel, in whose Paris bureau worked two of his friends whom he was now going to visit with his sister. In their home, Mala could rest and regain her strength, while with her brother she would tour for an hour or two each day and get to know this wonderful city. Sight-seeing could also advance the process of recuperation and release Mala's mind from the nightmares of the past.

Madame Jeanne and Erna received Mala with joy and motherly understanding for her emotional and physical condition, and even for her caprices. And, lo and behold: in contrast to her behavior in Kraków, Mala opened up to her caretakers in Paris, and happiness and friendship blossomed despite the difficulties of language. The new atmosphere returned the color to sunken cheeks, kindled light in half-extinguished eyes, and placed a smile on a face that had forgotten what a smile was. Her appetite also began to keep to a regular schedule, and the distinction in tastes of various foods aside from bread was again enjoyable. Seeing the cheerful recovery, it was decided: aside for urgent medical treatments that had to be carried out in Paris, the extensive physical rehabilitation (such as operations on the hump and teeth) would be postponed until Mala's return to Eretz-Israel, while here the emphasis would be placed on emotional rehabilitation. Because the goals that Zvi had set for himself in Poland (obtaining a passport and visas for Mala and taking her to Paris) were achieved with unexpected rapidity, and only half the period specified in his pass had been utilized to that point, he had time to complete the arrangements for the long journey, and at any rate, he would not rush to return to the Unit, but would dedicate most of his time to cultivating the renewed relationship between himself and his sister.

Telegram to Mr. Y. Poznański, academic secretary of Hebrew University:

"Please investigate the legal status of Mala Wróbel, who in 1937 received a certificate for studies in Jerusalem, and continued her studies before the war in the Faculty of Humanities."

"The investigation revealed that the *aliya* permit she received is valid and the student is authorized to enter Eretz-Israel" — was the happy content of the responding telegram from Jerusalem.

"We've jumped one hurdle in the race for your renewed *aliya*" — brother reports happily to sister. "The certificate you received in 1937 is alive and well. Your entrance to Eretz-Israel is open." In contrast to Mala's apathy in Warsaw and her complete incomprehension as to the reason for her brother's energetic activity to obtain the documents that would enable her departure from Poland and voyage to Eretz-Israel, she now changes her attitude and shows interest in the steps being taken on behalf of the supreme goal: her return to Eretz-Israel after seven years. The brother is pleased and wonders: what is the source of the change? Is this part of the process of recovery, or the result of that same process? Or did the Paris air (and not only that of Eretz-Israel, as the Talmudic proverb claims) make one wise?

"But how will we get there?" she asks.

"That's the next hurdle we have to jump. Don't worry, we'll get over that one, too."

"The *Aliya* Department of the Jewish Agency!" — an idea jumps into his head. "Of course! Why didn't I think of that before? I'll speak to Madame Jeanne. Surely she'll be able to do something about this."

Madame Jeanne laughed as if he had told a good joke. Then she looked at him as if pitying the simpleton son of the proverbial "four sons" from the Passover Haggadah: "What did you think? That I'd keep her with me until the end of time?" They both laughed, but at once became serious. "I'm sorry. This is not a subject for jokes. Don't worry, Zvi. Everything is already arranged. She's sailing from Marseilles on the *André Lebon* in three weeks. To be exact, on July 15. In short, there's no problem as far as Mala is concerned" — added Jeanne — "the only problem is y o u , Zvi."

"I'm the problem?!" he shouted. "For seven years the problem of Mala has been hanging over me, and for the past year I've been running around between Poland and Paris in order to solve it. Now that I've taken my sister out of hell and she's about to return to Eretz-Israel — suddenly I'm the problem? Really, Jeanne, you yourself said this wasn't a subject for jokes."

"Maybe 'problem' is not the right word. Maybe 'difficulty' is a better term. But the difficulty exists, whether you admit it or not."

"So what's the difficulty?"

"Mala sails shortly. Surely you will want to travel to Eretz-Israel together, but you are a soldier, and no civilian French vessel — such as the *André Lebon* — will allow a soldier in uniform on board, no matter what his rank, without presenting an official permit from the military authorities."

"Is that the whole difficulty? Even before the trip I discussed that with Major Silberstein, who was involved in every stage of the activities on Mala's behalf, and he promised to take care of any document that would be needed. That is the reason why I left that detail for the end, when I report to my Unit. Indeed, tomorrow morning I will go to the regular meeting place for the 178 vehicles, behind the Opera building (and if there isn't a ride available tomorrow, I'll go again the next day — that's what we always used to do) and I'll ride to the Unit with one of the drivers in order to report. Then I'll ask the Major for authorization to sail on a civilian vessel and a pass until July 15, because the pass for the Poland trip was only for one month and it will expire the day after tomorrow."

Indeed, the next day Ankori went to the 178 meeting point, to which they used to bring groups of soldiers for leave in Paris, while previous groups that had finished their leaves went back to the camp in the same truck. He waited until the afternoon, but no Star of David appeared on the horizon. Disappointed, he feared that the level of curiosity for Paris had expended itself and the destination for leaves had been changed, or that this was the weekly maintenance day. When 178 disappointed him again on the third day, he conjectured that perhaps a Moving Order had been received suddenly, as had happened often in the past. If so, how would he be able to find 178 in its new location? Despite his loyalty to the Unit's Command, the situation reminded him of the grudge he had felt in the past toward the NCOs, who were supposed to know where each soldier was and how to contact him, and who also had the duty to take care of him. This was already the second time they had ignored his absence and had not bothered to check where he was. The first time they had left him at the hospital in Udine, Italy: he had fled the hospital, burning with malarial fever, together with Johnny, who had also been hospitalized there. They hitchhiked across half of Europe in order to rejoin their Unit, which had moved from Italy to Holland. Now he was again left to his own devices — luckily this time the stay was in Paris and not in that miserable, remote hole. "They probably had their reasons" — he assuaged his anger — "but this time I need the Unit and its Commander urgently! My sailing depends on them!"

Suddenly a British military bus in camouflage colors appears and stops in front of him. A cheerful group of London soldiers (if one may judge by their heavy cockney accent) got off the bus. But who is the corporal getting off last? "Lord Almighty! It's Johnny, the 178-man, no one else but Johnny!"

"Speak of the devil, Johnny! It's unbelievable: just a few minutes ago I remembered you and our escape from the hospital, and as if from afar, you read my thoughts and came toward me. Congratulations for your promotion to corporal. As Napoleon said, 'Every soldier carries a marshal's baton in his kitbag.'" They embraced to the laughs and witty comments of the gang, four-letter words included in every phrase.

"Oh, Zvi, it's so nice to speak Hebrew again. I'll never forget those days I spent with you. Do you know what I'm doing in my British unit? I'm leading the gang around Paris, just as you led me around. And where am I starting? You guessed it! Place de la Concorde, of course, as you learned from your French book, and you led me that very same way, too."

"And what's that badge on your sleeve?"

"As a native of England, they put me in a British unit. You still have the badge of the Brigade?"

"Of course. Until the end."

'But Zvi, the end is already here."

"Yes, the war has ended. But we're still in the service. The end will come only when we take off our uniforms."

"I didn't mean that end."

"It's not important right now. Johnny, I need urgent information. Where did the Brigade move?"

"I see you don't know anything about what's going on here. Where have you been lately?"

"In Poland."

"Now I understand why you're completely disconnected from our reality! It's not by chance I'm in a British unit now. As sad as it may be, and as much as I don't want to be the one to give you the bad news, you should know:

The Brigade was disbanded.
178 no longer exists."

## XIV

The elegant hall, which in the past had hosted nobles and high-ranking officers in shining uniforms and powdered ladies, belted into ballooning crinolines under their fancy gowns, dancing to the rhythm of a polonaise or a romantic minuet — now served the British Military Mission to France. It took courage, Ankori complimented himself years later, perhaps even daring, to enter the historic Palais and, head held high, pass the British Military Police and request in the office, in contradiction to all-binding military procedure, for a personal conversation with the Major-General, Commander of the Mission.

The head was held high through force of will, but heavy doubts nestled in the heart. There could be no worse choice than this (although there was no other choice, because of the pressure for time), for the day on which to visit the British Military Mission in Paris — Monday, July 1, 1946. The radio and the newspaper headlines bombarded one on every side with the clamoring news of the severe steps of punishment taken by the government of the British Mandate of Palestine in reaction to the night on which bridges were blown up in Eretz-Israel by the Haganah three weeks ago. The government's actions had reached their peak two days previously, on the Sabbath of June 29 (called "the Black Sabbath"), and on Sunday, June 30, when all the leaders of the Yishuv and the Jewish Agency were imprisoned at Latrun, except for Ben Gurion, who was not in Eretz-Israel at the time, and Moshe Sneh, head of the Haganah Command, who managed to escape.

In such a situation, even if the general were to overlook the breach of procedure, could he really receive a Palestinian sergeant from the Jewish Brigade, with a blue-white-blue badge and a Star of David on his sleeve? And would he really do so, knowing that the soldier was going to ask for authorization from the army for a private voyage to Palestine on a civilian vessel, with the assistance of the Paris office of the Jewish Agency, that same Jewish Agency whose leaders were at that time under arrest in Latrun?

The fact is that the general did agree to receive the Jewish sergeant. Could it be that there are two types of British: the fair and honest ones who are the majority, while the others are sent to rule the colonies and the Mandate territories?

The British Major-General was visibly moved by the story of

the sergeant from the Jewish Brigade about his parents and little sister who were murdered, and about his older sister who had been exiled to a gulag of Siberia, while they, the two, the brother and sister, were the only ones of the whole family who survived. He was disturbed by the sergeant's exceptional request, the likes of which had not been brought to his desk throughout all the long years of his service in India, the Middle East, Italy, and France. Agitated, he rose from his armchair behind the desk filled with official papers and a battery of telephones, and vented his distress on the magnificent baroque armchair: he kicked it backwards with his heel with such fury that its four legs considered detaching themselves from the respectable seat and the Gobelins-upholstered backrest with the golden wooden frame — and to hell with Louis XIV for whom that furniture style is named!

The general stood in front of the desk and looked up at the ceiling of the large, regally decorated hall, as if asking, along with the composer of the Psalms, "From whence cometh my help?" and expecting an answer from on high. In the absence of help from the ceiling and from the higher power above it, he began to pace in agitation the whole length of the hall — from the writing desk to the elegant door and back again, his lips silently murmuring the opposite question to the one quoted in his memory from church: "How can *I* help you? How can *I* help you?"

"Did the other British Missions help you?"

"Certainly, sir. First of all, the Mission in Moscow located my sister in the Ukraine. Since 1941, after she left Siberia, I did not know where she was. Even greater than this: thanks to the Mission's intervention, my sister's right of repatriation was restored, and so she went to Poland, home as it were, except that the home no longer existed. On the strength of a leave pass I received from my commander, I went to Poland to meet her. And then the Mission in Warsaw helped me obtain a passport and visas for her. That is how we reached Paris. She already has a berth on the *André Lebon*, which sails on July 15 from Marseilles."

"And does she have an entry permit to Palestine?"

"Of course, here is the telegram confirming that." He presented the telegram he received from Jerusalem.

"If so, then everything is arranged. So what are you asking from me?"

"Because my sister is unable to travel alone after all she went through, I would like to request permission to sail with her on a civilian vessel, even though I am a soldier. The Jewish Agency will pay for the ticket."

After a moment of thought, the general returned to his armchair. His expression revealed that he had reached a decision. He called over his adjutant and dictated to him the text of a telegram. The officer instructed the sergeant to return in one week, on July 8 in the early evening, to the office next door and bring two photographs. Ankori wanted to shake the general's hand in thanks, but the difference in ranks did not permit that, unless the initiative came from the higher-ranking person. The general did not initiate a warmer farewell. After giving the order to the adjutant, he immediately buried himself in his papers, as if he had never met the Eretz-Israeli sergeant. The man of lower rank had no choice but to salute smartly, turn on his heel as in the best military exercise he recalled from Sarafend, and leave the hall. He would never again meet his benefactor, the general. His future efforts to thank him out of uniform, during his stay in London, were unsuccessful.

Only when he read the two documents, one in English, the other in French, which he received a week later in the office of the adjutant, did Ankori understand that the inner-military authorization in English had been granted by the Brigade headquarters that still existed in Ghent, Belgium, although it had no soldiers, while the French copy, addressed to the French authorities and to the ship, was signed by the Major-General with the addition of the Mission stamp and a photograph of the sergeant. And this is the order:

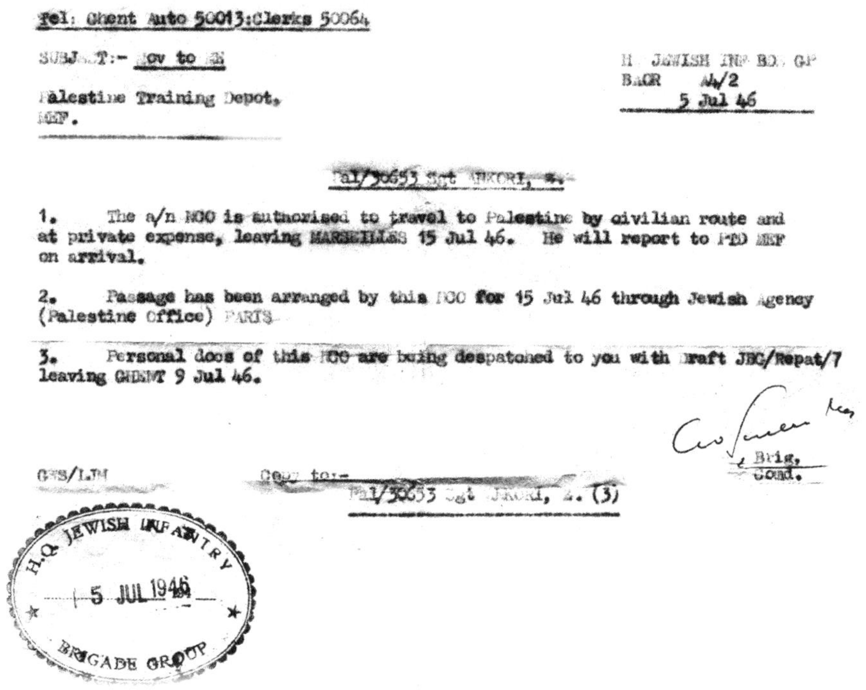

Pal/30653 Sgt. Ankori, Z.

1. The a/n NCO is authorised to travel to Palestine by civilian route and at private expense, leaving MARSEILLES 15 Jul 46. He will report to PTD MEF on arrival.

2. Passage has been arranged by this NCO for 15 Jul 46 through Jewish Agency (Palestine Office) PARIS.

3. Personal docs of this NCO are being dispatched to you with Draft JBG/Repat/7 leaving GHENT 9 Jul 46.

English document signed by Brigadier-General (name illegible)

TRANSLATION.

Tel: Ghent Auto 50013: Clerks 50064.

OBJET: Ordre de Mission pour Palestine.

HQ JEWISH INF BDE GP
BAOR  A4/2
5 Jul 46.

Palestine Training Depot,
MEF.

Pal/30653 Sjt ANKORI, Z.

1. Le Sous Officier sus mentionné est authorisé de voyager a Palestine par voie civile, et sur ses frais, quittant Marseilles le 15 juillet 1946. En arrivant il doit se presenter au PTD, MEF.

2. Le voyage pour cet Sous Officier a été arranger pour 15 juillet par L'Agence Juive (Bureau de Palestine) Paris.

3. Les documents personnels de cet Sous Officier sont "Soldiers Service & Pay Book". 3 copies de cette ordre de Mission en Anglais, et une copie en Francais avec photo.

A. G. SALISBURY-JONES,
Major-General.

French translation signed by Major-General A. G. Salisbury-Jones, with the sergeant's picture

> **MESSAGERIES MARITIMES**
>
> **FICHE DE CONTROLE** | **3ᵐᵉ CLASSE**
>
> Paquebot *André Lebon*
> Départ du *1 Juillet*
> Billet Collectif Nº-
> Nom *Mr Zwi ANKORI*
> Couchette *174*
>
> L'Agent,

Photo of travel ticket

From then on, things advanced with expected ease. Jeanne brought the military permit to the Jewish Agency clerk in charge of travel, and relying on it, the clerk immediately purchased a third-class ticket in the name of Zvi Ankori. The French copy of the permit would be presented on July 15 upon boarding the ship, and afterward would be deposited with the captain of the *André Lebon*, and "Bon voyage!"

❖ ❖ ❖

Beautiful is always the homecoming hour after six days of sailing on the summery Mediterranean Sea. After six days of sailing? No. After seven years of forced exile for Mala and five years of voluntary military service for Zvi — to both, the twilight homecoming to the foot of the Carmel was a hundred times more beautiful.

"Do you remember," Mala gushed, as if rediscovering Zionism, "how we stood here nine years ago, leaning on the rail of the *Polonia*, and counted the lights that seemed to slip down the slopes of the Carmel? It seems as if in the past few years, hundreds of new lights have been added."

It appeared that as soon as the *André Lebon* was tied to the wharf, Zvi's joy was actually diluted with sad nostalgia, in contrast to Mala's excitement at the sight of growing Haifa. "Yes," he thought aloud, "I was a youth of seventeen when I stood on the *Polonia* and saw Haifa's lights for the first time as if hypnotized, and now I am a man of twenty-six. You were the one who recalled on the ship two days ago, on July 19, that it was my birthday. On such a day one can and should search one's soul regarding the past crazy years: were they lost years for me, or did they mold image, character, and skill? Perhaps I'll write a book about it one day."

"Tomorrow we'll go to Jerusalem."

"You mean I'll have to start all over again?"

"Not necessarily. First we'll take care of your health. Then you decide: whatever you want to take from the old — take, and if you prefer to go in a new direction — go."

"Either way, it means starting all over again."

"No, it means starting to live again."

"I don't have the strength, Zvi, I am afraid...."

*EPILOGUE*
# Four Executions and One More Death

### I

All of a sudden the girl paled: "*Hesio?*" she whispered his Tarnów name. "*Is that you?*" Thus, on the first day of the war's end, in enemy country, they stood in embrace: Hesiek Wróbel and Baśka, the younger of the Fabian sisters, close neighbors in Tarnów, who had not seen each other for eight years. She had then been a child of twelve, and he a youth of seventeen about to immigrate to Eretz-Israel. Thus they stood in the center of Klagenfurt, embracing and crying.

THIS PARAGRAPH FROM one of the previous chapters ends the story that is almost unbelievable and bordering on hallucination, one of the unexpected happenings of the times. Hallucination? No, for the author himself was one of the three soldiers of 178 who, on the day of the German surrender, were the first to enter Austria in order to locate Jewish survivors, and he himself experienced the meeting with the first Jewish women he saw after the Holocaust. And, wonder of wonders, the two women, sisters, were from Tarnów, his hometown, and he and they lived and grew up on Bóżnic Street, just two houses away from each other.

After the soldiers and the women recovered from the surprise and excitement, two of the group stayed behind to guard the car and chat in German with the older sister. Ankori didn't part from the "little girl", who in the meantime had grown up and was now twenty years old, and who happily remembered and recognized him and continued calling him Hesio, as the girls used to call him then. The two went to sit down on a bench in the avenue and nostalgically bring up memories, as if they were a brother and sister who had found each other after a long separation.

At the very beginning, faithful to his mission, Zvi had told the young women that 178 would bring them over to Italy, either immediately or at any time they wanted, where they could go to one of the Jewish centers and remain there until they decided about their future. Personally (he added), he hoped they would choose to immigrate to Eretz-Israel ("illegally," as defined by the British), and he was willing to direct them to the proper address. Then came time for questions and answers, not about their wanderings or about the evil, and sometimes goodness, of humankind, but rather about childhood memories in Tarnów, in an effort to regain, at least partially, the time that had been lost. After a warm conversation, a heavy, embarrassing silence suddenly fell that was difficult to bear. The two feared the silence, even more than *the question of questions* that lurked behind the silence, and they knew only too well what it was and that it would have to be asked.

Finally, Zvi broke the silence — and asked. He asked directly, without embellishment and without going around in circles. To make it easier on Baśka, he did not allow his emotions to leave their stamp on his face.

— "What? You don't know?" — Baśka wondered, and fear filled her face because of the role that now fell on her shoulders against her will — the role of messenger of disaster and teller of a tale she wanted to forget.

— "No. In theory, that's strange. I know about the Warsaw ghetto and the other ghettos; I have worked in liberated concentration camps; I have cared for refugees and listened to their personal stories. But of what happened *in Tarnów* and of the fate of *my own parents* and the fate of *my little sister*, Gunia, I know nothing." To placate his conversation partner so she would not be afraid to hurt him with her words, he added: "Please, Basiu, don't worry about my feelings. I'm a soldier and I have seen a lot. I asked you directly, and you should also promise me that you won't spare me and will answer me directly, even if it is hard on you."

— "If so, Hesio, I will speak openly: *they are no longer alive*. Not your father, not your mother, nor Gunia. Unfortunately, I myself was an eyewitness to that act of horror."

So, not only did that day, the unforgettable May 2, 1945, bring Ankori to meet his neighbor from Tarnów who was saved from the Holocaust, but she also confronted him with first-hand testimony, chilling eyewitness testimony, cruel in her concise summary — "They are no longer alive" — of the murder of his mother, father, and little sister, in what was called in Polish jargon under Nazi influence an *Akcja* (read Aktzya) against the Jews of Tarnów. Later, he discovered that it was the first, but most brutal, of the three *Akcja*s that shattered Tarnów Jewry and left no remnant of it.

The war had apparently made Baśka more mature and wise beyond her twenty years, and she fully understood the shock that her interlocutor experienced on hearing this dreadful news. She thus waited until the frightening significance of her succinct statement penetrated his consciousness. Now, so she imagined to herself, would come the request for more details. And if so, she considered herself obligated to inform her friend of all that had taken place in Tarnów in those dark days, up to the last detail. In fact, her very statement "I was an eyewitness" sounded like an invitation to ask what she saw and when, and on her part, she would tell, yes, tell, tell everything without restraint. But contrary to what she expected, Hesio remained silent and asked nothing.

Again the intolerable, charged, depressing silence. When the silence extended beyond her endurance, Baśka tried to fill the time by recounting the history of the first period after the occupation — if only in order to talk, to continue the conversation, and not sink into the pit of silence that conjured up terrifying nightmares, fear of which never left her.

"All the Germans' steps and timing were calculated down to the last detail: first they closed the schools, the Polish ones too; then they burned or blew up all the synagogues, large and small; they ordered us to wear the 'Jewish ribbon' on our sleeves; and they appointed German commissars for each sizeable Jewish business, including my father's factory. The hooligans among them used to jump out from behind a gate and attack a Jew walking innocently in the street. They took particular pleasure in torturing Jews with beards and *peyes*, especially on the Sabbath, when they would walk to prayer services in some private house that temporarily became a synagogue. The friends of these perpetrators would photograph the "brave" acts, apparently in order to proudly send the photographs home. Once I even saw the abuse and humiliation of... No, I won't talk about it." Her partner in conversation did not pressure her. He sensed she was referring to the mistreatment of his father.

"Two things did not happen in Tarnów; a closed ghetto was not established until June 19, 1942. Earlier, however, immediately after the invasion, spacious homes in the Rynek were confiscated in order to house officers. The dispossessed, all affluent, were banished to the Jewish neighborhood. I remember that one or two were even housed in your home. And the other thing: the occupier did not damage the Jewish cemetery. This he left to the hooligans."

"Many young people, and a good number of adults, fled eastward" — Baśka continued — "mostly men. Only a few women dared to follow in their footsteps. I know that your sister Mala left — she always was brave — but I never heard about her again. We, I mean my older sister and myself, went in the opposite direction, westward, as did most of the girls with 'the right face', in other words, a *shikse* face, after they had obtained birth certificates showing that they were Polish or baptism certificates from some remote parish. The area we settled in — Klagenfurt — had an important advantage: many Yugoslavs had lived here for centuries, so it was easy for a 'Polish Slav' to mix among them undetected and find work."

Ankori listened with agitated attention, amazed at the sight of the lovely young woman sitting beside him. Back then, Baśka, a little "Smarkula", used to sit and chatter with the other girls her age on the entry steps to her house at the corner of Bóżnic and Koszarowa (Garrison Barracks) Street, practicing jacks or jump-rope as girls do. He, the "big boy", completely ignored her presence, while she apparently had her eye on the youth of seventeen, the topic of the entire street due to his upcoming journey abroad, to Eretz-Israel.

Ankori continued to remain silent. For some reason, a trivial question actually bothered him more than anything else for a moment: who are the "one or two" who were banished from their houses in the Rynek and taken into the Wróbel household, as in Baśka's story? Was it Shaul Spitz, son and inheritor of Leibchie? Perhaps Father was happy to receive him, above all out of gratitude to his departed father, patron of the young Aazik, who opened his library to him and instructed him in the ideology of Zionism. But in his youth, Father had been friends with Shaul as well, from the days of their *lernen* together with Reb Moishel Apter and in the *kloyz*. Or might it have been Reb Eltchie Baron, Father's former employer and friend from long ago? No, this was inconceivable. Such an experienced tycoon had undoubtedly found a way to get to Rumania, to his large petroleum business, and from there, with the assistance of his son, the well-known American professor, certainly continued to the United States. Who, then, were the people who came to live in the Wróbel home? And what became of them? Being at a loss to find an answer, the soldier remained silent. This time, Baśka interpreted his silence as waiting for details about the death of his parents and sister.

"It happened on June 11, 1942 (Baśka began), a Thursday. Unlike most days in the sub-Carpathian summer, there was a heat wave that day, so hot that one could faint. Of course it was not the Germans who had ordered the heat wave, but certainly the timing of the terrible act for Thursday was not coincidental, because since the beginning of the occupation Thursdays augured trouble. Accursed of all days, the Thursdays! Yet, despite the general anxiety and the fact that the residents of the Jewish neighborhood were ordered the day before not to leave their dwellings, no one (except perhaps for members of the Nazi-appointed Jewish Council and the Jewish police, who, willingly or not, collaborated with the Germans), would imagine that for this Thursday an operation of butchery unprecedented in its cruelty was being concocted in the minds of the German architects of murder. In the Nazi lexicon internalized by the victims, an operation of this type was a battle cry called *Akcja*, while among the Jewish public, the bodies of man, woman, and child shook with chills at the very mention of the term.

"In the early morning hours, all preparations for the *Akcja* had been completed, and the troopers designated to perform it had been brought in: scores of Gestapo men and units of Ukrainian collaborators (in black uniforms resembling the SS uniforms). A German military truck delivered, then went back and delivered again countless barrels of beer that were deposited in the courtyards of the Jewish houses and at their gates.

"And rightly so, for the architect of evil knew well the nature of his beast. What the uniform-wearers were expected to do on that day could be performed only in a state of complete sensory disorientation, and even the worst hooligans could not participate in the mission with a lucid mind. The beer was spilled like water, without limit, and it took an active part, even a central one, in the pogrom.

"Father (Baśka continued) urged me and my sister to take the 'Aryan papers' he had obtained for us with great effort the day before — running from place to place and obtaining them finally at great expense — and wanted us, dressed as *shikse* maids, to leave the neighborhood immediately. Unfortunately, he saw us return: the neighborhood was sealed, no one was allowed to enter or leave. Frightened, we hid in the attic above the third floor. The space was narrow and uncomfortable, but it had one advantage: Bóżnic

Street, on which you, Hesio, and I were born and grew up, sprawled at our feet in its full length and — yes, in its full terror.

"The Ukrainians, their cheeks reddened after they had poured the entire stock of beer into their guts, were even more excited than their German commanders at the opportunity to beat the Jews, torture them, and murder as many as possible. Organized into squads, they were given tasks with military precision. They began at the far end of the street, at the *mikveh* corner, and evicted the residents from their homes while screaming orders, pushing, and beating. Then they handed them over to other Ukrainians, who, using identical methods, forced the exiled Jews to run at a murderous pace to the street that turned left, while the sick and elderly kept falling on the street pavement, trampled under their brothers' feet.

"We could not see the rest from our observation point in our house, and only a few days later did we learn from those who were miraculously saved that the wretched were pushed at a run to the Rynek, forced to kneel, and most butchered on the spot, their blood flowing in two streams along the edges of Lwowska Street.

"When the Ukrainians had emptied the far houses and reached the middle of the street, the eviction operation passed to the central and northern section, including our home and yours. When we saw them, screaming and drunk (Baśka recalls, and even three years later the shadow of fear darkens her eyes), we understood that our end had come, and that this was the last time we would see our street. In the central section, the rioters went up to evict first the inhabitants of number 5, where you lived, and because our building and yours (both three stories high) were separated by just two huts and an empty lot where the country folk park their carts on market day, from the attic we could see everything that went on at the gate of your house, as if in the palm of our hands. The murderers discovered a full barrel of beer still standing at the entry to the building, and began to guzzle again, as if they were not drunk enough already. Then, with shrieks intended to frighten, whose sound reached our attic, they broke into the building. I did not recall that when your mother had opened the embroidery shop in your home, you had moved down from the second floor, where you had lived before, to the apartment on the ground floor. So I was horrified when I saw that the first man they dragged to the gate was your father. I'm sorry, Hesio, I cannot continue anymore" — she sobbed, as if witnessing at that very moment the bloody act that took place three years earlier. Speechless, her face awash in tears and averting her eyes from her Tarnovian friend, she jumped up from the bench and fled to her sister.

Ankori continued to sit riveted to the bench. Oh, how long he had awaited this story. And still, he felt that his head, unlike Baśka's, was empty of all thought, his heart lacking all feeling, his eyes dry. Suddenly he heard a woman's voice beside him. The older sister had come to finish the story:

"We saw your father standing at the gate, erect and calm, wrapped in a *tallith*, a *yarmulkeh* and *tefillin* on his head. Apparently they had caught him in the middle of the morning prayer service. The Ukrainians began to abuse him with beatings, kicks, and ridicule. But he stood like a statue and did not react, until the Ukrainians, astonished, released him and retreated backwards in fear, crossing themselves in awe. 'He is the Jewish bishop' — voices were heard. Due to the unplanned interruption, the German commander came, and when he saw his collaborators standing paralyzed, he pulled out his pistol and shot your father. Your mother began to scream, and the officer shot her, too. Lastly he shot Gunia, who screamed at the sight of her parents wallowing in their own blood."

"Perhaps death by shooting" — the sisters tried to comfort the victims' son and brother — "is preferable to the insane chase up the street to the Rynek, the humiliation of kneeling, and the beatings that the evicted suffered in the bloody square; either way, at the end of the day, most of them lay dead on the pavement of the square."

Apparently that last incident, and the sight of the Ukrainians, drunk to the point of losing their senses and exhausted no less than their victims from the murderous pace of the bloody activity from dawn until evening, convinced the German command to postpone the continuation of the *Akcja* until the next day. So the inhabitants of the last house on the street were miraculously saved, including the two young girls and their parents. All that night no one closed an eye for fear of the morning. But the murderers did not return. They moved on to another street, apparently following the advance plan for placement of the forces for the next day (since *Ordnung muss sein*, "Order must be preserved").

The *Akcja* continued for eight days. Eleven thousand people were butchered on the first day alone, and the same number perished in the seven days following. On June 19, 1942, a month that will eternally haunt the future generations, the neighborhood was closed into a ghetto. Dressed as Christian maids and equipped with "Aryan papers", the two sisters passed through the ghetto gate on their way to the unknown.

Ankori checked the pocket notebook he had received as a gift upon induction into the army, and the calendar attached to it. He often used the notebook to write down ideas for songs, while the attached calendar was rather special and rare: not only did it contain the Hebrew and Gregorian dates of the current year, as calendars usually do, but it also showed the dual dates for the five previous years and five years to come. So Zvi managed to glean the Hebrew date of the *Akcja* in Tarnów, and recorded it *the traditional way* in his notebook for eternal memory:

> Reb Aazik Wróbel, may God avenge his blood
> Golda Wróbel, may God avenge her blood
> Gunia Wróbel, may God avenge her blood
> June 11, 1942 — 27 Sivan 5702

Since then, Ankori never discovered any scrap of additional or different information aside from that terrifying testimony of the two sisters. As time passed, with no hope of discovering additional testimonies, he internalized, the sole testimony of the week-long

*Akcja* that the sisters gave him, teary-eyed, including the exact date of his family's annihilation.

The *yahrzeit* was thus marked on 27 Sivan. The Committee of Tarnów Jews in Eretz-Israel also decided on 27 Sivan as the yearly memorial date for all victims of the massacre of the Jews of Tarnów and the surrounding areas. The restraint that the son/brother placed upon himself was not violated for many years. Although he often spoke at the memorial ceremonies in Tel Aviv on 27 Sivan, and once or twice was also invited to speak at a memorial ceremony in Haifa, he never expressed his personal pain in public. He showed the same restraint when he participated in the production of a film on Tarnów Jewry. The only personal things he wrote were the four short lines, like a tombstone inscription, in his notebook on May 2, 1945, after his meeting with the two young women from Tarnów. Only the Discerner of all Secrets can know if, in caring for the refugees during the war, Ankori saw in the face of each man the image of his father's face, and in the eyes of each woman, his mother's blue eyes. And only the Discerner of all Secrets knows whether, when the soldier trained the youth of the camps, he saw on the face of every girl the face of his sister, sitting beside the youths who were listening to his words.

## II

And behold, forty years after the emotional meeting in Klagenfurt with the women from Tarnów, a letter from someone unknown to Ankori arrived from New York to his home in Jerusalem. Upon reading the address of the sender — Riverdale, the Bronx — the addressee did not know whether to laugh or succumb to nostalgia. Reluctantly, he did both. He chuckled — because from 1961–63, as a professor at Columbia University, he had lived with his wife Ora and their small daughters in an apartment in Riverdale, exactly across from the apartment building noted on the envelope. For a moment, he surrendered to nostalgia as well: for here, Gilat, their oldest daughter, had attended first grade at the school around the corner; from here they escorted Gannit, their second daughter, to nursery school each morning; and here their third daughter, Dahlia, was born. From here, Zvi used to go down to Broadway and take the subway to 116$^{th}$ Street, to his office on the pleasant urban campus of Columbia University in the heart of New York City.

But a moment later, he regained his composure, rid himself of the temptations of memory — and opened the envelope. The writer introduced himself as Martin Spett, "But in Tarnów I was Monek Szpet, or, if you prefer Yiddish, Moishele." A Holocaust survivor, after the war he had immigrated to the United States. In good time, he married and settled with his wife in Riverdale. The letter was written in English, his newly adopted language, since he said that he had forgotten Polish ("or perhaps repressed it", the recipient of the letter murmured to himself).

One Sabbath (Spett recounted), a certain neighborhood boy who had reached *bar-mitzvah* age went up to the Torah in the synagogue in Riverdale, and sang the blessings and the *haftarah* in the tune of Conservative synagogues in America. Spett then revealed to his friend, Benjamin Gumpel, who also lived in Riverdale and usually sat next to him on Sabbaths in the neighborhood Conservative synagogue, that in his mind he could still hear the tune that generations of *bar-mitzvah* boys in Tarnów had learned from Rabbi Wróbel. Despite the danger of doing so during the Nazi occupation, the rabbi, undaunted, had taught him, too, the words and the tune for his *bar-mitzvah* ceremony, and to this day he missed his rabbi and recalled him lovingly. The friend, on his part (Spett continues the story of that Sabbath), admitted that he also raises the name of his teacher at every opportunity. He also recounted — but the professor already knew what he said, for it was about him: receiving a second invitation to Columbia due to the chaos that the students' riots had caused; reinstating the chair in Jewish history; cultivating a choice group of doctoral students, today all professors and authors of historical research; conducting a university seminar in Jewish studies and Israeli current events, in which academics from outside Columbia also participated. The problem was that the professor, an Israeli, shocked by the Yom Kippur War, returned to Israel. Finally, Benjamin Gumpel revealed the main point: "The name of the professor is Zvi Ankori, and as far as I know he is also originally from Tarnów, and his Hebrew name sounds like a translation of the Polish name 'Wróbel'. Could there be a family connection here?"

From the darkness of the Holocaust, the image of his teacher rises before Spett's eyes. One Sabbath in the summer of 1940, Spett saw him returning from services, while German soldiers molested him all the way. In the evening, with the passing of the Sabbath, the youth recorded that drama by drawing the scene with ink on paper. Spett witnessed an even more frightening harassment in September of that year, when the rabbi was attacked on the way to a meeting with his pupil. Haunted by nightmares, Spett expressed his emotions in poetry. But his friend's conjecture that there was a family relationship between the two teachers would not allow him respite. Finally, he dashed off a letter to Jerusalem.

Ankori was thrilled when he read the surprising letter. The letter asked the professor to respond to the supposition raised by Gumpel, his former student at Columbia, that he was related to Rabbi Wróbel, who had been the writer's teacher in Tarnów. If the theory was correct, then Spett would send him a detailed letter about the period of his studies with the rabbi, the gloomy period of occupation, danger, and abuse of the city's Jews, abuse that touched his rabbi as well. Ankori immediately telephoned Riverdale, acknowledged that he was indeed the son of Reb Aazik Wróbel of Tarnów, and asked Spett for every scrap of additional information, even the most seemingly insignificant, about his father's life under German occupation.

But more than the letter itself, he was moved by two additional pages that he found in the envelope. He pulled out one page, on which was a poem that Spett had written in English.

In memory of Rabbi Wróbel, by his pupil:

MY RABBI

In the ember of September they came.
Like the locust, they came
To devour and destroy humanity.
The beasts of prey, as they were,
It was beyond sanity.
Sanctity and pity were unknown
To the conquerors of the innocent.
It was Shabbath morning,
With its golden aura of Autumn
Turning the leaves of the trees
To precious colors of a painter's palette.
Will the Rabbi come on this beautiful day
To teach me the *Ethics of the Fathers*?
"All the Jewish people will have
A part in the next world."
But the angel of death
Was waiting
With a drawn sword.
There he was, the man.
The gentle man of piety.
Wrapped in a *tallith*, not uttering a word —
Surrounded by the beasts
Playing him a fool,
Taking pictures of a frightened man
Whom they bounced from side to side
Laughing of their sport.
Was this his Judgment Day?
Will he have a part in the next world?

Ankori read the poem with deep emotion, and then once more.

Afterwards, he withdrew the second page from the envelope. It was a photo of an ink drawing that Spett had made after witnessing the soldiers' harassment of his teacher. In the picture, Reb Aazik stands upright, as if carved in stone, a giant compared to the two soldiers kicking him like a ball. But the rabbi, calm and strong, does not react to the abuse of his torturers. His body is wrapped in a *tallith*, and his entire being embodies a sanctity that ignores the defilement surrounding it. On his head was a black *yarmulkeh* of the type that Polish Jewish scholars used to wear in those days. For understandable reasons, Spett kept this childhood creation even after immigrating to America. Surely he showed it in public sometimes, and when he acclimated to his adopted country and language, he wrote at the bottom of the picture, for the sake of his American viewers: "Rabbi Wrubel's Tormentors".

M. Spett: "Rabbi Wrubel's Tormentors" — ink drawing
(*Tarnów, 1940*)]

The son studied the drawing for a long time, distraught. This was the first time his father's image, as it appeared in the first year of the occupation, was revealed to him in Jerusalem. He took an old photograph from before his *aliya* to Eretz-Israel, which stood as usual on his desk, and compared it with the drawing on the page. Wonder of wonders, the youth had "cloned" the likeness almost perfectly: the height, the powerful, upright body, and at the same time, the softness of the face encircled by a beard (that had lengthened since then). Here was the thin line of the eyebrows and the eyes with their direct gaze. Here was the straight nose (in contrast to the beaked nose that became the subject of anti-Semitic caricatures). And here was the high forehead and the scholars' *yarmulkeh* that concealed the bald spot. "Yes, that's how I remember Father, and that is how Spett saw him," acknowledged the professor in Jerusalem.

As a man of words, not drawings, the son attempted to compose a summary of the scene, at the center of which stands his father, tall, erect, and noble. But suddenly the little devil in his head, which often teased him and was mostly right, whispered that the wording he was considering was not his, but rather a recollection from memory of what he had heard from the Tarnovian women in Klagenfurt forty years ago. The meeting with them had been surprising and overwhelming. Just as he would never forget Spett's emotional poem and ink drawing, so the memory of the sisters' words would be preserved forever. This is what they had said:

> We saw your father standing at the gate, erect and calm, wrapped in a *tallith*, *yarmulkeh* and *tefillin* on his head. Apparently they had caught him in the middle of the morning prayer service. The Ukrainians began to abuse him with beatings, kicks, and ridicule. But he stood like a statue and did not react, until the Ukrainians, astonished, released him and retreated backwards in fear, crossing themselves in awe.

After noticing the similarity between the young women's report of the first hours of Ukrainian harassment on June 11, 1942, the harassment in the summer of 1940 depicted in Spett's drawing, and Spett's second report of harassment in his poem from September 1940, Rabbi Wróbel's Jerusalemite son was forced to ask himself about the final stage of these early incidents. The tragic end of June 1942 has already been told. But what about the persecutions of 1940 to which Spett testified: Did Reb Aazik escape his tormentors? Did the torturers tire of their mischief and retreat of their own accord? Or was it a third element that eventually ended the game? The Jerusalem resident hoped to receive answers to these questions from the initiator of the connection in Riverdale.

## III

"Despite the difficulties — characteristic of the times — mounting in our path, when we did not know what the next day would bring, my parents began to prepare my *bar- mitzvah* ceremony (Martin Spett recounts in his second letter), and invited Rabbi Wróbel to our home several times a week to teach me the text and the tune of the *haftarah*. I was pleased, but after I met my teacher and learned to like him, I became apprehensive of what would happen if the Nazis discovered, heaven forbid, that the rabbi was teaching me? All the schools had been closed, and private education had also been prohibited, on pain of death. Still, Rabbi Wróbel fearlessly kept coming and continued the *bar-mitzvah* lessons. The event was planned for December 1940. I asked my mother, how could we continue, with the danger of death hovering over our heads? Mother, completely calm, replied: 'God will help us!'

"My *bar-mitzvah* lessons thus continued. One Sabbath morning, I decided to go out to meet my teacher as he was walking toward me. When I passed the yard of his building, I froze on the spot. What I had feared had come to pass. There stood my good and noble teacher, wrapped in a *tallith*, and beside him German soldiers were kicking him and pushing him from side to side. One of the officers aimed a camera and gaily took a picture.

"When the rabbi noticed me, he cried out in Yiddish '*Antloif Moishele, Antloif!*' (Run away, Moishele, run away!) I turned on my heels and ran with all my might toward my home. I had only gone as far as the corner of the street when I heard a shot behind me. Chills ran through me when I tried to recall the incident to my parents; but my parents never told me if they heard or discovered what had happened to our beloved rabbi. Despite this, my *bar-mitzvah* took place on the planned date. The windows were covered with blankets so that the sound of the service would not be heard outside. A *minyan* quorum of ten men stood around the table, on which lay the Torah scroll, and I glanced continually at the door, hoping I would see my teacher enter the room. He had a central part in my celebration, certainly he would come. *He did not come.* I missed him and feared for his fate. Still, I read and sang the blessings and the *haftarah* without a hitch, exactly as my teacher and rabbi would have expected of me. After that I never saw the rabbi again, and my heart weeps that I will never see him."

It doesn't stand to reason that Spett was aware of the big bang he had caused with his story of the death of Reb Wróbel by shooting in December 1940. He continued to uphold his version, even when in a later letter Professor Ankori explained to him the chronological contradiction between his story and the testimony of the young women from Tarnów claiming that Aazik Wróbel was murdered on June 11, 1942, in front of their very eyes, at the beginning of the *Akcja* against the Jews of Tarnów, in other words, eighteen months later than Spett's date. Spett also repeated his story in his book, published in 2002 by the Manhattan College Institute for Holocaust Research, a Catholic institution in Riverdale, which contains his personal story during the Holocaust, as well as several of his later drawings and poems. The poem and the drawing from 1940 are not included in the book. Spett took upon himself the mission of visiting schools and colleges and speaking about the Holocaust to the generation that did not know the Second World

War or the Holocaust — a mission to which he dedicates all his time and energy, and in all his appearances, he speaks warmly of "My Rabbi".

Some time later, a third letter arrived from Spett, containing a copy of a photograph from a book on the Holocaust and a page of explanation. Apparently, while reading a book on the Holocaust, he came across a photograph depicting the type of abuse that was mainly the lot of religious Jews. In the photograph, a German officer — judging by the pistol in his belt and the club in his hand — and two of his soldiers, all three wearing military winter coats (December! Not like the summer uniforms in Spett's drawing of the first incident), are abusing an anonymous religious Jew, bareheaded against his will: his *yarmulkeh* had apparently flown off at a blow of the club by the officer, who is shown looking proudly straight at the camera (located outside the arc of the photographed event). The Jew has been forced to kneel and raise his arms high in a gesture of surrender. The frightening photograph reveals wretchedness and humiliation at their most extreme, although in fact it shows no violence; the violence is in the consciousness of the victim, who knows that it will arrive if he does not obey the Nazi. In the background, a group of Jews in their black garb is gathered. Were they brought here in order to witness the punishment of a Jew as a warning, or threat of collective punishment? Ankori, who had seen the photograph in several books on the Holocaust (including the Hebrew Encyclopedia) phoned Spett and asked for the reason of his sending the photograph. Spett threw a second bomb into the receiver:

"I recognized him at first glance: the forehead, the bald spot, the straight 'non-Jewish' nose, the eyebrows, and the eyes. *That is, beyond any doubt, Rabbi Wróbel, my teacher and rabbi! Unfortunately, professor, that was your father....*"

"Was or wasn't?" — asks Ankori, while he absorbs the chilling details of the photograph. "Before I attempt to bridge the gap between one testimony and another, I must verify that the anonymous German camera was indeed standing in Tarnów when it

FOUR EXECUTIONS AND ONE MORE DEATH 475

took the picture." The next day he checked with Yad Vashem. Yes, the photograph had been taken in Tarnów and it was preserved at Yad Vashem along with the rest of the material taken from the Germans. The photographer was anonymous, of course, and the Jew in the center of the photograph had not yet been identified. In a gesture of generosity or sympathy, the Yad Vashem laboratory sent Ankori an official copy of the photograph. But he did not seek to annul the anonymity of the victim. He was certain that his father would not have wanted to be seen in his humiliation and helplessness.

At that point, the son turned to address the contradiction between the two versions of the story.

Could it be that the girls, hidden in the attic as they watched the bloody chaos in the street below, heard the screams of both the evictors and the evicted, and feared that the *Akcja* was nearing them, were so shocked that they lost their ability to distinguish from afar the identities of the evicted?

On the other hand, was it not possible that the shooting the young Monek heard when he fled was not aimed at his rabbi but rather at himself, the fleer? The shot missed, but the frightened youth imagined that his rabbi had been injured. And what about his absence from the *bar-mitzvah* ceremony? The soldiers had apparently punished the rabbi for the warning cry to his pupil and perhaps imprisoned him for that, and thus he did not attend the ceremony. Did the soldiers' preoccupation with the camera paradoxically save the rabbi? Both versions were therefore possible, but embarrassingly, there was no way to harmonize between them. Faithful to the Sages' saying that "A man's student is called his son", the son as well as the student should recite the mourner's *kaddish*, but — woe — on different dates, one in Sivan, the other in Kislev. Were then *two* executions perpetrated on *one* man?

## IV

By coincidence, it was the *last* stage in the history of the Wróbel family during the Holocaust that the son learned *first*: the murder of the father, the mother, and the daughter; the place of the murder; and the manner in which it was carried out. The story of the tragic *end* was revealed to him when he met the two sisters from Tarnów on May 2, 1945. Only decades later, in Spett's testimony, would the scroll of history begin to roll back and uncover a small portion of the life of Tarnów Jewry during the *first* years of the occupation, and Reb Aazik's part in clandestine educational activity despite the draconian prohibitions. The destruction of all the synagogues and closure of the schools lent particular urgency to efforts to preserve, in the framework of the time-dependent limitations, the Jewish way of life, and to instill in the consciousness of the youth a reason (not in any way a justification!) for their suffering as Jews. Thus the Sabbath services continued with a *minyan* held in private houses, even though danger lay in wait for wearers of black when they walked in the street to services. On a Sabbath, a youth who had reached the age of majority might go up to the Torah and chant the *haftarah*, as befitted the *bar-mitzvah* ceremony. But the very presence of the Torah scroll in a private house (of the few scrolls that were miraculously saved when the synagogues were destroyed) could bring disaster upon the home-owner and those gathered in his house for the Torah reading. The same applied to study in preparation for the *bar-mitzvah*. There was great danger in the youth walking to his rabbi's house or the rabbi walking to his student's house, as Spett's incident witnesses. Thus secret methods were needed for Torah study and for exposing the children to the mysteries of the Hebrew alphabet. On the telephone from New Zealand, Giza, who had experienced Jewish life in occupied Tarnów, told Ankori about the "Torah underground" that his father had operated in the basement of his home, and he, the genius scholar, swallowed his pride and taught young children to read the prayerbook.

The command to study Torah is, of course, a permanent obligation under all conditions. But the command to preserve life is obligatory in the same way. "The information here" — mused the son/brother/Tarnów Jew, after long years of anticipation and fear — "much as I have awaited it, because of its self-evident importance, was not known to me before, and only now it was presented to me in a way the journalists call a 'report from the field'. Thus I learned the sad reality that prevailed in the first two years under Nazi occupation. But while those were external testimonies, what I'm missing is a *personal testimony* of members of my family, their feelings and their longings to save themselves from the vise. True, the days of escape eastward had passed and the flight there was no longer feasible. But the mail to the United States still operated, as long as that country had not declared war on Germany, and the connection with relatives there had not yet been severed. "Did my parents utilize it to try to obtain the clemency of refuge?"

In the home of Berele Wróbel (in America the name was Anglicized to Ben Wruble), in the mining town of Exeter, Pennsylvania — this was the brother who immigrated at the beginning of the twentieth century to the United States, and years later tried in vain to convince his brother Aazik in Tarnów to come join him with his family — there was an attic, and it was a treasure-trove of old, surprising objects placed there long ago and forgotten or thought lost. In the past dozen years, Sarah, Ben's eldest daughter, who continued to live in her father's house after his death, often used to go up to the attic, not actually to find a specific item, but to become intoxicated with the atmosphere of mystery there, which she recalled from her childhood days. Even so, never did she come down to the apartment empty-handed.

When she discovered that Zvi, her Jerusalemite cousin, had included in his first book a chapter on Grandfather Shloime and Grandmother Zlate, the parents of her father and of Aazik, she looked in the treasure-trove and found a precious item: a prayer book, published by the Austrian military rabbinate, that her and Zvi's grandfather had received during his service in the Austrian army a century ago and brought to America. She gave the prayer book to Zvi for keeps. Aside from that, she also took down from the attic and gave to Zvi two earthenware milking jugs that Grandmother Zlate, had used in Exeter, when her son purchased a cow for her in order to assuage her longings for her home village.

When Zvi visited Exeter again at the beginning of this century, his cousin presented him with a small yellow tin box, which still preserved a thin hint of the scent of cigars which her father used to smoke. "This is yours, Zvi."

The smell was not sharp enough to strike his nostrils, but it managed to filter into them. From the time Zvi met Uncle Ben (as he had always called Sarah's father) until this day, he remembered that the tail of an extinguished cigar regularly inhabited the corner of his lips, and the uncle who was supposed to be smoking never bothered to relight it.

At first, in Tarnów, the distant American uncle was a legendary figure in the imaginations of the Wróbel children, just as the country where he lived was distant and legendary. Only the "affidavit" episode that was repeatedly told at the end of the Sabbath had brought the man to life and anchored him within the family reality.

When Zvi made *aliya*, he was encouraged by his parents to correspond with the American branch of the Wróbel tribe. At that point, despite the distance, very close ties developed between Zvi and Ben and his children, particularly his oldest son Harold, his oldest daughter Sarah, and his youngest daughter Hannah who was exactly the same age as Zvi. They became even closer when Ben visited Israel for Passover of 1951, and the relationship was strengthened after Zvi and Ora went to the United States during Sukkot of that year. The uncle and his son met them at the airport in New York, and that very evening the four went to Exeter. Still, many years after that, with Uncle Ben no longer alive, a wicked mockery entered Ankori's mind at the sight of what he thought was an empty box and at its scent: "Couldn't Uncle have willed me a few cigars that he didn't get around to smoking before he lay on his deathbed?" Sarah guessed what her cousin was thinking: "Open the cover (she returned mockery with mockery), and look what's inside the box."

In the box, like dry autumn leaves, a dozen yellow postcards lay in disorder, the sort of pre-stamped shabby-looking postcards sold at every post office in Poland at a reduced rate. The postcards were strewn with ink letters in crowded handwriting (undoubtedly in order to contain a larger amount of text). The Nazi-ruled postal service permitted use of postcards only, not letters in envelopes. When Zvi recovered from his surprise, he saw that all the material was addressed to Ben Wruble and written in German in Golda's energetic handwriting. Although the name of the sender varied from postcard to postcard (repeating in order the names Golda, Aazik, and Gunia), the text was the same. The German censor's stamps were displayed on the front and the back.

Zvi was overcome. Finally the cache had divulged the treasure he had awaited for sixty years: *a personal written testimonial from the home in Tarnów in 1941*. The series of dates on the postcards indicated how urgent, how fear-stricken and pressured was the correspondence of the Wróbel home, isolated in Tarnów at the height of the Nazi occupation, with the major part of the Wróbel tribe in America. One postcard even rebuked what seemed to the writers in Tarnów to be their relatives' ignoring of the necessary urgency. "We know how busy you are with more important matters than ours, but please do not delay, lest your action come too late!" Was this a plea for the writers' lives or, heaven forbid, a prophecy of future calamity?

▼ ▲ Two sides of postcard from Tarnów
(specifying in its lower part the address of Mala in Siberia)

As astonishing as was the very existence of the correspondence (of which we know only the text of one partner, and even that sounds like a one-sided conversation with no hint of a reply), its content was ten times more incredible. They were in dire straits — that was the postcards' mute urgent message. Their Zionist principles, which had led Golda and Aazik to reject in earlier years the "affidavit" and the boat tickets that Ben had sent them, and their stubborn "Palestine only" declarations of yore dissolved when confronted with the fear of war and of the anti-Semitic steps that followed, and it was certain that worse would come. Escape from the city destined for a bloodbath became a question of life or death. Thus in each postcard the Tarnovian brother repeated his pleas to his brother in Pennsylvania that he should renew the "affidavit" from the past, and if it had expired, to quickly obtain a new "affidavit", so that he, Aazik, Golda his wife, and Gunia their daughter could sail to the United States and be saved from massacre. As for Mala, trapped in Siberia, the "affidavit" should be sent to the address of the American embassy in Moscow. There was no explanation of the reasons for the ideological transformation, but anyone who read the newspapers would understand that the British White Paper, in limiting *aliya* — just when opening the gates could have saved lives — had closed for this Zionist family their country of choice.

Tracing the postcard dates revealed that they stopped arriving in late 1941. Did Golda understand that there was no one in Exeter who knew how to read her German postcards? Or perhaps the entry of the United States into the war in December 1941, following the bombing of Pearl Harbor, stopped the arrival of mail from occupied Poland? Either way, their hopes faded. Not only were the gates of Eretz-Israel closed, but the only door to freedom was also locked. President Roosevelt, whom the Jews idolized, wrapped himself in silence, indifferent to their distress.

Wonder followed wonder! Hours passed, and in his imagination the son — "mama's boy" — accompanies his mother's emotion as she pours her heart into the ink of the letters and carefully composes each sentence, each phrase in clear German, and Father and Gunia who stood beside her were also struck with emotion, and her belief was their belief, and her illusion was their illusion. When he gazed at the handful of yellowed postcards, the son felt that he was embracing his mother with silent compassion and commiserated with her, placing into these cards all hopes to save lives — the life of Aazik, the life of Gunia, and her own life. But it turned out that from the outset, writing in German was a useless endeavor, as if the mother was writing to herself. Oh, how sad, how unrealistic and tragic was that box — a grave of correspondence that no one could understand or ever bothered to glance at again — a memorial to groundless hopes and the loss of those who cherished them.

## V

Indeed, hours passed and the son had still not finished his perusal of the postcards, although their content repeated itself from card to card: he checked them one by one and studied each postcard to himself, then read each sentence out loud, as if trying to show that the words were crying out to heaven. Suddenly — wonder of wonders! — underneath the last postcard his fingers felt a different touch of paper: an envelope! Four envelopes! He drew them out of the box, and the logo on them was even more surprising than the fact of their presence: COLUMBIA UNIVERSITY in the City of New York. The addressee of all four: Mr. Harold Wruble, Ben's son, a lawyer, writing in his father's name and sending his request from his office in Wilkes-Barre, a town adjoining Exeter.

The wonder continued. Three of the letters were signed by none other than Salo W. Baron, the greatest Jewish historian of his time, holder of a chair at Columbia and the man who, after the State of Israel was established, would found and direct the Center for Israel and Jewish Studies at Columbia.

The topic of the first two letters, as revealed by the replies, was seemingly simple: Ben's desire to send a package to Mala, who had fled just after the outbreak of the war to Lvov in Eastern Galicia, which under agreement with the Reich became part of the Ukraine in the Soviet Union. We can assume that in a marginal mining town like Exeter, it was difficult to contact the company that made the deliveries, and therefore Ben's son turns to Professor Baron in New York and asks for his advice. And another wonder: Professor Baron is willing to take the task upon himself, but Ben does not have Mala's address. As early as February 19, 1940, while Mala is still in Lvov, Baron presses Ben to give him the address immediately, because there is an order from the USSR to stop deliveries. A request from the professor was no small matter. Indeed, a miracle: Baron obtains an extension. But in July of that year, Mala is deported to a Soviet gulag in Siberia, and again there is no address.

Thus in the letter of February 27, 1941 — in other words, a year after his first letter — Baron informs Harold that he is returning the money Ben had entrusted to him in order to purchase an aid package for Mala. The sending of aid packages to the USSR has been irrevocably cancelled.

**Columbia University**
**in the City of New York**

DEPARTMENT OF HISTORY

January 13, 1942

Mr. Harold R. Wruble
110 Lincoln Avenue
Exeter Boro, Pa.

Dear Mr. Wruble:

First let me express to you and your family my heartfelt sympathy at your recent bereavement.

I am sorry to say that I have not heard from my family for over a year and, as far as I know, nobody has heard from Poland during 1942. The situation there is terrible, but there is no way of getting in touch with the Jews in Poland, except perhaps through the International Red Cross. You might request that organization to locate Eisik and his family for you. It takes at least six months before you will get a reply, but it would be better than nothing.

With kindest regards, I am,

Very truly yours,

Salo W. Baron

Letter from Prof. Salo Baron to Ben's son

Throughout 1941, Golda's postcards begin to flow from Tarnów, and they contain Mala's address in Siberia, similar to that which Golda dispatched to her son via the Red Cross. Ben does not know how to read them, but at any rate, it is too late. Towards the end of 1941, the postcards stop arriving. This fact disturbs Ben, for although he did not understand the content of the postcards, their very arrival was a sign of life. And now (he wonders), what does their absence signify? Worried, in late 1941 Ben rushes a letter to Columbia through his son — that is what emerges from Baron's reply of January 13, 1942, the third and last letter with his signature. This is the first time that the reticent Baron does not restrain himself from taking a personal tone.

It is not clear whether Ben took Baron's advice and contacted the International Red Cross, while knowing he would have to be patient, to gnaw on his fingernails and wait six months or more until receiving a reply from this organization. It is also unclear whether Baron himself contacted the International Red Cross, as he advised Ben to do. Either way, the two correspondents never imagined that not six but only five months would pass until the families of them both would no longer remain alive.

Four and a half years — with the war having already ended a year previously — would pass since the first letter, until Ben would receive another letter in the familiar Columbia envelope, this time not from Baron himself but at the initiative of Miriam Brownstone, his secretary. The secretary — who had in the past received and filed letters from Harold Wruble, the regular correspondent with Professor Baron on behalf of father Ben in Pennsylvania, and typed the text of the replies that Baron dictated to her — immediately realized the importance and urgency of the information contained in the letter that had arrived on July 29, 1946 from Europe to Baron's office, in his absence. Because she knew that it would be some time until the professor returned from his travels, she decided on her own initiative to pass on to Harold Wruble that very same day selections from the European message relevant to him and his family, and sent Harold a letter, the fourth from Columbia.

**Columbia University**
**in the City of New York**
[NEW YORK 27, N.Y.]

DEPARTMENT OF HISTORY

July 29, 1946

Mr. Harold R. Wruble
45 Bennett Bldg
Wilkes Barre, Pa.

Dear Mr. Wruble:

You may know that Professor Baron is away on an extended journey through South Africa, Europe and Palestine. Today a letter arrived from a friend of his who is connected with the J.D.C. in Europe. I think you will be interested in the following excerpts.

> "Yesterday a man came to see me about certain things and on talking with him I discovered he came from Tarnow. I asked him about your family. He said he knew them all. His name is Meyer Bodner, son-in-law of Joseph Henig, who owned a hair factory in Tarnow. According to this man your parents, Saul Spitz and Eisig Wrubel were all shot together with 11,000 Jews in Tarnow on the 27th of Sivan, i.e. June 11, 1942. He seemed pretty positive when I pressed him....."

Your father, may have received this news long before, but I thought that you might perhaps wish to have additional confirmation. To quote the writer of the above excerpt "... if you wish to oberve a Yahrzeit you now have a date. This is the most one gets now about missing people."

Very truly yours,

Miriam A. Brownstone
Secretary to Prof. Baron

Letter from Miriam Brownstone, Baron's secretary

The report that Eltchie Baron, Shaul Spitz, and Aazik Wróbel "were all shot together with 11,000 Jews in Tarnów", in other words, during the mass slaughter of the first *Akcja* in the Rynek — a report different from that which the sisters and Spett had given — shocked Ankori. The equivalence of the date lost its significance in light of the humiliation and the murder. In nightmares, he saw his father kneeling like in the photograph, multiplied 11,000 times by brutal force, but unlike in the photograph, he falls like everyone else on the pavement of the square.

The son of Golda and Aazik thus understood that for good reason the wondrous box had remained for decades in the deceased Uncle Ben's attic, and in it, a treasure of family history waiting for the son of the next generation to discover and give it expression. Now, the box commanded him to mourn *a third execution, in addition to the two in the street — the one as in the sisters' report, near the gate of their home, and the one, a year and a half earlier, as written by Spett — and this one, the third*, in the Rynek, was the cruelest of all.

## VI

Letters to Baron? Ankori wondered, astonished that his relatives dared to bother the professor with their problems, surprised at the professor's willingness to take upon himself such a seemingly trivial item as the sending of a package and to correspond on the matter from his office at the university. We must not assume that Ben or Harold, residents of a small town in Pennsylvania, had ever seen or exchanged words with the honored professor who lived in New York. Yet Baron understood that the issue was not at all insignificant and might be a matter of life and death, which overrode not only the Sabbath (as the Sages decreed) but also skimming a seminar paper of some student that would be kind enough to wait a bit. And was it perhaps the sense of brotherhood with those hurt by the war and deprived of any information regarding the fate of their families in Tarnów, including Baron's own, as he revealed in his last letter to Ben, that inspired, on the one hand, daring in the hearts of Ben and Harold Wruble to contact the well-known Tarnovian Jew and ask for his advice? Or was it the same sense of brotherhood that imbued the professor with willingness to render assistance, and raise it to the top of his daily agenda? Although the influence of these factors was great, each one alone and all together, the most important and decisive one was the link that joined the two parties even though they had never met face to face. That uniting link had a name — *Aazik Wróbel* — the older brother of Ben, who had immigrated to America; Aazik, who remained in Tarnów, had not seen Ben for more than forty years.

For the first nine years after Aazik — a village youth far from his family, alone, without a friend and without a home or bed on which to rest his head at night — came to Tarnów to study rabbinics, closed himself up behind the gloomy walls of the *kloyz*, which was his study hall and his synagogue, and which supplied a wooden bench in the back corner for bone-breaking sleep. Finally, pressured by the vise of the *kloyz* fanatics and their loathing of Zionism, he felt that despite his indebtedness to it, in the new hostile environment the *kloyz* was no longer suitable for him.

The twentieth of the Jewish summer month of Tammuz 5664 (1904) was the watershed that changed his life. The telegram that arrived that day from Vienna hit the Zionist community of Tarnów like thunder on a clear day: *Herzl was dead*, only forty-four years old. It seemed to everyone that in the heat of day and the burning sunlight of Tammuz, a giant bank of frost suddenly shrouded street and house, and froze the blood of the city and the blood of its Zionist residents.

With the telegram came the big bang. In contrast to the mourning, the anti-Zionists in the *kloyz* burst out in malicious joy, noisy and nauseating, and even the young scholars, Ankori's study-mates, continued to sit in sickening indifference, bent over their books of Talmud as the day before, pretending that nothing had happened. "This is the time for action" — Aazik declared, and closed his Talmud book, thumping the two covers of the tractate against each other, as if to say: *The End*. And ignoring the astonished looks of those present, he abandoned the lectern of honor at the corner of the podium, which had been granted to him long ago — a gift to the rabbinic prodigy for his scholarship — and with decisive steps, left the *kloyz*…

But only after the act did the practical questions begin to occupy Aazik's mind. In which direction was he headed? For no longer was he the village ignoramus of fourteen who, in 1895, with his mother's encouragement, left the remote Carpathian village for Tarnów, city of Torah scholarship; rather, he was a scholar of twenty-three, for whom years of intentional confinement between the pages of the Talmud had earned him a reputation as the "city *ilui* (prodigy)", and the title "Reb" appended to his name. Thus his mother's dream was fulfilled, that at least the oldest son of her family, a family of cavalrymen and horse merchants, would be a Torah scholar. But what of the son himself?

The gnawing questions following the spontaneous departure were too heavy to bear. What must he do and how should he react to the unfortunate split in the *kloyz* whose true self was revealed with the news of Herzl's death? How should he behave considering the unavoidable personal rift between himself and the fanatics? Perhaps the time had come, after nine years, to abandon the *kloyz* altogether? Or was it better not to burn all the bridges, but allot time in the *kloyz* only for study, and give up his privileged lectern and not so privileged sleeping bench. Thus he would free himself of all obligations toward the institution. And if he actually decided to abandon the *kloyz* altogether, as indeed was his inclination, then where would he go? Where would he find shelter in this city, known for the glory of its Torah scholarship but also for its shameful alienation of non-locals?

Yet the twentieth of Tammuz was not only the day when the watershed line was crossed in the story of Aazik's relationship with the *kloyz* and its fanatics, but also the day that miraculously brought an answer to his painful inner struggle and a solution to the difficult practical problems involved in leaving the *kloyz*. The redeeming angel was Reb Leibchie Spitz (known to the secularists as Herr Leon Spitz), a Tarnovian Zionist activist on the dividing line between the waning proto-Zionist "Hovevei Zion" period in the late nineteenth century and the dawning of "Herzlian" Zionism in the beginning of the twentieth century. It was his son Shaul who introduced to him Aazik, a friend and companion in Talmud study at the *kloyz* — this was the Shaul Spitz who was one of the three mentioned in the letter to Baron as a victim of the slaughter of June 11, 1942. A warm relationship developed between the elder Zionist activist of the city and the brilliant youth from the country, despite the age difference between them. Leibchie welcomed the lonely Aazik and invited him to his home for Sabbaths, and when he realized his talents and his desire to learn, he opened his rich library to Aazik and slowly began to serve as an advisor to him, treating him like his son. Indeed, Aazik needed advice and guidance at this time of crisis, and who if not Leibchie would give it to him. In a supreme effort, the youth succeeded in pushing through the swarming masses that filled the synagogue and the adjoining street in a spontaneous memorial to Herzl, and joined his patron.

"You came at the right time" — Leibchie surprised Aazik, before the latter managed to open his mouth and recount his doubts and difficulties. "I think a solution to your problem is about to materialize, and it is really within reach." The good friend must have deduced the distress of the innocent Torah scholar, or perhaps he recalled his own youthful experience, when he had also abandoned the *kloyz* and felt like he had just been born and did not know how to face the unknown reality outside the *kloyz* confines. Arm in arm, the two friends paced in silence toward the Rynek, where Leitchie lived. They stopped at the eastern side of the square, across from two large buildings that looked like twins. The first house, an older one, belonged to the wealthy Herschel Wittmayer, an importer of exotic fruit and spices that were called "colonial". The twin house was new, and belonged to Reb Elchie Baron, Wittmayer's son-in-law. A wealthy man on his own terms, Baron came from Eastern

Galicia, where he owned several petroleum wells, while in Tarnów he worked as a private banker and dedicated his time and energy to public affairs. "If it works out" — Leibchie declared, pointing to the Baron home — "this is the house in which you will live after you leave the *kloyz*."

Leibchie spoke quietly, almost in a whisper, as if revealing a deep secret in his friend's ear or as if apprehensive of the evil eye: "My friend and neighbor, Elchie Baron, whom you see each Sabbath sitting at the eastern wall of the *kloyz*, is searching for a teacher-companion to join his nine-year-old son Shulim. I told him at once, 'I have the right man for you.' He invites you to visit him this afternoon to become acquainted." To Aazik, there was something symbolic in the fact that precisely on the day of mourning — which in all aspects seemed to him a turning point in the life of the nation and in his private life — his patron had sent him this important message.

That very same day, Baron interviewed Aazik and found him to be a kindred spirit and suitable for the position.

Shulim was diligent and gifted, and his parents spared no amount of money or effort to develop his talents. He enrolled in school as was obligatory, but never sat on a school bench like other children his age, but rather — as did the wealthy, and particularly observant Jews — private teachers taught him in his home the subjects that were taught in school. Twice a year the boy was required to take external exams in the material studied in his age group's class. Now, as he approached high school age — eight years prior to university entrance exams and eight years before studies for rabbinical ordination — his father decided that this was the time to plan his son's pre-rabbinic education, as he valued equally the two goals: high-level general studies and high-level Jewish studies.

Therefore, concurrently with private teachers of general studies, the family decided to hire another private teacher who would prepare Shulim for the entrance exams to the Vienna Rabbinical Seminary, the most important institution of the kind in Europe. Thus the son would study simultaneously in two institutions of higher education in the imperial capital, and perhaps when he finished his studies (so the father hoped), he would be appointed city rabbi of Tarnów.

But this time — Shulim's parents thought — it was not enough to hire a private teacher on an hourly basis, who would come, give his lesson, and leave for home. Because the boy had never studied at school and had no friends, he needed a teacher-companion, who would share his room and through shared living conditions would develop ties of friendship, and not just instruction, with his student.

# VII

"A new period is now beginning for me" — Aazik rushed to write to his mother in Wisłok, and to make her happy, he wrote in large letters his city address, the first address he ever had: Herrn ELIAS BARON (für H. WRÓBEL), RYNEK 14, TARNÓW. (In the village, the single long street that stretched from one end of the village to the other had no name, and the houses were not numbered; it was enough to write the name of the addressee, and the mailman would know where that person lived.) In the same letter the son asked his mother for the address of his brother Berele, who had immigrated to America three years previously. Sitting on a comfortable chair beside a proper table, on which lay a folder with sheets of writing paper, envelopes, and rolls of two types of stamps, to Austria proper (including Galicia) and to the United States, encouraged the correspondence, which was almost impossible under the conditions of the *kloyz*. So the connection with the mother continued more intensively, and a warm exchange of letters began between the two brothers.

Berele, like his parents and other siblings, had never been to Tarnów, and this was the first time he had heard the name of Baron. Over the years, Aazik's letters would recount to his brother many details about the Baron home, about his hosts Elchie and Minna (née Wittmayer), and about their son Shulim, until it would seem to Berele that he knew them intimately, although he had never met them in person.

"A new period is now beginning for me" — the opening line of Aazik's first letter to Berele repeated the first line he had written to his mother. "Yes, a new period has begun not only in my life and in the life of my student, but, to a certain extent, in the lives of the boy's parents as well. They have welcomed me into the bosom of their family, and integration into the Baron home has offered me advantages that until now I did not imagine existed.

"See, Berele, how the wheel turns. After nine years of scarcity, during which I lived without a home, had one meal a day — the secret charity of the rabbi's daughter from the leftovers of her father's table — and slept at night on a rickety wooden bench in the back corner of the *kloyz*, now with my entry into the Baron home I am enjoying living conditions the likes of which I never knew before for comfort.

"From now on, I live in a room shared with my young pupil, enjoying as he does regular meals on weekdays, as well as a sumptuous meal every Sabbath and holiday. I sleep as he does on a soft bed, between white sheets, covered with a light blanket, and in winter both of us will receive warm feather quilts, like the one I imagine you, Berele, also cover yourself with on cold nights in America. Furthermore: my schedule in the *kloyz* prevented me any opportunity at the end of a day of *lernen* (meaning a late hour, after midnight) to share on my sleeping bench impressions and experiences with my fellow scholars: they had returned to their homes long before. But from now on, I can converse with my pupil-friend in an enjoyable, friendly chat before sleep, or fall asleep with a book in my hand, without fear of the yeshivah supervisor, who made sure I did not read anything the *kloyz* called 'forbidden literature'.

"When, before this amazing transformation, did I sleep like this? When, before your immigration to America, did you sleep like this? When in Wisłok did we both sleep like this? Come, let's answer honestly: never. There is no shame in poverty, and what's more, because of the poor quality of the land, the Ukrainians and the Slovaks in that part of the village lived in similar conditions. In our childhood, a soft bed was not even a dream, because we did not know that it existed. In the corner of the one-room hut — have we forgotten? — there was only one bed, that belonging to our parents, while we, the children, would wrap ourselves up on the large stovetop, like the peasant children. The warm embers that collected in the bottom of the stove kept the heat in the cast-iron sheets that covered the stove. Still, we were thrilled and proud that our father was a cavalryman in the imperial guard of Franz Joseph."

Until one day, in 1912, after eight years of sharing the room with Shulim, who grew up and became a young man, and passed all the exams with great success, Aazik informed Berele that Shulim had left home and studied for one year at the University of Kraków, and after that switched to Vienna, to the university and the Rabbinical Seminary, as his parents had planned, and never returned to his native city. But in contrast to his father's hopes, the son had no interest in the rabbinate. Shulim — now using a German name, Salo W. Baron — chose the academic life: first he taught in Vienna, and fifteen years after leaving Tarnów, he was offered a teaching position in the United States and was eventually appointed professor of Jewish history at Columbia University in New York. Aazik never saw him again.

Although Aazik's original pedagogical role ended and what was left for him was to follow from afar the progress of his student in the big world, the connection with the Baron home in Tarnów was not sundered. The former teacher was asked to assist the senior Baron in his community activities and was invited to continue living in the room in which the junior Baron had once slept. All that time, Aazik informed his brother of his doings, and in addition, of the goings-on in the Baron household in Tarnów, and thus it was no wonder that Berele considered himself familiar with this special home, as if he had lived there together with his brother. Possibly, this feeling of seeming acquaintance, no less than the other factors listed above, was what eased the brother's decision to contact Baron junior when the Second World War began.

In June 1914, when Aazik married Golda Weinmann, he left his room, which he had enjoyed for nine good years, as opposed to the nine years of wretched conditions in the *kloyz* — he left the room, but not the Baron home. The couple rented a modest apartment on Bóżnic Street, and there, in the first and only apartment they ever rented, they remained for the rest of their lives. Yet the relationship with the Baron family that Aazik had developed before his marriage was preserved afterwards. All his life, Aazik treated Elchie with respect and love, as a son loves his father. In fact, even during the lifetime of Shloime Wróbel, his biological father, whom Berele brought from Wisłok to America, Aazik considered Shulim's father as one who acted as a father to him, *in loco parentis*, and returned his love with love. The warm ties between the Wróbel and Baron homes in Tarnów — and especially between Aazik and Reb Elchie — deepened each year and grew ever stronger with Golda's custom of sending Aazik to Elchie every Friday to fetch that week's batch of newspapers to which the latter subscribed and which he had finished reading.

The two friends could not know that the day would come when death would also unite them, and that nine years after their deaths, the second generation, Shulim son of Elchie, and Herschl son of Aazik, would begin in 1951 a new cycle, although they knew each other in name only. Far from Tarnów, on the soil of America, the warm relationship between the two homes would be renewed in unique circumstances and in a new and dramatic reincarnation that the fathers never imagined. Aazik's son, who made *aliya* to attend the Hebrew University in Jerusalem and Hebraized his name to Zvi Ankori, earned a fellowship for doctoral studies at Columbia University under the direction of Salo Baron. And so, the one who had once studied Torah with Aazik taught his teacher's son.

Years later, when the time came for Professor Baron to retire, the former doctoral student (and later professor holding a chair at another university) was asked to take over Baron's chair and direct the Center for Israel and Jewish Studies at Columbia. Elchie had fifteen years to derive pleasure from his son's success. Aazik did not have that opportunity, unfortunately...

# VIII

June 11, 1942, which was 27 Sivan 5702 according to the Jewish calendar — the first day of the first Nazi *Akcja* that mercilessly slaughtered in one week, the majority of the Jews of Tarnów — more than any of the other days of horror in the Tarnów massacre reserves a place for itself in eternal disgrace for its brutality and for its number of victims (11,000 Jews in one day). For this reason, the Israel Committee of Tarnów Jews and the committees in other communities of the new Tarnovian diaspora decreed 27 Sivan as the yearly memorial day. This date is undoubtedly correct for most of the dead. Yet it is natural for the individual to search for and observe the exact date of the murder of his family. This is what Ankori did then, and this is what he continues to do even sixty years later. In the two testimonies about the murder of his father Aazik — that of the Fabian sisters as they told it in Klagenfurt to their fellow-Tarnovian the soldier, and that of the Joint representative's letter to Professor Baron, which included Aazik among the victims of that day — the dates overlapped and fit information researched by Dr. Chomet, the last leader of Tarnów Jewry, and published in his *Tarnów Memorial Book*. Ankori thus regarded the agreed date as the family date also, even though Martin Spett's story, which advanced the date of the murder to December 1940, continued to disturb him.

 The writing of the epilogue of this book was coming to a close. And yet, cautiously, the author still restrained within the depths of his soul the sigh of relief and satisfaction of successful completion of seven years of writing, despite the constant struggle with the recalcitrant computer. The illusion of the end and the anticipation of the long-awaited celebration of the achievement were suddenly deflated by a telephone call: Millek Korn was on the line. A Tarnów native and childhood friend, Millek had supportively accompanied through the years, stage by stage, the growth of this book, from its beginning until the almost-completed epilogue.

The telephone message astonished the listener on the other end with its urgency: "Zvi, stop!" — Millek's voice rose from the receiver, perhaps advising, perhaps warning — "You should delay the final chord until you read two pages of text I Xeroxed from a book and am sending to you. I also attached the title page, in case you want to peruse the entire book. You should know that the book can be found only in the Yad Vashem library. The material I've sent you will probably reach you in a day or two."

The new material arrived. At first glance at the title page, Ankori wondered at Millek's urgency. Truth to tell, he did not know what to expect. The subject detailed on the title page was important in and of itself, and addressed the massacre of Jews in Jasło, a picturesque little town on the Wisloka River that flowed north to the Wisla, and a distance of a one-hour bus ride from Tarnów on the road from the north.

But what virtue could he find in this book, a copy of whose title page he had just received? The book was one of many volumes in the series of publications of "The Chief Commission for Investigating Nazi Crimes in Poland". In the years since the end of the war, several such studies were published in this and similar series, and would that more like them appear, until the greatest crime against humanity that cast its shadow on the twentieth century was revealed in all its detail. The title of the book echoed Emile Zola's cry, in a kind of contemporary Polish version of *"J'accuse"*:

*Jasło Accuses —*

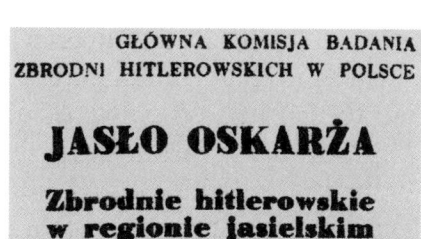

GŁÓWNA KOMISJA BADANIA
ZBRODNI HITLEROWSKICH W POLSCE

**JASŁO OSKARŻA**

**Zbrodnie hitlerowskie
w regionie jasielskim
1939-1945**

the title shouted bitterly, and the subtitle explained: "The crimes of Hitler's regime in the Jasło region, 1939–1945". Ankori knew that the Nazi crimes, the abuse, the punishments, and the murders that struck the Jews of Jasło and its environs were similar to those that took place in Tarnów. So what did Millek want to tell him by urgently sending him this material? Could it be that the book revealed cooperation between the Gestapo of Jasło and the Gestapo of Tarnów regarding the timing and method of their murderous operations?

Only when he began to read the first page of the text proper did Ankori realize that the cold, factual page, which recorded with no sentimentality or literary embellishment a list of Nazi crimes from the year of extermination, 1942, took him to another sphere and revealed a different aspect of the Nazi slaughter. Unlike the *Akcja*s that assailed the Jews of cities with large populations, such as Tarnów, in the countryside that stretched between Jasło and Tarnów, which was part farmland and part forest, a constant and cruel death hunt was in progress for lone Jews and isolated Jewish families who sought shelter in the area. They hid in forests or secretly were given shelter in the farmed region by individual Poles — in cowsheds, pigsties, or pits dug for them and expertly camouflaged. At night, someone from the house would sneak to the hiding place with a jug of water and potato dish. In these villages — some small, not appearing on any map, and known only to their immediate vicinity, and some large, which irritated the occupier with acts of sabotage and even face-to-face battle, such as that which broke out in the village of Swoszowa in 1940 — individual Poles, men of conscience and spiritual courage, rose up, ignoring personal danger (from the Nazi sword, or, yes, from the tongues of Polish neighbors), covered up for Jews, and saved quite a few. Silently they performed the rescue work, and thus, silent, unaware, they unwittingly earned themselves a place in Jewish history and on the list of Righteous Gentiles at Yad Vashem. Here are a few incidents of extermination from 1942 listed on that page:

* *"In Łubno forest — the page recounts — the Nazi police executed by shooting a Jewish family — two adults and a child. At the same time, in the village of Łajsce, a Jewish couple was shot to death, and their child beaten to death with a stick. This Jewish family hid at the farm of a local peasant. The corpses were buried in the forest."*
* *In the village of Kowalowe, the Gestapo of Jasło shot to death three Jewish women from the village of Skurowa."*
* *In the village of Szerzyny, the Gestapo and the Nazi police from Jasło shot to death forty-one Jews, among them ten children and eighteen women. As a warning against providing shelter to Jews, three men were hanged and five Poles were shot to death, among them four men and one woman."*

But the longest paragraph on the page hit the reader like a bombshell. Millek was correct in his alarm.

Oh, how much labor the author had invested in the thirty pages of the epilogue in order to reconstruct the three versions of the story of his father's execution, so that he felt they were not three variations of one and the same story, but rather three stories of three executions that annihilated his father.

Now came a fourth report; there is no doubt regarding the authenticity of the facts officially narrated therein, and furthermore, bearing the formal authorization of the Polish National Investigation Commission. And — woe! Suddenly, this last report turns the previous reconstruction on its head, and alas, it raises questions, questions, and more questions that drive one crazy.

Here is the report:

* *"In 1942, in the village of Swoszowa, Hitler's police murdered nine Jews. The young girls Feigenbaum and Szlama, Mr. and Mrs. Fratner from the village of Czermna, and two others, whose last names were not verified, were executed by hanging. A Jew from Tarnów — Assistant Rabbi Wróbel — and the Jew Chmajda from the village of Ołpin were also executed by shooting. The bodies*

*were buried on the site of execution. In 1946, the corpses were exhumed from their graves and transferred for burial in the Jewish cemetery in Biecz, Gorlice district."*

> W 1942 r. w Swoszowej policja hitlerowska zamordowała 9 osób pochodzenia żydowskiego. Powieszono dziewczęta: Feigebaum i Szlamę, mężczyznę i kobietę Fratner z Czermnej oraz dwie osoby o nie ustalonym nazwisku. Zastrzelono też Żyda z Tarnowa — podrabina Wróbla — i Żyda Chmajdę z Ołpin. Zwłoki pochowano na miejscu egzekucji. W 1946 r. zwłoki ekshumowano i przeniesiono **na cmentarz** żydowski w Bieczu, pow. Gorlice.

The mention of burial in Biecz allowed hope for additional information: did the tombs bear full names, not just last names? Perhaps they noted the exact date of the murder? Ankori called his friend Adam Bartosz, director of the regional museum in Tarnów, who had done much to disseminate knowledge of Tarnów Jewry's past and to commemorate the community's annihilation in the Holocaust. This was his reply:

> "I visited the cemetery in Biecz. There is nothing left there. The Germans destroyed all the tombstones. Today only an empty plot remains, surrounded by a fence."

Bartosz then relates that after the war, a memorial was erected in the cemetery, and at its top is a Hebrew inscription in memory of the victims of extermination by the Nazis. Underneath is a memorial inscription in Polish. In addition, symbolic plates, emulating large flat tombstones, were cast in concrete, to represent the graves. One original inscribed tombstone remained from the time of the disturbances, before the mass destruction began. The tombstone is a large, flat plate, like the new, anonymous plates that were designed to emulate it. While it was dragged, the original plate broke into three pieces and, being useless, was abandoned and forgotten. The inscription, engraved on it in an unskilled hand, commemorates a woman who hid in a bunker and was murdered. Unlike Bartosz, Ankori remarks that the Germans were not in the habit of destroying tombstones, nor did they have any interest in taking possession of them for reuse. This was done by the Poles (and citizens of other countries), who used the stone in construction and tiling. Bartosz attached photographs to his letter and sent them to this writer in Jerusalem.

Biecz Jewish Cemetery (*photographed by: Adam Bartosz, 2006*)

The hopes that Ankori placed in Biecz were not fulfilled. The Hebrew inscription at the top of the memorial refers only to the victims of Biecz, and ignores those brought to burial from outside; the burial site of the victims brought to Biecz from Swoszowa was also unmarked. Was a mass grave dug without the indication of names? Was the memorial actually placed on top of a mass burial pit, and no one thought to investigate and list the names of the buried? Had the bullet-ridden bones of the assassinated Rabbi Wróbel of Tarnów found their resting place there? Despite the generous assistance of the museum director, who of his own initiative photographed the cemetery in Biecz, Ankori remained alone in his grief, the questions ceaselessly grating in his brain.

He decided to ignore the seemingly trivial difficulty of the Polish report from Jasło, in which the title "assistant rabbi" was given to "the Jew Wróbel from Tarnów". The writer had apparently erred due to lack of knowledge regarding the difference of opinion among Tarnów Jewry. Reb Aazik Wróbel, the only Torah scholar by that name in Tarnów, had rejected this title due to his literal interpretation of a saying from *Ethics of the Fathers*, "Despise the rabbinate". Indeed, several times during his youth in Tarnów, his son had witnessed how his father shrugged off the fact that Christians related to him as an *uczony yevrey* (learned Jew) and called him *Pan Rabin*, as Hohorowski used to do, only because he was a Jew with a beard who wore black, as was traditional. But the text was also objectively wrong: no one in Tarnów had occupied the position of "city rabbi" since the death of Rabbi Meir Arak in 1925. At any rate, there was no "assistant" to the non-existent "rabbi".

But aside from the issue of the title, the pressing questions remained unanswered, and they were transformed diabolically into terrifying images that returned on sleepless nights and gripped the son as if choking him. Here, in December 1940, on a Sabbath morning, his father falls under punishing fire in the city street after horrifying abuse; here a volley of shots at the gate of the house, on the accursed morning of June 11, 1942, again cleaves the body of the father and the bodies of the mother and daughter; and again, later that day, they are killed a third time in horrible deaths in the *Akcja* in the Rynek; and now, for the fourth time, away from Tarnów, in the village of Swoszowa, the father is executed by a firing squad of the Hitlerite police. And where were the mother and daughter, who surely were deported or fled together with the husband/father? The report relates that the rest of the prisoners, all from Swoszowa and its environs, their names known, were hung. Only two of those hanged were unidentified. In his nightmares, the son imagines the Carpathian wind shaking two bodies on ropes. He goes out of his mind: could the unidentified hung bodies — unidentified, because they were not locals — be his mother and sister?

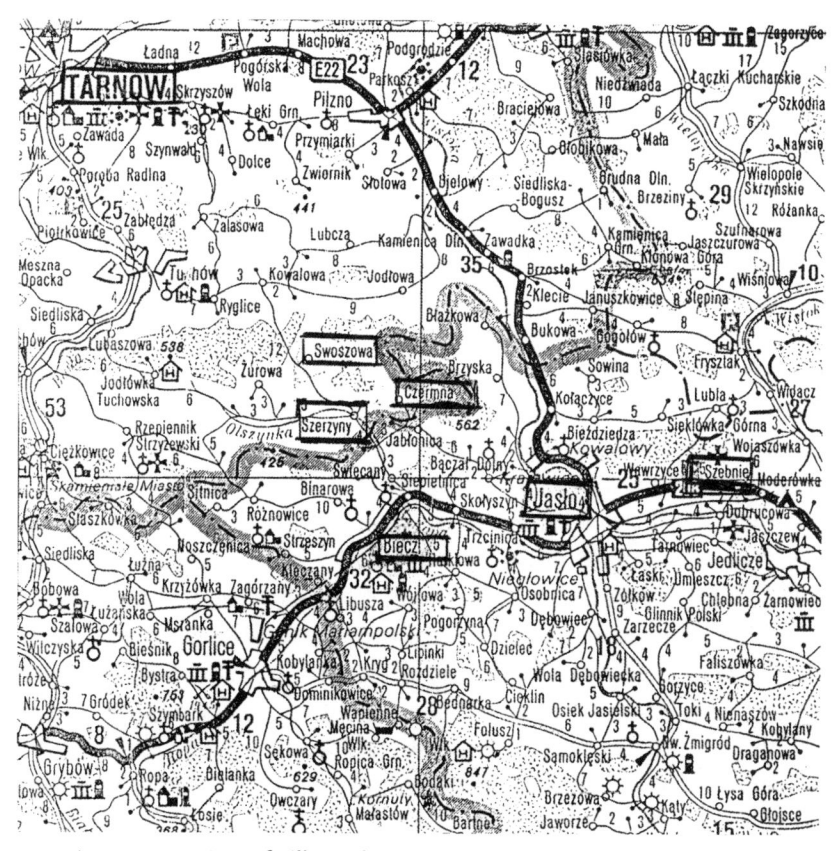

Map of villages between Jasło and Tarnów

But above all, the tormenting question of all questions: what were the three Tarnovians doing in the small village between Tarnów and Jasło? When and how and why did they go to Swoszowa? Did they manage to flee Tarnów, desperate to reach Swoszowa while the neighborhood was still open, before the first *Akcja* after which the neighborhood became a closed ghetto? The village was small but its name was whispered from ear to ear: a Polish brother and sister lived there, Władysław and Apollonia Kozak, who were being kind to Jews and trying to save them. One day, the Nazi police discovered the hiding place through detection or informing, and all those hiding were executed. And what of the seemingly authentic testimony of their deaths in the *Akcja* in Tarnów? Of course the witnesses, seeing Bóżnic Street empty of its inhabitants without knowing about the secret flight of the Wróbel family, included them in the total of the eleven thousand victims of the *Akcja*'s first day of slaughter. That was one conjecture. Reasonable? Who today could determine what was "reasonable" during that crazy whirlwind of killing, fear, and luck or…bad luck?

According to another speculation, no less realistic and no less dubious, the Wróbel family was sentenced at the height of the butchery in the Rynek death-square, to join those awaiting the caprices of fate: murder on the spot, a variety of strange and horrible deaths, or shipment to the crematoria of Bełżec. Reb Aazik, Golda, and Gunia are cruelly forced to run to the train station, pushed into the cattle car, and the engine already knows the way. In Jasło, the train stops for an hour. A change in plan? The Ukrainian guard, exhausted from the day's operation, murmurs: surely Bełżec must be full. He is correct. The train travels several miles eastward from Jasło and stops beside the Szebnie concentration camp. Here there are no gas chambers and no crematoria. After a day of organized registration, they shoot the prisoners. In the middle of the night, someone awakens a line of eight people who happen to be laying next to each other, among them Reb Aazik, his daughter, and his wife. In sign language, the guide commands complete silence and leads them noiselessly to a side gate that is not guarded. The

Ukrainian guard lies at the side, drunk senseless. They walk to a distance from which the noise of an engine will not reach the ears of the camp guards. The man beside the steering wheel introduces himself as Władisław Kozak. "Call me Władek." An extension of life before execution? Days or months? The end is the same as in the first speculation. The German police discover the hiding place: shooting, hanging, death. Later, Kozak is also caught, and pays with his life for his deeds to save Jews.

> W latach 1942—1944 w Szerzynach Gestapo z Jasła rozstrzelało za udzielanie pomocy Żydom małżeństwo Augustynów i Władysława Kozaka ze Swoszowej.

*In 1942-1944 (so reads the report of the National Commission) in the village of Szerzyny, the Jasło Gestapo executed by shooting the couple Augustins and Władisław Kozak of Swoszowa for aiding Jews."*

Yad Vashem awarded the Poles Władisław and Appolonia Kozak the title of Righteous Gentiles.

The riddle of the arrival of the Wróbel family in Swoszowa remains unsolved. Only its bitter end is known. There is no choice but to add the *fourth execution* to the three previous ones and to mourn all four.

> *"Four means of execution were entrusted to the Jewish court in ancient times"* — Reb Aazik taught his students from Tractate *Sanhedrin* of the Talmud.

"To the court", yes, but not to a situation in which court and judges, in the total anarchy, imposed on human beings strange and cruel deaths, the likes of which history had never seen, slaughtered in the name of the racial supremacy of the slaughterers over their victims. In those days when Reb Aazik taught that passage, he did not know that he himself would be tested with *four executions* of the kind that even Satan himself never knew, and that bullets would riddle his body, while before his eyes ropes strangled the necks of Golda, his wife, and Gunia, his daughter.

❖ ❖ ❖

All the testimonies, both oral and written, of the Wróbel family's disaster in the Tarnów Holocaust always related to Reb Aazik, and it was taken for granted that the name of the family's head also encompassed Golda and Gunia. Testimonies regarding other families were worded in the same way, and there was no one to object to the procedure. The only one who did not accept this rule was Sureh Weinmann, Golda's mother.

After the death of her husband, cantor-composer Zvi-Hersch Weinmann, in 1920 in Tarnów, Sureh immigrated to the United States with her three unmarried children, and was forced to leave her oldest daughter, the married one, Golda, mother of two young children, in Tarnów. Sureh settled in Boston, where her brother Lowa had lived for twenty years. "No matter, I have three children with me. One day Golda will also come and we'll go back to being one united family." But the dream of reunification of the family was the mother's dream only. Aside from Ephraim, who was twelve when he came to America, the two others were adults: Ben-Zion was twenty-three, Zippora was nineteen, and they had their own dreams. And so the unit quickly split up.

Ben-Zion, the artist and Hebrew poet, went to New York to join a group of Hebrew poets there. Then he devoted himself to painting, and never returned to Boston. Zipporah left America after three years and returned to Tarnów in order to go from there to Eretz-Israel and join a kibbutz. But the climate of Eretz-Israel was unsuitable for her, and she moved to Vienna, where she lived with her husband Tulah. Only the "little" boy remained with his mother. He would stay with her even after he married and gave his mother grandchildren. But before that, the mother was to take action. She would not abandon her dream, but she realized that it would not be fulfilled in America. "There is only one place in the world where we will reunite — in Eretz-Israel." Just before the outbreak of the "Disturbances" of 1936, she made *aliya* with her son, who was no longer so "little", and made her home in Tel Aviv. She was right. In Eretz-Israel, her dream began to reach fulfillment. Two years later, Golda's and Aazik's son and daughter made *aliya*, bearing the news that in autumn 1939, Golda and her husband and their small daughter would also come. Meanwhile, in 1938, after the Anschluss, Zipporah and Tulah also fled Vienna to Eretz-Israel. "In a year Golda will come, too. One more year to wait. Just one year and we'll be together again." And then, just when they were about to prepare for the journey, the war broke out...

It is unclear whether someone decided not to talk about the war and the Holocaust in Sureh's presence, or whether she herself repressed the questions and wrapped herself in silence. After the war, when thoughts and fears began to focus on the Holocaust — on who returned and who did not — again, without deciding to do so, everyone refrained from telling her what had happened. One day, without warning, Sureh surprised the people sitting at the table when she stopped some foolish conversation on a certain food with a somewhat aggressive barb, and hurled her question as a challenge to them all: "*Wi iz Goldeh* [Where is Golda]?" She did not ask what happened in Tarnów, how was Aazik, or other such expected questions. Only one subject bothered her: "*Wi iz Goldeh?*" She was perhaps even more aggressive than usual when her grandson Ankori returned from his service in the Brigade. Not a single word of welcome on the return of the soldier from five years of war. Only: "*Di bist du, un wi iz Goldeh* (You're here, and where is Golda?")" — as if he should apologize for returning alive and well, while Golda was not there. This time, too, no one recalls who stuttered first, in answer to her accusation, that "Golda is fine, and she'll be back with us soon", or who were the first to join in supportively in the same tone. So an irrevocable web of false excuses began to be woven around Sureh, and with it, an entanglement of fears of family members and friends that someone would appear who was not in on the secret of denial, and no one would want to behold the conclusion of Sureh's meeting with that person and with the truth.

That "someone" did in fact knock on the door. It was the joyous holiday of Simhat Torah, and the entire family, except for Sureh (who due to her age had stopped leaving the house) was participating in the celebrations at the synagogue. At the knock, Sureh opened the door, and there stood a Tarnovian friend of the family who had not visited the Weinmann home for quite a while, and had come now to wish her and the whole family a happy holiday. In annoyance, Sureh stopped the useless chatter, and asked directly: *"Wi iz Goldeh?" "Staitch wi iz Golde? Weist ir nisht? Di Daitschen hoben zi geharget fir yohr tzurick* [What kind of question is it — where is Golda? Don't you know? The Germans killed her four years ago]."

Felled by a stroke, Sureh sunk to the ground. The Merciful and Compassionate One would take her to meet Golda in the place where pure and tormented souls await their fate at the end of days, bearing witness on Israel's behalf.

So fell the last victim of the Gokhban-Weinmann-Wróbel-Ankori family, that was burned by strange fire on the accursed altar of the greatest enemy of Jews that history ever witnessed.

*IN MEMORIAM* — Oil painting by Ben-Zion in memory of his mother, Sureh Weinmann.]